Father Martin
and the Hermitage Mystery

Father Martin
and the Hermitage Mystery

David Bland

JANUS PUBLISHING COMPANY
London, England

First Published in Great Britain 2005 by
Janus Publishing Company Ltd,
105-107 Gloucester Place,
London W1U 6BY

www.januspublishing.co.uk

British Library Cataloguing-in-Publication Data
A catalogue record for this book
is available from the British Library

ISBN 978-1-85756-594-2

Cover design Janus Publishing

Printed and bound in Great Britain

Chapter One

The heavy flooding of the Thames Valley that followed the thaw after the severe winter of 1156–7 was, according to the perverse manner in which bounty and want are scattered on the human race, followed by a month of rain. Spring sowing was therefore rendered next to impossible – though the overwintering crops thrived in the early stages of their growth above the surface of the earth. And normally early fruits and vegetables were late. Then, after the Easter season, the sun burst through the residual cloud and appeared to be intent on seeking out and drying up every bit of the accumulated surface water from the previous six months of frequent precipitation.

As the low-tide level of the River Thames fell back to its normal range, and then beneath it, the bridgemaster was able to guide his team to strengthen parts of the substructure that were usually not accessible without constructing a coffer-dam. Martin, the preceptor of Bellins Gate, had learned how the vast elm mass of London Bridge had been virtually destroyed in the fire of 1136 and even after twenty years of new building his friend Peter the bridgemaster had pointed out that there were still incomplete and imperfect sections to the structure. Even those parts that had properly been completed, notably the decking over which so vast an amount of traffic and so many feet passed each day to and from the Surrey shore, were in almost constant need of repair or replacement.

Much as the college of priests of St Mary Overy relished their longstanding right to receive the tolls of users of the bridge in return for the duty to maintain it, they recognised their lack of talent in sophisticated methods of construction. They had therefore appointed Peter, chaplain at the church of St Mary, known as Colechurch, to be their bridgemaster. He had supervised the reconstruction of the bridge after the fire, and continued enthusiastically to develop his skills whenever opportunities such as this drought arose to be exploited.

1

Martin had been intrigued by Peter's explanation of how the most obvious way to strengthen discerned weak spots in the substructure – by reinforcement – was not really very satisfactory: 'We could just drive squared off trunks of elm into the riverbed next to the existing piers of the bridge, and bind them close to the great wooden stilts. This presents its own problems, however. If the additional timber is added upstream or downstream of the existing woodwork, it doesn't directly strengthen the roadway; and it increases the length of the tunnels through which boatmen have to align their craft. They have a very fine judgement to make, rowing in conflict with the combined forces of the river's changing currents and the wind. Yet if we add timber to the supports directly beneath the roadway, it necessarily narrows the gap and speeds up the tide race – which would be at least as bad for the watermen. The best solution for a serious weakness in a main structural member is to replace it; but for that the entire surrounding area has to be shored up, then the defective timber must be removed without damage to its neighbours, then the replacement inserted – and more likely than not, we'll find ourselves working in a confined space and at an angle that would make it awkward to use piledrivers.'

"If only there was an accessible material that was more reliable, more durable, than this timber!" Peter could not count the number of times his men had said this, or he had thought it. "There's no doubt that elm is the best for the purpose; no other wood lasts so well in the water, with comparable strength and load-bearing capability. We choose our wood carefully, too, and supervise the seasoning ourselves. Yet, once again this spring, the unusually low water level in the river at low tide has revealed elemental and animal forces of decay that are succeeding against our best endeavours."

For Martin, the answer to Peter's dilemma was obvious: "Throughout the land there are many massive stone buildings, and it is well known that the Romans and other ancient peoples built stone bridges over great rivers, as well as the miles-long aqueducts that still survive, even in England. The techniques for such construction have been lost, so our modern Christendom has only the timber bridge- building technology of our recent forebears. There is no insurmountable problem about building vast arches, as the current reconstruction of St Paul's Cathedral demonstrates. But I realise that those arches are not required to stand in a tidal river, and they will be expected to support nothing heavier than a roof that has to bear only the normal pressures of wind, rain and a winter's snow."

2

Peter had heard this possibility mentioned many times, and he restated again the conventional response: "To construct arches rising on piers set on the shingly bottom of a river would be next to impossible; but even if they could be built, the combined impact of tidal waters, flood waters and the constant pounding of traffic on the roadway would place an intolerable load on typical Romanesque arches such as they are installing at St Paul's and in the new priory at Smithfield."

Peter the bridgemaster avidly followed reports of experimental devices that were hidden within the structures of the cathedrals at St Paul's, Ely and Durham, where a kind of broken arch was being used. Instead of the semicircular arch that was standard throughout western Europe, the masons were testing out arches that came to a point. A single large keystone provided the cap to such an arch, and the more weight was put upon it – given that it was soundly constructed, of well-chosen stone – the firmer the arch became. The load from above pressed down on the keystone, pushing it more firmly into its dominant place over the two part-circles of stone that rose from the pillars to meet that keystone. The biblical references to the role of Christ himself, and of St Peter, as a headstone appeared to sanctify this form of design; and Peter took his being named after the follower who Jesus called 'the stone' as an omen that he would one day succeed in the building of a stone bridge.

"If the crucial question of the design of the arches could be resolved – and it is not yet proven that pointed stone arches on the necessary scale could be viable – the question of designing the piers or pillars on the riverbed on which the arches are to be built can be addressed. Here in London, on the tidal river, a stone imitation of the elm piers of the existing bridge could be attempted: we'd simply replace each vast collation of tree-trunks with a well-mortared and properly keyed-in structure of stone. That will take the main outstanding problem down below the surface of the water – to the river bed, and to the puzzle as to how the foundation of a stone bridge might be established in the mixed and moving mass of shingle that gave the Romans first their ford from London to the south bank, and then – so it is believed – a wooden bridge similar to ours."

On land, great buildings were put on a solid base: St Paul's Cathedral stood on the summit of a hard clay hill; Durham Cathedral was built on the native rock, high over the river; and Ely was a town, and now again the home of a developing cathedral, because it was a high hard clay outcrop in the fens.

Lesser structures were put on soft, even marshy ground. Peasants and the poor just relied on luck, not to have their ill-founded shacks blown over or washed away by a flash flood; but parish churches, abbeys and defensive works had to be set in marshy ground or on shaly soil if that was where God's work was destined to be done. There were well-known techniques for piling into building sites, with good timber buried beneath stone foundations. Sometimes it was possible to protect a building with drainage underneath it; and some kinds of ground took buildings better if rags, ash or animal remains were spread before the first stones were laid.

Peter pointed out that trying any of these things in the breadth of the Thames would be a different story from proving on land that they could be done. "The river is three hundred yards across, and the tide rises and falls at London Bridge by the best part of twenty feet when a high tide that is coming upriver is pushing back flood waters from the Thames Valley. The elemental forces that are at work in the water provide a more significant engineering challenge than does the sheer scale of constructing a bridge over the tidal Thames." Peter recognised that he faced two sets of problems, even in maintaining and finally finishing his existing wooden masterpiece: the constructors' problems of materials, design, workmanship and supervision; and the environmental challenges inherent in the river as a living system. Peter's skills were as a constructor; his detailed knowledge of the river he took from the preceptor at Bellins Gate.

On the first Monday in June, yet another low tide had displayed the need for more remedial work to be done to the bridge and one of the workmen had almost been lost in a clumsy incident at the point where repiling was already under way. So Peter decided, once more, to consult the preceptor about the river. He wanted to know if the preceptor's long-term research into the pattern of tides, winds, floods and consequent water levels had yet produced anything more than tide tables. If the preceptor's tables could show when there would be a succession of weak tides, which fortuitously combined with a prolonged period of drought throughout the River Thames catchment area, Peter could more easily construct a coffer-dam around one of the piers, pump out the water, and make basic repairs to his bridge. The lower the maximum predicted high-tide water level would be, the lower would the dam be required to keep the water out – less time would be spent on preparatory work, leaving more for construction on the bridge itself.

Before going to Bellins Gate, Peter waited for the tide to rise to the level at which the men had to cease working. He could not leave the site during work time once an accident had happened, because it is well recognised in the builder's world that good and bad things come in clusters, and idiots are inventive, so once something has gone wrong the coming few hours must be a period for special vigilance.

Once the men had dispersed to their dinner and the foreman had checked in the equipment to the Bridge House stores, Peter crossed to the northern shore, and turned right into Thames Street. The Fishermen's Row was still open for business, though the best of today's catch was at this very hour being prepared in hundreds of kitchens for the bellies of the better-off burghers and the clerics of the capital. Peter turned right again, down the narrow lane that led towards the riverbank, at the end of which stood the solid walls and the squat tower of the preceptory.

As the canons of St Mary Overy guarded their right to the bridge tolls so the abbot and monks of St Peter's Abbey, the West Minster, jealously defended their possession of this portal to the City of London from the river. By royal charter, Bellins Gate was the one point at which arrivals to London by river during the hours of the curfew could be allowed ashore. There were strict rules as to who might pass onwards into the forbidden city during the night hours, when the gates were locked and all fires must be extinguished or concealed beneath a *couvre-feu* (curfew) pot; all other arrivals had to remain in the preceptory overnight, and were released into the city at the legally permitted hour after they had declared their business and their goods, and paid the relevant toll.

Peter had encountered the previous preceptor, Aedric, some years ago, when he spotted the Benedictine by the riverbank, looking intently at the state of the exposed area of river bed on a day when – as in the current season – the low tide was especially low. At several points small banks of shale had been exposed by the declining waters, making the residual flow of the river divide into a pattern of small streams.

The preceptor had explained that he was interested in medicaments, and liked to exploit the low tide to look for elements that might serve in his potions, or as catalysts to their precipitation. Sometimes, he explained, copper or bronze, tin or zinc – even gold or silver – were exposed by the departing tide, just lying on the river bed, if one knew what one was looking for. "Herbs are more profusely accessible than rare minerals," the preceptor had explained to the bridgemaster. The conversation had then turned to the bridgemaster's art, and the two men had discovered their shared interest in the tides. The night's sleep of the gatekeepers at the preceptory was more likely to be disturbed if a high tide occurred during the night watches; so it was sensible to plan the manning of the *porte* (as the French-speaking state officials termed this access point to the city) to coincide with the potential incidence of business. Of course, some messengers and traders rowed up river at slack tide, or even against it, but these were relatively few.

In the course of his researches, which followed from observations that had been kept by his predecessor, the preceptor had noticed that tides were differentially significant, especially as to the varying exposure of the river bed at low tide in different seasons, weather conditions and states of the wind. A very strong high tide was the product of the moon combined with a gale from the east; and the total effect could be magnified further by coinciding with flood water flowing down the Thames from the west. A very low tide was the product of drought to the west, a mild breeze from the west, and the weakest phase in the moon's pull on the earthly ocean.

In their very first serious conversation, Martin had asserted that: "We can predict the moon and the tide, we experience the drought. But if we whistle for the wind, we will be ignored!"

The bridgemaster had silently wondered to what extent the preceptor's assertion was sound. "Is there no correlation between the state of the moon, the tide and the strength of the wind; or between weather that has already been experienced and weather that is to come?"

Over several years of similar conversations, Martin's predecessor had reported nil progress in addressing these questions, while the bridgemaster's success in repairing the massive construction over the river was visible to all. Peter of Colechurch had seen the last preceptor become seriously ill; his complexion became sallow, on occasions even hinting at a green tinge, and his movements became increasingly deliberate. He insisted that there was nothing seriously wrong, and spoke of a stiffening of the joints such as was common with those few who survived into the sixth decade of earthly endurance. There were times when he had seemed to be brisk and relatively well and he betrayed none of the thickened or permanently bent fingers that usually accompanied serious arthritic affliction. His back remained straight, and any problem with mobility seemed to arise more from a lack of energy than from any inflexibility of his legs.

It must have been three years or more since the original researcher on the tides had been called to his rest. Then Martin had been appointed preceptor and had gradually assimilated the import of the research notes that he found in his chamber.

Martin had not sought out the bridgemaster, which Peter was sure he would have done had anyone in the preceptory made any discovery of interest to the engineers working on London Bridge. So now he had come round to find out if there were even any tentative conclusions that might indicate that the research would provide some useful information for him.

Peter greeted the porter of the preceptory, gave his name and designation – as bridgemaster of London – and sought audience of the preceptor. He was directed over the yard to the tower, and to a small doorway aside from the access to the river gate. This door led to the spiral stair up to the preceptor's chamber.

"First level is the guardroom, second is the chamber, Father, and that's where our preceptor will be working," explained the porter. Peter set out to climb two flights, and found himself in a dimly lit little hallway with a large oak door facing him. He knocked, and Martin's familiar voice bade him enter.

The Benedictine monk who rose from a chair at the broad table to greet Peter was at most thirty years of age. He was smaller than the former preceptor, naturally sallow and with a sprightly manner.

"Ah, Father Peter, welcome. Pray take a seat." Martin offered wine. Peter commented that he had not been in this room since Martin had been in post, though he had on several occasions discussed the tide with the former preceptor. "I never met him," said Martin. "I was summoned from Gloucester to replace him; but he was certainly a man of many talents."

Peter settled into the high-backed chair and supped contentedly from his glass. Martin looked to the doorway – as was the custom in the preceptory, when a visitor was directed to the preceptor's rooms a servant was despatched to follow the visitor upstairs to check that all was as it should be, and that the guest was furnished with the hospitality of the house at the discretion of its head.

"How long have you been in this place now, Father Martin?" asked Peter.

"Just on two years, Father," replied Martin.

"And you were summoned from Gloucester? There was none in the great House of West Minster whom Father Prior was minded to appoint to this post?"

Martin guessed that there was a special reason for the question, related to the bridgemaster's visit to Bellins Gate.

Martin had looked out on the river several times that day and noted that again that morning the water level had been unusually low, and that even the tide that was now approaching full did not put the third step from the top of the Bellins Gate river stairs under water.

As a frequent user of the bridge that linked London and Middlesex with Southwark and Surrey, Martin was aware of the constant endeavour that the men from the Bridge House made to complete the bridge, while repeatedly having to revert to maintenance work. As the guardian of a *porte* to the city, he watched the river carefully and maintained the tide tables inherited from his predecessor. He needed to apply no conscious cerebration to reach the tentative conclusion that the bridgemaster's visit bore some relationship to the state of the river in this drought period, and to the opportunity that this must afford to Peter and his team to work on parts of the bridge that were normally inaccessible due to the depth of the river even at low tide.

Martin had laboriously decrypted the secreted parchments left by his predecessor, Aedric, and discovered much information about the height of the river at various past periods of drought, and the effect of wind on the height of the tide.

Martin had ensured that the monks who were allocated to work as supervisors of the *porte* were able to make the calculations that were necessary to predict the hour of high tide for at least fourteen days ahead. It was routinely necessary to check the moment when the flood was at its highest or lowest point once each day, so that the basis of calculation for future tides could be corrected if an error was perceived between the preceptory prediction and the actual time when the tide turned.

Martin had seen no direct use for the more comprehensive set of data that Aedric had also assembled, with great care over several years, to disclose the water level and the wind's direction and force, at high or low tide time. The preceptory's principal scribe, Brother Elias, had been enlisted by Martin to continue to note the level of high or low tide, whichever was reached first in the light of day. The level was measured by the amount of river bed that was exposed at low tide and counting the number of steps of the stair into the river that were covered when the water's flow slackened to mark the peak of a tide. If the level appeared to be significantly different from normal, Elias took a precise measurement of the water level, according to Martin's reconstruction of the system that Aedric had developed, and entered the resultant value into the record.

The servant had gone to fetch meat from the kitchen for the guest, who would soon miss his collegiate supper; and as the two clerics awaited the man's return Martin gave to Peter such an account of his predecessor's final illness and death as he had garnered from the monks who had served at Bellins Gate during that sad period. After depositing beef and bread on the table, the servant departed and Martin politely invited Peter to state his business. This he did:

"As we have discussed before this, I have one massive problem – in my capacity as bridgemaster – in that I can never tell how long a spell of weather such as this will last. So I have to err on the side of caution, always, in exploiting even the most favourable conditions for work on the footings of the bridge ... I found that Aedric shared my interest in the level of the water in the river, for very distinctly different reasons from mine. He was making observations that I hoped would lead to conclusions that would help me in my task ... Since he is long gone, I cannot now obtain his assistance on this earthly matter – though I shall certainly intercede for his soul, and pray him to intercede for mine – and so I must ask you, Father Martin, whether you or any of your brethren in the place know anything that goes beyond your predecessor's researches?"

"Nothing for your comfort, Father," replied Martin. "We have continued to note water levels that are higher or lower than the range that we regard as normal; and we have, of course, maintained all of Aedric's records about winds and tides. But apart from predictive tide tables, which are entirely sound provided we attain the necessary accuracy in our computations, we can make no predictions at all as to the state of the river at any future date ... We can say that if an exceptionally high tide should coincide with a high wind from east or west, certain effects can be expected; but we cannot even say that any given gust of wind is the last that will be experienced, even while a gale is in full force."

"You retain all of Aedric's work, then, Martin?" asked Peter.

"Both in the medical sphere and in that of ... Well, I suppose it is fluvial hydrology." Here Martin inserted Latin words into his French sentence, and Peter smiled assent:

"Yes, I suppose it is ... the study of the water in a river."

There was an element of sadness in the smile, for both men knew full well that it is easier to develop a clever name for a field of study than it is to make a significant advance within the subject matter. Martin perceived that it would be irrelevant folly to suggest to Peter that there might be some breakthrough in sight. It had taken him well over a year to recognise Aedric's tabular jottings as being reports on the state of the river, and Martin still had absolutely no idea how data that could be accumulated so easily could produce answers to the questions that predominated in the mind of Father Peter of Colechurch.

"I can see the importance of the information in relation to your duties, Father," said Martin. "But you have already built the bridge, including the great drawbridge that allows seagoing ships to proceed up river to Queenhithe and to the River of Wells ... so I do not see that you have any operational need for fuller or more precise information. You have mastered the river with the information that you already have."

Peter's smile indicated regret, rather than self-satisfaction, as Martin spoke. The bridgemaster's next point surprised Martin, who chided himself on not having thought of what was so obvious in the light of Peter's experience.

"Do you know how many men were lost, and how many were crippled, in the building of the bridge? Repair of the fire damage is not yet completed, but we are already spending as much time – and more trouble – on restoration and reconstruction of parts that were replaced after the fire as we are on new building or embellishment. I almost lost a man again today, down among the footings of the bridge. Will we lose lives every year, for the foreseeable future? Need we?"

Peter paused, hesitant to ride a familiar hobby-horse, but keen that the record would be unambiguous. He said:

"A timber structure has a limited life: each member has to be replaced as it reaches the point where it can be dangerous. The timber that is buried beneath the river bed or submerged all year beneath the water lasts longest, and the surface of the roadway wears out the quickest. Most unpredictable is the durability of the structures that lie between high and low water. Not only do these members suffer from salt damage and fresh-water plant growth, but the different seasons and small variations in the climate bring new life forms that batten on the bridge, only to be killed off in the next frost or carried away in a flood. Such creatures may burrow

10

into the wood to leave their eggs, and often the eggs pass into a grub stage during which the grubs eat the wood within the posts. I never know what alien activity is undermining my achievement, as I press on to complete the total project ...

"The present phase of maintenance work will be completed, to the extent that a passer-by will see the bridge as it is intended to look; but what he will not recognise is the extent of the differentiated decay. The only parts of the entire enterprise that will be there in a thousand years are the underground foundations, those that lie deep beneath the tideway. If the upper works are constantly renewed they could also stand for that thousand years, but even the main beams above the highest ever level of the river that remain dry beneath the roadway will decay every few hundred years, and every other part will rot or be eaten away faster than that – even if our constant worst enemy, the threat of fire, does not intervene, as it did a quarter of a century ago."

Martin looked up and saw the sky, framed in the inverted U-shape of the neat little window arch – and he recognised once more the answer to Peter's problem: stone arches!

"Roman stone bridges still stand, so I am told," said Martin.

"Exactly!" answered Peter. "As you have said previously when we have found time to discuss these matters, a stone bridge would be the answer to my prayers ... But the technical problems that face such a project cannot yet be resolved. The bridge that we now have is three hundred yards – in round numbers – from where the passenger enters at the Bridge House toll-point in Southwark, to the check point at the city gate above Botolph Wharf. Nobody in modern times – I think not even the Romans in their day – built such a long bridge. And the other crucial factor I discovered only when I made pilgrimage to Rome and happened to ask a naive question. The tide on the Middle Sea is negligible; literally insignificant. It is not a factor in fishing or in coastal construction ... Here, as you know, we have a normal tidal range of over a dozen cubits ... twenty feet, and exceptional weather conditions exaggerate even that disparity. No Roman bridgemaster was the conqueror of the elements to that extent, so far as I can tell! They may have used stone in some parts of their estuary bridges, and in the shoreline sections of the wooden bridge that some say they did build in London; but the deep-water sections of any Roman tidal-water crossings were certainly like those that I have inherited, built of wood. I myself believe that here at London the Romans had a ford, and that there were landing stages for boats to use at high water when the ford was impassable. I do not believe that there was a Roman bridge here – for the simple reason that I would have found the undecayed substructures in the course of my own work, and I have not done so!"

Martin respected the driving passion of this formidable man. Peter had already spent virtually the whole of Martin's lifetime on a single project, the reconstruction of London Bridge. Yet he was speaking as if the entire magnificent achievement was just a palliative, as if the real job that he wanted to do had not yet been begun. Martin also responded positively to the underpinning humanitarian objective that Peter had elucidated. So long as the bridge remained a wooden structure, men would regularly have to descend into the waters to repair and replace the timbers and their fastenings, and in that process would suffer injuries and mutilation, and orphans and widows would be left dependent on charity.

Martin hated those religious who regarded accidental deaths – particularly of the despised lower orders of the laity – as a benefit in that it supposedly gave a poor, honest fellow a faster route to celestial bliss. They asserted that the less time a person lived, the fewer sins he was likely to atone in purgatory. To Martin, the logical outcome of that perverted attitude would be to promote the death of infants, as they must go straight to their eternal joy if they did not acquire the means of committing sins. By contrast, Martin embraced the view that the human race is set on the earth to subdue and to develop God's material creation; not to be withdrawn from it before the individual has had the opportunity to make – and to enjoy – his or her contribution to the processes of farming, fishing or townsmen's work.

Martin felt that Peter was a fellow spirit, another priest who took the view that building good things in this world is God's work, the task of the creator carried forward by human hands. If human hands are unnecessarily mutilated, that is an evil. If there is a way of preventing such an evil from afflicting future generations, it presents a glorious and a godly opportunity.

The current preceptor recognised the goodwill that had lain behind his predecessor's laborious undertaking of the tidal and wind readings, and his linkage of these data to the phases of the moon. He wanted to help this impressive man effectively, as Aedric had evidently done before him.

"Did Aedric begin to undertake his researches on the river at your request?" asked Martin. The question came uncensored from his unconscious and he was slightly embarrassed by having posed it. Peter seemed to sense the thought process that lay behind the question: whether the research should be continued, or whether the time of the members of the preceptory would be better spent on other things.

"Decidedly not!" answered Peter. He told Martin that they had met when Aedric had been searching for metals, and how they had compared notes on their relative interest in the accessibility of the river bed.

Martin's talent to unravel mysteries was significantly dependent on his facility for non-consciously collating his visual perception of another person with the tone of voice and mannerisms, set in the location. What could which person have done, given the circumstances in which they were set? These questions resonated with other memories that were remote from the particular events. Somehow, somewhere, outside his understanding, Martin's perception of human situations went far beyond the evidence that can be gathered directly by any ordinary mortal of another. Martin had told himself in those cases when he seemed to be endowed with special percipience, that he was simply a living soul who interacted with other living souls in the common environment of humankind; he hoped that it was reasonable to presume that common shared instincts enabled him to understand more than he could hear or see.

To find that his mind was now being directed to search for answers to questions that lay within the elemental forces of time and tide, far beyond the urges and instincts of malleable mankind, was a different kind of challenge for Martin. He wanted to be of use to this impressive, caring, high-achieving priest; but how could he become so vain as to think that his modest ability to understand human error and ambition could be applied in a field of objective inanimate reality?

When Peter had completed his brief narrative, Martin enquired:

"All of Aedric's observations are recorded here, so far as I am aware ... would you care to take them into your custody?"

As he uttered the words, Martin was conscious that he did not want his visitor to accept the offer. If he did so, Peter would take the problem – and Aedric's work towards solving it – away from Bellins Gate. Martin felt that it would sever the connection of the preceptory with Peter of Colechurch's grand design. Of course, a pile of second-hand parchments was not necessary to stimulate Martin to develop further his own interest in the river and the weather, but as long as the parchments remained at the preceptory, and the clerk of the day continued to record exceptional high tides and low-water points, there would be continuity in the maintenance of the record of this river watch.

Peter gave the desired reply:

"No thank you, Father. I am sure that they are safe in your custody. I presume that I may refer to them, at need?"

Martin nodded assent, then said:

"I suppose that you collate all the weather lore? Things like watching when the midges or the dragonflies come out, when the middens begin to get their summer stink, how high the rooks set their nests, and the amount of white blossom on the thorn hedges?"

"Do you really think that the rooks build higher for a good summer?" asked Peter.

"They might, if they could foretell the weather," answered Martin "but I am told by woodsmen that they often repair old nests; and they don't look different to me, year on year."

Peter smiled. He was clearly of the opinion that the old wives who told such tales had no responsibility for important economic or military functions that could be spoiled by the weather.

"I think that some portents could have a more general validity than do others, as to the length and strength of a summer or of a frost. Many old men told me last autumn that the prolific nuts and berries were a sure sign that nature was stocking the larder for the poor; and they certainly needed it, in the harsh months that followed." Martin spoke tentatively, conscious that Peter had already displayed his scepticism at this kind of proposition.

"You'd go with the hawthorn, then, as a weather predictor, but not the rooks?" asked Peter.

"Yes, Father. Plants have to make provision where they are fixed; so nature might have given them instincts that are different from those of the birds and animals that can cover great distances in search of a subsistence," said Martin.

"That is an interesting thesis," said Peter, gravely, but with a twinkle in his eye. "If it is true, the longer-established a plant is in its location, the more experience it will have to display through its blossom, leaves or berries what is the severity or the splendour of the weather that is to come ... When I think about the high trees, the thick hedges ... there may be something in that! But I remain, at best, a doubter!"

"Then I will enhance your doubt, Father. If there is such knowledge, or understanding, it is in the species and not in the individual plant that manifests it. The old hawthorns did not display more abundantly than did the young this spring, when the hedgerows looked as if the winter snows had returned in renewed abundance. A seedling or a transplanted off-cut behaves like a miniature adult of its own vegetable kind; all their reactions are awake from first receiving the light as a separate plant ... unlike an infant animal, or a nestling bird, that must be both guarded and instructed by its parents before it can do anything." Martin had not deeply considered this distinction between plants and animals before, though it had biblical authority behind it in the Creation story, but as he formed his view, speaking out loud, he found it both defensible and intriguing.

"If you could but tell me, Father Martin, what could be the sure signs of a coming drought that affects the whole Thames Valley – such that I can sink the coffer-dam to build a pair of bridge-piers, even once every four or five years – you will bring closer to reality my impossible dream," said Peter. The voice was relaxed, almost casual; but the man's eyes burned with a powerful hope, even though the proposition was not credited by his meticulous intellect.

This priest could build a great stone bridge, in tidal water, if only he could anticipate the periods when he could be sure that the water level would be exceptionally low at low tide. The only force that could reduce to a minimum the flow of river water down the Thames – and all its tributaries above the Wallbrook – was the sun, banishing rain clouds and shrivelling the ground from which the myriad springs get their water. No man had ever controlled God's great light in the heavens; its daily appearance was a miracle, yet without the intervention of cloud and rain the sun itself was a certain killer. God's rain was equally as important as His sun, for all created life; but He gave or withheld the gift of rain according to a wisdom that was far beyond human understanding. Was it possible to penetrate that divine programme to the limited extent that was needed for Peter's plan? Aedric had been a much more accomplished practitioner of physic than Martin aspired to be, yet he had not cracked the divine code that governed the weather, so how could Peter of Colechurch, or anyone else, expect Martin to be able to do so?

Peter did not expect anything useful to emerge from this conversation, but he was hoping that Martin would provide him with the opportunity to widen the boundary of human accomplishment. Martin felt deep inside himself an urge to enable this extraordinary individual to realise his dream, which would spare the London and Southwark communities trouble, money and loss of life for centuries to come. It was a public work, a civic – or civil – work, and a work that would stand for the benefit of all; and it would be exciting to see how a stone bridge would be constructed. It would be sinful to give an undertaking to Father Peter that would quickly prove to be unsupported. Martin would let his imagination and his power of analysis address the issue, but he could not now claim that they would clear any access to a solution. Humility, not vanity, was the appropriate sentiment with which he should end this intriguing interview.

Chapter Two

The monks at the Bellins Gate preceptory managed no fields of crops to become worried about in the drought; the harvest that they brought in was gained in the form of ready money, tolls from travellers arriving in London from the river by night. But they maintained a neat herb garden, which had been much developed by Father Aedric. It lay next to their small burial plot, between the stout outer wall of the preceptory – which served as part of the city defences – and the high-tide mark of the Thames. Martin himself took a frequent turn at tending or watering the herbs, nostalgic for his days as a postulant in the Abbey of St Mary at Gloucester.

The day after Father Peter had paid his visit to Bellins Gate, Martin made sure that he was at the herb garden when the river reached its lowest point after the tide receded. This was the time when the water that he would draw from the residual main channel of the river would be least salty, and thus most acceptable to the many species that were showing their need for watering. The alternative water source was the small stream that entered the river from the preceptory latrine; it had flushed many fouler places before it served the final utilitarian purpose, and the vile trickle to which it was now reduced would serve neither as a fertiliser nor freshener for foliage. In principle, water could be fetched out to the garden from the well in the preceptory yard, but Martin did not want to be troubled by preceptory servants bringing the pails and disturbing his pattern of thought.

In retracing his steps down the shingle bank from high-tide point to the low water this early morning, and back again with a laden bucket, Martin looked for glints and hints of the metals that Aedric had sought to mix medicinally with the vegetation that Martin now tended. There were, indeed, sparks of reflected sunlight and strange dark specks among the mass of pebbles and grains of sand. Once a man had trained himself to know what to look for, this river bed could indeed be a fine hunting ground. It was not the sort of investigative work that Martin found the most congenial, though he preferred to search for materials here than seek enlightenment from obscure texts in a library of theological tomes. It was a pity, he thought, that Aedric had not passed on the fruits of his metallurgical observation to some other monk who could continue to supply the community with zinc or tin or copper from the spillages and throwaways of thousands of years of urban and commercial activity here at the heart of the London port area.

Perhaps Aedric had trained up a pupil who had found the task uncongenial and ceased performing it before Martin had come to serve as Aedric's successor. If he asked the brethren directly, they would tell him the truth, but if the monk concerned had so much disliked the work, monastic morale would suffer if Martin were to redirect him to it. The medicinal gains would be minimal, and if some element were sorely needed to treat an ailment, there was money enough to buy it. Indeed, Martin wondered if there was not something clandestine in Aedric's mudlarking; possibly this had been an extension of Aedric's trade in alcohol and narcotics with the hermit who lived in the marshy area to the east of the Tower, beyond the city limits.

As he carried the sixth bucket of water up the shingle bank, by now physically regretting that he had not opted to use the well and to exploit the servants as water carriers, Martin decided that he must ask the hermit about this possibility. The two men had always had easy, open conversation since they first met, because they both spoke West Saxon, the first English language that Martin had learned, and also because they shared a direct approach to life and an interest in medicinal plants. The hermit had bartered with Aedric, supplying the opiates that had eased the pain of the former preceptor's terminal illness. In exchange Aedric provided the hermit with distilled life-water to mix into various potions as a relaxant. Martin had recently donated the still to the hermit and in return the hermit now supplied several of the medications that Aedric had himself concocted and decanted for the preceptory's dispensary. Thus the hermit was becoming a more extensive producer of pharmaceutical preparations and Martin was becoming a mere customer, but the arrangement was efficient.

As Martin selected the plants that were to receive the final bucket of water for the garden this morning, he reviewed the purpose for which this neat array of plant life was maintained. Some of the herbs went directly and beneficially into the kitchen, but much of it went to waste, because Martin did not take the trouble to prepare from it the medicines that could be made. Sometimes he was far away when a plant budded, flowered, produced its seeds or otherwise reached the point for harvesting. On other occasions, not entirely by chance, he found that some harvested matter had rotted or perhaps dried out too much before he got round to considering the next steps in extracting its medicinal essence. He should have felt guilt at this waste of nature's bounty and of the training that Godfrey had given him, but he found it difficult to do so with any sincerity. In this great city there were doctors of physic and of medicine, who were far better at the healing and diagnostic arts than any monastic amateur. Rare and common herbs alike were available to be bought, pristine and prepared for use, in the markets. The infirmarer at Bermondsey Abbey was a much better pharmacist than Martin could ever be, and he was generous in supplying potions to other monastic establishments at need. And there was always recourse to the hermit, who grew a great range of useful species of plants on several of the marshy islets that peeped above the high tide on the north bank of the river between the hermitage and the semi-savage settlement of Weopping.

After the morning Office and breakfast, Martin collected from the larder a newish, and therefore reasonably clean, trug – a basket made of thin strips of wood – and set out for the hermitage. In just twenty-five minutes the walk took Martin back through centuries and layers of civilisation. For the first ten minutes the bustle of the city surrounded him. He passed through the Bye Ward to the west of the Tower, the strongest of the three castles by which the king controlled and protected the City of London, then by way of Tower Street to the Postern Gate, where even a Benedictine priest might be required to state his business if the guard was bored or under special instructions to be vigilant. Then, turning off East Smithfield to the right, down Knight-a-Gale Lane, Martin was in deep rural England even while the bustle of the city was audible. Once that hubbub had faded, and the harsh long grass and spiky shrubs of the riverside lowland fringed the shingle lane, it could still have been the time of the Romans or of their legendary precursor King Lud – the reputed founder of the city that was built on and around Ludgate Hill, overlooking the ancient ford that London Bridge had replaced.

Romans, Celts, Saxons, Vikings and Normans had not changed this topography, and the land had probably been thus before the earliest recorded civilisation had sent its troops out to explore the north bank of the Thames, with its treacherous tidal ditches and sandy quagmires. The lane was the proven dry-shod route to the tiny hamlet on Knighten Rise, the last point west of the Gravel Lane at Weopping, where a secure footing could be maintained by man or beast at every the state of the tide.

The hermitage was set back from the road, among thickets that in summer almost completely hid the ancient stone building from travellers on the lane and from voyagers on the river. The longstanding reputation of the place as the home of a holy man, who served humankind with healing potions, was a deterrent to any local person committing any offence against it or its occupant. The chances of any stranger breaking into the place or coming upon the hermit unawares were minimised by the defensive combination of stout walls, strong doors, massive bolts, geese and dogs.

Until a few years before, the occupant of the property had for a long time been a true hermit; a layman who, out of piety, had isolated himself from social contact and spent his time in prayer, fasting and the benign physical toil and mental effort of growing and refining his medicaments. The old man had heard people's complaints and pleas, and had silently handed them the potions that brought healing or relief. When he felt his strength to be failing, he had prayed for a pupil to follow in his humanitarian role. The answer to his petition had come in the improbable form of a sick sailor, set ashore by his captain in the marshlands so that the ship would not be impeded by the quarantine regulations of the port. The ship's master had told the man that once the vessel had been turned round at Queenhithe, the mariner's mates would recover him from the shore and tend him in the ship. Neither believed that was the true intention, or expected the man to survive alone for two days even if his shipmates had been able to find him again among the reeds and the sedge.

The old hermit had recognised the symptoms of the fever, and had gauged the inherent strength of the marooned man and the probability of effecting a cure. For a day and a night and most of the next day, the old hermit attended the young sailor where he had been left, under an elderberry tree. When the fever broke, and the man continued to breathe, the hermit had dragged him on a hurdle to the mermitage, sustaining him with drips of milk and medication for three more days until he recovered consciousness.

Communication was not easy between the hermit and his patient; the old man's native tongue was Middle Saxon, though he also possessed modest fluency in French. The younger man's knowledge of French was passive, and strictly limited. He was a runaway from the West Midlands, who had gone to sea as the sole alternative to starvation. He had no admissible identity; if the authorities took him up they might compel him to give his name and that of his lord, and return him to the capricious brutality from which he had fled. Alternatively, the arresting officer might take the fugitive as his own slave, impress him as a man-at-arms or just order him to be dismembered, and stick his head on a pike at the gate of the city as a warning to other serfs not to risk the same fate.

The hermit did not need to ask the man his origin, nor attempt to decipher his response. It was obvious what he was, a fallout from feudal absolutism, and thus a possible source of the contagion of freedom that every lord – spiritual and temporal – sought to eradicate from among his human livestock. The weather-beaten texture of the runaway's skin suggested that he had been at sea – and on a restricted diet – for a significant period, so the hermit correctly assessed him to be a marine fugitive, rather than a land-based churl who had escaped from a nearby manor. Consequently the hermit need fear no baying bloodhounds with an angry lord and horsemen in pursuit, looking for the sick man's hide; it was equally plain that any ship's company that the man had recently belonged to had taken a decision to dispense with his services, so they would be no more interested in him than the lords of Stebenhithe or Radcliffe would be. The young fellow had nowhere to go, there was nobody he could claim to be, if he recovered from his severe fever and its enervating aftermath. He was tough and, no doubt, modestly experienced and competent; but he was a blank page on to which the picture of a new persona and a new life could be sketched. It would be up to the fellow to decide if he wanted to take the proffered opportunity to be a new man – and his own man, under God – or whether to chance his luck elsewhere in an unsympathetic world.

The hermit broke his no-speaking rule when it was essential to do so for the instruction of the patient who, as health and strength were regained, seemed unquestionably destined to be his pupil. As if by some instinct, the stranger recognised the hermit's progressive weakness and acted in accordance with the signals that the old man made, first to do the heavy tillage and tend the fires, then to take in the harvest and chop or grind the medicinally useful parts of the plants. Finally the sailor learned to save and set seeds, and to mix the medicines.

For five winters and four summers this strangely effective and almost silent pupillage had progressed. Then the old man had died, and the younger found that the world now regarded him simply as The Hermit, so he had acted the part. He neither aped nor aspired to the religious aspect of the old hermit's lifestyle, to him incomprehensible, but he recognised the sense in being perceived by his neighbours as a holy man. During the years of his pupillage, the new hermit had attuned his ears to the throaty Middle Saxon speech of the Londoners and the people from the Tower Hamlets who came in search of medicinal aid. Most of the words that they used were similar to the nasally inflected vocabulary of his youth, and his growing comprehension of the causes that brought people to the hermitage door quickly completed his acceptance. The fact that he was the successor to a previous hermit quickly became redundant, for a hermit had been at the hermitage time out of mind.

The large dog chained very close to the closed door of the hermitage building was a clear sign to Martin that the hermit was out at his work in some garden. Before Martin had come in sight of the door, the geese had raised their warning of a stranger's approach and the dog had taken up a silently menacing stance – it would have to be killed before anyone got past it to try the door of the hermitage, unless the master returned and authorised the visitor to approach.

Martin had not encountered this fearsome mastiff on any previous visit to the hermitage, and concluded that there must be a reason for the significant heightening of his friend's security. Making no move that the dog would regard as an intrusion, Martin took in the carefully laid signs by which the hermit gave out his location to those whom he felt entitled to discover it. There was no water pot at the left side of the door, so wherever the hermit had gone to, he had not crossed a waterway to get there. The besom was set against the wall to the left of the water-butt, so the hermit had gone to the west. It was stood on its bristles, so he had gone south. This indicated that he was between the lane and the riverbank, somewhere towards the hamlet of Knighten Rise. Martin could not recall any garden there. It would not be a good place for it, because the cattle and the children from the cottages made heavy use of the sandy fields between the lane and the high-water mark. There must be something growing in the hedgerow, or perhaps even between the high and low-water lines, that the hermit was scavenging for his potions or perhaps for personal use.

Martin entered an enclosure across the lane from the hermitage, watched by three cows and four children. A well-chewed but still untidy hedge separated this enclosure from the next, and a hurdle marked the point through which countless generations of beasts had been led by variously gentle and brutal infant humans from one grazing ground to its almost identical neighbour. The second enclosure had no hedge or hurdles on its river side. It contained a tethered goat, a donkey left loose to roam, and a gaggle of children looking down the riverbank, their backs to Martin as he vaulted the hurdle. In so doing he discerned the hermit's shaggy head to be the apparent object of the juveniles' attention.

The approach of the monk was signalled by a small dog with a shrill bark, and the whole assembly turned to assess the cause. Martin was known to most of the children, for he had been involved in some of the most sensational happenings in Knighten Rise in living memory, events which outclassed the anecdotes of ancestral times that the old ones told in the dark winter evenings as families crowded together with cats, dogs and fleas under their blankets.

The hermit looked up as the younger children turned away from the river, and heard the greeting to "Father Martin". He grinned to the two larger youths who had been helping him with his task down the bank side, and told them that they might as well cease their activity for the day. The rising tide was approaching, and they had already taken the harvest of the shallows. The hermit himself would bait the traps.

"Six each. See you tomorrow?" said the hermit.

"You can be sure!" replied one of the youths, on their joint behalf. Six big fresh-water crabs would gain a farthing from a stallholder in the city; or a farthing each, if the lady of Chad's Well or the mother of the reeve at Stebenhithe or some other conspicuous consumer who lived east of the city limits could be persuaded to take them. While this season of high tides and warming water lasted, the crabs would come upriver and inshore, and whatever it was that the hermit put into his wicker traps captured a score or more of the creatures every day. The village men occasionally caught crabs; but they did not regard the hermit's semi-professional crab-catching as a competitive activity, as they would certainly have done had he caught eels, white fish, trout or salmon for the market. Modest netting for his own table, and for his beasts, was recognised as a necessity for the hermit's domestic economy. The fisher folk admired the cleverness of the hermit's crabbing technique, and sent their sons to help him, hoping that they would learn the art of constructing the traps and fortuitously discover the constituents of the bait that was proving so successful.

After a brief debate, conducted *sotto voce* as Martin covered the twenty yards between the younger children and the hermit, the youths agreed to offer three crabs to the Lady at Stebenhithe for a halfpenny; and the remaining nine to the fishmonger at the corner of But Lane, also for a halfpenny. The professional trader would be a hard bargainer, but the wily old woman buying for her own household would be even tougher. Each youth knew that the other would do well to get their price, as they crammed the crabs into their darned sacks and set off on their errands.

"So, that's today's crop," said Martin, counting eleven crabs in the basket that lay on the ground next to the hermit. The youths appeared to have taken more of the spoils than the master of the craft, but that was doubtless by his decision.

"Are these for your table, or for some medicament?" asked Martin. Almost any organic matter could be used as a treatment for something or other, but Martin had heard nothing of the use of crab flesh, or of crab shell, in the pharmacological context.

"Neither ... well, I could reserve one or two to eat ... but the majority will join their fellows from my water-butt in Walter of Eltham's shop cellar well before the city gates are closed tonight. His boy will be coming for them by the time the tide is half risen," said the hermit, adding:

"Even a reputed holy man needs clothes and cutlery that he cannot make for himself, you know!"

Martin knew that there was none of the Christian piety within this man that had made his predecessor opt for the life of a hermit. This fugitive conformed, without assent, to the requirements of the church, but within himself he combined the Old Religion with no religion. The surrounding communities had accepted his succession to the Holy Hermit and he made no shift to disabuse them of their error in transferring to him credit for all the attributes of his predecessor and teacher. He dispensed medicines and medical advice, accepting pence from those who could afford it in order to replenish the stocks of those ingredients that had to be bought. He continued his predecessor's habit of admonishing those whose lifestyle could be attributed as a causal factor in their ailments, and the recipients of his admonitions did not recognise that they were short on scriptural references or on instructions about prayer.

Martin always appreciated the hermit's frank manner of speech, which relaxed from attempted Middle Saxon to the fluency of his native Wessex dialect when he spoke to the preceptor, a fellow native of the Welsh border regions:

"If you want crabs for the preceptory refectory, Father, you'll have to give me notice. You can have them gratis, provided I know in advance and can tell Walter that he's to miss out on a delivery."

Martin inclined his head at the hermit's generous offer, and undertook to convey it to his steward.

"He'd better make his mind up quick," said the hermit. "The years vary, and this spring the crabs have been smallish after the cold winter; that always affects the sea as much as us land-bound creatures. My experience is that small crabs means a short season, that starts late and can equally end early ... so if you want the best of fresh crab meat set before you, decide soon!"

"In that case, next Monday," said Martin. "Will that do?"

"Yes, I'll tell Walter's lad not to come between Saturday and Wednesday. Walter will be peevish about it, and that will show that he deserves to be treated thus now and again ... You send my crafty friend Felix to collect the catch. If he comes with open baskets, he'll have a hell of a time getting a score of crawling, pinching, tough little bastards back to the preceptory!"

The hermit laughed at the picture that he had created for himself of Brother Felix in a lather over escaping crustaceans; and Martin decided silently that whoever came from the preceptory for this welcome variation in the diet would bring with him a couple of well-used sacks, such as the hermit's own henchmen had just departed with.

The hermit bent down beside the large wicker basket containing the crabs, and showed Martin a smaller wicker container that was woven to form the protection for a large earthenware pot. There was a wooden lid over the broad lip of the pot, secured in place by strings tied to the wickerwork and passed tightly over the large wooden cap.

"The village folk want to know what my bait is, so I make a great secret of it. That's the only reason for using this pot. Half of the healing art, at least, is the effect on the mind of the patient that the practitioner can exert. It's the same in other fields of life. Just look at the little kids now. They all know that their big brothers haven't got my secret, so they will hang around and watch, and listen to see if they can pick up anything."

The hermit had turned to face out on to the river, and spoke in a very low voice. Facing him, Martin was looking towards the bank and could thus watch the children without obviously doing so. They had fallen silent when the hermit had produced the secret bottle, and were giving his every move their rapt attention.

Martin turned his face sideways from the children, so that his own half-whispered sentence went past the hermit's ear and along the uninhabited shoreline:

"And is there a secret?"

"Oh yes, just stale ale. Crabs are like slugs. They are attracted to ale. So I just mix ale leftovers with anything: worms, berries, even rotted grain. Then I put it into the trap. That's just a one-way gate. Sometimes a crab gets out, as another comes in, but in general I'm in luck and my traps work well," said the hermit. Then he added with a broad grin:

"I'll tell 'em sometime, in my own good time!"

Martin returned the smile. Neither the hermit nor the villagers were disadvantaged by the little game that was being played out. The lads still took money home that they would not otherwise have earned, and the hermit's secret was a talking point during the backbreaking routine of fisher folks' daily lives.

"I infer that you need the mastiff," said Martin.

The hermit held his eyes, steadily looking into Martin's for several seconds. He did not need to acquiesce in words to that statement. The look confirmed Martin's suspicion that there had been some untoward incidents – almost certainly, more than one isolated event – to cause the hermit to feel the need to add terrestrial security arrangements to the traditionally sufficient inviolability of a dedicated place.

"You could have called on your friends, you know ... your fishmonger, or his boy, could have called at the preceptory; it's only two minutes diversion from his trip from here to the shop at But Lane," said Martin. He realised that the urgency in his quietened voice could have made his remark appear unduly admonitory when the hermit replied:

"It's surprising you say that. He did just as you suggest – and you were away at Oxford! You know how little I can afford to rely on other monks – even your henchman, that Felix – so I managed on my own ... And I've managed well!"

There was more of defiance than of confidence in the declamation, but it was self-evidently true that the hermit was in good health.

"Now that I am here, I hope that I may be permitted to help a friend – within the limited powers in my possession," said Martin.

"What errand brought you here today?" asked the hermit, changing the focus of the conversation in a way that Martin considered promising, as it could indicate that the host wanted to get back to basics.

"A fishing expedition. Not the sort you do here, but metaphorical fishing to see what medicaments you might have in sufficient supply to repair my stocks at Bellins Gate," said Martin.

"That I do accept!" responded the hermit. "A black monk with an outstretched palm ... or, as I see in your case, a three gallon basket ... is an entirely understandable caller."

Both men laughed. There were not many heads of monastic establishments whom a simple layman would dare to joke with, but Father Martin of the Bellins Gate preceptory was certainly one such. The hermit recited a list of what he had available, and they then discussed the relative merits of purgatives for patients to whom dysentery was already endemic.

"I've some of last autumn's juniper," said the hermit, "that helps wind, not the other thing ... and the motherwort has come through good this season, that's a fine relaxant. Then there's tincture of lovage, which has a cleansing and calming effect; and I've been able to get some bladderwrack ... that's a seaweed, whose pods contain a natural tincture that helps heavy neck cases ... not that you'll have any of those among your monks!"

"What about liquorice?" asked Martin.

"You mean, what does it do? ... or that you want some?" asked the hermit.

Martin knew the many uses of liquorice, from the treatment of coughs and asthma, through dietary problems to the alleviation of arthritis.

"I could use some," he said.

"Then you shall have some," responded the hermit.

The hermit had made no move to lead his visitor away from the riverbank, up which the tide was advancing noticeably.

"There's a good growth of catch-grass behind you," said the hermit. "You can harvest some now, before the dry spell shrivels it. That's a really good cleanser of the blood; and of the skin also. You get yourself the best part of your basket full of that ... and by the time you've done that, the tide will be at the mouth of my traps and we can leave them with no children to tamper with them."

So that was why the hermit was lingering. Martin decided to remain with him; it would take only a few minutes to gather a good batch of catch-grass, once they were on the move.

"Tell me, my friend, what are the uses of mineral ores in your art?" asked Martin.

"That's a tall order. It would take a brace of full tides, not just the rise of one, to go over that ground so far as I know it ... and there's much more than I know, that the masters of healing could teach of ... But I can give a few examples. Iron, for example, is good in small doses for biliousness or dizzy attacks. Sulphur clears the skin and the interior. Zinc is also good for erupted skins. Quartz, especially from flint stones, helps to stop bleeding and makes a powder for those who have much over-exerted themselves. Fuller's earth dries weeping skin. Copper and gold relieve the seizing up of the joints, and the pain that goes with it. Mercury calms the overly agitated. Tar made from sea-coal is another good skin treatment. Silver is sometimes effective in reducing warts, and can be taken – like iron – for headaches, dizziness or bilious attacks. But all metals must be used sparingly, for any gross accumulation is poisonous."

"That took all of two minutes!" laughed Martin.

Most of that lore he well knew, from his great teacher and from reading the papers that his predecessor Aedric had left at the preceptory. There had been some filings of metals in pots within Aedric's secret chamber on the top floor of the Bellins Gate tower. He did not recall reading that sea-coal was a metal, but remembered that he had asked the hermit about minerals; the medicine maker probably knew the differences between metals and other minerals, and assumed that Martin also did so when he added his warning against a build up of metals in any anatomy.

There seemed to be nothing that metal medicine could achieve that was not replaced or bettered, less hazardously, by herbal remedies. There was a special attraction attached to metals, however, for some people; a different and implicitly deeper science was engaged in the working of metals, from that which was required to make tinctures, possets and potions from plants. Thus there must be a temptation to think that the medicinal effect of the product was proportional to the effort of producing it – or to the rarity of the inert ingredient. Martin expressed this view to the hermit, who responded simply:

"I have neither the devices nor the wits to work in metals ... but I think you may be right. If I had to do all that extra work in the greater heat of a smithy, then I suppose I would expect greater returns and better results."

"But if the results were always better, ways would have been found to use metals much more," suggested Martin.

"Well, they haven't have they?" asked the hermit.

Since Peter of Colechurch had mentioned Aedric's metallic interest, Martin had wondered if he had been failing his community and denying his destiny by not having discovered and developed this interest of his predecessor at an earlier stage. He had taken some selfish comfort from the fact that none of his brother monks at Bellins Gate had pointed him in that direction, nor indeed had any of them reminded Martin that the primary criterion for his selection to occupy the preceptor's post had been his pharmacological and diagnostic apprenticeship. It was obviously not seen as being of great importance for the welfare of the reputation of the preceptory to sustain Aedric's active interest in the preparation of medicaments, and Prior Osbert also seemed to be unconcerned at the lapse of the resource that Martin had been summoned specifically to maintain.

Perhaps the changing times and the promise of social stability under the new king made it less important to recognise disease carriers as they passed through the *porte*, and to have a home-distilled selection of key medicines constantly accessible at the Bellins Gate preceptory.

The hermit's dismissal of the possibility of any mass use of metal-based medicines helped Martin to lay any ghost of conscience at not maintaining (or even expanding) Aedric's laboratory output from the top of the preceptory tower. In the time that was freed for Martin by obtaining medical supplies from the hermit, he had done things that interested himself, served the common good, furthered the interests of the preceptory and of its mother abbey, and caused no offence to the church or to its Heavenly Master.

Martin reassessed this comfortable conclusion at the same time as the hermit deduced that the water level had risen high enough for the traps to be free from infant inquisitors:

"Come, I'll help you to collect some grass, then I will tell you about my problem."

"A fair exchange," agreed the monk.

The children watched as the black monk and the shaggy hermit collected the grass. They were used to seeing the hermit gathering the ingredients for his preparations, for he was a local celebrity to whom all kinds of people came in search of relief for an endless series of afflictions. A local child could often get a coin from a rich and feckless searcher for the hermitage, and the children took it in turns to loiter in the mornings near the turnoff of the Hermitage Lane from Knight-a-Gale Lane. Even if no farthings were forthcoming, the children saw the horses and the garments of the patients or their attendants or their messengers, and could weave fantasies about them to bridge the massive deficiencies in their understanding of the passers-by.

Often the hermit went out to his island gardens, tending or harvesting his sometimes delicate crops. On such occasions the children would advise chance callers on how long they might have to wait for a consultation. For this purpose, all but the dimmest children learned the numbers one to six in French and the words *heures* and *retour*. Many of the callers were from the ruling race, and it was a constant source of gratification for the parents at Knighten Rise to hear their offsprings' accounts of the hermit's rough and ready responses to the importuning of the aristocracy. The more hauteur they showed, the less respect, or even understanding, they received. The parents pressed home, however, the message that any display of amusement on the part of the juvenile audience that gathered under the trees well away from the hermitage was contrary to the best interests of the community. The hermit was a churl, who just happened to have found a vocation that was of service to the elevated petitioners who came for his potions. The great accepted the abrupt manner and inadequate French of their herbalist, provided he delivered the desired unguent or elixir; but if they had seen that this caused pleasure to the local youth, the Norman lords might visit their wrath on a laughing child or its community. As Knighten Rise was independent of any lord, a true Tower Hamlet whose men were pledged to serve the crown in the defence of the city fortress, the community could not call on any local lord to defend them. Even with familiar outsiders, such as the hermit himself or the soundly trusted Father Martin or the local priest at Stebenhithe, Father John, the villagers knew that they must maintain a certain reserve. Safety first was the prime rule of communal and of individual survival.

When the monk's trug had been laden, the monk and the hermit went together towards the hermitage. One of the larger village boys waded into the rising water near the crab traps, but the others called warnings to him not to do anything that could get them all into trouble. He touched the top of the nearest trap, then declared that the water was already too high to do anything useful. He came back to shore, gratified at the recognition that the other children granted to his minimal explorations.

"Let's see what they're up to," he proposed, so the children followed in the wake of the two men.

The mastiff sat, at the hermit's command.

"He's a powerful animal, sure enough," said the householder whose property and privacy the dog defended. His tone was cautious. Martin guessed that the dog did not enjoy the full confidence of the hermit. As if he read Martin's thought, the hermit explained:

"When you were away from Bellins Gate – when the first was left here – I did nothing. When it happened again, I had to take comfrey to the Lady Angelina at Chad's Well. She was gracious, and I told her what had happened, and of my concern that what could happen twice at my hermitage could carry on happening. She said that I was right to be concerned, and took me to tell Sir Rulf ... He rode to the hermitage shortly after I got back there myself; and after assuring himself of my account, he said there were deep dark deeds afoot and he left me the dog for my protection ... I'm getting used to her now; she has quite a good nature, despite her size and apparent ferocity. I would not have dealt so well with a dog, I fear, as I do with this bitch ... Rulf has been back twice to check, but nothing else has occurred of the same kind. If what I think is the case is true, it would happen again on Friday or Saturday of this week!"

The man usually spoke much less than this, but also more clearly. Martin understood now where the dog came from, and how Sir Rulf le Court had become involved in the business, but he had no inkling what the business was. He said as much to the hermit.

"I know you don't. And I won't say a word until we are behind a closed door, in the middle of my hermitage," said the master of the place.

Martin followed him into the high stone structure that had the look of a chapel but the appurtenances of a great cookhouse or perhaps an ancient brew house. The far wall from the door was taken up by a great hearth with several braziers, and multiple chimneys rising above them. In the middle of the room stood a massive bench on which potions were prepared. The walls supported many shelves and against them also stood several presses and chests. The hermit's modest cot was at the end of the bench nearest to the fires, so that he could rouse himself relatively easily through the night to tend to continuous processes of distillation or rendering down.

The hermit closed the door, and both men took time to adjust to the almost-dark interior. Two of the high windows in the wall where the door was, the side of the building guarded by the mastiff, had their shutters pulled back, but the impact of the windows on the gloom of the indoors seemed trivial on so bright a day.

By feel as much as by sight, the hermit poured two mugs of ale from a barrel balanced on a trestle beside the hearth:

"Elderflower; it makes the late spring ale the freshest of the year!" explained the hermit, as Martin's sense of smell alerted him to an unusual odour emanating from the ale.

Both men drank, taking a deep draught, as if this action formed a bond between them, to consolidate their friendship as a prelude to the disclosure that the hermit was about to make.

Martin felt a pressure in his ears, a tension in the soft area between the top of his nose and his hard forehead, and a tingling in his fingers. Metaphorical midges filled his belly, and he held his ale mug with two hands for fear of spilling the special brew in his excitement. He was reasonably confident that he managed to show no sign of these involuntary physical responses to the possibility of getting involved in a new puzzle that could be dangerous as well as intriguing. None of the fires were lit today, so the stone building seemed almost chill. This could give him his excuse, if the hermit observed him to shiver, though the temperature of the air had nothing to do with it.

Since Martin's help had been sought six weeks or more ago, this case of wrongdoing could already have got out of hand. Once Martin knew what had been going on – or what the hermit and Sir Rulf had deduced to be going on – he could begin to make his own assessment.

The hermit did not sit. In his concern to tell the story clearly, he needed to pace the floor. The physical movement absorbed his surplus energy and left the appropriate flow of spirits to animate his exposition:

"If it had been in the crabbing season, like now, it would have been even worse; but it was bad enough!"

This opening could have been the start of any sort of a tale, but the manner in which it was delivered by a normally stoical individual made it clear that something truly shocking had taken place.

"I came back here ... it was when the frost had broken and the river had been very high, making it a hard struggle to get a ship up to your part of London – let alone past the bridge to Queenhithe or the River of Wells ... Well, it was early afternoon, time to get my dinner on the go, before I set all to rights outside ahead of the dusk ... I'd almost got into the house before I noticed it. Cloth in my water-butt. I grabbed it, to pull it out. I don't drink that water, or use it in my potions – I've got the well for that sort of thing – but I use it to stock my crabs, and later in the year I use it for watering if I need to, because it's handier than the well."

It was obvious that there had been more than a piece of cloth in the butt, or the story would not be worth telling, and the hygienic detail would have been irrelevant. Martin sipped the ale as the hermit came to the point.

"The cloth was clothes, and they were on a body ... a dead body, without a head, or hands."

"A man?" asked Martin.

"A youngish man," asserted the hermit. "Nine stone at least to heave out of my water-butt, without the parts I've mentioned. I had to get my head in there a couple of times, to make sure the other parts weren't in the bottom."

"You've buried him?" asked Martin.

"Yes, Father. I fetched Gutta, the headman from the hamlet, and we decided that neither of us wanted the sheriff or even Sir Rulf involved ... it seemed like a horrible one-off, then!"

The man had been buried in the burial ground at Knighten Rise, overlooking the small Thames tributary between the hermitage and the Weopping settlements to the east.

"What did you find out about the corpse? Were there marks? Possessions ... besides the clothes? Shoes or boots?" asked Martin. The hermit responded in reverse order:

"The feet were bare. There was no purse, nor dagger, nor belt to hang any on. If you don't count dismemberment as marking, there weren't no marks ... no stab in the chest, nor arrow in the side. He'd been killed by having his head off ... though perhaps the hands had been lopped off first. The arms were tied behind him, at the elbows ... He'd been a well-made man, in his prime; a soldier, perhaps, who'd got into the wrong hands in that horrible war they've had going on for so long over there ..."

"Which war?" asked Martin. The hermit seemed to be taking it for granted that the provenance of the corpse was beyond doubt.

"In Ireland, of course!"

"How do you suppose he was from Ireland?" asked Martin.

"From the cloth!" answered the host, and setting down his mug he went to a chest against the wall that faced the door. By this time, Martin's eyes were adjusted to the gloom, and he could see the brightness of the green dye of the bolt of cloth that the hermit was carrying towards him.

The type of cloth was unfamiliar to Martin. It was a blend of wool and linen, a fabric that was flexible and light, and yet gave considerable warmth. The hermit had folded it for storage in the chest. Martin felt a small corner of the material as the hermit backed away from him, unfolding the bolt of fabric as he did so.

The fabric thus revealed was a good yard wide, and several yards long. At each side – what would be top and bottom, assuming that the piece was wound somehow around the body – there was a bold pattern in a greyish colour picked out at a few salient points at each repetition of the design with simple stitchery in red wool.

"The material was somehow waxed before dyeing, so that these parts were left in the natural colour," said Martin, looking carefully at the pattern. "Then the stitching was done last."

"Aye, that's what I reckon. It's a very good job," agreed the hermit.

The pattern was based on a great spiral of incomplete circles, which was reiterated about every eight inches along either edge of the cloth. Although the pattern was visible in a shadowy form on the underside – as the hermit held it for Martin's inspection – it was clear which side of the material was for showing to the world and which side had faced the wearer:

"And you are sure that this pattern is Irish?" asked Martin.

"Absolutely!" said the hermit. "I can't swear to have seen that exact design – and I had never seen so green a dye before that shrieked at me from my water-butt – but I've seen a hundred men in things like that, in my days at sea ... the man I found here was in Irish dress; of that, I'm quite sure."

"From the way you phrase that, you suggest that you don't assume that every body found in Irish dress is an Irishman," said Martin ruminatively, looking enquiringly at the hermit.

"You follow me very well, my friend. This piece of cloth is unusual ... and it's undamaged, if you don't count a few bloodstains and a lot of muck. You could certainly clothe a few children from the unbloodied bits, or make a lot of towels ... so why throw away the cloth with the corpse?" The hermit's question was purely rhetorical. He assumed that the cloth was left on the corpse – perhaps, even, put on the corpse – to indicate an Irish connection, a thought that Martin agreed with.

"And why dispose of the corpse here?" he asked.

"I think that is an easier question to answer, if you presume that it was meant to be found. If you were to be intending to deliver this cloth – and its contents – to the King of England from a London-bound ship, you'd want to put it ashore at West Minster, or the Tower ... But if you'd struggled against flood waters up the Thames for a couple of days; and then found that there was a special watch set on ships that might sell goods illicitly in a time of great privation after the harsh winter, then you'd look to get rid of your extra errand as quickly as you could. I think that the ship's master heard from an outward-bound vessel that he had better be squeaky clean on his arrival in port, so he looked for any substantial building on the bank – or near to the river – and sent his men to see what my place was like. You can see it plainly from a ship's mast in the winter when the trees are bare. When they found my place, with nobody here, they made their deposit."

"And why the water-butt?" asked Martin.

"The corpse was already well stinking. I think they'd probably had it stored in something similar on the ship. I don't know if water does help to slow down bodily decay. But I do know that creatures like snails, that live in water, attack any flesh that is put their way, so even if the wet does preserve the flesh, the water creatures will speedily even up the situation." The hermit's answer showed the thought he had been giving to this particular conundrum over the past weeks.

Chapter Three

Martin stood holding one end of the long piece of light cloth that had served as shroud for the unknown dead man. The hermit stood almost at the door of his large single room, holding the other end. Despite the relative gloom, the blood and muck to which the hermit had referred were clearly visible disfigurements of a very fine piece of work:

"So, you and Gutta stripped the man, and buried him," asked Martin.

"We put him in a decent blanket; one of my own!" The hermit protested, mildly, at any suggestion that he would despoil the corpse cavalierly and bury it in a state of nudity. "All the village turned out, too," he added.

"But you didn't fetch the curate from Stebenhithe, or one of my monks," said Martin, "and I'll be bound that all the village was sworn to secrecy."

"Of course. I'd worked out most of what I've just told you by the time we buried the body. That was next day; for the night, we put it back in the butt, with planks over to keep off the foxes and the crows ... I drained the butt, after the burial. It took three men to help me pull it over, and set it up again. The staves are getting old; I'll need to replace it in a year or two."

He turned to the next serious incident.

"Five weeks later, I was roused before dawn by the noise of the geese. It was full moon, and I suspected there was a fox about. But the noise didn't quiet down as it usually does, so I got up and went outside and looked around. There was nothing to see close by, though the geese stayed agitated. I came back in, and stayed awake, and listened. I swear, I didn't hear a thing. Perhaps the goose noise covered any sound they made ... anyway, in the morning when I went outside again the rising sun picked them out ... Three heads had been set on stakes, facing my very door! ... And I think that two of them were ... had been ... women."

"You think it? You are uncertain?" asked Martin.

"One head was bigger than the others, and grey-bearded. The others were smaller and with longer hair. One, I think, was certainly female ... the other could be a youth; but I think more likely a girl ..."

"None of them was likely to be the head of your other ... deposit?" asked Martin.

"No, that man was younger than the man whose head appeared, and bigger than would fit either of the others." The hermit knew the things that he was sure about. After a brief pause, he added:

"These heads had been severed a while ago, perhaps last year. They were partly dried out, and they stank little ... not like the big corpse – that was much newer though it had lost all freshness."

"How were the heads displayed?" asked Martin.

"They were staked out, in front of my door. The winter ground was still soft; nothing like it is now. They'd not been hammered into the ground, else I'd have heard them. The heads were already stuck on the stakes, and somebody ... somebody had just pushed down on the heads until the stakes stood, with the heads then about three feet off the ground," answered the hermit. He began to fold the long bolt of cloth as he did so, as if the prosaic action calmed his recollection.

"What sort of stakes were they?" asked Martin.

"Oh, the ordinary elm that you'd carry in a ship's boat so that you can secure it to the shore if there isn't a stair or staithe to use," answered the hermit.

"So, a ship is involved, you believe, on both occasions?" asked Martin.

"Yes, and it could be the same ship ... or some of the same people. If so, I'm about due for another visit, because the full moon was over a week ago and the interval between the first and second visits was five weeks and a day."

The hermit prised the end of the cloth from Martin's fingers as he said this. He completed the folding and laid it on top of the chest from which he had drawn it. He returned to the barren hearth, took up his ale mug and helped himself to two generous pulls on the elderflower beer.

"Tell me, what did you do, once you realised what confronted you?" asked Martin.

"Well, I looked at the things, and took in what they were. I was sure that the men who had left them and their boat and their ship would be well gone, so I didn't look for them. I went to my water-butt. It was half full again, because the drought didn't begin immediately after the thaw, as you may recall. I was able to reach down in it with a paddle, and check that there was nothing untoward left there. I was going to the village, to get Gutta, when I met little Otrund." Martin nodded, recognising the name of a girl from the hamlet. "So she went to fetch him, and I went to the riverbank to seek signs of a landfall."

"Which you found?" asked Martin.

"Which I found ... The tide was well fallen back, and the footprints below the watermark hadn't been disturbed yet by the children's mud-larking ... They were bare feet, with wide toes – common sailors ... plus one pair of boots with a good heel: a man of status, just the one!"

"How many sailors?" asked Martin.

"Three came ashore. There'd need to be at least two more to hold the boat on the oars until it was well tied up, then to pass out that gruesome cargo. I was surprised how heavy the heads were, when we came to move 'em!" said the hermit.

"Did you find anything else?" asked Martin.

"Not on the riverbank, no ... So I came back here. Gutta had almost all the men with him, and the women and kids were there as well; all ooing and aahing at the horrible heads. And the dogs were sniffing at them, then backing off as if they were really foul ... We agreed that it wouldn't do to have a crowd around, if anyone came for a consultation ... and we didn't want the heads on display, either. So we agreed that Gutta would take them to Knighten Rise, but keep them safe ... I told him that any loss or damage would go hard for him, once the reeve was involved ... He said, he didn't want the reeve poking around, and I said that the reeve might torch his entire village if we were found to have kept this secret ... So eventually we agreed that I'd take Lady Angelina her comfrey a bit earlier than expected, and seek her advice."

From past experience, the denizens of Knighten Rise had learned that the le Courts of Chad's Well Manor could be relied on to keep their own counsel when it was in their own interests and that of their neighbours so to do. Rulf and Angelina le Court were prepared to treat the free community of Knighten Rise on its own terms and, indeed, to support its independence from the encroachment of the Abbot of the Holy Trinity of Aldgate who was given to claiming that Knighten Rise must be part of the old knighten lands and thus within his fiefdom. The Tower Hamlet community of fisher folk that was settled at the mouth of the small river that flowed to the Thames from Chad's Well was of use to the lord of that manor, and Rulf recognised this in his dealings with them. Martin had once been involved indirectly in the consolidation of that interdependency, and had secured the goodwill of both parties in the process.

Martin had returned from his foray to Oxford and his subsequent visit to Cambridge and Ely before this second incident, but he recognised that as the hermit had once turned to the preceptor in vain, he would have continued on the alternative path that had been available. The hermit told how he had presented the comfrey and the story to Lady Angelina, who immediately took the raconteur to her husband. That had led to the mastiff at the hermit's door, and the three heads being placed in an empty flour bin in the outhouse of Chad's Well Manor.

"So, Sir Rulf did not summon the reeve?" asked Martin. He sought the explanation, rather than a factual response that was self-evident – had the Reeve of Middlesex been called in to deal with the case, the outcome would have been very different from the story which Martin had heard.

"Sir Rulf will tell the king, direct, when the king is at West Minster," answered the hermit. "That gives us time to see if anything else happens. The heads had been dead for months, at the least, and they had died far away. Probably far to the west, in Ireland."

"You don't know that, about the heads," said Martin.

"Indeed not ... I concede that point. The heads could be from anywhere, as indeed could that headless body. Only the cloth comes from Ireland. Of that I am sure, and so is the Lady Angelina. She has Scots origins, and has met Irish folk many times. She shares my recollection of the circle-patterns. But it's a known fact that the bodies – or body parts – certainly don't come from here or hereabouts. Sir Rulf has made enquiry: there are no headless bodies, or bodiless heads, that the reeves of Middlesex, Essex or Surrey are trying to attach to their owners!" The hermit's assessment seemed fair enough to Martin, at first blush.

Martin would probably be welcomed at Chad's Well Manor, and Rulf might allow him to view the heads. Perhaps he would ask that, sometime soon; but Martin's first presumption was that all the body parts were simply signs, placed by someone who waited to leave a message.

There was a possibility that the person with the high-heeled boot, or his master, was unfamiliar with London and had on the first occasion been panicked into leaving the body at the most substantial building downriver from the port of London that was out of sight of the watchmen in the Tower and the nearby City Kenning-tower. Following the hermit's assumption that the ship that had brought the headless corpse did so under cover of a legitimate cargo, the ship would have proceeded to one of the many *portes* – the riverside landings, with a gate to the city – or hythes, where a ship could be harboured, off the main stream of the Thames. In that case, whoever was responsible for the deposit of the cloth signal and the body would have had ample opportunity to discover what sort of a structure the hermitage was. They could even have sent crewmen to spy out how the authorities were handling the discovery of the corpse beside the hermitage, while the ship remained in port.

Putting himself in the position of the depositor of the corpse in the water-butt, Martin presumed that he would for a day or so be busy with officialdom as the cargo was recorded and unloading began. That should have given time for the corpse to have been found, the reeve to be summoned, the investigation to begin and the story of the discovery to sweep through the riverside alehouses.

Even at a time when the flood water and the dearth of foodstuffs for delivery to London had reduced the number of ships demanding the dockers' attention, it would take three or more short early spring days to unload a seagoing vessel – long enough for the lack of any rumour to become significant. If the authorities had been informed, and were sufficiently sophisticated to be able to suppress rumours in order to spring a trap on enquirers, then it would be foolhardy to be caught by asking about dead bodies. Yet the depositor would find it hard to resist making any attempt to find out what, if anything, was going on at the hermitage.

Martin's series of assumptions all hinged on the presumption that the reason for dumping the body in the water-butt was ignorance of London. The sole function of the headless corpse had been to ensure that whoever discovered the cloth would give it special attention. Incidental information, such as the fact that the body was that of a youngish person, who had been subjected to needless violence, was peripheral to the main story. Yet it might have also served to support the supposition that there was an Irish dimension to the message, for it was known to all and sundry that Ireland had become a place of violence and sudden death.

Further following the hermit's line of thought, for want of a better, Martin conceded that the five weeks would indeed give time for a round trip to be made to some Irish port, or ports. It would allow turnaround time and perhaps trade negotiations as cover for more nefarious activity, and then the ship had come back to London.

The men from the ship had come ashore a second time, and checked that there was no guard on the hermitage, nor any stakeout around it. Then they had left their three grizzly markers.

The heads could not meaningfully have been left elsewhere; in themselves they conveyed no evidence of an Irish connection. Only by linking them with the other body and the bolt of green cloth could they possibly be understood. To leave the three heads at Tower Hill – or even in Chancellor Becket's own chamber – would be meaningless because the recipient would not have any reason to associate the two clandestine deliveries.

The error the first time round, in depositing the corpse at the Hermitage, had made it imperative that the follow-through also had to be there. The second incident had to be so blatant that, even if the occupant of the hermitage had simply disposed privily of the first deposit of human remains, it would have to be reported to the appropriate authorities.

Consistent with this line of thinking was the presumption that the heads had been recovered relatively recently from the site of some massacre or mass execution, which had occurred long before the killing of the younger man.

Lady Angelina had, on good grounds, confirmed the hermit's opinion that the cloth was Irish. Martin asked an obvious question:

"It would not take five weeks, surely, to make a round trip to Ireland?"

The hermit looked thoughtful, sat down for the first time since he had admitted Martin to his premises, and answered:

"Well, it's a good few years since I was at sea, but I'd reckon it this way. Clearance on arrival at Queenshithe, say one day; then unloading, three days. One Sunday, one feast, and four days to load; that's a total of ten days. Then you've a good day, perhaps more, to get out to sea from the port of London. After that, depending on the strength of the westerly and the Irish port you're headed for, three to six days. It can be less, with an east or south wind; but you tell me how often you get either of those, compared to a westerly. Now, coming back, of course, the same thing is in reverse; you can get back in three days from St George's Channel to Dover, and another two to London – if you are very, very lucky with wind and tide. Add that all up, and you'll find that you have twenty-three to twenty-five days ... and I've not included the Irish angle, yet.

"You don't just negotiate with one city reeve for access to trade in Ireland, you know. I know that's what King Henry wants, like many have before him; and he wants the reeve of every port to be a Norman that thinks himself an English subject – yet above the native English, and over the Irish or the Welsh or the Scots too! ... That's not stuff for me, but I know of it, like every man-jack along the river, and every honest seaman knows it ... anyway, whether or not King Henry's plans help it or not, the Irish situation is complicated.

"The Irish are essentially farmer folk; that's why the estuaries were open to settlement by outsiders. Like the old Romans, the settlers have stayed in touch with what they call civilisation by ship. It's ships that bring the arms and the bows and arrows – aye, and the slave collars and the man-shackles – that the settlers try to impose on the locals when trade does not seem to run to their advantage. It's just what the Romans did afore us, so there's no reason to say that it isn't the way of the world. And it's natural that the Irish don't like it! Look at me ... I didn't like what they did to me, ashore, so I went to sea; and what did I carry? ... I carried weapons to hold folk down, and I carried the things that they grew and the things that they made, while they were held down. That's what ships carry with their cargoes, Father Martin – the spirit of power and the wages they get from the use of power over poor folk!"

Martin had heard the hermit's account of his dash for freedom on previous occasions, and he had learned something of the independence of spirit that had led to the old hermit selecting this castaway to be his successor. Though not religious like the previous hermit, his predecessor had respected his wish for independence sufficiently to train him up in the skills of healing that had preserved the integrity of the hermitage through all the troubles of Stephen's reign.

The implicit political message in the hermit's declaration on the situation in Ireland was a complex one. Though enslavement and exploitation of the quiescent mass of the population was the way that the world was, some peoples – apparently including the Irish – were not yet persuaded of the universality and inevitability of the progress of civilisation. That, of course, was the true use of the concept of civilisation – a complex of cities, ruling the world, linked by trade and subject to the Law of God. The blessed St Augustine had shown how there can be a conceptual City of God coexisting with and within the visible network of terrestrial civic centre. The church, and Martin as a son and servant of the church, must support the mission of the church. Could the City of God exist, without the underpinning of the earthly city?

Perhaps the Irish had a way of doing that? Surely not! But there had been endless trouble about the establishment of churches in Ireland. The settlers from England, Normandy, Norway or Scotland were happy to accept the normal ecclesiastical jurisdiction over their churches. As towns were fortified on the river estuaries and harbours of Ireland, so the papally appointed primate, the Archbishop of Canterbury, demanded and received their dues and their obedience. The Irish had no right to object to this, let alone to add it to the list of their grievances against both the French-speaking and the Nordic settlers who were assiduously building a trade system that could draw Ireland into the mainstream of European Christendom. The Irish resistance to the evolution of the ports was dangerous – and possibly heretical, or even heathen – obscurantism, from the settler's perspective.

Yet deep within the hermit's observation, there was another possible interpretation. The Romans had not mastered Ireland, so far as was now known. Ireland had its own culture, and her ethics were provided by the ancient Church of St Patrick. Were these great values the true Ireland? Or was there merely a prevailing violent lawlessness that traded on Irish tradition as a sanction for its destructive attacks on the growing cities?

"So, whatever the cargo that a ship carries into – or out from – an Irish port, how many days does the whole trip need?" asked Martin.

"There you have me, my friend; I'm only guessing, now, because the situation has got a lot worse since I was regularly meeting seamen who'd been to Ireland. Then, the main half-dozen ports were almost as secure and efficient as Southampton or Dieppe ... but now, well, it's a different story ... But I will make a guess because I take your point. It has occupied my mind quite a bit recently, as you will imagine ... We have at least twenty-three days in what I have recounted to you already.

"Then, when you get near the coast, if you see a large number of small boats, you stand well off and get out to sea; enough little ships can overwhelm the biggest, if they catch it with sails furled and oars stowed. So you accept the odd inshore fisher boat as probably being safe, but that's all. Then you look for smoke, if you judge it safe to move inshore. No smoke means no city; no living city, anyhow. Chimney smoke, rising according to wind and weather in a disciplined way, that means a normal city. Black, thick smoke means unwanted fire, perhaps sabotage or a sacking. Fires outside the city mean an attacking or besieging army. I'd reckon that it's safest to cruise the coasts for part of a night and part of a day, to get an assessment of the fires. And you need one day of decent weather to gauge the amount of small boat activity to know how many folk are fishing for what ... And you always remember that the Irish, like the

Welsh, are not great sea fishers; they have fish enough on the rivers and close inshore where they can be fishers while not leaving their farms for long ... So if there are lots of Irish boats about, beware!"

The hermit emptied his beer down his throat on completing this sentence, and reached out to take Martin's mug, with his own, to the spigot on the barrel. He filled both and returned one to Martin before he sat, took another mouthful, rolled it round his teeth before swallowing, and continued:

"You won't be going to Ireland, of course, and nor shall I! ... But if I was master of a vessel charged to go to Cork or some such place, I'd want a day and a night of watching. Then, depending on the lie of the harbour, and how far the port may be up the tidal waterway, I'd decide whether to take the ship straight in, or whether to send a boat ... A reliable master of a big vessel is always ready to risk a boat's crew to save the whole enterprise. Sometimes it's the boatmen who are the survivors, if a squall or an enemy gets the ship, but that's not the usual way of it! Sometimes you'd send the boat into the port; sometimes you'll ask the men to land secretly, away from the port, and work out the lie of the land."

Again the hermit paused to drink, raising his mug in a pledge to which Martin responded. Behind his smile, he willed his friend to get on with his account. He did so, but with continuing circumlocution.

"If you feel safe to ride the tide towards the port, then begins the negotiation for access. You know more about that than me, being preceptor of a *porte* yourself, but I'd guess that most of the Irish ports that are still in operation – if any are – need to be sure of who the arrivals are before any portal is opened to them, or any men set ashore. If a town has been besieged by the Irish for many weeks even a dozen seamen may be too many for the town to resist, if they prove hostile. So the bona fides have to be verified, before the ship is secured and the gates are opened to it."

"And then?" Martin's interjection made it clear to the hermit that, while his attention to detail was appreciated, of greater interest was his summary. The hermit smiled, drank and replied.

"Then the trading begins. Remember, the Irish ports are tiny, compared to London or Southampton. So when the ship comes in, there are few men to unload, and fewer still to buy bulk cargo, so the local merchants have to wheel and deal to make up the purchase of even a modest cargo ... And it works the other way; no merchant has sufficient goods to fill a vessel. Even those who have stores for export might not have invested in barrels to contain them until they are sure of a safe shipment. So the goods must be collected, and priced, and packed and carted to the quay, then all the cargo has to be enshipped by a few men, including the ship's crew. There might not even be cranes, to facilitate the barrelage on board ... In such a situation, Sunday and the Saints may be less respected, but I'd say you'd be very lucky to turn round the ship in less than a fortnight."

"Which adds fourteen days to your twenty-three ... giving about the interval of five weeks that you have already noted!" It had been pretty clear from the outset that the answer must be of the order of thirty-five days, and now Martin had as full an explanation as he would ever need as to why a ship bound past his preceptory window for Limerick could not reasonably be expected to ride up the Thames on any tide sooner than the seventy-third after the one that was carrying it downriver.

"What sort of ship would go to Ireland?" asked Martin.

"You mean the design, the type of vessel?" asked the hermit. Martin nodded.

"Well, it has to be big enough to go right out to sea, through the highest seas known to man ... The harbours and rivers are great and good, so there is no natural constraint on the size of ships. But too big a ship is useless, because of the smallness of trade – and of the traders' resources – in the Irish towns. So I reckon you'd want a fully decked ship. That's less likely to take on water in high seas ... and if you're economising on crew as well, you want that sort of a vessel ... So, I'd say one of the smaller fully decked ships, probably one low in the beam, to ride the waves without too much buffeting on the hull from the wind."

Martin saw ships of every design and from all of western Europe, including the Mediterranean, pass his preceptory in panorama with every tide. Often they moved under oars against the tide, or thus stressed the urgency of their errands at the slack water of high or low tide. He could easily call to mind the sort of solid, smallish ship with almost no poop but a fully planked-over cargo space that the hermit speculated would be the best. It was not certain, of course, that such a vessel would have brought the gruesome messages – or indeed that Ireland had anything to do with the whole business. But if any more messages or follow-up came, then the small ships of that design that were on the Thames at the relevant time must be a focus for investigation.

"If two and two make about sixteen, and there really is an Irish connection – as that cloth certainly betokens – then you are due, if not overdue, for another sign or symbol," concluded Martin. The hermit assented:

"That's what Sir Rulf thinks, as I do ... So he's got his own men, and the village men – and the lads, for that matter – on the lookout. He is keeping a night watch with his own men and some of the bigger riverside children. That is part of the reason why I have such a large audience for my crab catching – the smaller kids are released from helping at home, to some extent, if they swear they are river watching ... looking out for anyone from a vessel making an unsolicited landfall between where the little river runs into the Thames past Knighten Rise to the east, and the lands of Trinity Abbey to the west of us."

"Sir Rulf has still not invoked the sheriff, then?" asked Martin.

"That's right," replied the hermit. "He thinks he's close enough to the king – and to mighty folk, like your prior – to take the risk of keeping the secret. He said that's why he has custody of the King's Wardrobe, whatever that might be!"

Martin concluded, silently, that the hermit was being disingenuous. Rulf was one of the guardians of the Wardrobe Tower, a solid stone structure near Baynard's Castle in the City of London, where the king kept some of his most valuable records, along with redundant regalia and a stock of armaments. Any man the king trusted to guard this resource, and to maintain the inventory of it in good order – and the weaponry in working order – was certainly rock-solid in his loyalty. But it was still bold on the part of such a man to undertake to keep a secret from the king's officers, even if his motive was to serve the king effectively and in the least troublesome way.

The problems of settlers in the Irish towns had become acute recently; Martin himself had received refugees by way of his *porte* at Bellins Gate, and there had been much talk about the need to force the Irish to conform to the same dispensation as had been imposed on England since the Norman Conquest. But the reign of Stephen had left many acute problems closer to London than the west of Ireland, and these had to be settled before it was safe to consider launching a war beyond the shores of Britain.

France was far more susceptible to dominance by the regime of Henry of Anjou than was the Celtic fringe of the British Isles. As by far the greatest lord of France, Henry II of England had every reason to look to his French lands for resources. He had done homage to the French king for his lands and had checked out the fidelity and effectiveness of his lieutenants and reeves and castle constables. He had monitored the castle building programme, and had endowed churches and chantries in places where the clergy's support required to be consolidated. Now he could decide on the direction in which to seek expansion of his realms.

The Scots had made successively deeper incursions into England during Stephen's reign – taking Durham, approaching York and temporarily occupying Lancaster. Henry's highest foreign policy objective was to secure his unquestioned sovereignty over what was loosely termed Northumbria. His decisive actions in that area had already borne fruit, and emissaries of the Scots king were negotiating about where and when he should meet his dear brother-king Henry so that he could formally acknowledge England's overlordship of Scotland. This would enable a tidying-up treaty to be negotiated, under which it would finally be determined which lands north of Hadrian's Wall would be retained by Scotland, and which would in perpetuity be designated as English Northumbria, or Northumberland.

King Henry fixed on Chester as the site for the Scots' humiliation, because in so doing Henry could make it clear that the Earl of Chester was very much the subject of the English king; and if Earl Ranulf thought once more of changing that status, he would die branded as a traitor.

In Scotland the feudalised lowlands provided a barrier between England and the still-tribal highlands, but the Welsh tribal alliances – the loose principalities – meant that pre-feudal social structures reached the border with England. On the English side of the Welsh border, in the southern part of the Severn Valley, Earl Robert of Gloucester had been able to maintain a rough and ready control around his western base at Cardiff Castle and thus maintain forces strong enough to defend the frontier. The Earldom of Chester had been established by the conqueror to keep the northern Welsh out of England. Earl Ranulf had played this game according to his own rules, during the troubled reign of King Stephen, including making informal mutual defence pacts with his neighbours in Wales, and reputedly on occasions encouraging Welsh aggression against the undefended English Marcher territories that lay between his lands and those of Earl Robert. This disruption of coherent English government had interrupted the Anglo-Norman assault on Welsh independence.

Martin had personally witnessed the aftermath of several ugly incidents on the Anglo-Welsh border, during his novitiate at the Abbey of St Mary in Gloucester. He had heard many tales of the nobility and the culture, the savagery and the superstition of the Welsh. It was self-evident, now that England was a united power again, that the monarchy would not tolerate the continuance of anarchic conditions a few hours' walk from significant county towns – Cardiff, Gloucester, Worcester and Hereford – or from the principal westerly ports of Bristol and Chester. The Welsh showed every inclination to resist being drawn into the feudal economy. Henry's advisers suggested that allowing Wales to remain free would simply prolong the agonies of a moribund cultural inheritance whose day had ended when the mailed fist secured the bridle of a horse whose rider had been equipped with stirrups. Knights and their auxiliaries would ultimately subdue Welsh bowmen, even in the remotest valleys; it would take time, but the powerful signal of a Scots king coming to Chester – on the Welsh borders – to pay homage to the English king, in a great show that was to be paid for by the equivocally loyal Earl Ranulf, would surely settle the minds of the princes and chieftains of the Welsh to recognise the need to compromise with those whom they were pleased to miscall the Saxons.

The Irish had no significant history of Saxon invasion; their most ruthless attackers for well over a millennium had been the Norsemen, from whom many of the Anglo-Normans who settled in England with the Conqueror were descended. If settlers come to Wexford or to Waterford as subjects of an English king – whether their latest journey began in Rouen, Bordeaux or an English port, and regardless of whether they asserted French, Viking or Jewish ancestry – they were accounted as English in Ireland. The power that purported to have the authority to grant the settlers a civic charter was English. Now that England had a powerful king, the logic shared by most courtiers suggested that once the Scots and the Welsh frontier problems were resolved, the continual demands of the church and of the merchants in Ireland for an end to anarchy and bloodshed must be heeded.

The opportunity to secure Ireland might free up lands that could be allocated to some of the old soldiers who had served Henry and his mother. The conundrum of how to provide a pension for landless, tough military men who were no longer needed for battle was a problem for every successful conqueror. The Romans had given captured land to long-serving legionnaires, thereby planting colonies of loyalists on the new frontier territories of their empire, men who would be capable of securing their land against both external aggression and local rebellion. Henry II had shown a strong tendency to leave established landlords in place, provided they promised him their full support for the future. So additional lands had to be got elsewhere with which to reward those who had been loyal to himself.

The Welsh, the highland Scots and the Irish did not have any system of land-lordship that was similar to feudal land holding, so there was virgin territory for the English king to appropriate and allocate, in the way that his great-grandfather had redistributed all of England after 1066. Henry only had to establish his sovereignty over the territory, and the knights whom he assigned to be or to serve the new landlords would do the rest.

The objectors to the expansionist policy reputedly included the Empress Matilda, the king's close counsellor Chancellor Becket, the Papal Legate Henry of Blois, and Queen Elinor who acted as Regent of England during her husband Henry's absences in France. This party argued that creating and sustaining trading bases around the coast of Ireland was very different from seeking territorial mastery of the hinterland. The land was mostly low lying and served by large rivers, but the further inland an invading force went, the longer and more vulnerable would be the army's supply lines – men on campaign would move into an unknown land of bogs and woodlands and even if they were well supplied and enjoyed a spell of good weather, the Irish could retreat ahead of them until supplies were reduced and the weather returned to its notorious wetness. Then the Irish could turn and fight.

The oppositionists argued that if the Irish ports were a valuable base for trade, then they should be developed as such. By all means give them garrison troops, who could build up the city walls. Send merchants to Ireland with civic charters and material assistance, such as skilled men to construct quays, jetties and cranes. Encourage coopers and shipwrights to settle in the new or restored Irish ports. But never confuse the affordable colonisation of ports with the territorial occupation of a vast hinterland.

Cutting across both arguments were the views of Archbishop Theobald of Canterbury. Universally well respected, the Archbishop had strong opinions on Ireland that were reinforced both by the rights of his position as primate and by his increasing distrust of his own archdeacon, Thomas Becket. If Becket was becoming inimical to the interests of the church, then his position must be exposed and undermined. Becket was a first-class lawyer – that had been the basis for Theobald selecting him as archdeacon, despite Becket's reluctance to proceed from the diaconate to the more demanding commitment of being ordained as a priest.

Since Becket had become the king's chancellor, his obligation to his former patron – Archbishop Theobald – had progressively been ignored, apparently without conscious consideration or any regret. Becket was now the king's man, and only a few dared to whisper that affections that could so easily and so totally be transferred from Church to Crown could equally readily veer in another, or in the reverse direction. Becket's reputed opposition to any adventurism in Ireland undoubtedly strengthened Theobald's contrary view, and it ensured that the Archbishop had sided with the interventionists.

Theobald's basic proposition was that several popes – and especially the present, English-born pontiff – had confirmed the Archbishopric of Canterbury as the ecclesiastical overseer of the Irish towns. This award reflected longstanding papal disenchantment with the independent attitudes of the native Irish church. The Irish clergy supported their kings in their intermittent campaign to compel all settlers to accept Irish rather than English hegemony, provided that the Irish kings included ecclesiastical as well as political autonomy among their objectives. In order to maintain their trade with the Irish, settlers in several ports had decided to regard their obligations to the See of Canterbury as being dispensable. The Irish towns, in short, had stopped paying church dues – cash – to the occupant of Lambeth Palace. The reduced scale of charges that they remitted to the indigenous Irish hierarchy enabled the leaders of that robustly individualist ecclesiastical structure to reinforce its independent attitude in relation to the centralising tendencies of the Roman curia. Theobald was an advocate of strong intervention in Ireland because he believed that it was necessary to extend the King of England's writ in Ireland, to enforce the papal grant of overall ecclesiastical primacy to Canterbury. Theobald was believed to have been the primary influence that persuaded Pope Hadrian of this point of view, and once that papal decision had been clearly stated, Henry of Winchester – Papal Legate to England – was forced to back Theobald's recommendation to the king.

Martin had heard all this as political chatter from his fellow West Minster monks, from the passengers through Bellins Gate, and from the many contacts that he had made in and around the City of London. The bowyers, such as Father Zebedee's churchwarden Wilf, and the fletchers, the smiths and the pikestaff turners were all building up stocks of weapons in the expectation that the Crown would soon be placing orders. Ship owners kept their elderly, storm-damaged vessels fully rigged in creeks down the Thames, ready to lease them to the monarch for a tidy sum if an army was to be conveyed to Scotland or – as was seen to be the greater likelihood – to Ireland.

In this context of warmongering and expectation, the message that the headless body had been intended to convey would probably be of material significance – if it could be rendered comprehensible. Martin was inclined to accept the assumption that was shared by Sir Rulf and the hermit that the other heads were simply a reinforcement of the original, as yet incomprehensible, announcement. So deciphering the message that was apparently conveyed through the cloth, and to a lesser extent by the brutal means by which it had been displayed, was crucial to this entire mystery.

The time was right for another sign to be revealed; the same period had elapsed since the second incident, as between the first and the second. Any secret agent with his wits about him would realise that since the two incidents had both passed without gossip getting out, very confident agencies of the state must be controlling the situation, agencies who must be ready to pounce, if anything further should occur, especially if the landing was gifted at the same spot as the previous pair. At the very least, charges of murder and of the desecration of corpses had to be addressed – secure grounds for arresting anyone who came ashore there with apparently clandestine intent. The authorities then could pursue their enquiries with all the passengers and seamen from the boat safely locked up.

Martin thought this interrogators' dream unlikely to be achieved; he did not expect the perpetrators to follow up their calls at this lonely spot with one more that must surely provoke their seizure. By all means, let Sir Rulf protect this excellent fellow, the hermit, and all his health-giving materials, but Martin could not envisage that this waiting game would bring about the resolution of the puzzle. He saw no point in saying this – he had not been a monk for a dozen years without learning that it is worse than counterproductive to challenge other people's notions on the basis of mere hunch, even if instinct has in the past been proved right.

Thus he allowed the conversation to dwell briefly on the hermit's estimation of the likelihood of another deposit being attempted, and the chances of Rulf's man making significant arrests. Then Martin declared that he must go, and that he would depart secure that the hermitage was properly protected.

"So, you have no need of a little monk; though I will nightly offer prayers for your continuing safety, and for the poor souls whose bodies are so crudely desecrated!" said Martin.

"That means you're off then; well, I think you are correct in what you say. It's a matter of watching and waiting for the present – waterside folk are good at that. Then, if something stirs that shouldn't, the armed men can pile in; they're good at that!" The hermit's radicalism was again displayed, unself-consciously, and he simply switched the topic thereafter. "So, let's get you your potions. You'll already have missed Vespers, Father preceptor, but if I stir my stumps you'll beat the City curfew bell and be back at Bellins Gate for Compline-time!"

Chapter Four

No exceptional night call from the *porte* disturbed the preceptor of Bellins Gate, who had to rise only for the regular rounds of nightly prayers and thus was thoroughly refreshed the next morning.

At Matins, he made a silent prayer of confession, admitting that his feelings of suppressed excitement and general well-being were derived from an inner certainty that he would become embroiled in the matters that the hermit had disclosed to him on the previous day. He added a prayer of thanksgiving for the opportunities and the abilities with which he was blessed. Then he tried to give his full attention to the ordered routine of the Divine Office, and after that to the worthy reading that accompanied the monks' breakfast in the refectory.

Martin almost succeeded in closing his mind to secular issues, but he was conscious of a sense of relief when he accompanied Brother Elias across the preceptory yard and up two levels of the tower by way of the stone spiral stair. There it was his custom to review the preceding night's business, agree on any specific memoranda that would be useful in the future if questions were asked about any of the travellers, and note the conditions of wind and weather.

As Elias copied the entries from the slate on which they were first jotted, into the neat version that would be deposited in the Muniment Room at West Minster Abbey when the scroll was full, Martin told him of the recent conversation with Father Peter of Colechurch. Elias was interested in this revelation of the use to which the daily data could be put, for he had been charged with keeping the Bellins Gate record of high and low tides for some while and had seen Aedric devote great attention to the topic.

"We are well into a dry time now, Father," he said, anxious to demonstrate his comprehension of what Martin had told him, "so the river will reduce in outflow quite soon. We will want to know, if the dry weather persists, how low the river goes – and how long it takes to fill up again, after the rains come."

"From what we saw of the floods after the last thaw, it would seem that the river rises faster than it falls for lack of water," said Martin.

"Yes, Father, and that must be very worrying for the bridgemen, down there in those little dams that they make on the river bed. They have to wait so long for the river to reduce; and yet a flood can come at any time," said Elias.

"You must have watched the men going about this sort of work often, then, Brother?" asked Martin, trying not to sound surprised.

"Yes, Father. I've been at West Minster and Bellins Gate together for almost thirty years, so I have seen virtually all the reconstruction of the great bridge ... though I had not really thought about the matters that you have learned of from Father Peter," said Elias.

There had only been two arrivals by way of the preceptory in the previous night, both well-known merchants who had been gone at first light to get a good start to the day's business. The daybook and the ledger were quickly completed, with no special memoranda. When the job was done, Elias went to the window and looked out at the river. It was almost low tide. No breeze ruffled the surface of the water, but Elias reconstructed in his mind's eye the many combinations of wind, weather and tide that he had observed from this eyrie over the past eight or nine years since he had been despatched from the abbey to become scribe. These varying conditions must affect bridge builders no less than they dominated the activities of seamen. There are lots more ships than bridges, Elias told himself. There's only one bridgemaster in London but you can meet a dozen ship's masters in any one of a dozen inns, even now when the shipping business was still poor after that awful past winter. So one is bound to hear much more of ships' responses to wind and weather, than of bridges and their stresses and strains. Nevertheless, he felt that he should have associated all the sights that he had seen, and the myriad seamen's anecdotes that he had heard, with his long observation of the reconstruction of the great wooden bridge. He would not let relevant information slip him by in future. He wondered whether he should express this determination to Martin, then he decided that his young preceptor would better be impressed by the proof of his commitment displayed in neater and more informative columns of numerals than those that Aedric had left for posterity.

Martin looked at Elias's back – the squat shape in the black habit, the squarish head, with the fringe of steely-grey hair between the thick neck and the flat top of the tonsured pate. There was no need to speak about his thoughts; they were on – or in – the river, as Martin wished them to be. The preceptory could keep accurate records, without Martin himself having to do all the work.

He chided himself for moving on to think that all he needed to do was accept the praise when the project proved successful. Not only was that vain, and therefore seriously sinful, it was even more obviously absurd. Any success arising from keeping the tide and wind records would depend on the user of the information, and on his overwhelming triumph over the elements to achieve a wonder of construction. Compared to that achievement, the preceptory contribution would be comparable to that of the spit-turner at a feast. Such thoughts restored Martin's sense of perspective on the great project that Peter of Colechurch had in contemplation, and he redirected his attention to the green cloth at the hermitage.

Rummaging along the pile of odd ends on the table – a process that caused Elias momentarily to look back from the window embrasure – Martin found an off-cut of parchment about an inch square, and on it he drew the circle-inspired pattern that had recurred on the two edges of the cloth. Martin had recalled the pattern many times over the previous twelve hours, and drew confidently. When he had finished, he was displeased with his effort. The twirl simply did not look right, yet Martin was sure that he had captured the configuration precisely.

He dipped his forefinger in the ale-jug and tried to replicate the design, this time at its actual size on the tabletop. He was pleased with the result, until he compared it with the drawing. Then he recognised that he had made the identical design; the same intangible error was apparent in both representations. He wiped the beer stain from the table with his sleeve – now very acutely aware that he was under observation by Elias – and tried once more to capture the Celtic tracing that had looked so simple on the bolt of green fustian. As he made the first semicircular movement of the beer-sodden finger, Martin felt his action inhibited by an impulse that declared that it was not for him – or for any alien – to capture the message that the design encapsulated. It was not a message – it was an identity code. The identity might be collective rather than personal; it might be the livery of a noble house, or the mark of a clan or a caste, but equally it could be specific to an individual.

Martin challenged himself to rationalise this assumption, as he looked up to meet Elias's enquiring eyes. He licked the beer off his finger, and wiped the stalled attempt at depicting the design off the table.

"I won't spoil your working area, Brother," promised Martin. "I am trying to work something out. Just leave me be, and decide for yourself how best to organise your observations ... It would be helpful if you could maintain some continuity with Aedric's way of keeping the record, which you have kept up so carefully, but some development of the range of records is clearly desirable."

Elias nodded assent, pleased to be given this job in preference to being despatched to the small scriptorium to continue copying Prior Osbert's third treatise on personal purity. He opened the second chest, the one not used for the preceptory records and receipts, and pulled out one of the second-hand scrolls on which Aedric had recorded his observations. He brought it to the corner of the table farthest from Martin, and studied it carefully, leaving Martin free for his own thinking.

The fact that the pattern could be remembered but could not be drawn from memory had led Martin's unconscious thought to its strange conclusion. The greatest lords had devices to depict their status – devices worn by their servants, carried before them on banners on occasions of state, and carved in stone to certify the identity of an entombed grandee. These devices were most often recognisable objects: a lion, a star, or a sword – or they were combinations of colours, such as a chequer of blue and gold. It was a very far cry from heraldic achievements to think that that piece of cloth carried in its pattern a similar mark of identity or of affiliation, yet once his mind had raised the concept, Martin found it to be irresistible.

The next challenge to tax himself with now became obvious: had he drawn on some suppressed memory of actually hearing that the Celts used fabric patterning to identify themselves? One heard so many stories of past times and of faraway places, of mythical beings, historical figures and biblical patriarchs. Joseph's ultimate crime, in the sight of his elder brothers, had been to accept from his doting father a distinctive coat of many colours. This recollection re-emphasised the possibility that a fabric could convey a subtle message in this age, even as it had evidently done in the time of Joseph in Egypt. Was it the case that this complex of general knowledge had become synthesised into Martin's insight on the bright green fabric rather than any tale that he had heard relating specifically to the Irish?

Martin looked at the sleeve of his own habit, damp from the ale. The black Benedictine dress was itself an assertion of distinctness and of affiliation, as was the green habit of a Templar priest, or the cross on the Templar Knights' tabard. The green dye that had been used on the fustian was of a brilliance that Martin had not seen even on the best vestments and altar hangings in the great abbeys. So, the colour itself must be significant, even without the distinctive pattern. It indicated remarkable skills, if it was indeed proven that the dyemaster was possessed of secrets that had not been penetrated by his colleagues in France, Italy, Germany or England. In turn the level of skill might indicate that the cloth was not Irish at all, but from some more advanced territory that was already subdued by the trading nexus of the Earthly City.

Perhaps the pattern was Irish, but the cloth was not? This supposition could quickly be dismantled. The Irish did not have the resources to buy expensive foreign cloth, nor did they have the reputation of putting much value on such imports, even if they could have afforded them. More germane to the immediate issue was the fact that the pattern appeared to have been set on the cloth before it had been dyed; which either located the dyer in Ireland, or the Irish pattern-designer in a dyehouse somewhere on the continent. The Irish had been intrepid travellers throughout history; Irish priests had converted Wales, parts of northern Britain and much of central Europe to the Christian faith, and St Brendan had followed the Vikings to great islands far to the west of the mapped world. There was no problem about imagining an Irish dyer or designer working in Pisa or Sluys, that was entirely plausible; the difficulty came with the export to Ireland of the produce of such an expatriate undertaking. Ireland was increasingly no-go territory for alien imports, and the complexity of getting goods from an expatriate workshop into tribal Irish territory was no less than for any other items in trade.

If the thing was Irish, it was made in Ireland.

The bell tolled to call the monks at Bermondsey Abbey, over the river, to Terce – the Office said or sung in every convent at the mid-point of the morning. Elias and Martin rose together to go down to their own chapel, as one after another the abbey, priory and nunnery bells of the metropolis each declared their agreement with the sexton at Bermondsey that the time for the service had come.

Martin slipped the small square of parchment into his cuff before he followed Elias down the spiral stairway. There was a source of information on Ireland that he could tap on his own account.

As soon as the Office was ended, and he had once more with penitence acknowledged his lack of full concentration on the performance of his central duty as a monk, Martin made his way through the city, west along the riverside to Garlic Hill. There he hoped to find the relatives to whom Fulk Joiner and his family, refugees from Galway, had gone from their overnight stay in the preceptory several months earlier.

Garlic Hill was a short, relatively steep street near Queenhithe, between the riverbank and the merchant areas around Cheapside. Most of the properties were occupied by craftsmen and traders whose produce was largely used by the marine trade: oars, barrels, rigging, sailcloth, ships chandlery and victuals.

Martin asked after the joiner's shop, and was told that there were three. At the first, his request for Cousin Fulk was met by a blank look and a courteous suggestion that the brother must be mistaken. At the second, the journeyman who had turned from his planing to ascertain the monk's business brightened and referred Martin on to the third joinery workshop.

"You'll be meaning the man from Ireland, with the baby grandson. He was there, but he's moved. They'll be able to tell you where; it can't be far, because he's back here often enough, borrowing tools."

Martin asked the name of the master joiner who was Fulk's cousin.

"Simon," answered the man, taking up his plane again and spitting on the right hand that would resume the delicate steerage and control of the depth of cut as the left hand repetitively drove the boxed blade forward. His master clearly did not encourage the waste of time on conversational irrelevancies, and he had anyhow given the monk all the information he had on Simon's importunate relation.

Martin thanked him and made his way to the entrance gate higher up the street, over which hung a large, crude but effective wooden effigy of an adze. An elderly man came towards Martin as he leaned over the gate, looking into the yard that fronted the street with the covered workshop beyond:

"Master Simon Joiner?" asked Martin.

"Aye, that's me. What Benedictine brother requires to know it?" asked the man.

"I am Martin, Preceptor of Bellins Gate ... I recall your cousin Fulk and his family, who passed through our *porte* towards the end of last year; before the great frost."

"Yes, they did so! And all dues were paid, that were called for!" declared Simon.

"Indeed so ... and now I would like to seek some information from them, that may help me in a matter of some concern," said Martin.

"Information?" asked Simon, still suspicious of any grasping cleric.

"Yes, I do assure you. Information and information only!" declared Martin. "Where may I find them?"

"Well, Tom and his father-in-law have both gone to the bottom of the river!" said Simon. The twinkle in his eye as he uttered this further defiant statement gave Martin the clue that here was a challenge. The men clearly were not drowned; if they had been, the neighbour's journeyman would have heard of it and Simon would not look so cheerful. The explanation came at once – it would have been shameful not to have got it, thought Martin, considering his recent conversations.

"Ah, they have got work with Peter of Colechurch, then. I know him! And you have been generous with your tools, for that has enabled them to get this work ... Well, it was low tide when I left my preceptory, so there's at least a couple of hours before Peter's foreman will stop work for the day; then they will go to confirm their attendance on the payments register at the Bridge House – followed, perhaps, by a mug of ale on the way home."

Simon smiled in a much more friendly way, as Martin revealed his understanding of bridgemaster Peter and his work:

"Well, there, Brother! I'd thought you just an ordinary monk, coming to take off decent folk more than they can afford, and I may have been mistaken! I rather hope that I was, for it's good to meet a man who seems to be what he's meant to be." Martin looked past Simon as the joiner thus implicitly stigmatised the generality of his fellow religious to avoid giving tacit assent or denial to this commonplace tradesman talk.

Martin let the sentence hang in the air for a moment, and Simon recognised that the monk had no wish to acknowledge it. This is a wise young fellow, he decided:

"You're really in luck, Brother. Fulk's daughter Joanne is here, showing Baby Fulk to my own grandchildren. Will she have the information that you require?"

"It's quite possible, yes," said Martin.

"Then come in and see her; provided you can stand the smell of baby, and all that women's talk that goes with it!"

Simon conducted Martin through two busy workshops, in which eight or ten men and youths were at work, and beyond into a yard with fruit trees. At the further side of the yard was a house, quite a large one, with an upper storey in half-timber obviously added over an older stone-walled hall.

"There's fourteen of us in the household, not including occasional visitors and distant relations escaping from foreign troubles that they should never have got into!" explained Simon, justifying the scale of his house in relation to the extent of his dependent family.

"Are they all in the business?" asked Martin.

"I've three sons here, all married, and two daughters married to journeymen. With their children and me and the wife, there's above a score of us," explained Simon. Evidently, children did not count among the fourteen – that was the adult complement of the household.

"And I've two daughters married away from home. That's seven children alive and well and five long buried – God rest their souls!" As Simon delivered himself of this piety a knot of small children, ranging from around ten years to a toddler, came from the house to greet the patriarch. Clearly they considered neither their grandfather nor a black-robed monk to be any kind of ogre. Small hands reached up to lead Martin to grandma, while the oldest girl explained to her grandfather how the newest baby was thriving despite a recurrent tendency to a prolapse of the great bowel.

The former hall-house had been greatly altered by Simon and his wife Wanfran. A floor had been constructed above the great room, necessitating the addition of external buttresses to support each of the four main beams that carried the interior weight of the upper structure. While the original hall would have had a pitched roof rising to some dozen or even fifteen feet above the earthen floor, the new rooms left the hall only seven feet in height and new windows had had to be cut through the walls between the buttresses. Three of the windows in the first room, that covered most of the floor area of the old hall and accommodated the great fireplace, were wide open. The three closed sets of shutters each had a small glazed aperture; Simon had evidently prospered at his trade to be able to afford such luxuries.

Four women were sitting on stools in a semicircle round the fireplace where two large iron cooking pots were suspended, and half a dozen girls stood with them. An older woman was easily identifiable as the matriarch, even if she had not been seated on a high-backed chair to the left of the small fire. Seeing Simon and a monk enter, with their attendant gaggle of grandchildren, the older woman stood and the others immediately followed her lead:

"This is Father Martin of Bellins Gate preceptory, my dear ... Father Martin, my wife, Wanfran ... Cousin Joanne you say you know ... my daughter Joan ... my sons' wives ... the girls." As in other things, so in making these introductions, Simon was economical in a hierarchical manner. The daughters-in-law were not his kin – though their children were – and he did not deign to present them by name.

One daughter and one of the daughters-in-law were not there, Martin worked out; they were likely to be at work in the washhouse or the stillroom or the pantry.

"Welcome to our home, Father ... it is Joanne you have come to see, I gather?" said the mistress of the house. Martin had guessed from the woman's name that her French would be that of a Saxon who had learned the tongue after her marriage at sixteen – it was fluent but far from grammatical. There were more and more mixed marriages, as the centenary of William's conquest of England approached, but the language problems within such marriages often left the Saxon party – especially when female – at a disadvantage. This woman, however, did not seem in any way to lack confidence or self-possession, for she had brought a good dowry, in the form of this site, into the marriage with a good-looking Frenchman whose English she mocked more freely than he mocked her French. The family's prosperity was in no small measure due to her assiduous maintenance of her family links with leading citizens of Saxon origin. Simon himself had not been slow to learn the advantages of addressing such commissioners of major structural works in Middlesex English and Wanfran had been a better teacher of her tongue than Simon had of his own. On this occasion, though, Martin's hosts assumed that a monk in his important post would be exclusively a French speaker, and so kept the conversation in the rulers' language.

"Will you sit, Father?" said Wanfran, pointing to her own chair.

"You are kind, madam; but I wish to trespass far on your generosity, and ask if I could have a brief, private conversation with Mistress Joanne ... with yourself and Master Simon present, of course!" said Martin.

"My husband has important work to do today," said Wanfran, casting a telling look in the direction of her man, "so you may have to excuse him from the conversation."

"Yes, indeed. The carters will be here at dawn tomorrow to take the main beams for the new roof at St Benet's and we have a problem with knots where dowels must go ... If you will excuse me, Father, I'll be off!"

Simon did not wait for Martin to release him but left quickly. He evidently fully trusted his wife, both to manage the visitor effectively and to report accurately and in full on the discussion between Martin and Joanne. His excuse about the dowel holes might have been true, but it was certain that if he had wished to do so he could have left one of his sons to carry on the work – as he was no doubt doing, perfectly adequately, during the preceding minutes when engaged with the monk.

The women still stood in their semicircle, one of them holding the baby who was obviously Fulk's grandson and the victim of the commonplace problem that the small girl had found so interesting.

"Keep the baby," said Wanfran to the daughter-in-law who held him – in Middle Saxon, Martin noted – and then she invited Martin to come with Joanne and herself "into my parlour".

The further part of the old hall had become a separate room, with a door from the hall leading into a small passage with a door on each side – "Storage" explained Wanfran as they passed – and beyond the further door was a parlour of which a court lady could be envious. When they do well, thought Martin, these city tradesmen certainly do themselves well!

Both shutters were closed, but in each of them a glazed area let in a trickle of daylight. Wanfran evidently found this level of illumination sufficient for conversation, as she did not propose opening a shutter or lighting any of the candles on tall sconces that Martin was able to discern as his eyes adjusted to the relative gloom. The furniture was good: oak armchairs, a table with various pieces of sewing in progress (they will certainly need more light for that, Martin thought) and, by a fireplace against the end wall, a great chest at one side and a press at the other. There was no bed. Like the hall, this was a day room only, though it was possible that apprentices and unwed journeymen brought in bedrolls at night and slept before the dying fire in the winter months.

"Do sit, Father, please!" said Wanfran, indicating a chair. "Joanne, you go there, facing the Father." Wanfran herself moved to a chair where she could see both of them in profile against the limited light from one window, while her face was in the shadow cast by the other window behind her.

Martin sat and was surprised to find that the chair was cushioned. The room smelled of lavender – it really was luxurious. Martin wondered how many other merchants or master craftsmen in this great city could afford a similar setting for their wives' private entertaining; probably quite a lot, though Martin had not realised that such rooms existed. There were powerful incentives for the trading classes to press forward the outer limits and the range of activities within the Earthly City. It was, indeed, difficult to imagine how the Heavenly City could provide a reward comparable to that which a successful tradesman could eat, touch, feel and smell in this world. But now was not the time to develop that theme, even in his own mind. Martin waited until the women were seated, then he asked Joanne:

"How are your father and Tom?"

"Well, thank you, Father."

"The baby looks well; but one of the children told Master Simon that he has a problem," said Martin.

"Lots of babies have that problem. If you shove the parts back, in the proper way, they learn to stay there and all is well!" declared the experienced older woman. Joanne made no comment, but replied to Martin's question.

"He's a good baby, and he is growing well."

"Where are you living now?" asked Martin.

"Nearer to Queenhithe; just down the hill. So that Dad and Tom are near to the work and the accommodation doesn't cost too much."

"I was glad to hear that both are engaged on the bridge work ... Is it congenial to them?"

Joanne hesitated, then said:

"Dad is glad to have the money; so is Tom ... but they would both really like to be trading on their own. It isn't easy to start with nothing ... without heavy tools, or any money for timber ... so we have to go step by step ... and we are doing so!"

She gave an air of quiet confidence. Martin proceeded to his errand:

"I have sought you out because you may be able to help me. A friend of mine has received, by a mysterious route, a bolt of cloth. It is in a brilliant green, such as I have never seen before in human artifice. It is like a young oak tree's leaves, when they have first fully opened in the spring ... and on this cloth there's a design. I have tried to capture it, but I do not seem quite to be able to understand how the whorls, or twirls, are made. Please look at this, and tell me if there is anything familiar to you about it."

He wondered if in the dim light she would be able to make anything out on the scrap of parchment that he handed to her, but Wanfran wanted to see it, too. She stood up and hurried over to open one of the shutters, calling on Joanne to come to the light.

The women's heads came close together as they pored over the small ink sketch. Wanfran's head came up first; she turned towards Martin and declared that it meant nothing at all to her.

"But then, you didn't come to ask me, did you, Brother?" This was accompanied by a gentle smile that indicated the softer side of the formidable matriarch.

Martin moved closer to the window, where Joanne was still looking at the design:

"I suppose you think it may be Irish, Father?" He nodded a silent response. "Well, it could be, but I've never seen it done like this. There's always a repeating pattern and the actual shape of the individual components is – well, it's sort of changed, by the repetition."

Joanne had the cunning eye of a woman for such matters, and Martin at once realised how drawing the pattern had eluded him. The shape that he had tried to capture emerged from the pattern, and was an integral feature of the pattern. The design that he had in his memory was the whole fringe, which was itself carefully proportioned to the width of the piece of cloth:

"Could you draw me the nearest thing that you have seen, in Ireland, to the pattern that has this shape within it?" asked Martin, wondering if his somewhat convoluted request was clear enough.

It seemed to be, because Wanfran was instantly clearing an area of the tabletop, saying to Joanne:

"Come and find the sewing chalk for me, then you can show the Brother what you mean."

Joanne picked up the block of chalk, and found a point on its surface that was prominent enough to leave a thin trace on the dark tabletop. Then she drew the central design of the fabric's twin strips, about the actual size that Martin had seen it at the hermitage. She drew about fifteen inches length of the pattern, to get in two complete versions of it. She had the confident style of a woman who helped the men with chalking out shapes in their workshop, as well as one who lined up the seams of her own garments. The pattern that emerged from her drawing was of very similar design to the one on the fustian at the hermitage, but there were several subtle differences that resulted in there not being anything closely resembling the near circle that Martin had previously presumed was the central feature of the artwork.

"Are there many patterns of this kind?" he asked.

"As many as you like," answered Joanne. "Some are handed down in families and villages over generations."

"And are the designs of about this breadth?" Martin set his thumb and middle finger over the design, bridge-like, with the distance between the finger point and the thumb on the table roughly the same as the width of the design on the green fabric.

"Yes, Father. There is always a border, beside the main design. Always there is a border nearest to the outer edge of the cloth; only sometimes is there a second border." With a thicker edge of the chalk Joanne ran a line alongside the pattern that she had sketched out on the wood; and as she did so Martin was even more convinced that the pattern that he had seen yesterday was from Ireland. He removed his hand from the table as she drew the thicker line, then said:

"That convinces me that the cloth that I saw is likely to be Irish; that is the general view of those who have seen it already ... Now, you tell me that such a design may delineate a person's family, or native village ... Might the colour of the cloth also be significant?"

Joanne looked at him in some surprise and said:

"Well, the cloth is the natural creamy grey of wool and flax fustian, surely? Do you not mean the colour of the design, Father? That is often embroidered in strong colours, if the threads are available. It is not uncommon for chieftains to have gold thread in their stitchery, and good green colours, such as you mention are quite common."

"The cloth that I saw yesterday was the brightest green that I have ever seen in a human artefact ... not the design on it; that was grey, picked out in black stitch work. The cloth was green," declared Martin.

"That I have not seen. I have seen an ochre-dyed fabric; and priests wear robes of black lamb's wool, as do the better-off widow women ... But I have not seen any material such as you describe, Father ... And, did I hear you correctly? Did you say that there was a grey pattern picked out in embroidery, as if the design itself is not sewn on?" Joanne was clearly thinking carefully about all that Martin had said, no doubt berating herself for not having taken his original reference to the greenness of the cloth at face value.

"Yes, that is correct. I think that some sort of waxy substance was put on the untreated cloth, making the pattern; then it was dyed, leaving the natural colour where the wax had been. Then the wax was taken away and the design finished off with the needle," answered Martin.

"I've never heard of such a wax!" declared Wanfran. "It would certainly make the fortune of the dyemaster who could develop such a technique. That is very interesting indeed!"

It was clear that her entrepreneurial instincts were stimulated by this concept, and neither Joanne nor Martin doubted that for the coming weeks the women and children of the household would be roped into making experiments with all the waxy substances that the household could discover. Joanne, too, might undertake her own trials as a means of contributing to the accumulation of the funds that her menfolk and, in time, her baby would need to establish and maintain their own business amid the competition of a great capital city.

"Have you seen such a fabric in Ireland?" Wanfran asked Joanne the very question that Martin was about to put. Her self-interest lay behind the point, but as it coincided with Martin's interest in the green fabric his look towards Joanne indicated that he, too, sought the answer.

"No, I certainly have not; and I beg leave to doubt, Father, that any fabric could thus be dyed – especially in Ireland ... I would hazard that there is fine stitching, where you thought you saw just the background cloth colour. It would be much simpler to do it that way and the Irish have plenty of time for detailed handiwork – much more than they have resources for such novelties as you have been speculating about," said the young mother.

"Let us set aside my manly ignorance about how the fabric may have been sewn or etched on. May I take the chalk?" With the block Martin began to sketch out the design that he remembered. He tried to replicate what Joanne had done, in producing a couple of repetitions of his memorised design. The second was more like the original than the first, so he made a third and asked for a rag to remove the first. He wiped off his least successful attempt and made a line down either side of his pattern.

The result was not an exact replica of the distinctive design that he had seen at the hermitage, but it was close enough, and it bore a family resemblance to what Joanne had drawn.

Martin decided that it would be fair to elucidate the reason for his enquiries. He told the women how the fabric had been found, and succinctly begged the women not to tell anyone else of the incident. He did not mention the follow-up delivery of the severed heads.

"Was the whole body wound with the cloth, top to toe, as with a burial winding-sheet?" asked Joanne.

"I do not know. If the body was transported from Ireland, then brought ashore, then put into and taken out of a water-butt, I don't suppose that it would be too clear how the fabric had originally been applied," answered Martin.

Wanfran challenged this:

"A winding sheet, if it is really tightly bound – as it should be, to keep everything together as decay sets in – should have remained in place. We often use twine or linen strips, in my family, to ensure that everything is tightly bundled."

"The Irish would certainly do the same," said Joanne. "They greatly respect the dead, and often inter sidearms with a corpse. They would not be lax about winding-in a dead man, if the intention had been an honourable burial."

"Decay had not gone far on the corpse in question and there were no signs that it had been disinterred from an honest grave," said Martin, guessing that the hermit would have mentioned it, if there had been evidence to the contrary. "The cloth was worn as a kind of single-piece skirt and cloak, folded but not pinned ... Is such a garment worn in Ireland?"

"Oh yes, but only – so far as I have seen – in the natural colour of the fabric. In wet weather, which is most common in Ireland, pigskin jerkins and trews are the most common men's wear – not unlike the leathers that you have seen my uncle and cousins wearing as you passed through the yard here. The patterned cloth is more for festive occasions, a formal and celebratory attire," said Joanne. "Aunt, if you have a bolt of cloth that you could let me use, I'll show Father Martin how the Irishmen wear them."

Wanfran was doubly interested, in the murder mystery and in the technological opportunity that Martin might have stumbled on, despite Joanne's scepticism about the idea. There might be some clue in the use of the fabric to how it lay and thus to the purpose that the design was meant to serve. She went over to the press, and opened the lower doors of the cupboard to reveal a pile of bolts of materials in different colours.

"How wide is the beam of the fabric that we are to imagine?" asked Wanfran.

"A yard, or perhaps a little less," answered Martin.

"Let us go for a yard, then ... and linen, you say, Brother?" asked Wanfran.

"Yes, a linen and wool mix, I think."

"That too would be a novelty to me, but I accept your word, Brother." Wanfran continued to speak to Martin with the form of address that applied to all monks, despite the equally persistent demonstration by Joanne that within the premises at Bellins Gate, Martin was known as Father preceptor.

Wanfran straightened up, holding a roll of blue cloth a yard wide, and asked Joanne how long the Irish had their bolt for wearing. Joanne had no idea, but Martin estimated the length at well over five yards. That amount was duly rolled off the long cloth, and another couple of yards which allowed Joanne the play necessary to wind the lengths of material first high around her breasts, then like a skirt about her posterior, and finally over her shoulders like a cape. The woman needed pins to hold it in place, "but you could do it just by folding, if you know how," said Joanne. Wanfran reluctantly conceded that it was feasible, but thought that the thing would hang better if a few good brooches were used, particularly at the shoulder.

"Yes, they do have a brooch there," agreed Joanne.

"So they probably have pins where you can't see them!" declared Wanfran, apparently keen to assume that mere men could not be expected to fold a garment properly, in defiance of both gravity and their own innate untidiness.

Joanne and Martin exchanged a glance, indicative of a shared dissent from the old woman's point of view, and broke the contact quickly to avoid smiling and thus attracting Wanfran's attention to the silent interchange.

"I think that the man was dressed when he died, though he had no brooch or belt when he was found, here in England," said Martin. "That looks very similar to the way the cloth was on the corpse."

"I'll take it off, now, Father, if that's all right?" said Joanne. She did not enjoy being likened to a headless corpse, even for purposes of forensic illustration. The older woman carefully divested the younger, checked that the pins had done no damage to the cloth, and rewound it on to the wooden batten that gave form to the roll of cloth:

"We can conclude, then, that the fabric was – is – Irish; and that the wearer was dressed for a feast, rather than for combat, when he met his end," said Martin. The two women assented, then Joanne asked:

"May I tell my father of this, Father? He knows much more than I of the habits of the Irish people; he may be able to offer you further guidance."

"Certainly, if he can be of any assistance, I would be grateful," said Martin.

"My husband knows nothing of Ireland, or the Irish, except alehouse gossip and a few sad snippets from Fulk, so he cannot help you with this matter ... but he does deserve to know the business that is transacted under his roof," said Wanfran.

"By all means tell Simon, but under the same seal of secrecy as you are yourself bound by," said Martin.

Within two minutes Martin was out of the yard, striding down the gravel surface of Garlic Hill, keeping well away from the noxious trickle in the deep ditch that was normally much more salubrious due to the outfall of a spring just south of Poultry. The drought had killed the spring, and the stench of the ditch grew daily. Within fifteen minutes he was back in the preceptory, in good time for the midday Office and then dinner.

Chapter Five

After Vespers that day, as the monks filed out of the refectory on completion of their supper, Fulk came to see the preceptor at Bellins Gate.

The elderly joiner seemed to be depressed, rather than listless as he had been on his exhausted arrival in London as a refugee from Ireland. The intervening months had not dealt kindly with him. His cousin Simon had been generous with accommodation, food and advice for the arrivals at his gate. He it was who had got work for Fulk and Tom, in place of two of Peter Colechurch's disabled bridge builders, and he had made the introduction to the widow woman whose house they now shared. There had been limits to his generosity, however; from the outset he had made it clear that his sons, sons-in-law and the rising third generation were more than sufficient manpower for his own firm. Fulk and Tom had recognised that they must shift for themselves and that the bridgework was their best opportunity for the time being.

Tom had adapted well to the work. Fulk felt his age – and a lot more – when the work got heavy, and the high of parts of the bridge, especially at low water, gave him a vertiginous sensation. With the arrival of the baby, both the father and grandfather were determined to ensure that the child had a better chance in life than as a refugee pauper. The grandfather, however, found the means of making the fortune physically demanding and – for a master craftsman with his greater and more precise skills – somewhat demeaning. Increasingly Fulk felt nostalgic for his own business in Ireland, even with all the troubles that seemed endemic there. He recalled the high hopes in which he and his young bride had opted to make their lives in the colony at Galway, and he remembered the many good times they had enjoyed together with the baby Joanne and her brothers, even though the boys had died young. His wife and sons lay in the churchyard where he had intended to join them when his time came.

Coming to England had seemed to be necessary; things had got just too out of hand in Galway, as the Irish from around the town had increased their pressure on the exploitative little city of French and English artisans and tradesmen. England had proved singularly uncongenial for Fulk, especially as the adaptability of his daughter and son-in-law to their changed conditions reminded him forcibly of the resilience with which he had long ago confronted the challenges in Galway, and made him feel old. London provided no demand for his skills as a constructor of cranes that could raise the largest barrels from the depth of a ship's hold, with only four men in the treadmill; nor did anyone respond with interest to his notion of building a great swing that could carry four adults in its boat-shaped cradle and move forty feet from end to end of its arc. So he was doing little better than journeymen's work on an immense project, whose design was complex but whose individual components were big and rough-hewn.

Fulk was led up the spiral stair to the great chamber on the second floor of the tower of the preceptory where Martin greeted him warmly.

"Master Fulk; it is good to see you, and in evident good health," said Martin, recognising that the man's spirit was obviously less robust.

"Thank you, Father. Yes, I am well ..."

Fulk let the sentence die, but Martin decided that it was not yet the moment to say "But?", and allow the old man to itemise his mental and spiritual ills. The fellow had come to give Martin information. It might not be relevant, but a man of Fulk's stamp would not venture into a house of religion on the pretext of bearing intelligence unless he had something substantial to impart.

Martin offered him a seat and a beer; he accepted both, but was reluctant to take either until Martin had himself sat down and taken a sip from his horn of ale.

"Joanne has told you of our conversation today," said Martin. Fulk took the invitation to develop his extension of the earlier dialogue.

"I've seen green cloth, like you described to my daughter," said Fulk, "And with a pattern like you said ... It betokens the household of the King of Leinster, not the royal family; their colour is red ... well, a purpley sort of red, like a too-ripe plum."

Fulk gulped some beer nervously, and inhaled as he did so, provoking a coughing fit. It took him over a minute to regain his normal respiration, and Martin urged him to drink more of the ale to assist him in regaining his equilibrium.

"Assuming as I do that this young man was probably one of that household, or that we were meant to conclude that he was from that establishment, what inferences may we draw from the deposit of his remains – with his garment – in a water-butt near to the Tower of London?"

Martin had not told Joanne where the body had been found, so the fact was new to Fulk. He looked searchingly towards Martin for a moment, as if he might glean further information from the preceptor's expression that would enable him the better to frame an answer that would please his host. Martin was the first person of any standing to have sought out Fulk or his daughter since their arrival in London, and the old man was anxious to establish the best possible basis from which he might exploit the connection in the future. Gaining nothing from Martin to help him, he responded at some length:

"Well, Father, it's like this. The king thereabouts, in the far west of Ireland, has the same problems as all the other local rulers. He recognises that his people could perhaps gain by preparing goods to sell to the town merchants for exports. They all want imported goods and the only way to pay for them is by exports. Not even the King of France could last for long if he used his treasure to buy things with. But there's the old guard of clan chieftains and the priests, who want to keep out foreigners and drive away the aliens who have been suffered to settle in the past. So there are parties at his court, as there are at every other – some of them are consistent in their views, while others chop and change as they judge it to be advantageous for themselves."

Fulk paused, and took a tentative swig of his ale, anxious not to choke once more.

Martin offered no comment, just looked steadily at his visitor, so Fulk resumed his recital:

"I was one of the guild masters of the town – as the only recognised master joiner in the place, that was no great honour – but it did mean that I knew what was going on. The town provost, who we elected each year on St Stephen's Day, acted for the town in the negotiations that always seemed to be going on between different groups of the king's men and the town. We never saw the king – we were always dealing with factions, Father, and we never knew if they really represented the King, nor yet whether he could actually control them and make his own decisions if he chose to."

"Was the king the same person all the years that you were in Galway?" asked Martin.

"Oh no, there were father and son, then two usurpers, then another son of the original – who said he'd been king ever since his brother died, of course! That one was still there when I left. He had the reputation of being physically ill-favoured, but clever; and gifted in music and poetry – that the people set great store by."

Fulk took a more confident drink from the horn of ale, leaving Martin to digest these dynastic and cultural facts. A king who was keen on music and on the oral traditions of his people – whatever the Irish equivalent of Nordic saga-telling might be – would probably want his courtiers to be apparelled in a traditional manner. It was unlikely that an Irish monarch would have one of his own men dismembered and dumped in London in easily identifiable court dress, unless the man had been accused of acting as an agent of the English!

Martin's excitement at adducing this explanation quickly evaporated. Without the head, identification of the man as an English agent – simple identification of any kind, indeed – was virtually impossible. If the man had been of unusual stature, or had some physical peculiarity that would have disclosed his identity to an English controller even in his headless state, the hermit would have noted it, but no such mark or deformity had been mentioned. Thus it must be assumed that the body was not meant specifically to be recognised; the message was of a generic nature.

Though the body had been left at the hermitage, it had evidently not been consigned for the hermit when it had been shipped from western Ireland; its deposit in his water-butt was probably fortuitous. The sign could have been intended for Archbishop Theobald, who maintained clandestine relations with the parts of Ireland where his primacy was under challenge. Agents of the Archbishop, returning from Ireland, had passed through Martin's preceptory more often than the monks were aware; of this, Martin was in no doubt. The Archbishop's palace at Lambeth was easily reached, right by the river. Alternatively, it would have been possible to dump the message in Canterbury. Theobald could not be ruled out, but it would have been easy to dump the body on his doorstep, so Martin was inclined to exclude him as the target.

The intriguing question was what event or report had caused these desecrators of corpses to make their move at this time – or, more precisely, to have determined on it about three to four months ago?

If the move was in reaction to an event in England linked to the king, that must have happened at least four months ago. Yet four months back, the great frost had not yet broken. The king and his court had been at Winchester. Ireland had been under discussion; but it was generally believed that no firm decision had been taken about whether or not to accede to the demands for which Theobald was rumoured to be seeking more explicit papal sanction.

If the intention had been to impress Henry of Anjou personally with the corpse, then London was not the place to take it. The gesture could surely have been made at Winchester or at the king's newly reconstructed palace in Oxford where he now resided. To make the display where the king could not view the corpse must surely mean that he was not the recipient of the coded signal.

Martin knew that decoders of messages to the king travelled with the court, to decipher the cryptic documents that came to him from all his lands in Britain and France. All these, once decoded and understood were forwarded to the royal archive at West Minster or stored more securely at the Royal Wardrobe. When the king was on his travels, much information still came to his permanent base, and only the gist was passed on by his confidential clerical team.

Following this train of thought Martin came to the recognition that some agency wishing to challenge those of the king's councillors who advocated action in Ireland might try to get their contrary message into the routine briefing that went out from West Minster to the peripatetic monarch.

If the courtiers who had remained at the palace were as able and as committed as the king needed them to be, they would tell the king the answer to the puzzle when they notified him of it. To send him simply a report that said "headless body deposited, apparently in Irish dress, apparently with significance that we have not grasped", would invite his angry contempt. Of all rulers, Henry II least liked unresolved mysteries; he demanded hard facts on which he could base decisive action.

Martin had become acquainted with a number of the men whom the king had drawn into his confidential circle. He knew some of them well enough to have discussed with them this matter of the deposits made at the hermitage, but it was not Martin's secret to disclose. Sir Rulf le Court was also a solid king's man, and acting in a way that could prove detrimental to him would not be sensible. After all, Sir Rulf was only doing what Martin had concluded any other reliable servant of the king would expect to do: keep the mystery under wraps until the meaning as well as the circumstances of the signal could be conveyed to the king.

Even if the hermit's assumption was correct, that the deposit of the messenger-corpse at the hermitage was a hasty and incompetently handled action, the follow-up deposit of the heads had been a deliberate attempt to make the best of a badly executed task.

Looking at Fulk's furrowed brow above the drinking vessel obscuring his mouth and nose from where Martin was looking at him, Martin thought of the even more wizened heads that had been staked out as the secondary message.

Perhaps those corpseless heads had been fellow citizens of Fulk, and had suffered in the massacre that he and his family had feared and fled from? It was possible, even, that Fulk could know the faces – if they were still recognisable. As Martin had not himself seen the heads, he had no idea how badly defaced or decayed they had become. A positive identification of any of the unfortunates might be irrelevant to unravelling the meaning of the message; but it could pinpoint their provenance and give corroboration of the presumed source.

"There is another worse aspect to the findings at the place where the headless man was found," said Martin. "At a later date, as if to reinforce whatever message the first incident was set to convey, three severed heads were placed on stakes at the same place ... I have not yet seen these remains, though they have been kept above ground and not buried, as the first corpse was ... Would you be prepared, Fulk, to come with me tomorrow to see these things and tell me if they have any similarity to anything that you have seen in Ireland?"

With their working hours governed by the daily advance in the hour of the high tide, Martin knew that Fulk and Tom would have to cease work on London Bridge around the middle of the next day. In midsummer they could be called back to work in the evening on days when the high tide was in the forenoon, making early afternoon work on the substructure of the bridge impossible. As the season of split shifts had not yet begun, the men could walk to Chad's Well and back while the work site at the bridge was submerged.

The old man readily agreed to come to the preceptory as soon as he could get release from Peter of Colechurch, or the foreman, at the end of the next morning's work. It was not spoken, but understood between them, that Fulk would invoke Martin's name if his superiors proved to be reluctant to permit him an early release.

Thus it was that even before Martin had finished his dinner in the refectory on the next day, Fulk and Tom together presented themselves at the preceptory gate. Fulk was wearing the same clothes as he had on the day before, and Martin knew that these were not a joiner's working leathers. Tom was also cloth-clad, and both men had simple strong shoes on their feet, so it was clear that the two men had been home to clean up and change clothes before they came east along Thames Street to Bellins Gate. The craftsmen expected to be kept waiting by high-ups, and the sound of the droning voice emerging from the open shutters of the refectory confirmed to the arrivals that Martin was properly engaged in the monastic routine. The waiting men heard the voice come to an end, and Martin's voice giving thanks in Latin; after which Martin led his small community out into the yard.

The three men passed out of the city by the Ald Gate, headed east along the Stratford Road, then took a lane towards the south alongside which were several makeshift hovels in which masterless, landless men and their families eked out a precarious existence on the basis of the fathers' casual employment in and around the capital. No such hovels interrupted the hedgerows once they had come within the Manor of Chad's Well; Sir Rulf made no bones about clearing out all forms of squatter, settler or itinerant.

"This is Chad's Well," said Martin, as they came into the cultivated area that surrounded the hamlet. "There is the convent to St Cedd, where holy nuns reside ... and beyond the village, on the border of that good woodland that you see ahead of us, there lies the manor house and somewhere adjacent to his home Sir Rulf keeps safe the severed heads."

The mention of Sir Rulf caused a slight stiffening as of nervousness in Tom; even though he knew of no Sir Rulf. Tom's father-in-law, being slower to react, saw the younger man's reflex and forced himself not to appear to share it; his apprehension at the probability of having to address a real noble showed by his adopting a swagger that was much more conspicuous than Tom's reactive posture.

So the three men came to Chad's Well Manor. A servant came forward to see what was making the dogs bark, and demanded to know their business, trying to be courteous to the monk while keeping the commoners in their proper place:

"I come to see Sir Rulf – or the Lady Angelina, if Sir Rulf is not at home," said Martin. He spoke in French, even though the man had accosted them in Middle Saxon. Fulk and Tom had less Saxon than Martin himself, and he preferred that his companions should follow the entire proceedings.

"Master is out," said the man, more deferential after the language of the ruling classes had been deployed. "Lady is at home!"

Martin had continued walking in the direction of the house as this interchange took place, demonstrating that he knew the layout of the property and had every right to be there:

"I will announce you!" said the man, suddenly hurrying off ahead of them.

"That won't be easy for him to do," said Martin to his companions, "since he's not asked who we are."

The man, in fact, had remembered Martin from a previous occasion; it was the recollection that had spurred him into action. As a result, Lady Angelina emerged to greet the monk as Martin and his companions arrived at the manor house:

"Father Martin ... it is a long time since we met ... and a while longer than I expected, since I assured Rulf that you were bound to become involved with the peculiar goings-on at the hermitage by the river!"

Having declared her own prescience, with a warm smile for her guest, she looked towards his two companions and back at Martin, seeking an explanation of their presence.

"These are Master Fulk, joiner, formerly of Galway in Ireland and now in refuge in London; and his daughter's husband, also a joiner – and now a proud father – Tom," said Martin.

At the mention of Ireland, the lady's eyes had narrowed. Martin had, indeed, come on the errand that she had predicted and without any need of a summons from Sir Rulf.

"Will you come into the house, and perhaps take some refreshment?" she asked.

"Certainly madam; we shall be most grateful for such attention. But first it may be most convenient – if you are willing – for Master Fulk to see certain things that your husband has safe but not, perhaps, in the house?"

"Yes, Father, of course! Get that gruesome bit of the proceedings over with and then, perhaps, we can chat a while," replied Angelina.

She led them herself, with the manservant and the dogs in attendance, to a barn close to the stables. Within the barn she led them to a small chamber, constructed under the loft and furnished with a solid barred door:

"We have had a night guard here, since these things have been here," she said as the servant pulled back the heavy wooden bolts at the top and bottom of the door. The man swung the door open, with the manner of a conjurer on the completion of a complex trick, and stood aside to let his mistress lead her visitors into the room. Tom hesitated, then Fulk, as if they feared that the door would close on them, forgetful that if they were thus imprisoned Angelina, who had preceded them, would be their hostage.

The room was extremely gloomy, with only a thin illumination reaching it from the open barn door. Angelina opened a large, crude chest and said:

"Each is wrapped separately. They are quite heavy. I suggest that you take them one at a time to the doorway."

"Or one each!" said Martin. And thus it was that each man picked out of the chest and carried past the waiting servant a cloth bundle whose sickening contents he knew, although he had not yet seen them.

In the entrance to the barn was a trestle table, that could have been used for the preparation of the produce that was normally stored in the barn; or it might have been set up specifically for the purpose that it now served.

After Martin, the other two men set down their bundles on the table, and Martin began to unwrap that nearest the left.

"It's a youth!" declared Fulk.

"Not just any youth, surely," said Tom. "That hair colour is the smith's family, of that I'm sure."

"Then this must be the middle boy," said Fulk.

Tom turned away from the group to be sick. The smith had declined to leave Galway when Fulk and his family had fled.

"I can't leave the men's weapons unfettled, can I? I can't leave the gate locks to seize up – especially in the open position – can I?" The smith's arguments had been irrefutable. So his family had remained with him, three sons and two fine girls, and one of the family, at least, had been reduced to this.

Fulk turned the drying flesh from side to side, ignoring Tom's nausea and pleased at his own comparative stoicism:

"Yes, it's that boy. There's enough of his nose to see the shape that it was, though something's got the eyes, so you can't compare the colour."

Martin busied himself unwrapping the second head. It was of a young female adult, with black hair that had crudely been cut short – perhaps at the time of death.

"I don't think I know 'er," said Fulk. Tom looked up and agreed.

"Nor me."

Finding something other than his own discomfort to concentrate upon greatly steadied Tom, who came close to see what might be made of the final bundle that Martin was now opening up:

"My god!" said Fulk.

"It's Master FitzSimon!" said Tom.

"Who is – was – FitzSimon?" asked Lady Angelina.

"He was the Provost of Galway for longer than anyone else – perhaps six years!" Fulk had taken hold of the head, which was in a more advanced state of decay than the others, and he twisted it about as he had done with the first one, trying to discern detail of the features:

"It's very badly rotted," he said at length, "but I've no doubt it was him, look at the teeth! No doubt at all! Unless he had a twin brother, and that doesn't bear thinking about!"

Fulk put the head down and picked up that of the unidentified female:

"Well it isn't one of the Smiths, that's for sure; and it ain't a FitzSimon either, for he had no daughter ... No, this one leave me beat ... she may not be from Galway at all, of course, but the other two are; and all three are crying out to highest heaven for a Christian burial and for revenge on whoever did this awful thing to them!"

Fulk's stoicism had lasted as long as he had been usefully engaged in the process of identification. Now, a severe reaction was setting in. These two – or perhaps three, if the woman could eventually be identified – seemed to indicate the fate of those who had stayed in Galway when the wisest and the most cautious had departed. Fulk was glad that his family had left, for otherwise Joanne might not have lived long enough to have delivered her baby. But he was ashamed also, at his failure to participate in the common defence and he was embarrassed at his recurring nostalgia for a community that he could, with some justice, be accused of having betrayed. And a community that probably was no more – the timber quays that he had helped to extend, and the cranes that he had designed and built, could be standing idle in a ghost city or be burned on Irish hearths.

Fulk shook himself, and unashamedly let his tears course down his face. Tom patted him on the shoulder and shared the old man's feelings of dismay and impotence.

"The heads will properly be buried when the king's officers have investigated, as they must. The names that you have given will be of material benefit in that process," said Angelina encouragingly.

"Will we get the help that we need to live securely in our homes in Ireland?" asked Fulk.

Tom looked surprised at this question from his father-in-law. They were all having a struggle to succeed in London, but the young man had thought that the coming of the baby had alleviated Fulk's bitterness. Now, as Fulk looked at the head of his old leader from the Guild House at Galway, his real feelings poured forth:

"I'm just an alien here in England, lucky to get a journeyman's work. I can't go back to France as a master-craftsmen either: I was never free of the guild in my home city because I chose to go to Ireland – where our duke, your king, told us that there was so much opportunity! So I'm nobody nowhere, with no more prospects than the rest of FitzSimon has – wherever that may be!"

"Nay, you've got Joanne and the baby – and me, for what that's worth. You have the skills, and I still have much to learn from you, to pass on to our descendants," said Tom.

"Skills are an embarrassment, to an unfree man. In Galway I was an equal citizen in a free community – a true coming together of brave spirits who were bold enough to turn a creek and a few hovels into a new Bordeaux. We gave our free days to digging the town ditch, raising the ramparts, strengthening the stockade and building watchtowers because of the Irish, but my skills were needed in all of that! My barrows and spades brought earth from ditch to mound. My stakes formed the stockade. I made the gates, and the structure of the watchtowers. And all the time my cranes drew the cargoes from the vessels that came in greater numbers until things were really sour, just a few years ago."

This kaleidoscopic recollection and self-justification did not exactly tally with Tom's own experience. The younger man was not twenty-three years old, and he had been permitted to marry his master's daughter immediately his apprentice years were completed, but only because of

Fulk's fears for her safety. With a tough young man at her side, armed with modest skills and a lot of self-interest in the marriage, Joanne's chances of surviving an incursion of Irish to the town – or flight from the town – were bound to be better.

Tom's grandfather, a Bristol merchant, had been caught on the wrong foot as he had supported Matilda's cause, against King Stephen, before Matilda's half-brother Robert of Gloucester had made the south west of England safe for their supporters. With his last possessions and his children, the merchant had fled to Ireland. In Dublin, he found the King of England's party too much in control of civic affairs, so he had sailed on to Galway.

The settlement of Galway, far to the west of the main trade routes around Europe, had an excellent sheltered inlet that cut deep from the wide Atlantic into the central west coast of the island. Galway Bay was well served by rivers and had a vast natural inland waterway system close by, in the form of Lough Carib and its feeder streams. A good quarter of Ireland could be accessed by coracle, skiff or longboat from Galway, subject always, of course, to the *laissez-passer* of the local chiefs and kings. If internal rivalries in Ireland, or Irish chauvinism against the settlers, inhibited trade, then the economic basis of the whole venture would be undermined.

Tom was born within a month of the family's arrival in Galway, to the merchant's only daughter. Tom's father had subsequently become disenchanted with serving the role of his wife's labourer, giving his energy to her family business and seeing his wife take part in endless disputation with her brothers while he was left to mind the shop. So he had bought a boat and begun conveying goods around the harbour and up the river. He took great pains to acquire some Irish, which he declared was not difficult to do if you realise that there's no French or Nordic element to it, and address the language in its own terms. He also took on the weather on its own terms, and one February day when Tom was seven – and then the oldest of four children – his father simply failed to return from a storm-tossed crossing to Kilcolgan. At thirteen Tom had been put to the apprenticeship with Fulk. Through all his life he had been conscious of family hardship, civic discord and external threat. He had not been encouraged to follow his father in learning Irish or trading on a personal basis with the surrounding community; instead, he had been put to learn an urban craft.

As Fulk's work in ship repair declined with the disappearance of trade, so there was less demand for piling to consolidate the staithes along the waterfront, or for new cranes. The only experience that Tom had of these great engines, throughout his apprenticeship, was assisting his master in making running repairs that hardly seemed necessary. A few people wanted extensions or alterations to their premises, or a new bed, a table, some stools or a chest. There was no turner in Galway, so Fulk had made himself a wood lathe that turned in a balanced manner on the pull of a bowstring, so he could make turned banisters for the half-dozen buildings with stairs, or produce ornate legs for the half-dozen chairs that constituted a good year's demand from the struggling community.

There was plenty of work to be done on the town ditches and the stockades, the gates and the riverfront defences, but the town authorities had less and less means of paying for the work as the years went by. The plea of necessity was a powerful influence on Fulk, so he had worked a lot for little reward.

He dreaded his own daughter's rape, and the burning of his small timber yard, so he gave what he could not sell towards the strengthening of the town. His apprentice learned from a very early age that Joanne shared his own scepticism about the viability of defending the town with fewer than three hundred able men if a serious siege were set to the place. This perception was commonly held, so that the decline in trade became the excuse for those who could do so – the able-bodied – to remove themselves to more prosperous ports, and the defensive capacity of the town declined with the population.

When King Stephen's son, Eustace, had died and that disastrous monarch took Matilda's son as his heir, several of the Galway citizens who had fled from the English Civil War now reckoned that Galway was a more dangerous spot than Hull or Bristol and they also took their muscle and their money out of the struggling settlement. The coming of peace in England was a good time for refugees to return to their former homes.

Tom's graduation from apprentice to journeyman – fully qualified craftsman – and his marriage to Joanne, had coincided with the first serious Irish assault on the town. The gates were not forced, and the attackers had no experience of how to mount a ditch and drive defenders from a well-designed stockade, so the Irish withdrew until they could obtain the guidance of a compatriot with successful invasion experience.

In the meantime those who could afford to do so began to sail away from the beleaguered town.

Only after a second, more determined and more professional – though still unsuccessful – assault on the town did Fulk recognise that the count of the dead and wounded meant that such losses could only be sustained for six days, on the assumption that the invaders would only challenge the walls at one point at any time. If multiple assaults were made, whether feints or serious attacks, the place was already indefensible with the resources available.

Joanne and Tom had already made it clear that they were keen to take their chances elsewhere, so when Fulk had decided on the inevitability of defeat – in this siege, or the next – they endorsed his decision to withdraw, respectfully but urgently. Joanne's pregnancy was the deciding factor in Fulk's decision to abandon the little that was left of his business. Tom felt that the family's departure from Ireland had been inevitable, that there had been a generation-long build-up to the crisis that they had fled – only just in time, as these grim mementos made clear.

"How long ... do we know when they died?" Tom asked.

Martin knew of no method by which such a question could convincingly be answered from the sight – or smell – of the human remains, beyond the obvious facts – that flesh leaves the bones in a few years or less, according to the state of the ground, and that the bones turn to dust in thousands rather than mere hundreds of years. So a clean skeleton, found underground, is likely to be from a death decades or more ago.

In these cases, the flesh on the skulls was rotted, but it was impossible to say whether through natural decay or ill usage. Some damage might be inadvertent, an outcome of transporting the skulls over the seas, though the violent deaths all the victims had suffered must be assumed to have damaged them before and after decapitation.

"We know from your account that these people – or rather, the two males – were alive on the feast of the Holy Trinity last year, for that was when you yourselves took ship from Ireland," said Martin. "So the longest that they can have been dead is just less than a year; from July, perhaps. The least time that they can be presumed to have been dead is six or seven weeks, since they were ... er ... allocated for despatch here to London. Beyond that, it is guesswork, until we have the story of what occurred in Galway, and the date of those unhappy events."

"The town is gone, then," said Fulk.

"Not necessarily," answered Angelina, to the surprise of all three visitors. "These people could have taken a ship – as you did – and been less lucky with their selection of master, or have been attacked by corsairs. Again, they might have ventured outside the town for some purpose and been taken on the highway."

"There are no highways in the west of Ireland, madam," said Fulk. "The rivers are the highways; otherwise there are just tracks, and many of them lead nowhere, to deceive strangers." The passion had gone from his voice, leaving it a depressed monotone.

Tom remembered the good times – periods of peace and fair weather, when he and his master had collected other men together and had rowed upriver to select and fell timber from the abundant forest. They lived well on fine fish, trout and salmon, as they rough-dressed the trunks and major branches of the trees before setting them to float downriver to the town, the crane and the waiting timber yard. In such times, life in Ireland was idyllic; the tragedy was how frequently and how damagingly human jealousies and ambitions – and the invocation of arcane rights or traditions – had undermined the joys of that existence.

The land was unhappy, in Tom's mind, but it was far from unlovely. Now was not the time to argue with his father-in-law, with these skulls still before them on the crude plank of the trestle table.

"I think that we have seen all that we need to see, my lady," said Martin. "May we return the heads now to their secure hiding place?"

"There is no need for you to do that, Father. Sigbert will tidy up for us." With this, Angelina nodded the instruction to her servant and turned towards the house with rapid steps that the men hastened to follow.

At the house a maid appeared, to whom Angelina spoke in a dialect that none of the men could recognise or understand, though Fulk thought that he detected an almost Irish element in it. He shook himself once more, ordering his mind not to permit itself the fantastic conceit that this lady's connection with Celtic affairs might not be entirely innocent. Martin knew her to be of Scots-Norman origin, and the maid to be a native Scot. Fulk's instinctive linkage of the Scots Gaelic intonation with Irishmen's talk showed a good ear and an accurate memory, though for the moment he attributed his reaction to paranoia, which he would describe as fearful fantasy when he recounted the incident to his dutiful if independent-minded daughter.

Ale was offered to the guests and they stood with their mugs in a semicircle around the seat that Angelina occupied, beside an open window at which she had been sewing.

"I had told Rulf that he should consult you, even though that ragamuffin of a fake hermit had said that you were away at Oxford – no doubt, on some nefarious errand to Beaumont," said Angelina to Martin.

"Oxford was indeed the butt of my journey, madam; but I went to the old priory at the castle, not to the royal palace."

Angelina paused briefly, to give Martin time to enlarge on his reasons for going to Oxford, or on his experiences there. Always willing to indulge an ally, within reasonable limits, Martin delivered an extremely economical elucidation:

"Prior Osbert, as you know, is a great bibliophile. He had an agent in Oxford, for some time, searching for materials. I was able to facilitate the return of the best of them to West Minster."

"I see ... as far as you are willing to let me see," said the shrewd lady. "I doubt if Osbert of Clare would dispense with your services for the best part of a month – in appalling weather – just to collect a few mouldy pages of parchment ... but life is full of strange incidents; though few are so singular, do you not think, as the objects that your men have just identified?"

In including the joiners in the conversation, Angelina moved from the general to the particular.

"Father Martin, will you please record, at your preceptory, all the details of the Provost FitzSimon, and the boy Smith, and of their kindred and antecedents, that these good folk can give to you?"

This request implied that the le Court household was without parchment or ink. The presence in the surroundings of scores of ducks, geese and chickens made it improbable that the lack of a quill was the inhibition against a cleric writing in this illiterate establishment.

"I would happily do so, madam, but would it not be easier for Sir Rulf if the record was kept here, at Chad's Well? Surely the holy sisters at the convent have ink, and skins to write on?" Martin did not question the probability that at least one of the shrewd women who made up the small, well-endowed and thus beleaguered religious community could write as well as any male scribe.

"Of course, that is a much better idea," said Angelina. She looked out of the window. The sun was still reasonably high. "You men would have time to tell your tale to the holy sisters, and get back to London before the gates are closed, if you go now ... will you do so, for the peace of your former provost?"

"Of course; we will do what we can," said Fulk.

Angelina clapped her hands, and again spoke to the maid in the evocative and tantalisingly alien dialect. Martin detected the name Sigbert – a jarringly un-Celtic sound – and inferred that the fellow was summoned to conduct the joiners to the convent. Martin was familiar with the way to the nunnery, so it was clearly the lady's intention to separate Martin from the commoners and to enter into a confidential conversation with him, while Mother Anne or fat Sister Osyth took the men's deposition.

Less than five minutes later, Martin was seated on a stool next to Lady Angelina, the two alone in the spacious hall.

"I take it that Sir Rulf will tell the sheriff – or the king himself – what has transpired as soon as the next incident occurs; or shortly, even if nothing else happens?" said Martin.

"Too late, Father. Rulf has gone to the king – to Oxford, where we believe him to be, on his progress from Winchester to Chester." A smile hovered around Angelina's eyes and mouth; there was something that she was supposed to keep secret, but Martin would easily tease out of her if she did not offer it directly. He made a guess:

"So the third incident has occurred! It was about due!"

Angelina screwed up her face, in mock disappointment at his percipience breaching her secret, then she laughed openly, before saying:

"Yes indeed, Father ... two nights ago."

"But the hermit told me, only yesterday, that a night watch was being kept," protested Martin.

"And so it is, and so it will be – to deceive the hermit and the scoundrels at that fishing place, and to entrap any more men who come ashore there illicitly," said Angelina.

"But Rulf has already got the big fish?" asked Martin.

Angelina told how, two nights ago, not long after dusk as the tide reached full flood, a boat had put ashore. It had come further west than the village folk had been deployed to look out, so only Rulf's men from Chad's Well had been aware of it. Four men had got out of the boat, carrying a struggling thing wrapped in sailcloth. The boat had been secured to the bank by stakes, and the men had then carried what appeared to be a living prisoner to the road. Rulf had himself shoved the boat adrift, cutting off the escape of the landing party, before leading his men in the pursuit of the interlopers. At odds of eight to four, it had been a brief contest, though one of the seamen had wounds from which he had died overnight.

Expecting to release a man, the raiding party had ordered the sailors to put the bundle on the ground. As they did so, one of the uninjured men tried to run away. The dogs got him within five paces, and made a fair mess of his legs before they were driven off with whips. In the light of the next morning the superior doublet that he wore proved him to be the ship's captain, and he had been taken by Rulf to Oxford, where he would face up to the king's justice:

"And the prisoner?" asked Martin.

"Turned out to be a particularly fine billy goat, that went berserk as soon as it was free, and butted four men – two of each side – before it fled the scene." The village lads, inevitably, had secured it the next day, and it had made a fine supper for the community. A living stray animal would be claimed by an owner, a dead one could be claimed for carcass value, but a beast that has been consumed is irrecoverable. So the people of Knighten Rise had taken the gift-goat into their own mouths, as quickly as they could, and all trace of the animal had vanished by the time one of the Chad's Well villagers had been sent to Knighten Rise purporting to be in search of a goat that had escaped from his own yard.

Angelina laughed as she described the incident, then she became serious again:

"The paraphernalia that came with the goat were less amusing. They have been taken with Rulf and the captain to Oxford, so you will have to make do with my description of them. There was a stake and a rope, to tether the goat – presumably somewhere near the hermitage. And there was a sort of copper mitre – like a bishop's mitre in shape, but much taller – that had been fitted to slip on to the goat's horns ... I know that it is bizarre, but this whole series of incidents has been beyond normal behaviour, as you are well aware, Father ... Then there was a special sword. Rulf and I are convinced that the intention was to sacrifice the goat ... having brought it many miles – perhaps even from Ireland – for the purpose."

"And provided with a martyr's crown, perhaps?" said Martin. He smiled at Angelina, to encourage her to keep her confidences flowing as he evaluated this next step in the sequence of events. Biblical and classical images of the scapegoat were inescapable; the ancient human tradition of sacrificing a goat to propitiate the god's wrath against sinful, stupid mankind was so deeply engrained in many traditions that occasional human sacrifices, or the victimisation of an individual for the common good, was likened to the use of a goat for the same purpose.

Did this mean that the first body, the headless young man, had been a human scapegoat? That situation could not apply to the other corpses; their severed heads were evidence of a bloody massacre, not of selective victimisation – their use as reinforcement of the importance of the message had been the significant feature about them.

Martin enquired if there had been any design or engraving on the goat's crown. No, said Angelina, it was simple, crudely burnished and recently shaped thin copper sheeting.

"I don't suppose anyone got anywhere near trying the crown on the goat to see if it actually fitted?" asked Martin. Angelina agreed with his supposition. Nobody in her husband's party had been able to hold the goat for any purpose.

"Is the sacrificing of goats a common Celtic pastime?" he asked.

"Not among the Scots whom I have known, but I have heard of goats paraded by the Welsh, and of rams given metal horns – or horn covers – as a sign of their virility and of their owners' pride," she replied.

"So, it is not impossible that a more complete Celtic culture, such as that which Ireland has retained, could include the ritual use of goats ... It is an ancient Bible tradition as well ... Joseph had a coat of many colours; Joseph was scapegoated by his brothers – they told his father that wild beasts had taken him, after the sacrificial blood had been smeared on the coat ..."

In thinking out loud, Martin had opened up yet another new prospect. Perhaps the young man had not been executed as a traitor, or wantonly sacrificed as a scapegoat. Perhaps he had died in battle, or from accidental poisoning, and his body had been used, as the massacre victims' heads had been used, simply because it was available. His dress could be the analogue of the coat of many colours, and the crowned goat could be the guide to such an interpretation.

Alternatively, the crowned goat could be an insult, an indication that the King of England was seen as a goat – a brute beast, albeit the wearer of a crown. The latter possibility must be kept in view, but Martin did not rate it highly. He much preferred the softer interpretation that distanced the users of dead bodies from the murderous acts that had reduced them to mere carcasses. The perpetrators of the blasphemy had been prepared to sacrifice a goat – but men kill goats by the thousands every day, so the circumstances could be discounted in comparison to the deed. Killing a goat for meat – as the people of Knighten Rise had done – might seem more natural than the ritual slaughter of a sacrificial beast, but from the goat's point of view, or from God's, there is no material difference between routine and ritual butchery, especially if the flesh is consumed after the event. Practitioners of ancient religions could have believed – and heathens might still believe – that their gods demanded blood sacrifices, but Christianity taught of a unique and final religious sacrifice, though it demanded men's lives in crusades and other campaigns on a large scale and apparently in perpetuity.

These considerations were profoundly challenging intellectually, but did they further the purpose in hand of coming to an understanding of the three-phase message that was apparently to have been completed with the slaughter of the goat in the hermitage clearing?

Martin turned the questioning to the latest event:

"Where is the dead man from the landing party?"

"At Knighten Rise, and six feet under."

"And where are the two men who have not gone with the supposed captain to Oxford?"

"Safe, locked up at the Wardrobe ... but you say the supposed captain," said Angelina, suddenly anxious. "Why do you say that?"

"Did the man utter a word in French, or in English, before he was led away?" asked Martin. Angelina believed not.

"Did Sir Rulf compare his hands, face and limbs with those of the other men?" asked Martin.

Angelina seized the drift of his questioning, and her anxiety increased. Rulf had not done these things. It was just conceivable that the men had changed clothes in the dark. They had been securely incarcerated for the remainder of the night after they had been seized, but they had not been bound.

"I must ride at once to the Wardrobe!" said the loyal wife, jumping up from her seat.

"You will not do your business today and return before curfew, my lady. May I suggest that we go there together tomorrow? Come for me at the preceptory after Matins, and we can investigate who is whom in good time ... The men will not be spirited away in the night, if the place is strong enough to hold them safe!"

Angelina was convinced of the folly of rushing out at once, though Martin's words also raised in her mind the irrational fear that if she left the interview until the morrow she could indeed find that the men had vanished. Rulf's orders to the guards at the King's Wardrobe had been very clear, and they had been given in the name of the king. The prisoners would still be available for questioning and inspection in the morning, and since Martin evidently knew the signs to look for in distinguishing a common seaman from a master mariner – which Angelina could only guess at, in terms of rough hands and sun-burned skin – Rulf's interests would be better served by Martin's presence

The assignation for the following morning was duly agreed, and fixed for the Wardrobe after Terce to give Angelina time to ride comfortably into the city after doing essential household chores while Martin also carried out the routine business of the preceptory day.

Martin then took his leave of Angelina, making the sign of the cross in the direction of the barn that held the severed heads. He called at the convent, to be warmly greeted by the sisters of the community who were quietly agog with the details that Osyth had written down at Fulk's dictation, and then he and the two joiners set out for a brisk walk back to Ald Gate. By maintaining a fast pace, Martin minimised the chances of the joiners asking questions that he could not answer, or engaging in speculations that were more likely to confuse than to assist him. He obtained precise directions to the widow's toft at which they had established their lodging, so that he could contact them directly if he needed to. Sending his good wishes to Joanne, he bade them farewell just inside Ald Gate, where he had vouched for them as joiners going about legitimate business under his personal supervision. It was only when he walked down the Bye Ward of the Tower that he realised that a settler who had spent over twenty years trading with the Irish might know about ritualised use – or abuse – of a goat. He would have to raise the question when he next met Fulk.

Chapter Six

As Martin approached the Royal Wardrobe, ascending a short, steep slope from the riverside bulk of Baynard's Castle, he was surprised to hear the call of a corncrake. Surprised, for this was a bird of the open field, never a city dweller. Martin stood still and heard it again. It must have been at least three summers since he had encountered the sound, and memories of the years before his life in London flooded back to him as he stood still at the side of Knight Rider Street, just listening. The sound came again, a little unreal – or probably a little false. Martin had looked around as he had listened, and he had seen no bird vaguely reminiscent of the corncrake. The sound seemed to come from within the stone tower ahead of him.

At least as big in circumference as the gate tower of his own preceptory at Bellins Gate, though more massively constructed and a storey higher, the Wardrobe Tower was surrounded by a walled bailey. Access was by a gate at the northern end of the compound so, as he approached from the river side, Martin had to go round the perimeter, giving him a fine opportunity to verify the height and apparent strength of all the walls. The ditch, mound and wooden stockade of earlier times had been replaced in Stephen's reign by stone walls set on top of the consolidated earthen mounds. It would not be easy to capture the Wardrobe, even if the king's enemies should gain control of the surrounding city. The massive bulk of the partially reconstructed Cathedral of St Paul towered over the Wardrobe complex, from the summit of Ludgate Hill, but even if some blaspheming rebel placed his archers on the cathedral roof they would be able to do only limited damage to the well-shielded defenders inside the high walls of the Wardrobe.

This was definitely not an acceptable habitat for a field bird. Martin looked at the passers-by, covertly, as he made his way up to the gate. He had allowed ample time for his short walk from Bellins Gate, because of the likelihood that some acquaintance would stop him for a discussion of preceptory business on the way. No such diversion had occurred this morning, so Martin had been able to count the six ships at the *porte* of Queenhithe, to observe the timber barges at Broken Quay and to see how little grain there was in the warehouses around the mouth of the little River Wallbrook. Now that he had become sure that the screech that had caught his attention was a human imitation and not the utterance of a lost, confused or demented bird, he was attuned to discover whether there was any response.

No suspicious person was apparent as he strolled up to the gatehouse, nor was there any visible idler looking towards the gatehouse from a safe distance. The porter told him that the Lady Angelina was not in the Wardrobe, nor was she expected. The monk could not be admitted to wait for her, because he had no authority there.

"When she does arrive, tell her that Martin of Bellins Gate will wait on her presently," said that person; and he took advantage of the waiting time by making a complete circuit of the Wardrobe, starting by reversing his former route around the eastern face of the complex and then walking as close as he could to the western walls back to the gate. Several alleys of small houses abutted directly on to the walls of the bailey that enclosed the Wardrobe, but they could quickly be cleared away if any assault was intended against the fortified structure. They were not high enough to serve as platforms for an attempt to scale the walls.

The Wardrobe looked secure, and at no point around its circumference did Martin see anyone loitering with intense interest in the premises. Nor did he hear any corncrake, real or imitated.

He took his time over the perambulation, a good twenty minutes. When he returned to the gate the surly porter had become obsequious and ingratiating:

"I didn't mean to doubt you, Father, when you was here before ... but you can't be too careful these days, and orders is orders ... but her ladyship has come, with Sir Rulf's password to let her in, especially to see you, she says. So come right in, Father, pray do."

The man had opened the main gates to admit the solid cob on which Angelina had ridden pillion to her servant, the taciturn Sigbert, from Chad's Well into the city. Jousting practice in Cheapside had delayed their progress, more because of Angelina's interest in the proceedings – and the possible disclosure of information that could be useful in making her side-bets at the joust itself – than because of the partial obstruction of the thoroughfare. One of the Wardrobe gates had been closed, and the other of the pair of great wooden doors had been left ajar to admit the lady's expected guest.

The porter directed Martin across the yard to the door at the base of the tower. As in the Tower of London, this access point was some dozen feet above courtyard level, approached by an easily demolished external wooden stairway. There were window embrasures from that level upwards, but it was evident that there must be at least two dark levels of unlit storage space below the entry floor, ample even for a king's stock of reserve weapons. The four storeys that had slit windows – most of them being visibly shuttered – would provide sufficient accommodation for archives, and for the robes and regalia that kings and queens neither wanted to destroy nor to convey on their endless progresses around the realm.

The yard surrounded the great circular tower, providing a cleared space to guarantee the occupants sight of any approach to the main structure from any angle. Against the high outer walls, but less tall than them, were various lean-to buildings: stables, stores, and half a dozen cottages for the staff.

Martin climbed the springing wooden steps, still listening for the corncrake. It would be good to pinpoint the angle of the tower, if not the actual slit, from which the noise was emanating intermittently.

Before Martin reached the head of the stair, and the wooden drawbridge that led from the landing to the doorway of the stone structure, the servant Sigbert came out to greet him and to apologise for the earlier refusal of the porter to admit the monk. There was no point demurring; Martin merely nodded a couple of times while the man gabbled on, as he led the way through a small hallway into the main chamber on the principal floor of the tower.

All the shutters here had been opened, and a fire was being kindled with a great deal of smoke by two liveried attendants of some antiquity. The old men seemed ineffectual at firelighting, and Martin hoped that they were better at storekeeping; they would certainly not be effective guards for desperate prisoners.

Angelina rose from her seat by the table and came towards Martin, who begged:

"Please do not add to the apologies I have already received for not being admitted earlier. The man only did his duty, and for that should be commended."

Sigbert grunted his approval at this fair comment, and was ordered out of the chamber by his mistress. Some mistresses would have a servant whipped for such impertinence; to agree with the upper classes unnecessarily could be construed as going far beyond the permissible range of servile communication. Shouting a warning to one's master in an emergency, or whispering gossip or even a suggestion when it was solicited were tolerated, but making gratuitous comment, favourable or otherwise, was always an offence. Men and women lost their tongues for it, and Sigbert would be fortunate if he had heard the last of the matter.

Martin accepted the seat offered by his host, and as he sat a younger man in the same livery as that of the elderly firelighters brought in ale, bread and salt. Martin broke off a piece of the bread to eat, touched the salt in token acceptance, and accepted the ale with a smile. He was being received as an honoured guest, in final quittance for any offence that had been given by his earlier rebuttal at the gate. As Rulf's representative, Angelina was evidently the ruling power – under the crown – in this place.

The man who had brought the offerings set the tray with the loaf and the salt cellar on the table, and stood by Angelina's chair. Both the lady and the servant looked at Martin, without speaking, as he washed the piece of chewed bread down his throat with a sip of slightly vinegary ale. He put the mug down, with a rather definite gesture that indicated that he would be little inclined to drink more, at which Angelina said:

"Shall we take a look at the prisoners, then?"

"One thing first," said Martin, so the lady settled back in her chair. "Do you know sufficient of the Celtic Scots tongue to talk confidently about the brown field bird?"

"The brown field bird?" Angelina repeated Martin's question in English, and then said some words in Scots.

"Would you please repeat those words, loudly, as if finishing some piece of conversation, as we approach the door of the cell where the men are held?"

She looked Martin in the eye, as if to say: "I'll do it, and I'm too proud to seek an explanation of the request," and simply bowed her head in assent.

So they stood, and the servant led them to the broad spiral staircase.

If he had then turned downwards, Martin's hunch about the source of the birdcall would have been invalidated. There were no apertures from which a clear sound could be directed to the outside world from the lower levels. But the man led the way upstairs, two levels, and into a chamber the same size as the first. Various chests, some piled one upon the other, all made of crude planks of oak, occupied much of the floor area and there was a doorway in the wall in the position where the great chimney breast had been in the main hall.

"That little room's all stone, floor and ceiling, because it's built in with the fireplaces and chimneys," explained the servant.

"So prisoners cannot do it any harm," said Angelina.

The solid door, complete with a metal lock and two great wooden bars, also contained a spy hole. Martin looked into the hole, and at first saw only a small square of daylight: an opening the size of a large cobblestone went right through the courses of stone to provide a channel for light and ventilation to this oppressive little cell. As he became accustomed to the gloom, he saw the shapes of two men – and something, perhaps even the eye of one of them, then came to block the spy hole from the inside.

"Now, my lady," whispered Martin, having turned his back to the door, and in a massive contralto voice Angelina declaimed the strange foreign sounding formula.

Three armed and armoured men had followed the small group of investigators into the room, and they now proceeded to bar the door to the stairs as a prelude to the prisoners being let out of their confined cell. Angelina commanded the door to be opened, the wooden bolts were removed and the liveried servant unhooked the large iron key from his belt and turned it – with some difficulty – in the heavy mechanism of the lock. Even then the door was stiff to open, and the two guards had to tug hard to gain access.

Despite the ventilation that the cell enjoyed, the opening of the door brought a rush of noxious air into the larger chamber – it confirmed that the cell was not fitted with any latrine or oubliette. Such a facility was not to be expected, so high in the building, but it meant that the prisoners would leave behind them a stinking memorial to trouble for some time for any users of the main room. The servant opened the window shutters one by one, and with each increase in the level of lighting the contents and layout of the room became more clear:

"Come out of it!" bawled one of the guards. The prisoners did not need to understand French to know that the words were addressed to them, and it did not take significant cerebral powers to realise that the most likely order was for them to move into the larger room.

The prisoners came forth, shuffling because their limbs had been cramped for three days. They were dirty and unshaven; but even so it was clear that the taller one had a much more tanned complexion than the other.

Martin pushed back the sleeves of his habit, so that his wrists were exposed, then he put out his hands at elbow height, showing first the palm and then the back of the hand uppermost.

"Do this!" he said, in French; then he winked to the Lady Angelina. She looked startled at this intimacy, then took in his meaning.

"Do as he says!" she added, in Scots. The taller of the two men looked towards her in surprise, then did as Martin did; the other man followed suit.

Things were not quite as Martin had suspected. The tall, very dark man had the rough hands of a seaman, with no little finger on his right hand and the tips of two fingers gone from his left. His legs and arms were skinny but muscular and his eyes faced the far wall steadily. His expression was resigned, long-suffering.

The other man had much smoother hands. The right was larger than the left, with hard skin at the junction of each finger with the palm, while the toughened skin on the left hand was at the base of the thumb. Here was someone used to wielding a sword in the right hand, with the strap of a shield in the left. There was notably more fat over his muscles on arms and legs; he was fit, but also he was used to a good table and probably a soft bed. This man must be the originator of the incidents, or the agent of that higher personage. The big man had shown in response to Angelina's words that he was a Celt, and almost certainly a common seaman. He was a big, useful fellow, however; one who might well be willing to engage in desperate activities for extra pay or the chance of sharing in some loot. His fingers might have been lost in shipboard accidents or in combat.

The smaller man had lighter-coloured hair, thinning at the crown and receding over the forehead, suggesting that he was probably over thirty. His blue eyes flashed from the monk to the woman, to the guards, to the servant, to the ceiling, to the outstretched arms of his fellow prisoner, to his own extended palms, and back to Martin.

Martin put his own hands down to his sides, and after a moment of hesitation the big man did likewise; then the soldier or gentleman followed. Martin guessed that he must be well on the way to realising that the relative status of the two prisoners had been correctly assessed, and that that of their absent companion had also been brought into the equation – and that necessarily the heat would turn on himself. The big fellow – and the man who Rulf was escorting to Oxford – might not be able to respond to French or English interrogators, even under torture. They might know enough French to respond to orders, at sea or ashore, or they could have had a captain who spoke their own dialect. Martin however recognised that the minions would probably have no material knowledge of the intentions and plans of their masters, nor even be able to describe the deeds they had taken part in in any language he could understand.

If an Irish interpreter could be found – and such must be available, among the Irish exiles, refugees and expatriates in this great city – maybe the big man would disclose what he knew, preferably by bribery rather than torture. It would be of limited value, except as corroboration or refutation of the conclusions that the investigators could derive for themselves. Martin reckoned the other prisoner would be a tough nut to crack. Personally he abhorred the idea of effacing or deforming a human body in order to extract information from the spirit that it contained, even when the inquisition was conducted in a holy cause. He hoped, in this instance, as in others, to gain what he needed without the authorities needing to apply more forceful methodology. The resolution of this question rested with the prisoner.

Even if a prisoner gave full co-operation and told the full facts at once, however, a cautious investigator might still try torture to see if the account remained the same even under extreme stress. A statement that was too pat, too glib or too loquacious could be suspect, so it was a matter of careful judgement for a prisoner to make, as to what it was wise to confess and in what manner to frame his remarks. Anyone organising a complex crime, or a rebellious action, or sedition against a government, was well advised to use people who could simply not make useful statements, such as henchmen with no knowledge of relevant languages. The approach needed careful use, for the arrival of large numbers of tongue-tied, well-armed visitors would be highly conspicuous: such resources could only be used in small numbers for brief, specific operations where the sea would give ready access and escape.

A foray by small boat from a ship in the Thames came into this category.

"Well, my friend, you have been given thinking time by the servants of the king himself."

It was Angelina who spoke, in a clear and authoritative voice that was notably lighter than the jocular contralto with which she had referred to the brown bird before the cell door had been opened. She was determined to extract the meaning of that particular ploy from Martin before he left the Wardrobe, if it did not arise naturally in the course of this interrogation. She now assumed the role of her husband's representative, one which every upper-class wife had to adopt in his frequent absences and one which Queen Elinor had developed with powerful effect in recent years.

"Tell me, then ... yes, it is you I am addressing ... tell me who you are. What you are, I know; and some of what you have done ... You will tell the rest; for we will not let you die until you have done so. Whether you live or die, when all is known, is the king's business ... Do not think that you will return to that chamber, to decide your own fate. I have told you – that was thinking time, and you will have no more of it."

Martin marvelled at Angelina's *post facto* rationalisation of the blunder that had left the expedition's leader shut up in a cell with a common seaman for three days. The leader had no reason to know where his other companion had gone, but assuming that the man spoke only some savage tongue, the leader could be complacent about the outcome of any investigation on him. Now Angelina had reconstituted the scenario, with the removal of the second man to Oxford presented as a feint.

Martin had no doubt that the fastest horse remaining in Rulf's stables, with the best rider from Chad's Well, had set off for Oxford within the hour of Martin leaving the manor house yesterday. The messenger might even have departed while he himself was still at the convent at the northern end of the village, and a possibly false recollection of hoof beats heard while he had been with the sisters now flashed into his mind. Angelina's appearance on that bulky, aged carthorse that had been complacently lipping straw in the courtyard of the Wardrobe was now explained. It would be in the lap of the gods whether Angelina's messenger reached Rulf before Rulf met one of the king's inner circle, but it was highly probable that Rulf had by now received the revised version of the story – urging him to be cautious as to which prisoner was which – before it was brought to the personal attention of the monarch.

Angelina was evidently determined to do all she could to retrieve the situation, and rescue Rulf's standing at court by discovering the true facts on his behalf here in London. In the meanwhile he would have to make up his own story as to why he had brought a relatively insignificant man, together with the goat's crown, to Oxford, but Martin could easily see how an account could be constructed. Rulf could report that the prisoner who had been conveyed to Oxford was merely a sample – the key man had been kept in London for questioning near the scene of his blasphemy and possible witchcraft. He could mention that the horned beast was the symbol of suppressed religious movements in England, of which Martin had recent bitter experience. The clerics of Henry's court might also construe a diabolical meaning from the addition of a goat to the murderous rituals.

It would be deeply unfortunate if Archbishop Theobald, with or without the connivance of his archdeacon, Becket, should convince the Pope that the Christian Irish were sunk deeply into heresy and even blasphemy as well as canonical disobedience. To demonise a subject people and their actions can create a self-sustaining myth; every accident to the occupying force can be put down to the work of the evil eye or the treacherous mind, and any brutality that is perpetrated against the alleged Satanists becomes a defensible work of piety.

All of this thinking would fall apart if the man standing nervously before Angelina and Martin among the King of England's muniment chests was not the leading player in the landings that were clearly a key part in some carefully planned – though initially ill-executed – plan or plot.

The imaginative leaps of Martin's mind – which carried him over vast chasms of ignorance or concealed facts to conclusions that could be tested through questioning – depended crucially on his assessment of the people involved. Martin had merely watched the two men, while Angelina had addressed the one who was palpably from a higher social order. The seaman had been looking at the back of the other's head, in evident relief that he was not the target for interrogation. There was continuing anxiety in his demeanour – he might yet be at risk of the rack or a beating – but it was plain that he had little love for the other man, and that his anxiety was on his own account.

The leader affected in his posture a degree of self-control that was not sustained in the seaman's flickering eyes or in the frequency with which his tongue emerged to moisten his dry lips. He would certainly talk, sooner rather than later. The more that his residual self-confidence could be eroded at this point, the more abject would be his mental state when he made his confession; and the more information might be gleaned for Rulf to present to the king in justification for his purported stratagem of deliberately leaving the key witness at the Wardrobe.

Angelina was counting the seconds, wondering how to force the pace with the prisoner, short of ordering rough hands to be laid on him, and hoping that Martin would intervene to resolve her dilemma.

Martin did so, but in a manner that she had not anticipated. Nor indeed had Martin himself. From some deep well in his memory, he recalled travellers who had arrived at the Bellins Gate *porte* over a year ago. He had enquired of them whence they came, and the oldest man among them had replied with words sounding like *'on ayran'*. This had quickly been elucidated by others in the group to mean 'from Ireland'; though Martin thought that the old man had been asserting himself to be Irish, rather than from Ireland.

Martin pointed to the seaman, and tried to recall the old Irishman's exact phrase as he attempted to utter it in a rising tone to imply that it was a question: "*On ayran?*"

The man looked surprised, and as if by a reflex he answered "*Ap cum rag.*"

Martin had heard similar to this in Gloucester, even at the little lazar hospice outside the town that he had served for some time. The man was saying – rightly or wrongly – that he was "of the companions": a Welshman.

Welsh traders and seafarers had done well in the chaos of Stephen's reign. The north and mid-Welsh coasts had been fully controlled by the Welsh princelings, though they were mostly associated in lucrative alliances with Ranulf of Chester, who controlled the mouth and hinterland of the Dee. The Welsh had sold passage to Ranulf's men in their expansion of his domains northwards, they had traded with and supported the Scots in their incursions into Cumbria, and they had traded on their own account with the Isle of Man, Ireland, France and Spain. The fairs in the major English towns along the Welsh borders had become significant shop windows for the Welsh to sell both their native produce and their Mediterranean imports on to English midlanders. Martin had himself seen the range and variety of these goods, as a monk of Gloucester Abbey and thus a resident of the city that was effectively the capital of the borderlands. In the years when English merchants were suffering from the closure of ports and the rapacity of the warlords, the Welsh had increased their share of the market. Now the tables were turned and Welsh seamen were finding less normal work in this fourth year of postwar reconstruction in England – more risky activities might well prove attractive.

Angelina looked in surprise from the seaman to Martin. She had had not supposed Martin possessed so great a range of linguistic knowledge.

Martin had kept the other prisoner's face well within the periphery of his vision, and as the seaman uttered his three syllables, Martin shifted his focus to the leader. The man looked angry now, as well as exceedingly anxious. His eyes flashed towards Martin, met the monk's ready gaze and then dropped to the floor.

Angelina accepted a hint of a nod from Martin as the cue to return the questioning to the prime prisoner.

"You are no Welshman, I presume?" she said, in French, "nor yet an Irishman, though you may be from a settlement on that island." She deliberately ended her question with a statement so he had no need to answer at once – even if he was sufficiently softened up to do so. The more they could find out before the formal interrogation, the less obfuscation he could create. A few minutes of good luck and careful management of their present advantage could save significant time later.

"Whoever you are, and whatever you are, you know enough Welsh to give orders in that language ... which would indicate that if you are a seaman at all, your home port will be Chester!"

Martin's assertion was a shot in the dark, based on the assumption that Earl Ranulf had less to lose by stirring up Anglo-Irish problems than had any other influential figure who had contacts with the Welsh. By his reference to Chester he hinted at the man's possible master without naming him – the grandee who would shortly be host to the king and queen.

A hint of a grin on the prisoner's lips, showing the tips of his teeth, told Martin that the fellow understood some French, but equally it suggested that part at least of Martin's guess was wrong. Perhaps he did not speak Welsh? If so, the seaman would have to understand some other tongue, at least well enough for simple instructions. Alternatively, the port of origin was not Chester.

The blessed St Patrick, apostle to the Irish, had been a Welshman taken to Ireland first as a slave; while David, the missionary to the Welsh, had been an Irishman. The connections over the short but stormy seaway between Wales and Ireland had been close and continuous since the Roman era. The principal carriers of goods – as well as terror – around those seas for the past five hundred years had been the Norsemen of Man, who had also established bases in Ireland. The prisoner's grin, almost arrogant even though his posture was deferential with his gaze towards the floor at Angelina's feet, was that of a man from a rapacious and masterful race. The Manx and Irish Vikings had retained their own language, so if this man was one, the French he knew was probably just enough for trade, and perhaps a modicum of Irish or Welsh for the same purpose. But, as was also probable, the sort of trade that he undertook in England was illegal or illicit, conducted with merchants of Viking or Saxon origin, rather than with Norman settlers whose dependence on the conquering power made them more likely to obey embargo regulations and to pay tolls. If so, the common language that he shared with a Welsh crewman would likely be a simple form of English.

Martin had picked up several regional versions of English over the years. He had grown up speaking the Welsh border Wessex dialect of the local peasantry, alongside his native French. He had worked hard to understand the Middle Saxon of Londoners, and even the Essex variant when he had been in that county. He had heard, and partially understood, the more strongly Viking-influenced English of Lincolnshire, but he could not use it for an interrogation, even if these men had a common tongue something like it. No doubt an interpreter could be found, but Martin knew that Angelina would prefer no outsider other than himself to become embroiled in covering up Rulf le Court's apparent misjudgement in taking the best-dressed prisoner to Oxford.

Martin beckoned Angelina to the other end of the room, out of the earshot of the men. He hoped that the move would stimulate the impression in the prisoner's mind that his interrogators – a woman and a monk – were useless and did not know where next to build upon their false assumptions.

"What was the build of the prisoner who Rulf took with him to Oxford?" asked Martin.

"Smaller than either of these; he was older and had a sickly complexion ... Since you alerted me yesterday to the possibility that I now take as fact, I have decided that the doublet that he wore was loose upon him. How could I have been so unobservant?" She required no answer, and Martin proffered none.

"It is the style of the doublet that I ask you now to recall, if you can. I know that you saw it only briefly, and not ... not too critically ... but I wonder if you could give me an impression as to whether it was most plainly Celtic, French or Nordic."

Martin did not invite Angelina to speculate on the garment being of native English origin, though Saxon dress still retained its distinctive style and foreigners who used English ports could well have bought clothing there.

Angelina was definite that the origin was Nordic.

"Do your Scots linguistic skills extend to Norse?" asked Martin.

"As yours do to Welsh!" answered the lady.

"Fewer than a dozen words, then?" he asked.

"Very much fewer," she confirmed. "Do you think him a Viking?"

"His colouring is consistent with that, as is his attitude ... He grinned, when I made the assumptions that he spoke Welsh and hailed from Chester," said Martin.

"Yes, I noticed that. He reacted as if you were wrong on all counts," said the lady.

"Exactly so ... and if he does not speak Welsh, the Welshman has to understand something else, at least as a language of command. I do not think it is French, or we should have had some reaction from him ... So let us gamble for a few moments on it being English ... If he is a Manx or Irish Viking, he will speak English in the manner of the Severn Valley – or in the Cumbrian way, or like a Chester man. I do not know how they talk in Cumbria; but I can speak West Saxon with any man or woman. So let us try that dialect on the prisoner ... the seaman."

"He is expecting the questioning to be focused on his master. He knows that we have recognised them for what they are," said Angelina.

"All the more reason to put the pressure on the man ... apparently ... while we attack the confidence of our Viking. You watch the principal, while I talk to the subordinate; and you shall judge the moment to round on your main suspect once more."

Martin said this as instructions, as he did daily to his little troupe of brethren at Bellins Gate. There was no arrogance in his manner, but there was no room for questioning the command. Angelina silently compared Martin's style favourably with the excitable, changeable but repetitive manner in which her own lord gave instructions, and nodded her acquiescence.

This interchange was conducted in the corner of the room furthest from the stinking hole in which Rulf's prisoners had been held, and between the participants and the captives was the piled welter of crude chests that largely obscured the view of each group from the other. Thus the prisoners could not tell which of the participants in the conversation – the grand lady or the monk – was doing the most talking. Angelina recognised this point, and, as they returned, Angelina to the fore, she turned and said to Martin in French:

"Since you know some of the crude tongue, Father, I desire you to ask the question for me."

The monk recognised her goodwill, her good sense and the speed of her intellect. By making it seem that Angelina's attention would also be directed to an activity that she had ordained, the primary target might perhaps fatally relax his defences. His grin when under direct questioning showed he was neither trained for this experience nor wary of it. Under torture, he might well be as brave and as inarticulate as a male mute swan; but already he had shown himself to be significantly susceptible to this soft-handed approach, the clever way of coaxing information. He would probably try to catch the eye of his shipmate, to encourage him into silence or fiction – most likely, the former – and hear what the man had to say for himself, rather than realise that he would be better gauging what he could from his interrogators' body language.

The leader raised his eyes to the lady's face, then to Martin's as he evidently understood her. Martin caught this motion, trivial though it was, while already appearing to give his full attention to the sailor. Then he asked, in English:

"What language of command does this man use towards you? What speech does he use: English, French, Welsh ... what?"

The question appeared to the simple man to be staggeringly irrelevant and unthreatening. It was almost a conversational matter, such as a priest might ask of someone whom he met taking the shade by a hedgerow, or among the revellers after a wedding.

"Your speech ... as you have just spoken to me!" The man's reply was broken and hesitant, but clear enough.

"Were all your ship-fellows Welsh?" asked Martin, realising that he probably had not captured the correct terminology but that the man must understand.

"Master and men, yes ..." said the sailor, looking at the other prisoner in a way that indicated that there was a huge distance between all the persons thus mentioned, and this man. So he was not the ship's master.

"Is your ship Welsh?" asked Martin.

The man seemed puzzled by the question; and he hesitated before he said, "I've told you, master and crew, we're Welsh."

"But the vessel ... the boat ... the craft." Martin used all the variants that he could think of, around the terms *boot* and *shiff* avoiding the Latin *navis* and the French *bateau*. The man smiled in recognition, part way through this imaginative digression, and waited courteously for the monk to finish before he said simply: "His."

He did not look at the other prisoner as he spoke, as if he recognised that his assertion would incriminate the other much as it reduced the pressure on himself.

"From which port?" asked Martin, seeking to discover the home base to which the principal prisoner had attracted a Welsh crew. The man obviously latched on to the word port which he evidently associated with the *portes* or entry-points from the Thames to the City of London, for he replied:

"Queenhithe."

"Is that where you were going to?" asked Martin.

"Yes ... and coming from. It's where we are based ... as you asked," said the sailor.

The concept of a London-based ship, with a Welsh crew and an Irish Viking charterer, took only a fraction of a second to slot into the range of credible situations that Martin had encountered since he had been preceptor of the Bellins Gate *porte*. Norsemen had mastered the trade of the North Sea and the narrow seas around the British Isles, besides far further afield. The Vikings conducted their own armed expeditions, but they used crews of slaves and of freemen from all the maritime provinces of Europe in the way of ordinary trade.

"How often do you go to Ireland?" asked Martin.

"Six or seven times a year; perhaps more ... It depends on the trade and the troubles," said the man.

"Troubles in Ireland?" asked Martin.

"Troubles here, troubles there ... where aren't there troubles?" asked the man.

"You left Wales because of troubles?"

"We left Wales for work!" That at least was a robust and sufficient answer.

"Is this your first London ship?" asked Martin.

"Which ship?" asked the sailor.

"The ship that you landed from, with the goat," explained Martin.

"No."

"How many London ships were you on ... before this last one?" asked Martin.

"Two; *St Bede* was a good ship, and had a good trade. William of Ypres wanted both, so our master disappeared, mysteriously, leaving a fatherless family. We were sent with the ship and its cargo – that had been bound for

London – to Sluys. Then we were put in a boat bound back to London, with a groat apiece and a warning not to blab ... That was when us five companions – Welshmen all – decided we had to look after ourselves. So we did. Rhys ap John knows the arts of navigation, and I'm a good sailor – a sails man with a nose for the wind ... So we sold ourselves as a complete crew ... that's over three years ago now ... to a merchant of Rouen who was doing business with Ypres – but was clever enough to be able to carry on coming to London, when Ypres fled after King Stephen died."

The Welshman spoke in a sing-song sort of way, but his English was clear enough – a mix of East Saxon, West Saxon, Middle Saxon and poetic licence. Until that moment he had been engulfed in the gloomiest of expectations, now he saw hope that abject submission and ample information could see him out of this place – and not on his way to an early death at the hands of some minion of the state.

"Then there was the *Jolly Annie*, but that wasn't a happy ship, despite being called after a whore – long ago, I'm told – from Southwark ... pardon me, madam and Brother, for mentioning the fact!"

Martin was aware that interrupting the man's story, even by telling him to cut it short, would in this mood of confession lead to even more detail. He was familiar with this characteristic of the nervous human being. People naturally seem to think that by adding more circumstantial detail to a core story – whether that central proposition be true or false – they increase its credibility. Angelina was too amused at his assumption of her feminine shockability – and too concerned not to show dancing, humorous eyes to the other prisoner – that she, too, remained silent for the Welshman to fill the silence that followed his apology. The lack of any acknowledgement increased the man's flow of spirits sufficiently for him to recognise the need to proceed to the next chapter of his career:

"She sank, the *Annie*. Just off Deal ... in Kent. The wind got up, and I knew we'd be taken on to the sands, with the tide all wrong – there's bad sands, sir, if you just turn south when you think you're free of the Thames mouth ... Anyway, we decided not to try for Dover, where it's pretty exposed to a south easterly anyhow; Deal's worse, but it was nearer. We'd have to beach the ship. The new owner didn't like it!"

The prisoner saw a look of enquiry on Martin's face, and explained:

"The new owner was a Frenchman; he'd bought the *Annie* with a payoff for doing some work for King Henry, and thought that the cash plus the connections would build up his business on the sea. Anyhow, he came on the voyage with us ... him and his whore, as was ... He told us to stay out to sea, she agreed we should come to land. He started raving on, so ... he was quietened, and when the *Annie* broke up on the breakers, he wasn't able to get ashore with the rest of us ... We walked back to London, thanks to the charity of Holy Brothers like your good self ... The whore swore for us to the port reeve, as to what happened, and now she lives with Rhys ... all very cosy, until this last accursed landfall!"

The Welshman looked around – anywhere but the direction of his master – confused as to how best to bring the tale down to the present:

"Your name ... your own given name" asked Martin. The man seemed surprised that it had not been taken already.

"Hew ... Hew ap Hywel ... of Glamorgan."

"Well, Hew Fitz-Howel, tell me how your shipwrecked company came to be working for this person ... what is his name, by the way?"

The Welshman appeared hesitant to say, as if that would more surely invoke the wrath of the smaller man than anything he had said up to this point.

"Oskar ... Oskar Fitzlief, in your terms!"

It was the master, not the man, who spoke. He recognised that an account was going to be given, whatever he wished. He had never realised that the taciturn Celts of his crew, who always gabbled their obscure tongue to each other, could speak English so well as Hew now demonstrated. They might, for all he knew, also know enough French or Norse – or Irish – to have formed impressions about some aspects of his activity that would be unhelpful for him as a prisoner of the English state. He felt, from the monk's manner, that it would go more favourably for him if he did open up to these representatives of the authorities.

Oskar Liefsen, in Viking terminology, Martin told himself ... That was at least linguistically credible. If it was his given name or an alias by which he was generally known, that would be fine. If it was an instant untruth, concocted to allow himself time to plan his way out of this situation, he must be made to pay for it.

"Is that so?" asked Martin, in Middle Saxon, looking still towards the Welshman.

"Aye, it is so!" said Hew.

"I swear!" said the man called Oskar.

"Now tell me, Hew, how your crew came to be employed by this man," said Martin, again. He knew that the first rule of interrogation is not to let a prisoner or a witness deter you from getting an answer. His aim was to get Hew as quickly as possible to the point in the story at which it would

111

become desirable to hear the two men individually, but if the broad background and antecedents could be provided by Hew, there would be less for Oskar to prevaricate upon when the focus of the enquiries inevitably shifted to him.

"Well, there's not been too much work of late, you know. It was getting bad before the winter, because your new king hasn't make his mind up whether he's going to be fighting in France, or Scotland, or Chester or Ireland. Then came the winter, but by then we was working for ... him, there ... It happened like this at Michaelmas last year, when we got back from Deal."

"If you're a seaman, you need someone you can trust on shore ... Well, trust isn't the word perhaps ... If you don't have a wife and family, then you need somebody ... somebody who owes you more than you owe him, who you can destroy if he betrays you while you're not there!"

Hew looked at Martin, to check that his story was still following lines that the monk welcomed, then proceeded, once he was content that he still held Martin's attention, notwithstanding his master's indication of apparent willingness to speak now.

"We use Sewel of Dowgate for this. His mother was of the House of Rhys – the great Rhys, prince of South Wales before the Normans came to spoil things ... perhaps even before the Saxons, for all I know! Anyhow, the Normans took her as a girl, and in the end gave her to a merchant for his wife. She taught her son a love of Wales – though not our language, which she reckoned would be taken by the English as a sign of improper ambition – and, well, he helps Welshmen who find themselves in London."

Martin thought it absolutely impossible that Queen Matilda and William of Ypres would not have identified an informal Welsh consulate in their metropolis, during the reign of Stephen. This Sewel must have become embroiled in the rumbling conflict between Richard, Earl of Gloucester (a favoured bastard of King Henry I and the loyal supporter of his legitimate sister Matilda), and Stephen, the usurper of Matilda's throne. Earl Richard might have taken more of Wales into his jurisdiction and have ruled his Welsh dependants more ruthlessly, had he been relieved of the preoccupations of fighting the civil war against Stephen. So for the past couple of decades it had been in the interests of Welshmen to keep Richard in power at Gloucester, Stephen in power in London, and let the two reduce England to a debilitated condition that left most of Wales to its own arcane political system. Sewel might have been a double agent, a double-turned agent, or merely a timely turncoat, but if he was still active as a city merchant in this fourth year of the reign of Matilda's son, Henry II, he must have been able to convince Matilda and her son of his present loyalty and of his consistent past sympathy for their cause. Most probably he had overtly supported Stephen, paying the king's official levies on trade and offering extra cash for the favour of remaining in business alongside William of Ypres, while also spending money on Matilda's cause. Donations have always been the way for tradesmen to gain monarchical favour, whether they come as military levies, cash for the privy purse, entertainment or sumptuous goods for display. Sewel would need to be a successful merchant indeed, to be able to buy and retain the favour of both sides in and after a protracted war, but Martin knew it to be possible.

Sewel doubtless helped Welshmen who could help him, in Stephen's reign, and now. Such a man, who must have been acting beyond the mere fringes of undercover activity in Anglo-Welsh affairs, would also be in constant danger of being drawn into the machinations of the Scots, Irish, Manx or other foreigners, even if he did not initiate the contact. Such a background made sense of the sailor's simple-minded tale.

"Well, Sewel knew of someone that needed a crew, to man a sort of ship that's got a different cut of sail from the French sort – or perhaps it's Saxon – that most of the ships that use London have ... It's a sort of low, part-decked ship, like you see on old gravestones of captains from last century ... With one big sail, square cut; and a lot of rowing expected, if you have a serf crew ... Well, we aren't serfs ... that's why we're seamen! So they wanted someone that could find the places – that's Rhys – and someone to find the wind, which is me. The other lads – well, they're OK once they've sobered up away from port. The only other thing you can say for 'em is that they know what they're up to about a boat, and they know they need looking after on shore if they don't want to end up chained to an oar!"

A trade in men was well known to keep the Viking mercantile marine supplied with cheap labour. Drunken human oxen with sea-weathered clothes and complexions would be obvious targets for alert recruiters who, feigning friendship, would ply their targets with drink to reduce their resistance. Even a paid-off Welsh sailor in a strange city would be susceptible to the agreement that he'd be safer sticking with his fellows and looking forward to the next voyage with officers whom he could rely on.

Again the sailor looked for guidance from Martin's expression, and found sufficient reassurance that his account was of interest for him to continue:

"Those Irish ports aren't all deep enough for a modern ship, nor can their quays take stuff from a high ship's side ... but the real reason for using a Viking rigged vessel, of a longboat sort of shape, is because the Irish are less likely to regard it as the enemy as compared to a ship with high sides and a full deck and more manageable sails."

Martin could extract a full account from Hew of the various voyages that he had made to Ireland with Oskar at any time. At this stage then only two items of information were needed. Martin asked him:

"You've been off the ship now for three nights; this is the fourth day. Where will she be? Under whose command?"

"She'll be where we left her, I'd guess," said the sailor. "We've been ashore in Ireland for up to a week more than once and the ship has laid in the roads on an anchor – if there ain't a mooring post, such as we used at Rotherhithe Reach this time. She'll be snug enough there, beaching at low water and riding the tide; there's been no hard weather since we landed."

"And the commander?" asked Martin.

The sailor looked confused, casting a glance towards Oskar. The Norseman was the giver of commands. So what was this question? Was the monk trying to wrong-foot him? Martin took the confused look as incomprehension, and rephrased his point:

"Who will be minding the ship, while you men are ashore?"

"Oh, the lads! ... And there's Hela and the bairns, and the old woman."

The other prisoner shot another angry and rather anguished look towards the sailor as Hew made this revelation, rendering it unnecessary for Martin to ask whose 'the bairns' might be. Oskar must be the father, Hela the mother, and the ship would be a home as well as a place of business and, quite probably, a base for politically sensitive activities.

Hela would be worried by now. With young lives at stake, Oskar must have given exact instructions as to how long she should wait for him, and he would have been firm in his order to save the family if circumstances dictated that this was the prudent course of action.

One option now would be to ask the port reeves to search for and impound the vessel before it could be moved, though whether Hela could command the Welsh crew effectively, given that Rhys was somewhere near to Oxford and Hew was in the Royal Wardrobe, was open to question. Some instinct of self-preservation might, however, drive the remnants of the ship's complement.

The option that Martin preferred required the separation from now on of the two prisoners. He would take up the next hour – or more, if necessary – with Oskar, discovering what he could be encouraged to reveal that might conceivably lead to him being restored to the bosom of his family. On the basis of the evidence that was to hand, Oskar had probably been embroiled at least in the desecration of corpses, and possibly in the grizzly events that had led to the decapitated heads. If all the deaths had taken place on alien territory – Ireland, for instance – the king's justice might not demand that Oskar should be penalised in England for his part in those events; especially if he could be of use to the English in the coming years. He could perhaps be induced to recognise this in the forthcoming, more intensive session of questioning.

"The ship's name, you've forgotten to tell me that," said Martin.

"*Star Lady*," said Hew. "Oskar Liefsen says that it can mean the Blessed Virgin for the pious; and for himself it means Lady Hela."

Chapter Seven

Ten minutes after Hew had been returned to his cell alone, Oskar stood before Angelina and Martin in the small privy chamber of the keeper of the Wardrobe.

"*Star Lady* ... Lady Hela ... you have navigated deep waters, in life as well as in the sea, my son," said Martin. The prisoner was older than himself, but he used the clerical form of address to the laity unself-consciously as a means of reassuring Oskar that he was to regard himself as one of the church's children who was capable of achieving redemption.

Angelina had followed the Welshman's English patois reasonably well, though much she had found too complex for full comprehension. Martin had spent a full five minutes reviewing with her what Hew had said, and what he had learned and guessed from it. Now Angelina expected a conversational French that would allow her active participation. The extent and quality of the Viking's French was not clear, but he had shown some comprehension.

"Who was the brown bird – the whistler from the tower – you or Hew?" asked Martin.

Oskar looked him steadily in the eyes for a couple of seconds, as if he was trying to access the innermost part of the monk and determine whether the hope that had flickered in the latter stages of the interview with Hew would now be shattered or fulfilled. He seemed to get no reassurance from Martin's steady return of his gaze, but it was enough to make him opt for frankness. The Welshman had given so much away that any other course of action would be a waste of effort. If Oskar now said anything that either of his interlocutors considered to be mendacious or even misleading, they could – and probably would – hand him over to the tormentors who would not be too concerned at the condition he would be in after they had finished with him.

"It was I." The French was poor, but clear.

"And I can therefore assume that it was Nordic rather than Welsh ears that were meant to be alerted to your presence by the sound?" continued Martin.

"It's easier for me in English," said the prisoner; "I didn't understand your French – though I realise that's your prime language ..." Oskar was confused as to how to get out of this gaffe. He could be understood to have criticised Martin's French; but the way he had tried to get out could be inferred to be an attack on Martin's English, though the monk did not seem upset. Angelina looked peevish; she felt cheated that this prisoner, too, was going to use English. Martin would again have to take the lead in the questioning and although Angelina was satisfied that he would do most of it better than she could, there were things that a woman could pick up that a man would not. Again she must limp along in the tailwind of the dialogue but she would make sure that she asked enough questions of Martin as it proceeded to be sure of the validity of each step on the way.

"English it will be, then ... so long as I am convinced – and the Lady Angelina is convinced – that you are being fully co-operative with us ... so tell me, at once, what was the purpose of the birdcall?"

"It was just a wild shot, like the bird itself does, when looking for a mate. It flies to the breeding country, then it settles and shouts, and it moves on and settles and shouts until there is an answer," said Oskar.

"I heard no response," said Martin.

"No," agreed Oskar.

"Was it Norsemen ... or Irish, you would have attracted, if an initiate had heard you?"

"A what?" asked Oskar.

"An initiate – someone who knew the meaning of the call," Martin explained.

"Oh, it'd be someone from Leinster, Norse or Irish. At least, that would be the friendly hearer. Munster or Connaght folk might know the call as a Leinster signal, and take that as a hostile sign ... or they might say to themselves that it sounds like an Irishman in trouble," said Oskar.

"Leinster?" asked Martin. "Munster?"

"Kingdoms of Ireland," said Angelina, keen to show that she had kept up so far.

"So you would expect a Leinsterman – or a woman maybe – to report the call to others in London?" Angelina managed the sentence in heavily accented English, and Oskar replied with his very different intonation:

"Yes ... there are several such people in London, besides me ... But I am the agent-general of King Diamuid of Leinster in London ..."

"To whom the Lady Hela bears what relationship?" Angelina interrupted, keen to display the relevance of her intuition to the slow discovery of the truth.

"She is his half sister," answered Oskar.

"By a Nordic concubine ... hence her name!" Angelina was smiling at her own insight.

"Yes, that is so ..." Oskar looked bemused at this leap in the conversation.

"The former concubine is the old woman on your ship?" Angelina intoned this as a question, because she had lesser confidence in this assumption. But it was correct, as the prisoner confirmed. While this family tree construction, based on feminine intuition, was going forward Martin felt a growing irritation. He could not deny that the information was of relevance, but he would not have given it priority in this interview. Before Angelina could get on to ask the ages, sexes and dispositions of 'the bairns' he dragged the conversation back to what he believed to be the essentials:

"Galway is not in Leinster, I think?"

"No; it's in Connaght – or Munster – depending on the power position of their kings," said Oskar. Martin then summarised the situation as he saw it:

"Yet you know why I ask of you about Galway ... so we need not waste time establishing that point. Three months ago – as soon as the great frost had disappeared – a headless body in Irish cloth was deposited at the hermitage near the Thames. Six weeks ago, heads from Galway – plus one so far unidentified person – were staked out there. And most recently, you were taken carrying a goat there with some nefarious intent. The connections that we have full understanding of are Ireland in general, Galway in particular ... and you! ... I had presumed that you had maybe mistaken the hermitage for some other place; or that you had picked it almost at random, on sight of a stone structure from the river. But neither of those possibilities remains viable, now that we know that your vessel is London-based. So why were the signs and portents – conveying proof of past crimes – deposited at so eccentric a spot?"

Oskar had given full attention to the monk's words, though his eyes had repeatedly moved from Angelina to the speaker and back again. He did not want to have too many insertions of female logic into the dialogue; he found them disconcerting. He recognised that his wife and family would be drawn into the cognisance of the English authorities; but as far as possible he wanted his business and wider responsibilities to rest on his own shoulders only. The monk had brought up the central issue with which the English had become concerned. It was easily addressed, man to man, so Oskar did so:

"The heads have been identified ... er ... individually?" asked the Viking.

"As I said; two have, yes," answered Martin.

"That's better than me; I only knew one of them, but that is the one that he would know," said Oskar.

"He?"

"The hermit, so called ... Simon, the founder of the Galway settlement, and father of FitzSimon who was left with his mother and the other children when Simon did his deal with the King of Munster and fled the country," explained Oskar.

"The hermit is a younger man, from middle England ... True, he was a seaman, but he is several years younger than FitzSimon was when he met his fate ... of which you must now give us an account," declared Martin.

"The hermit ... a younger man?" Oskar seemed very surprised indeed at this.

"Perhaps a little older than yourself, but not significantly." As Martin said this, Oskar's expression changed and he asked:

"This hermit then, must have been the pupil of a former such person?"

"And the former hermit kept silence, even with his pupil, except to explain those aspects of his medicinal work that could not be conveyed by display. There was no personal conversation between them: not even an exchange of identification," Martin explained.

"May I ask, Father, how many years has Simon been dead?" asked Oskar.

"I am not sure, precisely; I think about five," answered Martin, looking for an opinion from Angelina as she had used the services and the concoctions of the hermitage for many years.

"You are correct, Father Martin; some five years is the time since I have been aware of a change in the hermit ... The new person is much less holy than the last, but in the preparation and prescription of potions he is perhaps better than the one that the prisoner calls Simon."

Angelina addressed her remark to Martin, but instead of delivering it in her usual brisk French she gave it slowly in seriously fractured English so that the Viking should fully understand it. He now must accept that the intended recipient of the silent messengers – for she assumed that the goat was due to be slaughtered before the hermit had seen it – had not been alive to understand their import. Not only had they been wasted on a common Saxon seaman turned herbalist, but the hermit had called in the authorities, who had kept watch until the culprits returned with their next piece of mischief.

Martin had rapidly revised his assessment of the situation – the Viking had specifically brought the evidence of murder and mayhem in Ireland to lay it, literally, at the door of the hermitage.

If Simon had been alive, had recognised the implications of the headless corpse and then of the bodiless head of his own son, and had subsequently seen the sacrificial goat, all the guilt that had brought him to sublimate in his dedicated task of healing the sick would be reactivated and reinforced with hideous daily visions and nightmares. The longer that he lived on this earth, in the knowledge that there were people who linked his past with his present, and the butchery of his own son – among others – with him, the more would his pain and earthly anxiety grow. If he knew that he would indubitably be assigned to hell on his death, then he would live as long as he could, despite the distress that his refreshed memories generated. He might have hoped that by devoting his life to prayer and pharmacology he might create some substance on the positive side of the scales of divine justice. The Viking's deliveries to the hermitage door clearly countered that hope by showing that people were still dying in this Year of Grace 1157 as a consequence of the offences he had committed decades ago. If Simon had recognised his own son at all – and there must be a fair prospect of that – then he would have realised that he had died only recently. The continuing cries to Heaven from young people like the others whose heads had been staked out beside that of FitzSimon must far outweigh the gratitude of recipients of knitbone or comfrey from the hermitage garden. Simon was to have been reminded of his offence, but there must be a current reason for the reminder.

Far from wanting the English government to be aware of the warnings to Simon, Oskar had taken the risk of landing illicitly before reporting to a London *porte* to deliver each of his messages directly. If he had smuggled ashore marketable goods in this manner, discovery would have led to his own execution. If Oskar had not been able to land at the hermitage, through the presence of a portreeves' patrol boat or of guards on the riverbank, his secret cargo of human parts could have been discovered by the officials of the port of London. So he had taken huge risks – greater than Martin had hitherto recognised – to deliver his messages.

The perspective was changed, also, by the evidence that FitzSimon's head had been placed before the Hermitage door precisely because it was FitzSimon. That made it indisputable that the first incident – that of the headless man – was a planned foretaste for the second. Oskar must have had FitzSimon's head, or access to it, before acquiring the headless young man.

Martin summarised these thoughts in brief French sentences to Angelina, before he said to Oskar:

"The living Simon – if indeed he was the hermit – would by now have been extremely aged. What gain was expected from renewing his guilt?"

"He could have sent letters – or better still, gone to Ireland – to prove that Galway was granted to the settlers by treaty with the king in the west ... He could confirm who received tribute, and that it was paid every year, not retained in the town chest, as is commonly alleged ... The Irish respect age and a truthful tongue, no less than do my own people; and we have dealt well with them time out of mind!" Oskar appeared quietly confident now, in his still alien-sounding English speech. He interpreted the removal of the interrogation into this comfortable chamber as a very positive sign, he appreciated the acuity of both his interviewers, and he was gaining confidence that if he handled the situation sensibly he might yet avoid a personal disaster.

"If he had told these things, and had been believed, what would have been the effect?" asked Martin.

"The King of Connaght would have to abide by his father's treaty ... even though Simon gave the document to be destroyed by the Munster men."

"Why?" Angelina's ear was more closely attuned now to the Viking's English and, although she found it hard work, comprehended most of it. This interjection exactly matched Martin's thought. It arose within the logic of the conversation, not from that extraneous feminine departure from concentration that Martin found irritating. He relied greatly on his own inner thoughts, which often jumped beyond the point that was provable with available evidence; but he could always retrace where his mind had gained its substance; he could never similarly reconstruct a woman's progress to an intuitive remark, and he recognised this as confirmation of the properness of Holy Church in promoting the celibacy of the clergy and the positioning of women in subjection to their men folk.

"For money, madam ... what other reason could there be? ... Simon had sunk all his considerable substance in the Galway venture. The King of Connaght was ... concerned ... at the success of the colony. The King of Munster saw it grow in a way that was not mirrored by the settler ports in his own domain, and he feared the complete subjugation of his territory to Leinster and Connaght – though those two kingdoms are bitterly opposed, which is the only way that Munster survives anyhow."

Martin found these Irish territorial politics incomprehensible, so he asked Oskar:

"Name to me a place in the middle of Ireland. Let that be where you are standing, and point around you to these kingdoms and cities ... The lady and I are unable to follow what you tell us, until we know the locations and the relative sizes of these places."

Oskar considered for a moment, then he said:

"I have never been there, but the Rock of Cashel is the mid-point of Ireland and there all kings can convene with their nobles and heads of families in peace." Oskar extended his left arm. "To the rising sun is Leinster, on whose shores are the main Viking ports. To the north," Oskar here half-turned to indicate that he was describing the territory behind his back, "is Ulster; that is a divided place, but wealthy. To the setting sun is Connaght, a land of great rivers and high seas that run far into the land. And to the south is the area of Munster."

"Munster faces to France?" asked Martin.

"No, to the Great Ocean ... as do Connaght and the north of Ulster. Ireland is to the west of France as it is of England," explained Oskar.

"So, only Leinster faces England?" asked Martin.

"Yes ... that is why it has the best trade, and the most sheltered ports – though the seas can be evil enough! ... The waves in that sea – the narrow sea, as we call it – are frequent but low, while on the great ocean they could engulf this tower itself ... You have to handle a vessel very differently, between Consore Point and Malin Head, than within the protection of the land masses of Britain, Ireland and the Hebrides."

"Again you must help my slow wits – how much of the Irish coast lies between these points that you name? ... Half?" asked Martin.

"Oh no, Father, at least two parts of three; maybe three parts of four ..." answered Oskar, speculatively.

"So you tell me that most of the Irish coast faces no proximate land?"

"Most of it faces no land at all, Father; which is what makes the open sea no good for fishing of the ordinary kind. Inshore, at the many inlets and down offshore when it is calm, the fishing is good. But on the deep – the real deep – then it is better to hunt whales; and walrus for the ivories! That was the great objective of Simon. Galway is well sheltered in the greatest of the western bays; but it is also the port equidistant between the points I have named – Malin and Consore – and can thus address itself most completely to the great ocean."

"You say this as if there is a great drawback to that situation," said Martin.

"Yes, Father, there is. You can't always give your full attention to the ocean. We are landsmen by nature, who venture to sea but always need our landfall. Our home harbour must be safe, from storm and tempest and from the rapacity of man. It needs good governance, strong defences, and a secure relationship with the neighbouring countryside, whence all daily necessities – except the fruits of the sea – must be obtained." Oskar was becoming almost as prolix as the Welshman had become under encouraging questioning; and what he had to say was much more relevant to the interests of the hearers.

"Galway minus Simon ...?" Martin needed to give this modest steer to Oskar's now fluent explanation. The Viking's English was no better but he had dropped the previous anxiety to avoid all slips and thus he was more coherent:

"Galway – with or without Simon – was always a marginal venture. Connaght needs a port, and it has a good one at Sligo, only a day's sailing from the safer ports of the Ulster coast, if you approach it round from the north. Galway's port is more sort of central, but is thereby harder to access from the seaward. The Munster kingdom has an interest in developing Cork and Limerick to trade with the west, in so far as the west of Ireland itself has trade for anyone ... The King of Connaght doesn't need Galway; he has Sligo. There's a Viking trade in walrus and whale from the northern isles – from Iceland, and from the Faroes and Vinland and Man, so we don't need a great fishery ourselves, we let the settlers do it ... If there was a great whale and ivory factory at Galway, trading direct to London or Bordeaux, that would not be good for the Viking trade in general. We have survived very comfortably from Irish ports which serve Irish interests and our own. The Galway venture was different; it was conceived as a base, located in Ireland – but facing out to the endless Great Ocean, whence it would collect the fruits and ship them on to London or a French port."

"So the local Irish – and the Irish Vikings – would get no benefit from it?" asked Martin.

"Well, they'd have a market in the town for local produce, wouldn't they? ... And there could be work for strong men, butchering the whales or the walrus, salting fish and portering; but that would all create a centre of wealth and power out of control by the local ruler – and such things never go down well ... because at some point the tolls and taxes that the town pays to the king stop being enough ... So he sacks the town, or undermines its prosperity in other ways. But Galway never really succeeded. It never had the fleet of dozens of whale-catchers needed to support an export trade, and similarly with the ivory ... The Munster people saw their chance, and bought off the founding father even before their relations with Leinster broke down. Then they spread the legend that Galway did not really pay all its dues to Leinster anyway; and because Simon was gone, taking the charters and the recollections, things went from bad to worse for the townsmen."

Oskar's eyes sought in Martin's face any sign of the monk's reaction to the recital, then he glanced towards Angelina before he added:

"It was rumoured, of course, that there was a woman in the case; one who seduced Simon from his wife, for the King of Munster ..."

Neither of his hearers commented. Martin simply asked:

"In what year did Simon reputedly renege on his people?"

Oskar noted the word 'reputedly'. He would be astonished if there was any doubt about Simon's treachery or its cause. Even if the monk knew something to the discredit of the story generally accepted in Ireland, nothing would restore the reputation of the man himself.

"More than twenty years ago ... Before Hela was born ... before the last great frost – the last before the latest winter, of course! I reckon it must be well over the twenty years, but not two score; less than twice twenty!" The Viking's power precisely to enumerate was evidently limited to small numbers. Around thirty years was the best assumption to make, thought Martin; that would give Simon the age to have had a grown-up son, yet be young enough to have some series of adventures before he had fetched up penitent and equipped with advanced knowledge of medicines in the hermitage, long enough ago for few people now to remember his arrival.

Simon had probably arrived at the Thames-side as the hermit around the same time as Fulk the joiner had gone to the new town on Galway Bay full of hopes for the future there. The town's officials had recruited Fulk through a campaign in France to attract new inhabitants; they might have been forced to look so far afield because those in closer ports and inland cities had probably learned how doubtful the future of the Galway adventure was.

"One wonders if Simon would, indeed, have recognised his son after such an elapse of years. I never saw Simon, so I cannot infer any similarity of their cranial construction ..." Martin ruminated aloud in French. He did not wish to embarrass Angelina by asking her directly – in front of a prisoner who might understand more of the language than he admitted to – whether she could draw any such inference from her memory of the dead hermit and her brief sightings of the skull:

"I have thought of it much, Father, these last few minutes. The hermit was wild in appearance, and his filthy hair could have been white. But there could just have been something ... yet I know I may be imagining it; so much of a family resemblance rests in the tissues of the skin or the chin, and more in the cast of the eyes! ... I cannot give any useful response," she said. It was fair and honest. She asked a few points to elucidate what she had followed in the English answers from Oskar, then said:

"Why should the man Simon do such a thing ... assuming that the basic accusation of treachery could be sustained?"

"Lust for the woman hinted at, I put low among the likely reasons," answered Martin. "The feeling of frustration at not achieving the grand objective – nor seeing it as achievable in the near future – would be very active in corroding the commitment of many men. Perhaps, too, the other townsmen became irritated with one who believed he was their chief and continually called on them to undertake ventures for which they had insufficient resources ... Or perhaps his wife was a shrew, his children precocious and the same spirit of adventure that made him first go to Galway led him to seek an escape from such cloying demands."

Martin knew that men – and sometimes, women too – left all that they had for a religious life or for a life of crime, for a crusade or for service in a mercenary army. It was not just ill-regarded have-nots, such as the present hermit had been in his youth, who ran away to sea or sought admission to a monastery; merchants and nobles sometimes chose to decamp. Adventurers of this kind, who survived their escapades, would not be welcomed back by the families who had adjusted their affairs without the renegades, so they ended up as monks or mendicants. What made the difference between becoming a monk and being left to beg a living was usually the possession of a bag of coin. Entry to a convent, with a place in a dormitory and a seat in the refectory, a Christian burial and medical attention in later years, depended on the prior being content with the terms for access. The talk would all be of pious intentions, true repentance and an active desire to be fully involved in the worship and the work of the holy establishment; but nobody doubted the importance of the money-purchase offering for the monastic pension.

Martin had known a few men who had been through such phases of life. His own great teacher had gone along such a path, though the first step had not been a betrayal of a family so far as Martin was aware. Other monks had frankly told of children left behind after an outbreak of wanderlust, stress, frustration or irrational ambition dragging them from a happy but humdrum home. In other cases, rivalry for influence or inheritance, or the loss of family estates through war or mischosen civil alliances, made a man literally a soldier of fortune and his sister of necessity a whore. Martin had no basis at all on which to evaluate the mind of Simon when he made his decision to leave Galway, but the action was consistent with a recurrent pattern of human performance.

Angelina was far from satisfied. Her own upbringing, in a family of Norman knights that had imposed itself upon the Scots nation, had taught her that people can never escape being what their birth has made them – a knight continued to be bound to defend the conquests of his class; a chief was bound to defend his native tribe and territory; a clansmen was bound to chief and clan; and worst of all, a landless, clanless scavenger for survival could only hope for modest security if he became the unquestioning indispensable servitor of a master who might still feed and clothe him if he lived long enough for his physical prowess to fade. In her world, anyone who abandoned his place in that scheme of things was a traitor. She had learned, in the years living with a husband whose manor was two miles from London city, that the Earthly City has groups who exist outside the feudal and tribal categories that she had known in her youth; that was precisely why she felt uneasy with the hermit and the free fisher folk of that hamlet near the hermitage.

Villeins were needed to work on the manors. Labourers were needed in the towns, but under the complete control of masters who were themselves responsible in all things through their guilds to God and the king. Anyone else must be a vagabond. That the creator of a town should take flight from it, pursue goodness knows what devious paths, with or without the encouragement of a seductress, and then masquerade as a holy man – notwithstanding the good that he did as a healer – was as perfect an example of anarchy as this female pillar of the conquest settlement would ever wish to expose and condemn. But Angelina also recognised that Oskar was not party to whatever had led Simon to do whatever he did: Oskar could have been no more than a nurseling, so interrogating him on the evil or idiocy in the old hermit was pointless. She simply shrugged as expressively as she could, and nodded to Martin to indicate that she would prefer him to decide upon the next line of enquiry.

"The heads have obviously been dead longer than the headless body. Did you have the heads first, then the body? Or did you discover the heads afterwards, after you had set the body in the water-butt?" asked Martin.

"The first. We rescued the heads – ten of them – from where they were posted outside the port of Galway, as a warning to vessels to shun the port," answered Oskar.

"The port survived the massacre then?" asked Martin.

"It depends if you consider a dozen killings a massacre or not ... A niece of FitzSimon, his sister's girl, had a vision of the Blessed Virgin by a pool in the river. The girl should not have been there alone, but word is that she was somewhat simple ... that may explain the vision, as well. Anyway, she insisted that she'd seen it, and other youngsters went with her – against their parents' orders, of course. So the local Irish started coming to see, and some of them claimed also to see the water shadow or trick of light that was at play. Then the children started fighting: was this a manifestation for the Irish – it was on indubitably Irish land – or was it for the settlers in the town, who had seen it first? ... Then an old Irish woman said she had seen it herself, in her youth, which made it Irish, but invalidated any idea that it could have been the Holy Virgin's intention to deter the founding of the town. So the Irish kidnapped a group of the town youth who had gone to see the vision despite the danger. FitzSimon and two of the fathers went to negotiate for the release of the children. Nothing was heard of them in the town for a week; then the heads appeared at the roads, where the channel to the port comes close to the shore. That's far enough away from the town for the watch not to see anything on a darkish night ... and we arrived the next morning, before the town had decided what to do. So the heads were still there ... three men and seven children, including the girl who was the cause of all the trouble."

"Your original reference was to ten heads; but you also spoke of a dozen killings," said Martin.

"Yes, Father ... three other parents claimed a missing child, but their heads were not returned."

"I see ... and were the bodies ever recovered?"

"No, Father ... so they kept the heads at the church, in hope of getting the rest, instead of burying them. That is how I was able to get them, later," said Oskar.

"I see ... we will come to that presently," said Martin. "Now tell me, where did the headless body come into the story?"

"It is not part of the same incident at all, by origin. The man, Michael McDiamuid, was a cousin of my wife and an emissary of Leinster to Munster. His head was returned to King Diamuid – his kinsman – with a challenge to meet to fight, in circumstances unfavourable to the king, who is constantly challenged by factions even within his own family. Indeed, the death of Michael was probably due to one of his own relatives who fled to Munster for refuge.

"Diamuid asked me to go under a flag of truce, to seek terms. I received contempt, and was given the rest of the corpse in a barrel; they said it would pollute their soil to bury a McDiamuid in their kingdom! ... When I told King Diamuid of this – I did not bring the body, to let him vent his temper upon it – he raved but had no policy. I offered to dispose of the body at sea, and he agreed. So we sailed for London, with a cargo of whalebone, ivory and salt fish ... and a rotting corpse with no head, in a barrel of vinegar and water. The Welshmen didn't like it ... they said that only a man who dies at sea should be buried at sea ... I inclined to agree, for we are landsmen, not mermen; so I agreed that we would bury him ashore ... I did not want to have to explain a headless corpse at Queenhithe; they'd probably command it to be buried at sea anyhow, after holding us up with endless inquisitions. So as we came up river I remembered the story that Simon of Galway and the hermit were one and the same ... I think it is commonly known, among the London Irish ... Anyway, I decided to lay the corpse at Simon's door, to remind him of his Irish escapade ... And I thought that was the end of it!"

"But five weeks later you were back, with the heads that time ... Why was that?" Martin's question took for granted that it was Oskar who had committed the multiple desecrations, and Oskar made no attempt to deny it:

"The situation of the people in Galway gets no better. They have men enough to guard the narrow compass of the walls, because they have pulled back the limits of the town itself to where the strongest ramparts already were. But they do not have the resources to withstand a long siege, after the awful winter that affected Ireland almost as much as here ... I had promised to return, with much needed supplies. They could pay for them with earnings from the fisheries, but there are few ships that will call there now. The place is remote and dangerous, and if the Irish mounted a determined attack, there might not even be a living town to receive a vessel at the end of its perilous journey."

Martin and Angelina evinced continuing interest, so he proceeded:

"I reported to the burgess council – there are only six of them remaining, including the provost. I told them that the conflict of Leinster and Munster might strengthen Connaght temporarily, but that this would give Connaght no particular reason to attack the town. Indeed, if the townsmen showed friendship to Connaght it might strengthen their situation ... They heard of my gift to Simon, with grim humour, and it was the oldest councilman – and the only one who had personally known Simon – who suggested that we could follow up that donation with the remnant of the old man's own son ... And then we thought of the goat, to suggest to Simon that the son had died for the father – a true scapegoat ... The goat was due for slaughter anyhow; the world requires few mature billys – as you well know."

As with rams, bulls, boars and stallions, billygoats are infinitely more ungovernable than the female of the species, so only adult males needed for breeding are kept. Martin and Angelina both assented to this commonplace of animal husbandry and Oskar took encouragement from their endorsement of the obvious to develop his point:

"It could just be possible that Simon – the hermit, so I thought – could have had some documentation of the proper payment to the O'Connor King of Connaght, of the agreed fine for the setting up of the town, and of the tax due for the erection of the walls and the staithe; and of the tolls that were fully paid for the early years – before the present continuous record that now had been established ... If not, he could still make a deposition of that information upon the head of his own son – quite literally! Even O'Connor Diamuid would respond to such a declaration in a positive spirit; especially if he has any regrets about the killing of mere children in a dispute over a holy vision – or holy fantasy!"

"There was to have been a fourth trip?" asked Martin.

"Not in the sense of bringing some further token from Ireland, no. The idea was for me to set up the goat sacrifice near the hermitage, then Edmund the Skinner, Provost of Galway, would call upon Simon to do the right thing," answered Oskar.

"Is Edmund here in London, then?" asked Martin.

"No, I know an elderly man who has long been a jongleur who lives near the Creppel Gate to the city, and for half a mark he would act the part of Edmund to a level of perfection that the actual Edmund would never emulate!"

Martin wondered what range of dramatic roles, for what deceitful or subversive purposes, the jongleur was willing to portray. Everybody acted a part in life – Martin was conscious of the extent to which he himself acted out his different roles as monk, administrator, friend and investigator of the unusual. The idea of someone acting out a false identity for money, to benefit a third party, was nevertheless a novelty to Martin. The idea intrigued him.

"When was the jongleur to visit the hermit?" asked Martin.

"I didn't ask him," answered Oskar, "but I thought that next week would have been a good time."

"Ten days after the third incident?"

"Exactly so, Father." Oskar's positive response seemed to conclude a phase in the interrogation. The outline of what he had done, and what he had intended, and the reasons for it, had all been stated. Martin found the account generally credible, with the sequential components of the story hanging together to make up the whole. Oskar seemed himself to have relaxed now that the broad outline of the tale was told. Details would no doubt be required over the coming days, and he was sure that his ship would be taken and the crew and passengers cross-questioned to validate his story, but he had no reason to worry that the little that his crewmen knew would gainsay his account. His wife's preoccupation with her children – the newest only five weeks old – had kept her and her mother well away from his conferences with associates; in any case the women would tell nothing through loyalty, but above all through their absolute ignorance.

"If the jongleur had found Simon at home, Simon afraid and contrite, Simon willing to assist with a notarised statement ... the account would not have gone to Galway, would it?" Martin spoke his challenge slowly, his tone at first seemingly reassuring to Oskar. Oskar's face relaxed further, then contorted with anger and a sudden renewal of fear: the monk must have guessed he intended to use the information for his own purposes in the complex and cruel world of Irish politics. If these Celtic kingdoms of Munster, Leinster and Connaght were in ever-shifting but fundamentally hostile relationships with each other and with the settler ports, the key facts about the history and the potential future viability of a port in Connaght might be of as much interest to O'Connor of Connaght as to the townsfolk, and therefore of value also to his most powerful rival, the King of Leinster, and to the balancing power in Munster.

The King of Leinster, through alliances with the Viking settlers in his own kingdom, and beyond, had strengthened his position over the trade routes. This London-based Wexford Viking was one of the few remaining links of the Galway community with the trading world. Since he had acted as a messenger of the King of Leinster to Munster, his trips to Galway – in Connaght territory – were equally likely to have been authorised by Leinster, probably to gather information. If Galway could be made a dependency of Leinster, in the heart of Connaght, King Diarmuid would have a major coup, and so would the associate who delivered the prize to him. Of course, the King of Connaght would be under pressure to bring the place under his own governance or to destroy it utterly. But if it was boldly defended, the well-armed and provisioned townsmen, with only a few reinforcements, would be all that was needed to deter O'Connor from wasting his lightly armed men in attacks on impenetrable walls.

Thinking through Oskar's account, it made most sense to Martin if he first established his status and loyalties. His wife was a royal bastard of the Leinster royal house; he had served that king in a sensitive negotiation, had brought back an unwholesome and unwelcome response from Munster, and yet been able to persuade the king to react constructively. Oskar had been granted a certain degree of independence to own and manage his vessel from an alien base with an alien crew; so he must enjoy the trust of his king, and plainly political priorities were covered by his trading that were ultimately much more important than trade. There might, indeed, be commercial profit enough to make voyages to Galway worthwhile; but the political content of the undertaking would be of greater value to Oskar and his backers than any walrus ivory, whalebone, shell or salt fish. On this analytical foundation – rickety, but more secure than entertaining any possibility of Oskar being a free agent – information of value would probably first be presented to Oskar's patron. If King Diamuid put it into the hands of the Galway citizens, to use against Connaght, then that would be a distinct political act ... But there was no information to be traded, because Simon was long dead.

Oskar gave no spoken answer to Martin's question, which had been uttered so slowly and with such clarity that Angelina had easily understood. Equally unmistakable was the meaning of the unspoken reply. Any deposition by Simon, if he had been still alive to have given one, would not have gone to the benefit of the City of Galway.

"Did the goat, or the copper crown, or the sword – or even the rope tether – come from Galway?" asked Martin.

"No." Oskar was prepared, defensively, to address questions of fact. He might have given away his position with King Diamuid, but he would never speak about his undercover activity under interrogation.

"When were you last in Galway? When you were given the heads?" asked Martin.

"Yes. That was when I was given the heads."

"Have you been in the farther coasts of Ireland – Munster or Connaght – within the past month?"

"No."

"From which port is your present cargo brought?"

Oskar met Martin's eyes after this question was uttered, for the first time after the tone and orientation of the questioning had shifted. He hesitated a moment, then said:

"Dublin."

"That is a shorter voyage than from Galway to London?"

"Aye, but still tricky, if the shallow seas are tumultuous!" The embellishment of the answer, the implicit explanation of why a Dublin trip could take as long as a Galway voyage from London, refocused rather than deterred Martin's further questioning:

"Dublin's a much greater city than Galway? ... Yes or no!"

"Yes."

"With well-established merchant warehouses, stocked by your own people?"

"Yes."

"So a boat – a ship – can be unloaded speedily ... and the goods for the return journey are already gathered into bags or barrels in the warehouses above the quays?"

"I suppose so ..."

Oskar recognised the direction of the enquiry. This slight monk is even more wiry of brain that he is of body, he thought. The monk recalls my indication that much of the time of a Galway trip is gathering together a cargo once you have cleared the vessel of the imported supplies. He has worked out that the same thing need not happen in Dublin; any more than it need do in London, now that William of Ypres has gone and the London mercers no longer hide their stocks in barns and attics all around Middlesex.

Oskar looked at the ground. The monk might even know – he could certainly find out – that there had been westerly winds for the past month; weak ones, that had brought no rain to break the English drought, but which had been enough to get a vessel from Dublin to London within a week. There was no point, therefore, saying they had waited on a wind; if anything there had been less wind these past few days, when they had sailed, than in the preceding fortnight. He could assert that he had waited for a specific cargo; but that could be checked out, and Oskar could not think of any item in his manifest for which it would have been sensible to wait a fortnight. So he just looked away from the woman and the monk, anticipating that the questioning would become more difficult to handle as it entered the political arena. This monk had let Oskar give the whole prepared cover story – a good one, and largely supported by actual events – and had now made it clear that he knew the underlying purpose for which the trading activity had provided a pretext and some payment. So Oskar steeled himself to parry all questions about his doings ashore in Leinster in the proceeding month.

Lady Angelina was acutely aware that this was an area of questioning that her lord – for all his recognition of her intellectual abilities, and despite her noble origins – would consider it inappropriate for her to dabble in.

Martin now adopted the same tone of voice as he had used to shift the enquiry into this phase, that was so much more challenging to Oskar as it became of concern to Angelina, and said:

"Until this moment, knowing as we do that Simon the hermit is long dead, I had assumed that the greatest guilt of you and your crew was one with which the ecclesiastical courts should properly deal; the offences of the desecration of corpses by delivering and displaying body parts at the hermitage. The secondary, but grave offence was the intended blasphemy of sacrificing a goat – a cloven-footed beast. I could have interrogated you on that basis, and on that basis we might have been able to recover your leading hand Rhys from the king's justice ... I might have been able to plead mitigation for you, because of a desire to help the orthodox Catholic people of Galway in their struggle with the heterodox Irish ... But it now appears that you are the confidential agent of an Irish king who is your kinsman by marriage. I can question you no further! This is the king's business ... Lady Angelina, your husband was absolutely correct to ride to the king, even with incomplete information and accompanied by a prisoner who can tell him nothing material. We must await the king's command, and his officers shall decide what is to be done with this fellow!"

As he spoke, Martin thought of his one face-to-face encounter with Henry of Anjou, the heavily built, red-faced, able King of England. Henry would not break a man who would make himself useful, as Oskar undoubtedly would be able to do ... unless the king's mother, or Becket the Chancellor, took Oskar in charge. They were opposed to any venture into Ireland, and would not want the king to make any allies there. While no friend to each other, the empress and the chancellor could rely on others who were equally set against the Pope's demand for an expedition to Ireland – including the Pope's Legate to England, Henry, Bishop of Winchester. The Legate would certainly be supported by his nephew, Hugh, Bishop of Durham, who was beginning to rebuild his estates after decades of Scottish incursions and exactions from Northumbria. Hugh Pudsey wanted a strong English military presence north of Hadrian's Wall, and saw no benefit in diluting the available resources through opening up in Ireland. Henry II would be angry, if he ever learned that one of his subjects had allowed a potentially useful agent to be disposed of before the king had the option on his services. The chief blame would go to whoever actually gave the order for disposal – if that were to happen – but Henry would also reckon that Martin should have prevented that outcome.

Martin wondered why he should worry about this, why he felt concerned at this distant intimation of possible disfavour from a remote and busy monarch. After all, as a servant of the church, Martin could not directly be punished by the king; and why should he care to bask in royal favour when his evident duty was to the greater and more glorious service of God?

The answer lay, he felt, not so much in his own human frailty as in his interest in his fellow men. This nosiness was a God-given attribute, which he saw no point in denying. He had been made a man, and among humankind he had proclivities that could be of service to the species. The race was subject to principalities and powers; and the forces of anarchy were palpably more ungodly than were responsible emperors, kings, princes and lords. So it behoved a godly monk to serve a well-intentioned king, especially if that helped to steer the king's actions in a beneficent direction. There was no neutral ground with any monarch – he who is not visibly for the king must be presumed to be actively or passively against him. Henry would list Martin as one who had proven himself willing actively to serve the monarch, if indeed Henry could still recall his meeting with the preceptor at Bellins Gate. Martin found himself very profoundly wishing not to change that favourable impression by allowing Oskar to be disposed of by anyone other than Henry. Martin did not question whether the king might wish to use Oskar: that was not his place to suggest, but he found himself determined not to bear Henry's blame for allowing the concept to be unattainable because Oskar had been despatched as a nuisance or petty criminal who had desecrated the remains of dead Irish residents.

It took no calculable time for this new pattern of conclusions and concerns to take possession of Martin. His final words to Oskar were addressed in French for the benefit of Angelina, and the look with which it was greeted showed she shared his recognition that the case was one for extreme circumspection.

Angelina was less reassured by Martin's reference to Rulf's current situation. It all depended on whether her messenger had found her husband before he had reported with his prisoner to the king's courtiers. If the prisoner was presented as the principal, Rulf would lose standing when it was proved that the best-dressed of the survivors of the landing party was just a Welsh sailing master who knew nothing of why he had exchanged clothes with his ship owner. If, on the other hand, Rulf had been able to exhibit his prisoner as the messenger was instructed to propose should be done – merely as one of a landing party whose activities were discreetly being investigated, in London – then Rulf could be criticised only for flamboyance in rushing to the king with his story when, some might say, he should have stayed in the capital to superintend the investigation. That challenge could quickly be disposed of – both the Middlesex shrievalty and the king's courtiers at West Minster could conduct an investigation and come to conclusions, if that was the whole of the matter. Rulf could argue that he had recognised the Irish connections of the incidents, at a time when the king's decision on Irish policy was awaited, so leaving the king alone to decide whether or not to take note of what might prove to be a useful pawn on the Irish chessboard. The pawn must be kept safe for the king – Rulf's career, Oskar's life and Martin's freedom to indulge his interest in the doings of his fellow men would all be in jeopardy, if the wrong moves were made in the coming days.

As soon as possible, King Henry must himself know who and what Oskar was, then he could assess the use that he might make of King Diamuid's Viking. The Sheriff of Middlesex might be displeased that the prisoners from the *Star Lady* were kept from him, but in due course he would realise how far greater would have been the royal displeasure if he had intervened with ineptitude. To hold the situation and the prisoners, at the king's pleasure, was the safest course; so it must be followed:

"This man must be held, secure. Can you ensure this, my lady?" asked Martin.

"Segregated from the other ... the Welshman?" she asked.

"Certainly; and from all conversation with guards or with passers-by, through the medium of birdcalls!" said Martin. Angelina looked sharply up towards him.

"You have something in mind, Father," she said. She did not actually ask him to reveal it, but he said:

"When we have this prisoner secure, we will still have a great deal to do to get all ready for when your lord, or another king's man, comes to take possession of this prisoner."

They spoke *sotto voce* in French; but the object of their discussion could be in no doubt that it was his own imminent fate that was their subject. By his repetition of the word *prisonier* Martin was ensuring that the well-attuned ears caught a French word that the hearer was likely to recognise.

Angelina said that she knew of a place without a window where the prisoner could be held. It would be a grim existence, but necessity drove a hard bargain for Oskar. He would metaphorically be in the dark about the whereabouts and treatment of his wife, his children, his ship and his crew, no less than he would be in ignorance of his own prospects as he sat and slept and voided his system for an indefinite period of indistinguishable days and nights in a confined and unventilated glory hole. The uncertainties would sap his morale, yet they would also reinforce his desire to stay alive, to do what he could for his loved ones even if he was himself beyond human pity or assistance. Ten minutes earlier, Oskar had let himself think that he was close to persuading the monk of his simple good intentions, but now he saw that this had been entirely illusory. The monk had seen through the picture that had been built up, and out of the other side. Beyond lay an uncertain future which the Viking felt would be more heavily influenced by this black monk than was comfortable.

Chapter Eight

Angelina ordered the guards to bring the prisoner and she led him out between the two burly servants of the Wardrobe, without a glance in the direction of the monk. A few minutes later she returned.

"What is your plan then, Father?" she asked. She had decided not to express her heartfelt gratitude at the conclusion that Martin had made to the interview with Oskar; that could indicate her own weakness, and her anxious recognition of how close first Rulf and then she could have come to making a disaster of the proceedings after Oskar had been taken.

"That you should hold him secure here, until the king or the king's man directs what shall be done with him ... And by the king's man I mean the person the king whom sends specifically to deal with Oskar, not just an official with the general warrant of the king; not even Chancellor Becket, or your mistress the empress!"

Martin's quiet simplicity was far more impressive that any shouted or insistent command would have been. Angelina again found herself comparing his manner favourably with her husband's; but this ratiocination simply induced her to recognise that her fate was inextricably linked to that of her noble lord, and that it was his handling of this matter at the king's court that could determine their future position and prosperity. Again she prayed that her messenger had reached Rulf before he had encountered anyone of importance on his arrival in Oxford.

"There is more for me to do, Father?" Her manner was almost humble, certainly ingratiating. A layman, or a monk with lascivious tendencies, could have received her meaning as a sexual invitation. Martin wondered fleetingly if this was the case, as the flutter of her eyelids was slightly disconcerting, but he decided that such could not possibly be intended, and he replied:

"Yes ... For this you need the City Watch to be invoked, but secretly. Tell the bishop's captain at his house by St Paul's that there are things in the Wardrobe – secret things, being held for the king – that could be subject to a specific threat of robbery. The robbers' signal may be the sound of the corncrake ... do you know it?"

Angelina nodded assent. Still there was that in her eyes that Martin found unfamiliar and challenging, but he now found it less easy to assume that it was a fleshly wish – it could be her way of showing relief at a narrow escape from committing the serious error of underestimating Oskar. Martin proceeded with his advice:

"If the guards could act unobserved, but keep watch all around the outside of the Wardrobe, they may entrap a human bird ... I do not know if it is likely, but my guess is that Oskar did not make the birdcall merely on the offchance of some fellow Viking – or some allied Irishman – hearing it and taking note. If we can assume that Oskar is an important agent, he will not be unsupported in his base city of London ... We could find out some of his affiliates by interrogating his wife or her mother ... or anyone else we find on the ship who is not a Welsh crewman or a babe ... but I prefer not to have to depend on such sources. It is most likely that Oskar keeps most of his doings secret from his kin, for their own safety."

"Should I go in person for the bishop's guardsmen?" Angelina's voice still had a breathless tone that again disconcerted Martin.

"With servants, yes; but you should enquire first for the bishop. I believe that he is out of London, with his close confidants, so there is no danger of him demanding fuller details, or taking over the situation. Then you can enquire for the captain, and they will bring to you whoever has been left in charge of the guard. He, in turn, will be empowered to levy a watch from the wards of the city in the name of the First Baron of London, the Lord Bishop. You must instruct him carefully of the need, and of the absolute importance of secrecy. A watch is needed, from daybreak to curfew, daily until the king has decreed the disposition of his wares ... or muniments, or whatever you judge it best to call them using the most misleading truth that you can conceive."

The conspiratorial smile with which Martin unaffectedly ended this suggestion provoked from the woman another peculiarly direct smile in return, that reawakened his apprehension about the nature of the intimacy that was on offer. He would and could resist all such temptation, but he rather liked the woman and found dealings with her interesting; he regretted that he would hereafter have to be consciously circumspect in every sentence or gesture that he addressed to her. A monk should be

7

so with every Daughter of Eve; on this topic of absolute sexual purity,
Prior Osbert of West Minster was the greatest living authority, particularly
dwelling on the reciprocal duty of females to adopt virginity as a lifelong
vocation if they entertained ambitions for sanctification. Martin felt
himself in danger of relapsing into another smile which Angelina might
misunderstand, if he let his face reflect the thoughts that Osbert's arcane
but orthodox views caused, so he deliberately switched his thinking to the
next steps that he could undertake.

He should just walk back to his preceptory – or more probably, crawl
there – begging for forgiveness for allowing worldly concerns that did not
even affect his House or his Order take over his life for much of yesterday
and today. It was about noon. However, if he hastened to West Minster
now, in defiance of his duties at the altar and the prayer desk, he could
be at the abbey gate for dinner time.

Once at West Minster, he could opt to enter the abbey and seek an
interview with Prior Osbert, to unburden himself of the irregular but
intriguing activity and discovery that he had become involved in over the
past 60 hours; or he could go further, to the royal palace on the former
Thorney Island, and there seek out whichever courtier of his acquaintance
was managing the king's business. Prior Osbert was close to the king,
would certainly have some interesting comment to make on the matter of
the body parts left at the hermitage – and would certainly take charge of
the political dimension of the business. Similarly, even the friendliest of
the courtiers would wish to put his own stamp on the affair before the
king's instructions could be received from Oxford. Such a course could
simply cause problems, and could serve to mark the preceptor down as a
mere minion in the eyes of the king. So Martin turned his face away from
the west, and walked east along Carter Lane. He had turned his back on
the higher authorities that he should, perhaps, report to. So long as he
kept all formal responsibility for the affair in the hands of Rulf, and
assisted Angelina in her wifely duty to correct her lord's over-hasty – if
natural – early reactions to the evidence, he would stimulate no flurry of
unnecessary activity and arouse no jealousies that could become raw if
blame were allocated at a later stage. The decision to leave a sensitive
matter directly in the king's hands might not actually please any of the
king's friends, but it was a decision that they must all applaud publicly.

Martin turned left in St Paul's Chain, right into the churchyard and
crossed the open space to reach Cheapside. The jousting which had been

141

in preparation when Angelina had ridden that way in the morning was now in full sway, so Martin had to deviate by way of Bread Street and Love Lane to reach Aldermanbury and the ancient royal palace that was now used for the offices of the Portreeves of London.

Something had to be done about the *Star Lady*; she must not be found to have slipped her moorings and quit the Thames before the king had taken his decision about Oskar. Martin was reluctant to tell the story surrounding the ship to his own prior, or to a West Minster Palace official at this stage, yet he was going to tell it to the relatively minor city official he was now going to see. Necessity is the mother of invention, and on his walk to the Reeves' Hall, Martin had concocted a story that included an imaginative component but no untruth.

Any fear that the clerk would have been drawn to the jousting vanished as the *gendarme* at the entrance greeted Martin and said:

"He's in his room, with the shutters closed and candles lit ... says he can't work for the noise of the crowd!"

The soldier seemed cheerful enough about missing the sport himself.

Martin entered the gloomy room, with its high Saxon features; it was one of the finest rooms in the city, but it had the orphan air of a place whose glory days are past. Its allocation to a bureaucratic functionary ensured the place was maintained, but the grandeur of the architecture somehow clashed with the keeping of port records and court reports of trade and tax disputes. This seemed especially to be the case today, where shafts of sunlight entering through the cracks in the shutters revealed the dust particles that danced in the air high above the pools of light created by the clerk's tallow dips.

"Ah, Father Martin, you are welcome. You must excuse the gloom of this place; I am unable to concentrate if I hear too fully the baying of the mob!"

The clerk Edgar had been poring over papers on his broad table, and he rose and advanced round the table to greet a welcome guest. The two men – the host a monastic runaway, who had fathered a hopeful family and made a significant secular career for himself – had worked together successfully to resolve a couple of awkward incidents in the few years since Martin had become preceptor at Bellins Gate. Martin's unexpected arrival might just be a courtesy call, or a visit to deliver returns of passengers entering through the *porte* for which Martin was responsible; but there was always the chance that he had something to impart that

Edgar would find more challenging and interesting than if he had accepted the chance of standing with his sons watching inept city apprentices pretending to be knights.

"Ale, Brother?" As an ex-monk, Edgar was given to displaying his ecclesiastical erudition. As a monk and priest, and head of his subsidiary house, Martin was properly addressed either as Brother or Father, and Edgar alternated them according to his own mood and criteria.

"Indeed, yes, thank you!" The bread and ale Martin had been offered at the Wardrobe had not been such as to refresh him. He realised that he was thirsty, and told himself to slake this appetite circumspectly. Edgar's ales, from a nearby brew house, were slightly more acid – less malty in taste – than the normal Benedictine ale, yet they were deceptively strong.

Martin took the horn of ale and seated himself. He asked courteously after the wife and children that should not exist, and Edgar spoke with enthusiasm about his elder boy's developing literacy:

"He'll make a good reeve's clerk, perhaps even reeve of a good manor or clerk to a sheriff, if my connections hold good once he has the years as well as the skills to carry off that role!" declared the proud father. To be a literate layman was a rare and valuable skill. Martin knew that Edgar desperately wished for his children to have normal, secular lives. He would hate to see a son take up the life that he had himself fled from, after a series of beatings for challenging the manner in which the monastery dealt with a questioning mind and a querulous temperament; still less would he choose for one of his daughters to enter the drudgery of a nunnery.

Edgar then looked expectantly towards Martin for him to state his business, hoping that he had some of substance. The preceptor of Bellins Gate spoke diffidently.

"Well Edgar, I have a responsibility to observe the passengers through my *porte* and to hold any whose apparent medical condition would be of concern to the city ... but I have no authority – or responsibility – for vessels that do not put persons ashore there."

Edgar agreed that this was indeed the situation, and he shifted his posterior to get greater comfort in his chair and enjoy Martin's tale. Martin then delivered the fruits of the imagination that he had applied to editing the truth during his walk from the Wardrobe of the current king to this palace of his ancient predecessors:

"There is a ship that has been lying for four days now near the Rotherhithe riverbank with a couple of children aboard ... It might be wise if the infants were, perhaps, kept in isolation from others of their age, until their freedom from a rare infection has been verified."

Edgar's interest had declined when the monk stated this business. There was certainly no excitement in hearing about other people's infants' diseases. As a parent, Edgar had shared his wife's anxieties at jaundice and whooping cough and the pox, scarlet fever, croup, colic and diarrhoea; but the rest of the world cared no more for Edgar's anxious paternal moments than he found that he did for other people's. Parents in general – including himself – would be ready to cast blame on to the civic authorities if a new sickness was loosed among the pot-bellied, dyspeptic, coughing and sneezing juveniles of the metropolis. It behoved him therefore as the chief civil servant to the portreeves to take action on the basis of the information that Martin gave, but it would be thankless work, with a good chance of something going wrong.

"What do you propose?" Edgar made this sound like the weary question of a preoccupied official. Martin smiled at him.

"I can't always bring you cases of blood and guts, or matters of state security, you know!"

"I do know it, Brother ... Yes, we have to act – that is, I do – but I would welcome your advice on what to do." Edgar managed to smile as he said this, hoping that if he helped Martin to solve this little problem and they avoided censure for letting infection loose upon the city their friendship would continue and bring more exciting interchanges in future.

"The boat – the ship – is at Rotherhithe. I suggest that a reliable boatman should be got to convey two women – the mother and grandmother, as I have heard it – and two children up the River of Wells and the Oldbourne stream to the landing nearest to St Bartholomew's Priory at West Smithfield. Let the children then be put, with the women, in the care of Prior Thomas and his excellent associate Father Frederick, with the strict charge that none of them shall leave their place of safety, nor shall any but the canons of St Bartholomew's enter it, until all infection is absent from both children ... or they be dead."

Martin had no reason to think that the children were even ill, but the mention of the possibility of one or both of them succumbing while in quarantine strengthened his story, and the bait was taken.

"There would be no risk to the boatman ... or to the guard in the piquet boat, who would be needed to compel the women to go as directed?" asked Edgar.

"I think not ... and so I pray!" answered Martin, conscious that his avoidance of direct lying was cosmetic: he sinned in not clearly telling the truth.

"And the ship?" asked Edgar.

"Is the *Star Lady*, a part-decked Viking vessel, based in London but of Irish origin and used in the Irish trade. The crew are Welsh, and should be placed under sureties for good behaviour to be found by Sewel of Dowgate who recruited the crew," said Martin.

"So you've encountered Sewel as well, Father? ... A slippery silver fish he is, and always will be. He uses that gilded tongue – backed with gold in the palm, for those who will take it – to keep himself well clear of trouble. So there must be more to this matter than sick infants after all, Father Martin? Ah, you don't need to tell me! ... I sense just a glimmer of a suspicion in your very unusual mind, that I hope you will share with me when you have more than a shred of evidence!" said Edgar.

Many items of evidence of Sewel's non-mercantile activities were collected in Edgar's memory and shared with the portreeves' sergeant over several years; but there had been nothing to nail him with, and officially he had an unblemished character. Edgar was sure that once Martin had garnered new evidence on whatever crime or misdemeanour he thought Sewel was contemplating that was hard enough for official channels to be invoked, they would be. He guessed that the quarantine of the children – while it could, indeed, be desirable on medical grounds – would have the added benefit of getting them and the women well away from the suspect crewmen.

Edgar's own sources in the city and its *portes* could deliver information on the *Star Lady* – origin, ownership, past cargoes conveyed, tolls paid – much of which would already be in the records kept in this very room. Other, less obvious channels of communication could be tapped for evidence of Sewel's connections with this particular vessel and its crew, and with the Irish trade, in which Edgar had not known Sewel to show any particular interest in the past. Collecting and collating this information would take Edgar a day or two, while the women were kept secure at St Bartholomew's and the vessel was put somewhere from whence it could not slip out to sea. That was an important assignment for the sergeant;

many ships had been impounded at London in the period of William of Ypres' ascendancy, and there were still chains at Broken Wharf where ships could be immobilised and suitable means of shackling a ship to the shore could be improvised. Edgar's mind was already racing through the details of the operations that would enliven the coming afternoon for the sergeant, the guards and himself; and he gave Martin courtesy and conversation, without concentration, as the monk finished his ale and inwardly congratulated himself on the degree of success of this little ploy.

The women would be kept safe away from the ship, while the ship and its crew would also be secured by the city authorities, but no word of the great matters that Martin had learned from Oskar needed to be released either at the Reeves' Hall or at St Bart's. Nor could the city authorities now say that the preceptor had improperly failed to bring them into the business: the ship and its entire remaining complement were to be taken in charge on his advice. If the king should demand the ship, it would be granted to him; so the king's interest was also better secured. The city officers could ask what questions they liked of the Welsh crew, and they would discover nothing of what Oskar had disclosed at the Wardrobe.

Martin thanked Edgar for the ale, and Edgar thanked Martin for giving him and the guards an afternoon of activity that would be far more interesting than the joust.

Edgar set about implementing his plans, and Martin decided to compound his sins of the day by undertaking two more errands before he went in true penitence to the preceptory chapel for Vespers. It was understood in the preceptory that its head was of necessity frequently summoned from his devotions to deal with the earthly concerns of the *porte* and of its mother abbey, and consequently the little convent of priests and lay brethren maintained the work and the worship of the establishment punctiliously – if not enthusiastically – during the preceptor's often unannounced absences. Martin's problem of conscience related only to his own indulgence of his personal inclination to apply his mind to terrestrial affairs, and in that area he had a workable compromise with the Almighty that he expected to maintain through this active day.

Martin set off east from Aldermanbury, by way of Cateaton Street and the Jewry to Poultry, thence to Dowgate – where he wondered which of the substantial merchant complexes of shop, warehousing, yard and hall, belonged to Sewel the Welshman – and into an alley that cut through eastwards to Bush Lane. There was the modest widow's toft, an enclosed yard with buildings, where Fulk Joiner and his family had obtained lodgings.

The men were at home for their dinner, and they rose together from the bench by the trestle table to greet the monk when the confused widow showed Martin into the small house that had been her original married home. She now shared a newer hall with her married son and his extensive brood, and it was on his insistence that she had abandoned her plan to live in the small house, so that it could be let for revenue. The old woman looked regretfully at the clutter left by three adults and a baby in the space that had been her own, then she left the black monk with her tenants, and returned to give news of the visitor to the family in the hall.

Martin accepted a seat on the one stool that the cottage boasted. Joanne sat on the floor, nursing the sleeping baby. The two men returned to the simple bench, and Martin wondered why joiners had not done better for themselves than this in the matter of furniture. As his eyes adjusted to the gloom of the cottage interior, he saw a well-made bed and a crib; so he guessed that the other crude items of furnishing were those that had been let with the house.

He declined the offers of food and drink that were hesitantly made by a family still conscious of recent abject destitution, and insisted that the men should finish their dinners. They did so noisily. After Fulk's second profound belch, Martin asked Tom to watch from the door that none of the widow's household came near enough to hear what was being said, while he asked the men to do him a favour.

"What favour, Father?" asked Fulk. He anticipated that it must be connected with those grim skulls that had given him a restless night of bad dreams and he was not too keen on seeing them again, or in any other way getting involved with them.

"If I give you two pence, would you two good fellows be willing to argue – rather loudly – in alehouses where you have reason to believe some Leinsterman might overhear you?" Martin's request intrigued all three.

"Argue? What about?" asked Fulk.

"A corncrake," answered Martin.

"The little bird?" asked Joanne, in surprise.

"The very same," said Martin.

"Two pennyworth of ale ..." said Fulk, ruminatively.

"Two quarts of ale apiece, Dad – and a penny for meat!" said Joanne sharply.

Her father smiled at her.

"You're right, of course," he said.

"One penny and four farthings is my offer; use it as you will," said Martin. "All that I ask is that Tom declares that he heard a corncrake in the vicinity of St Paul's this morning – between the cathedral and Baynard's Castle, in the area of the King's Wardrobe – and you, Fulk, are to deny it. I want the two of you to dissect the probability of such a nervous bird straying into the city; with you, Tom, declaring that it is so and you, Fulk, opposing him."

"And it's Leinstermen that you want to hear us saying this ... in French?" said Fulk.

"Since that's your language of conversation, it's the language that you must use!" answered Martin.

"The Leinstermen I know of – that are to be found in the Jewel Tavern, on Botolph's Lane – are not likely to understand French!" protested Fulk.

"If you stuck to your argument long enough, and invited others to take sides, I dare say someone would translate the tale for those who don't understand it in the original," said Joanne. Then she asked Martin directly the question that her father had hesitated to pose, "Is this to do with FitzSimon's head?"

"Indirectly yes ... but I cannot reveal how; for that's the king's business and it is safest for us all if I tell you nothing of it," answered Martin.

Fulk and his daughter received this response in silence, and Tom turned back from the doorway to exchange a glance of enquiry with his wife. Her expression told him nothing, though her silence warned him to keep his own tongue still; he returned his attention to the yard, where the inhabitants of the hall had all turned out to see what could be seen at the cottage as it was favoured by the unusual dignity of a visit from a monk. Tom turned his face once more into the cottage, and reported the interest that was being given to their affairs.

"We'll be off out soon, to put an end to their speculation," said Fulk.

"I am, of course, here to conduct a service of purification after childbirth," said Martin. "You may invite the neighbours to witness it, if you wish."

Fulk did not so wish, but he recognised that this would scotch imaginative rumours from their landlords, so he made sure that the four farthings were tucked into his belt in a fold of his shirt, and the penny was safely concealed with the rest of Joanne's cache of housekeeping money, before he told Tom to go to the landlords with the invitation.

The widow and her family came to the cottage door, and listened as Martin intoned the prayers that made the home clean after the perils and traumas of childbirth, with the attendant release of Original Sin into yet another descendant of the fallen Adam and Eve. The families repeated "Amen" after the priest half a dozen times, then he left, walking in a consciously ceremonious manner over the uneven ground to the heavy wooden gate. The widow's son, who had not sought for his own wife and children the benefits of this kind of religious benefit, felicitated the lodgers on their good fortune in having the acquaintance of such a cleric before his family returned to their part of the compound, content that they fully understood the reason for Martin's visit to the household of Fulk the joiner.

The entire proceedings, not least the religious component that had sanctified his home and his grandson, put Fulk in great good humour, and he begged leave of his daughter to take her husband "to a certain alehouse".

With an admonition to both men to be careful, she assented with a smile, though her concern for their safety was real enough, and she would not have wished either man to go alone to the Jewel. As with every exiled community, the London Irish refugees and the Irish trader community kept in touch with affairs in the land that they had left. Men who would draw a dagger on sight of each other on their native turf accepted a certain superficial mutual toleration here in London, where the portreeves would certainly mete out serious punishment for alien inter-communal brawling – especially if English heads or bar stools were broken in the process. Thus in taverns located in alleys and lanes close to the riverside, groups of Welsh, Irish, Alemanians, Norsemen and even Italians were to be found swapping stories and rumours, or listening silently to the flow of conversation as they wondered if any of this stale news might work to improve their own situation.

Fulk and Tom had heard of the Jewel alehouse from other Galway émigrés whom they had encountered in London. Fulk had been once alone, and once with Tom. They had seen no one they knew, nor had anyone accosted them as acquaintances. They had understood little of the conversation around them, conducted as it was in English, with occasionally audible mutterings in Irish, which to them was even more incomprehensible. They had picked up no word about Galway, though

149

there had been mention of Wexford and Dublin, of Connaght and Leinster, and of endless strife.

Entering the house well after the dinner hour, they found it full, but the landlord knew how to maintain his business and waved Fulk to a stool by a table at which two stolid old men were seated with mugs before them. A potboy fetched a second stool for Tom, before the quart jug that Fulk had ordered had hit the surface of the table. The wooden jug was made like a small barrel, of wooden staves bound together by softwood hoops. When it was brim-full, as now, beer would be lost in trying to pour it out; so Fulk dipped his earthenware mug into the ale, as if it were a ladle, drank and then poured a mugful for Tom and then himself. As he set the mug down, he declared:

"You're absolutely wrong, you know. It's quite impossible; they never come into town!"

Within two minutes the two old fellows had been drawn into the dispute about the corncrake. One of them supported Fulk; so, in the way of bar-room conversation throughout the ages, his companion was willing to allow the possibility that Tom was right. They drew others into the conversation, including the landlord, and the discussion came to focus on whereabouts in the city it was that Tom claimed to have heard the bird. One old man said it could be expected on the fringes of Portsoken, or around Faringdon, where the city embraced the fields and an echo of the bird could have come from some tall building; but at Carter Lane, in the shadow of St Paul's with the bustling port a few hundred yards to the south, it was not feasible to hear a corncrake. There was then considerable discussion about what other sort of bird Tom could reasonably have heard in that unwooded place, and Tom had difficulty in keeping his face straight as he solemnly denied one suggestion after another. Eventually the conversation died and other topics emerged in the small groups who had come together for a chat. Twice Fulk re-opened the topic, to ensure that new arrivals to the pub also heard his account of the sound of the corncrake near the Royal Wardrobe – without any mention being made of that actual building – and all too soon the four farthings had been spent and the mugs were drained for the final time.

"I'll sleep well tonight!" said Fulk, with considerable satisfaction, as the two men made their slightly unsteady way homeward. They were in good time for the curfew, but Joanne had become anxious behind her well-barred door. She greeted her father and her husband warmly, and did not protest when the older man declined bread for supper:

"I'm full enough, lass!" he said, and the cheerful manner in which he did so brought her great comfort.

After making his stately exit from the widow's toft, Martin turned north to Tower Street – away from his preceptory, which was down by the river – and walked briskly to the postern gate in the city wall, in the shadow of the outer defences of the Tower. The watch nodded him through the gate, and he increased his pace to arrive at the hermitage in less than quarter of an hour. The mastiff was still in place, and she growled professionally at Martin's approach to the door. While Martin stayed beyond the reach of the tethered hound, the hermit appeared in his doorway; today was a medicine mixing day, as the amount of smoke from the vent had intimated to Martin would be the case:

"Ah, Father. Come on in. It's one of my busy days at home. I try to save these tasks at this time of year for the rainy days; but we don't seem to be having any, so I've a backlog of indoor jobs to catch up on." The hermit spoke quietly to the huge bitch, as Martin passed her and entered the stiflingly hot building. Three fires were burning, each giving heat to an array of cauldrons, pots and pans. The hermit was indeed making up for lost time. Although the broad chimney was a good one, the air inside was laden with smoke, steam and the heavy scent of a variety of herbs and vegetable compounds being boiled, braised or simmered.

"I'll be taking a dip in the river before dark; and I'll be sleeping outside, because the fires have to run all night for some of these brews!" The hermit anticipated his visitor's comment on the oppressive atmosphere in the workshop. He than said:

"I've asked you inside because I guess that your business is confidential."

Martin raised an eyebrow at this; it was true, but how could his host be so sure of it? Again the hermit addressed the point without verbal solicitation to do so:

"The crabs went to the preceptory this morning, by the hand of Walter's lad. I had crabs enough to let him have some for the shop as well, so he was quite content to deliver yours. The season will soon be over; but it's been quite a good one, with the dry weather after the floods ... Anyhow, I know that our ordinary business has been done, so you're here for an extraordinary reason; and unless I'm a Viking, it's to do with the Irishmen!"

"You're not wrong, my friend," replied Martin, and he briefly recounted the salient points from Oskar's testimony about the former hermit. The old man's pupil listened in silence, then he said:

"We've all got the secrets we'd rather not carry with us! I don't judge him; and from the way you tell the tale, you haven't done so either. That's proper ... So your question is, did Simon – as you call him – leave any documents about Ireland lying about the place?" The hermit beamed at his own percipience.

"I don't know what they're about, but besides the herbiaries and the *Materia Medica* and the *Book of Psalms* there is a packet of papers that he left. I'll really need to get in the river, after I've fetched 'em!"

To Martin's surprise the hermit removed his long doublet – he wore no other garment in this stifling environment – revealing a wiry body with a prominent paunch. He then walked into the chimney breast, between two of the fires, and climbed up the smoky, steamy chimney. Within moments he was back, coughing and rubbing his eyes, black with soot which had also fallen in small amounts on to the hearth:

"I keep my flues well swept but you can't stop accumulations," he panted. "I shut my eyes and took a deep breath as I went in, but you still cop it!"

In his hand, the hermit held a blackened linen bag secured by a drawstring. The bag was carefully sewn and reminded Martin strongly of the bags in which many of the documents had been stored in the Wardrobe.

"It's a proper deed-bag," said the hermit, "with real deeds inside it too!"

He handed it to Martin, who had some difficulty releasing the drawstring; the hermit had clearly not attempted to refer to the documents in several years, if ever. Martin had never enquired, but he recognised the probability that his friend was illiterate. That would be a useful attribute, if it had ensured that these documents were in good condition through neglect.

Once he had the bag open, Martin pulled out one large and a dozen small parchments and some pieces of bark. The large parchment, obviously a significant charter, was in a language totally unknown to Martin. The chances that it was Irish were good, but it was tantalisingly difficult to determine how to prove that presumption without handing over the charter to some other person or agency. Unfolded, the document spread out to about two feet by eighteen inches with, stitched to the bottom left corner, a small parchment bearing tiny characters. These were in Latin, apparently a summary translation of the principal document. If so, it was, indeed, the grant of civic status, harbour rights, wharfage and walls with gates to the City of Galway. The smaller documents, written in Latin or French, appeared to be accounts, precisely the kind of record that Oskar had hoped to terrorise Simon into releasing.

If Oskar had been sent to look for these documents, his controllers must know about them; and if one side in the war of dirty tricks was after them, probably their opponents would soon learn of the quest and try to beat the Leinstermen to the goal. Indeed, they might already be on the way.

Martin looked up at the grinning, soot-stained face of the hermit.

"So it's what you wanted then?"

"Yes ... may I take it? I'll make sure that it gets to the people who need it, those who Simon left behind." Martin was not quite sure how he would achieve this, but he had an idea as to what to try first.

The hermit nodded:

"It's no use to me!"

"They ... the people who sent Oskar, or perhaps their enemies ... they may come looking again," said Martin.

"And I can tell 'em I ain't got nothing, can't I?"

Both men laughed at the mockery of a Middlesex dialect, in which the hermit pretended to be a total ignoramus. Then the hermit said that he must mend his fires and get his swim, while Martin must carry the documents into the safety of his preceptory well before curfew.

"They probably had the crabs for dinner, while you were gallivanting around London," said the hermit, "but they may have set a small 'un aside for your supper."

Crab was indeed the supper menu, for Martin and for all his brethren at Bellins Gate. The preceptor made a resolution to confess his offences in full on the next morning to Father Zebedee, of St Swithun's church at London Stone. Zebedee was a sound priest; his absolution would carry due weight in the celestial tribunal where Martin's activities would one day fully be evaluated. Zebedee's lack of affection for the Benedictine Order would ensure that no word of Martin's irregular conduct became known to the hierarchy of West Minster Abbey. At his next routine confession with the fellow-priest to whom the duty was allocated by Father Prior, Martin could confess the lack of attention to detail and the concupiscent thoughts that detracted from his pursuit of the monastic ideal; but he would not confess to confessing out of turn, nor repeat the list of the sins that Zebedee would have referred to the ultimate authority. Then Martin ate the crab, untroubled by conscience, and ascended to the chamber on the second floor of the rivergate tower where he reopened the linen bag and inspected its contents with care.

The summary stitched to the great charter was clear and succinct; and as Martin could not comprehend a single word of the main text in Irish he soon set it aside. Most of the chits of parchment and of treated tree bark bore series of numbers and cryptic combinations of letters such as: 'ii. xi. xviii. Thos. Jas.'

Whether Thomas gave James eighteen of something on the second of January, or Thomas and James together received something on that date, was unclear. The two and the eleven might not be a date, though it was likely. Transactions had evidently been completed, of sufficient significance for a written record to be made of them. There might be tally sticks somewhere, confirming the detail and specifying the components of the transfer or cash that the records appeared to refer to.

Simon the hermit would surely not have retained these records unless the clear pen strokes had a value that some other person would recognise and be able to exploit. The Royal Wardrobe where Martin had spent the morning was crammed with documents and souvenirs, held not for sentimental value but as reference points to fix the stamp of royal authority on past evidence that might at some point be of relevance to the present. The same motive caused the continual expansion of the muniments and the library of West Minster, and of every other monastery in the rapidly growing network of such houses all over England. Where a document proving title to some land or possession of the rectory of some parochial church was unavailable, the monks were not above providing a substitute; nor were priors and abbots rigorous in forbidding their enthusiastic subordinates to char, soil and grey such documents to impart an appearance of antiquity to them. The documents referring to the foundation of Galway were almost certainly not forgeries, so they should indubitably be in the City Chest there, available for the townsfolk to use in promoting the security and the prosperity of their venture.

Some of the smaller bark pieces seemed to be fragments of a single document, and these Martin pieced together to find that he did indeed have four of the six segments into which a crudely folded bark page had become split. The original piece had been some seven inches by three –

quite large for a bark writing tablet – and it had been folded for concealment, down to a size of less than two inches on the longer side. The bark must have suffered badly from being folded, even when relatively newly treated. The folded document had subsequently been much rubbed – in a purse, or even a shoe, by being carried about in some place of concealment – and it had many times been opened and refolded, until it had split along the folds. Martin turned the bag inside out, and found a few tiny fragments of bark that he laid on a sheet of new parchment on his table, moving one and then another in juxtaposition to the mass until he convinced himself that they probably did constitute what remained of one of the two missing segments of the sheet. No writing or number was visible on either side of these fragments of bark; nor was there any sign of the final missing section of the document.

By matching the pieces as best he could – before tackling the faded writing – Martin concluded that he had before him the lower half and the upper left sixth of the document. The lesser fragments could convey nothing, so he abandoned any attempt more precisely to co-locate them and began trying to decipher the faded words on the four more substantial remnants of the late Simon's sheet of notes. He dismissed the thought that the name Fulk was there on the lower left segment, and forced his eye to focus on the adjacent faint forms. There was an 'a' ... definitely, an 'a' ... with a 'b' following and an 'r'. Before the 'a' was another stroke; a 't' perhaps? An 'i'? An 'f'? FABR ... the Latin for joiner is *faber* and the Fulk who Martin knew was without doubt a joiner. Martin could not prevent his eyes from giving him the same message as his mind wanted to discover on the page: Fulk fabr; Fulk *faber*. Fulk the joiner was undoubtedly mentioned, along with Thomas, apparently a butcher, Guil a leatherseller, Stephen mason, Hugh tailor, illegible a smith – presumably the parent of the youth whose head was in the chest at Chad's Well – and another Thomas who as a 'mag mar' was likely to be a ship's master.

Imagination was called upon, in significant amounts, to reconstruct the list of names and occupations from the residual markings of thin ink on the discoloured and decaying piece of bark; but once the reconstruction had been made, Martin was convinced by it. Even in the mood of high excitement that this apparent success had given him, Martin was quite unable to discern another letter – not even a dotted 'i' – when the sound of the bell from Bermondsey Abbey, across the river, told him that his own preceptory bell would almost instantly chime in with its summons to Compline. It was a relief to break off an intense concentration that was completely stymied, once the names had been copied from the rotten bark on to a parchment offcut. In the order that they appeared on the document, they were:

Thos. mag.mar
Guil. cor
Steph. strucr.
Fulk. fabr.
Tho. trucr.

A quick visit to Fulk would readily confirm or quash Martin's reconstitution of the list of names. If the other names were indeed Fulk's companions in the guilds of the City of Galway, it would be a further demonstration of the authenticity and antecedents of the more viable parchment documents that had been in the linen bag.

He went hurriedly down the dark spiral staircase and over the small yard of the preceptory. The beautifully structured simplicity of the familiar Office of Compline drew the unshriven preceptor fully into the contemplations of a Benedictine. His mind switched completely from a terrestrial task that could be taken no further forward on this God-given day, to the eternal verities on which he must rely for a 'quiet night and peace at the last'.

On re-ascending the spiral stair, Martin had no thought of stopping off in the great chamber to make another futile and frustrating attempt to read what was no longer accessible to the human eye. God had chosen that it should not be revealed to Martin, now or ever in this mortal life; so be it. The morrow would enable him to find out from Fulk the circumstances if not the substance of the document that had evidently at one time been regarded by Simon as both secret and sensitive.

With that confident expectation, and the promise that he would call first on Father Zebedee to make his confession, Martin completed his bedside prayers and was soon deeply and comfortably asleep. The day had been a full one, and the dreams that he was never to recall reviewed the events at the Wardrobe and the hermitage with surreal minuteness. They helped greatly to sharpen his wits, ready for another busy day.

Chapter Nine

On the morrow, Father Zebedee was not enjoying one of his better days. He had suffered a debilitating stroke some years before Martin had first met him. Though he survived with the help of a faithful concubine, and served his parish well with the support of devoted laity, there were many days when he found both communication and physical movement difficult. Within his dysfunctional frame, a shrewd mind and a generous temperament were hyperactive, and it was to both of these resources that Martin habitually addressed himself in their encounters. On the days when Zebedee could say the least, Martin was more loquacious and revelatory than he ever was with anybody else. This was not by conscious decision, nor was it a determined attempt to help Zebedee to compensate for his inarticulate condition. Martin merely found himself sharing with Zebedee's mind the things – both facts and ideas – that presented themselves to his own consciousness. Often he felt Zebedee's reactions, without the need for words. This mode of communication denied Martin the explicit advice or admonitions of the older secular priest, but the glint of warning or expression of encouragement in the still-bright eyes were unmistakable.

Martin sat facing his friend, the light from the unshuttered window falling on his face. Zebedee, in the shadow, was a looking, listening, almost immobile presence.

Martin asked if Zebedee were willing to hear his confession. The eyes did not glare a negative, so Martin proceeded briefly but with telling explicitness, to relate the specific offences that he had committed against the Rule of St Benedict and against the spirit of monastic seclusion from the affairs of sinful man.

"So, Father, thus I have sinned!" On saying that concluding formula, Martin shifted his look from Zebedee's eyes to the old man's right hand, in time to see the forefinger move a tiny way down, then sideways. Zebedee had made the sign of the cross, doubtless at great cost in mental effort and material stress, and Martin was absolved of his sin by as good a priest as was to be found in all Middlesex.

Martin then told Zebedee of what had drawn him away from his duties – the full story, from Fulk's arrival in Galway through the tribulations of the town before and after Simon's defection, to the time when Fulk fled to London and the subsequent deposits that were made at the hermitage. He explained the documents that he had recovered the previous afternoon, and told how he was going to see Fulk in search of confirmation of his reconstruction of the writing on the page of bark.

Zebedee necessarily heard Martin out in silence; then Martin shared the silence as he reviewed mentally the chronological reconstruction that he had just formulated for the first time.

Zebedee seemed to be giving Martin no sign, either of approval or of inhibition. The finger that had twitched to give priestly comfort remained immobile whenever Martin looked down for a signal from it. It was to be inferred, then, that Zebedee judged Martin's proposed course of action to be logical and appropriate.

"If I have read the bark page rightly, and my understanding of the documents is correct, they should be with the people of Galway ... But would I be right to send Fulk with them, back to a place of danger? I know that he is deeply unhappy in London; but should I make a proposal to him that he will probably welcome as duty?"

Since he was not expecting a spoken reply, Martin was as much shocked as intrigued when Zebedee croaked in reply:

"Baby!"

Zebedee's woman, Hilda, hastened into the room to attend to the man on whom her modest comfort was dependent. She must be totally attuned to his voice, thought Martin, because he had been sure that he had heard a rattle of pots from some outer room just before Zebedee had spoken.

Reassured that Zebedee had not summoned her, and that he was not suffering a 'turn', Hilda left the men together with an admonition to Martin not to stay too long and thereby tax the old priest's strength too far.

This intrusion gave Martin a few moments to analyse what the unexpected response by Zebedee had been intended to convey. The parish priest had become accustomed to his own disability to the extent of having learned always to give the most obvious message, and those about him had discovered this after many misunderstandings.

Reviewing his own account of events in Galway and at the hermitage, as just delivered to Zebedee, Martin verified that he had mentioned the subterfuge of 'purifying' the cottage where Fulk and his family were living. Indeed, he had listed the element of cover-up that had sullied the religious observance, during his confession to Zebedee. So Zebedee was aware that Tom and Joanne had a baby – Fulk's grandson.

"Now that there's a baby – a third generation – Fulk will not mind the danger so long as the future of the family is safe ... is that what you tell me, Father?" asked Martin.

Zebedee moved not a muscle in reply. Since he had demonstrated that he could mount a sign if he had been determined to deny Martin's inference, Martin concluded that Zebedee had advised him that Fulk should be told of the documents and given the chance to offer to take them back to their rightful owners in Galway.

"I'd better do as Hilda orders, and leave you to rest; it will be best for your people if you have recovered by Sunday," said Martin. He only just anticipated the trivial movement of the right index finger, but had no doubt that it once more indicated the sign of the cross and Martin took increased confidence in his own judgement as he walked the short distance from London Stone to London Bridge.

Martin well knew that it was improbable that he would be able to find Fulk at his work on the bridge, where he inevitably would be at this stage of the tide in full daylight. Nevertheless, he found himself unable to resist the urge to try to find the old Galway settler, although he knew that a few hours could make no significant difference to the assumptions that Fulk could confirm or deny. Thus Martin approached the bridge, which as a cleric he could transit free of toll, and he began to look for men at work upon the wooden structure. In doing so, he failed to note the presence on the roadway of the clerically garbed figure of the bridgemaster:

"Father preceptor," Peter called in a formal manner that was modified by his friendly smile.

Martin turned to greet him:

"Good day, Father Peter. I see that the river is low; indeed, exceptionally low, as we agreed might be the case as this dry weather continues."

Peter was standing by the parapet at the side of the bridge and as Martin joined him they both turned to look upstream, to view the broad plain of mud, gravels and stones through which the small central channel of the

Thames continued to flow. It was a sizeable river nonetheless, compared to any of its tributaries, but at this state of the tide and in such a prolonged drought, it did not look like a force that could deny the ambitions of a constructor of the force of Peter of Colechurch. Martin made a remark on these lines to which Peter replied:

"Treat the earthly elements – especially fire and water – as you would treat the temptation of the devil himself! Whenever they seem mild and co-operative, there is their greatest danger; they make us forget that their elemental force, once released and gathered to its full potential, can destroy any man or anything that men can build. Fire and water are always extreme dangers; and if we remember this as we light even the smallest fire – or drink water in a way that avoids us choking – then we will be able to bridge oceans or to harness the heat of the sun itself ... but all must begin, continue and end in the full awareness of the maximum destructive power of these elemental enemies."

Martin could not discern whether Peter meant that fire and water were enemies of each other, or were equally Peter's enemies; so he asked. Peter replied:

"Now that's a question that properly puts me on my mettle! I'd meant they were enemies of each other. A fire can't live if too much water is applied to it; while the necessary amount of fire can dissipate any amount of water into steam ... I know, you'll tell me that the steam stays in the air – you can see it and feel it, when it is reduced to water vapour – while a fire is totally gone when it is extinguished, and some fellow or some trick of the sunlight is needed to generate new fire ... But nature fights fire with water ... and this river is so low now because the great fire of the sun scorches the land ... Have you experience of a great, permanent desert, Father Martin?"

"No, my friend," replied Martin. "My old master at Gloucester Abbey had been in the Holy War in the Holy Land, and told me many stories as we worked on his medicaments, so I have a picture in my mind ... He also said that day and night are much more nearly equal in duration, all through the year. I do not think that I would be too comfortable with that!"

Peter turned to look speculatively at the small Benedictine, and said:

"Oh, you've managed the shock of the change to London after Gloucester. The word is that you have another string to your bow, too, that is useful to your own prior and to Henry of Winchester ... Yes, having the Bridge House at the Southwark end of the bridge and the governorship of the way vested in a Southwark convent does rather give one access to the tales that always swirl around a great man such as Henry of Blois ... I reckon that you'd adapt just about anywhere; and make the contacts that count, by making yourself useful to the men who matter. That's the lesson that life has taught me ...

"Books and the lore that skilled constructors, masons, carpenters and shipwrights can pass on to you: they all give you facts and theories and methods to test. That learning – that kind of learning – comes from other men; from their experience in coping with the problems that arise in living in this world. Life itself teaches other things – that we can't live on our own, with any confidence of survival; so if you have to live with other men, attach your interest to the biggest noble you can find and make yourself useful to him! Even kings do this. Once any man is the greatest in one sphere, he must go off and seek glory – even reflected glory – in some other ... As a monk, you are supposed to eschew all of that; but here you are with me, and we are both hoping that you will find the formula that will enable me to schedule works right in the bed of this river – yes, even at the bottom of the residual stream that we can see there now – and make the boldest statement in stone, of man's power over nature, that has ever been delivered!"

Martin recognised the magnificence of Peter's ambition; but also the possible implications of vanity. Was the bridgemaster suggesting that he – Peter of Colechurch – was the greatest man in Martin's environment, and that Martin should give him adoring service as a would-be weather foreteller?

Martin looked out over the river, hoping for elucidation; it came from Peter:

"A man who is asked to solve problems for Henry of Blois, Henry of Anjou and Osbert of Clare, should not have much of a problem in working out an answer to my modest conundrum!"

So Peter had positioned himself well below those who had used Martin's forensic talents. He went on to explain his thinking:

"Great men like great achievements, and great projects. If a king sins, he wants to draw God's attention to his penitence through the construction of a great abbey. He doesn't usually trifle with a small chapel, or a receptacle for the widows of his victims ... Though Stephen did both, of course, building the vast Trinity Abbey church for his burial place and then the widows' foundation at St Katharine's. My bridge ... the bridge in my mind, that will replace this one ... that will be a project great enough to secure the support of the king himself! Once that is achieved he will see how it is impossible to wage unnecessary war; when the men and the metal and the skills of all can be used for glorious peaceful projects!"

So this was Peter's deeper motivation! He believed that works of civil engineering, if sufficiently grandiose, could take the king's attention from military engineering and strategy. Like every other English subject, Martin knew how important the control of castles had been throughout the troubles of Stephen's reign. Since Henry II had succeeded to the English throne, ensuring that all castles were in the hands of his own loyalists had been one of the ruler's preoccupations. Loyalties had been tested by the speed with which castles had been surrendered to the king, and new castles were projected wherever the local loyalties were questionable. Within the past two years, a string of castle-building projects had been launched to protect the king's French lands, and the withdrawal of the Scots from Northumbria had been greeted by Stephen's nephew, the new Bishop of Durham, with a spate of castle reconstruction to reinforce the frontier region. Martin could not believe that one bridge, however great or grand it might be, could replace fortification as the major engineering preoccupation and investment by the kings of Christendom; but Peter's was an ideal with a defensible predicate that Martin was disinclined to dismiss.

"I don't expect a man with your connections to hear and simply to agree, but I do ask you to an another man's honest reason for his plan!" This plea from Peter was perfectly acceptable to Martin: it was a more modest statement than what Peter really thought, for human nature is thus constructed, but it was a point on which agreement was easy to concede.

Looking down upon the bed of the Thames from his elevated position on the bridge, Martin thought of the many streams that he had crossed on his way up that river's valley to Oxford during the previous winter. Most had been reduced to a trickle because of the winter frost. The side valleys had filled with snow and ice marked out the banks of the brooks. Martin had left Oxford with the thaw, enabling him to take a boat for the return journey and to experience the thrill – and the danger of a fatal spill – of moving with the fast current of a river augmented by a veritable torrent of water from each of its lesser tributaries. Between the frost and now, the streams had all received a vast amount of water, all passed on through this one river – between the great wooden legs of the bridge that they stood on – down to the sea. Twice a day the tide pushed that water back – so what became of it? It just stayed there, backed up in the tributaries and in the streams that fed them, and in the brooks and ditches that fed the streams. It was logical, therefore, with no tidal pressure and no rain for some weeks, a vast water-holding area in the tributary valleys was at present simply not in use.

Without letting Peter observe his line of sight, Martin looked carefully at the channel on the river floor by which the Wallbrook joined the main river, almost directly beneath the bridge. The presence of the bridge, and of the deep channel to Queenhithe, clearly affected the way in which the diminished dribble of water from the lesser river joined the main stream. But north of the deep channel, where the Wallbrook could be said actually to cut through the bank of the Thames, less than a tenth of the U-shaped gap in the bank of the Thames was occupied by the flowing water. Looking for the high-tide mark, Martin calculated that perhaps seven-tenths of the aperture was occupied at a high tide. So in these drought conditions, it was likely that a huge volume of tidal water would rush up the Wallbrook twice in every twenty-four hours to scour out the filth not carried down into the Thames by the insufficient stream.

So it should be possible to make two measurements ... in theory. You could measure the number of gallons of water that it took to make the very mouth of the Wallbrook – say, the last foot of its course as a separate river – from one-tenth to seven-tenths full; then multiply that by the length of the river. You'd have to allow for it tapering off, of course; but if it was open to anyone to compute so vast a number, and to add to it similar estimations of the capacity of all the brooks and streams that discharged into the greater tributary, a figure for the water-holding capacity of the Wallbrook system could be devised.

You could also test the force of the tide, by seeing how far various objects placed in the Wallbrook – or within the tidal range on its banks – were pushed up the stream by the tide, before the ebb either deposited them or carried them down to the Thames.

Martin decided that he had better develop the theory very much further before discussing it with Peter, and enough of his attention and too much of his time had already been diverted from his search for Fulk. He turned to Peter and said:

"I came here hoping to meet one of your carpenters, Fulk, a refugee from Ireland."

"He's a good fellow; strong, and he knows his craft. He doesn't get on too well with the others, though. He sticks to French – won't even try to speak English – so they regard him as a bosses' man, even though they know he's escaped from the trouble in Ireland. His son, Tom, is much easier in temperament, and he is doing quite well at English."

"Son-in-law," Martin corrected.

"Ah, that explains why they don't look alike, and have different attitudes ... When I have to lay men off, after the season, I'd thought to keep Tom; but not the other. What you say rather tends to convince me of that ... But what do you want with the older man?"

Peter would obviously the more readily facilitate Martin's encounter with Fulk if he was told the reason, so Martin gave it in the simplest possible way:

"I have news of Galway – the place where Fulk came from – but it needs explanation that a Galway man alone can give me. There is a list of names – including his, I believe – that he can be particularly useful with."

A monk charged with managing West Minster Abbey's city *porte* could legitimately have direct communications with foreign ports, but it would be unusual. The abbot, prior or cellarer at the main house would normally deal with external relations; and the cellarer exclusively with suppliers. Hence, Peter felt sure that the message Martin spoke of, and its elucidation, were really for somebody senior in the secular world. This could be someone, such as Henry of Winchester, who held both ecclesiastical and secular offices, but it would certainly be to the secular arm that Martin's information would be delivered. This little fellow was up to something big; and since Peter had big ambitions of his own, the bridgemaster reckoned that it must be worth his while to speed Martin's quest:

"If it was Tom you had asked to see, I would have had to refuse you," said Peter. "He is working in the coffer-dam, and the lads down there would take it as the worst sort of bad luck if a woman or a celibate enters that place."

Martin forbore to ask how Peter, as a priest himself, coped with that problem, though he expected that Peter would answer it, for he must have been aware that the question would spring to the front of Martin's mind. Since Peter did not do so, and he was obviously not a woman masquerading in a priestly cassock, Martin inferred that Peter was telling him that he was in defiance of his vow of celibacy. The application of celibacy to secular priests – those who lived among their parishioners, in rectories and vicarages, who were not members of the religious orders – was relatively lax, as compared to the intolerance of sexual licence shown by the likes of Martin's own superior, Prior Osbert, within the monastic system.

In mentioning that no celibate would be tolerated in the coffer-dam, Peter might be explaining why he held the city benefice of St Mary Colechurch and was not one of the regular priests of St Mary Overy, the collective owners of the bridge and Peter's employers in his capacity as bridgemaster. If he had taken the oaths as a member of that college of priests and in consequence taken up residence among them, concupiscence would have been impossible. Peter allowed Martin no time to challenge his declaration, saying:

"But Fulk is not of an age to work down there, though he is fit enough, it seems, for any task. He is preparing some joints down at the Bridge House. Do, please, come along."

Peter started off fast towards the southern end of the bridge. Martin, following behind, was left with the distinct impression that Peter was avoiding the possibility of the conversation continuing as they proceeded. Peter, indeed, already regretted making a remark that might seem boastful or even improper to a prim preceptor. Many clerics who lived in the shadow of great men, acting as their clerks and remembrancers, were pernickety straight-laced sort of people, over-anxious to maintain their image of probity at all times. By contrast, others became gluttons, drunks or lechers if they felt that they had the confidence of tolerant masters. In Peter's view, Martin was probably in neither of the obvious categories, but he was nearer to the former than the latter. So Peter was a little concerned that Martin could at some time put in a word detrimental to Peter's plan, on the grounds of unsteadiness of character. Peter just hoped that Martin had not taken the plain implication of his injudicious remark, admitted to himself that it was an exceptionally faint hope, and decided that the best course of action was to let the subject go no further. Once Martin was talking to Fulk, Peter's personal life would cease to feature in Martin's thinking; and if Peter maintained good relations with the preceptor of Bellins Gate, there was no reason why one odd comment should become burdensome.

The preceptory tower was easily visible from the bridge, just a few hundred yards downstream from the bridge on the north bank. Peter could not avoid future contact with so close a neighbour as the preceptor, so he just had to hope that Martin would let the remark fade in his memory if he found it improper.

The Bridge House yard was at the peak level of operation, due to the demands that the bridgemaster was making to take advantage of the low water levels in the river. Cottagers had been tempted to come from the Surrey villages to provide labouring assistance, fetching and carrying, sawing and rough-hewing timber with axes or adzes, freeing the more skilled and experienced men to work in the coffer-dam or to do the finishing jobs. Fulk was fitting together timbers by mortise and tenon joints, to ensure that they could be perfectly put together on the bridge itself. The day was warm, the morning ale ration was consumed and dinner was in the distant future. Fulk was used to working a full day and his resources of energy were still ample to sustain that demand, but he felt his age a lot more in this merciless heat than he had done on a typically damp Irish morning. Even on really dry days in Galway there are zephyrs of Atlantic air which invigorate and refresh a hard-working artisan. Here in Southwark, Fulk felt that the air seemed to be trapped in a stillness that became full of heat from above. With the rising tide would come a salty tang to the air and a hint of cooling, but there were several hours to wait yet, and the relentless bounty of the sun would in the meantime draw deeply on Fulk's physical resources.

He was not sorry, therefore, when his workman's instinct told him that the boss was making a beeline towards him. He looked up and saw Father Martin of Bellins Gate in the wake of the bridgemaster. That made this the third day running when the priest had sought him out. This business with the sickening skulls was clearly preoccupying the priest about as much as it was preying on Fulk's mind. The joiner did not flatter himself that his remaining in Galway could have prevented the slaughter; he could, indeed, have been among the victims. Nevertheless he felt something much more profound than embarrassment at having taken the self-preserving option. Of course, he wanted Joanna and the baby to be safe, so they must stay in England, at least until Ireland was pacified. Fulk felt uncomfortable at the thought of staying with them, though they quite plainly expected him to be in their household until the end of his natural life. The thought of his end always revived the desire to be buried with his wife and her beloved lost children. That meant going back to Galway, but Fulk was not sure that he was ready for the challenge.

FitzSimon had assured him that his shop and home would be kept secure against his return; but what was the current value of a promise from a man whose mouth was now with the rest of his head in an outhouse in Tower Hamlets? Fulk had shaped and set the timbers of the building himself. He had put every dowel in the floors and walls, made the stairs, doors, shutters and furniture, and had carved the wooden mugs, trenchers and spoons that even now were gathering dust in Galway. Every bit of that house was his, because he had made it, from the wood shingle roof to the brushwood matting on which the footings of the wall timbers were buried beneath the ground. He loved it, and he wanted it; he saw it as clear in his mind's eye as the two black-robed clerics occupied his physical vision.

"Fulk, Father Martin wishes to consult you. I think at this time of day the quietest place around here will be St Olaf's church," said Peter. Then to Martin, he added, "I trust you find what you – and your principals – need."

With a knowing sort of a smile, he turned on his heel to return to the task from which he had defected when he saw Martin on the bridge. The thought of what Big Bert might do in his absence made him break into a trot, and all thoughts arising from his conversation with Martin were pigeonholed in his brain.

Fulk led the way to the much-rebuilt church that commemorated one of the greatest Viking martyrs. By contrast with the Bridge House yard, the church was a haven of cool air and quietness. Two men hastily stood up from their kneeling position against the south wall of the church, and hurried out as soon as Martin was clear of the entrance.

"Dice ... they're from the yard. I'd wondered where they went," Fulk explained the men's presence, the reason for their posture and the cause of their shamefaced look, all in his first monosyllable. The joiner looked rather pleased, and Martin inferred that he welcomed having gained the small leverage over the men that this incident might have given him.

Martin immediately stated his business:

"Fulk, do you know these names? ... Thomas Butcher, Thomas Mariner, Guillaume Leathers, Stephen Mason ... and a Smith ... what would his name be?"

"Jedediah; the father of the lad we saw ... or perhaps it would be Jed's father, William. If the list goes back as far as William – Guillaume – the leatherseller, the smith then was probably old Will; because the son – Edmund – took over the tannery a good dozen years ago now."

"You do – or did – know them all, then?" asked Martin.

"Aye, for sure; I'd expect my name to be listed with theirs ..." said Fulk.

"It is!" Martin replied.

"They – we – were the guildsmen of the city. Simon, the provost who got us our Charter of Liberties from O'Connor of Connaght, was keen that the crafts as well as the Guild Merchant – that was really just him – should be seen to govern the town. He reckoned that it would attract others and it did – a few, anyway – before he effed off. Sorry; forgive me my language Father, but that's what he did!" Fulk was embarrassed at using the indicative first letter of the common obscenity but Martin smiled indulgently and exploited the joiner's confusion by asking:

"How, and why did Simon – er – eff off?"

Typically for a man of his age and class, Fulk began by answering the question that Martin did not ask:

"Now when would that be? Joanne was not quite born; and we still had Nigel, I think ... Yes, the town walls were still partly house walls – you know, with a blank side to the outside, and palisades between the houses – before we'd finished the first full set of wood walls ... It'd be around a score of years ago; take a few months off Joanne's age, and you've got when it happened."

Martin knew that it was best to let older people reminisce in their own way, and only intervene if their recollections moved far from the topic. Anyhow, in this case, Fulk was confirming Oskar's testimony that the incident had been over twenty years ago though Oskar had indicated that it could be significantly more. Martin reckoned that Joanne could well have a more precise knowledge of her own age than did her father, so he could check it with her if the exact timescale of the incident became a material factor.

Fulk paused, appeared to realise that he was not actually answering the question, wrinkled his forehead in concentration and said:

"The how is easy. He took a skiff that belonged to Thomas – the ship's master who you named just now – and rowed the night tide down to the sea. He picked a time with a light north-westerly wind, so the sea would carry him south to Limerick, or Kerry, and therefore to Munster, in the end ... That's where he went! ... And why? ... There were various tales: he fled from his wife, he fled to his whore, he fled from his debts, he fled to a great bribe for betraying us ... there were lots of stories flying about, and they all contradicted each other!"

"Did he betray you?" asked Martin.

"Yes ... well, we thought so!" answered Fulk.

"How so?"

"Well, you see, everything was his idea, and people came because of him. I did, and the other joiner who came later to compete with me, he did too ... He left – the other joiner – after Simon went. There wasn't work for two, and being the guildsman I got the town work ... I gave him the chance to work for me, on the walls, but he told me to bog off! He said he was a master craftsman, better than me, and he wouldn't demean himself!"

Fulk gathered spittle in his mouth, ready to eject it in a simple indication of contempt, when he remembered that he was in a church in company with a priest. It took him two swallows and more embarrassment to dispose of the spit, while Martin pretended not to notice but prepared a question that might again exploit Fulk's evident embarrassment:

"What do you think about it, now, after all these years, yourself?"

"Well, I've left Galway too! I feel badly about it; my heart wants to be back there, but my head still says no ... At least, I've brought Joanne here to have her baby good and safe. Simon left his family. That must mean he doesn't care for 'em so the story of the other woman might be true." Here Fulk's face became less wrinkled, as if he had come to the resolution of a major puzzle; as Martin imagined he would look when he had resolved some difficult design problem in his woodworking. "But I think he just got too melancholy ... I think he felt guilty at bringing folk there – like the other joiner – for whom there wasn't work enough ... not with as many kids as he had!" Fulk had probably never before thought of such a sympathetic explanation of Simon's defection, let alone articulated the concept in words. He looked relieved to have got it off his chest, however, as a man looks when he has made the long-delayed confession of a serious sin.

"So ... you think he went simply because he could no longer stay?" asked Martin.

"Yes, I suppose I do, when you put it like that," said Fulk. Then he fell silent, and Martin realised that even if Fulk wanted to ask him what became of Simon in the end, he would not have the temerity to ask a priest such a question. Nor would he demand to know what the list of names, that included his own, portended, nor yet the purpose of Martin raking over all the old stories. So Martin would have to volunteer the explanations, giving him the opportunity to work on Fulk to agree to take the documents back to the city:

"Would you believe that Simon is buried in the parish churchyard of the place where his son's head is now kept? ... At Stebenhithe?" he asked. Fulk looked surprised, but nodded. He would believe it, if Martin said it was so. Martin explained how Simon had spent his last years as a hermit and healer, and enquired:

"Did Simon show any interest in health – or in religion – while he was in Galway?"

A cunning look passed over Fulk's features. He was now going to give Martin old gossip that he had heard about the Provost of Galway in the days of Simon's dominance, the sort of thing that is all too often whispered about leading figures:

"Well ... he could write! ... So folk said he was a runaway monk! He never said anything in my hearing that supported that and he wasn't particularly churchy. Well, he wouldn't be, would he? ... Some said he'd only gone to Ireland because it was out of the reach of Citeaux, but they'll say anything, won't they?"

"Yes indeed," agreed Martin. But the mention of a specific monastery – the headquarters of the expanding new order of white-habited monks – lent verisimilitude to the proposition. It was not usual for merchants to be able to write, even if they could read numerals and the names of their trading counter-parties and of their principal classes of stock in trade. If Simon was well known to be literate, gossip would quickly attach to the most obvious explanation. After all, it was how Edgar, the portreeves' clerk in London, had gained the skills necessary for his job. Briefly, Martin speculated on how easy Edgar found it to get Oskar's woman into quarantine at St Bartholomew's Priory, then he redirected his attention to the matter in hand:

"And medicine ... potions?"

"Oh no, not so far as I know ... but there were rumours! ... Some said that the woman he was supposed to have gone off with was the Irish witch from up the valley ... But she had left a year or two before Simon went, so if she had bewitched him, it must have been a potent spell, to have kept possession of him for so long and then caused him to leave all that he seemed to value!"

"So you are dubious about the story of a woman leading him astray?" asked Martin.

Fulk looked troubled, rather than pleased, when Martin gave this evidence of having confidence in his judgement. Some other factor, as yet undisclosed, had presented itself to Fulk's consciousness.

"Come on, my friend; tell me what is in your mind. We are in church; I am a priest ... I could grant you absolution, if it is something on your conscience," said Martin.

"No, it's nothing on my conscience," said Fulk, in a rather hoarse whisper, "it's on his ... or was, I should say. It'll be in the account books up there anyhow." He pointed to the church roof, indicating heaven. "Why do some men get thrown out of monasteries?" Fulk looked Martin defiantly in the eyes as he delivered this rhetorical question.

"But Simon had children, surely?" said Martin.

"Aye ... they do ... some of them! But that doesn't stop 'em doing other things too. My dear wife used to say it didn't matter so long as they stick with their own kind and I suppose she was right, in general." Fulk's thoughts had apparently returned to his late wife; his eyes had a faraway look. Martin brought him back to Southwark, and the present:

"So, no woman! I take your word for it. Now, what would you say if I told you that the Charter of the Liberties of the *Urbs Galvacium* has been found, at the place where Simon died?"

"And it's just turned up now?" challenged Fulk.

"No, somebody knew where Simon had left some secret documents – in a niche up in the chimney, in fact."

"Aye, he would pick a place where even a child burglar would know to look! That's Simon sure enough!" Fulk was satisfied of the authenticity of the documents on the basis of the consistency of the choice of hiding place with the joiner's estimate of Simon's character. "You said documents, more than one ... one of them had my name on it?" Fulk's brief moment of self-satisfaction was succeeded by a note of concern – was he somehow incriminated, or recorded as a debtor in the discovered parchments?

"That's just a fragment – a bark fragment, in fact – that just seems to list the leading townsmen. It had been hidden somewhere folded over and it had been carried about folded, because it is badly frayed," said Martin.

"I'd like to see it," said Fulk. He did not doubt Martin's word, but he could discern the letters that made up his own name, and he wanted to see them on this bark memo sheet from his past.

"Come to the preceptory when you have had your dinner, and you shall see all that is to be seen!" promised Martin.

"Right, I will, Father! Now I'd better be back to my work. My ganger can't fault my joinery, and I don't want him getting at me for absenteeism, which he might, even though the bridgemaster himself in person told me to speak with you!"

Fulk was striding towards the church door before he finished his sentence. At least he'd have something to mull over as he continued fine-shaping the huge joint that he would work on for the rest of the day. Martin let him go, then himself left the church and walked down to the riverside, to get a rare view of his preceptory from almost exactly the opposite side of the river. The small stream that flowed into the Thames a few hundred yards to Martin's right was exactly opposite the *porte* on to the river that was the reason for the existence of the preceptory. Its oval tower was a distinctive landmark – an embellishment of the long curtain of wall that ran from the White Tower in the east to Baynard's Castle in the west, with just the well-guarded outflow of the Wallbrook breaching it. The great bridge was built into the walls, and it was protected by gates and by the huge drawbridge section of London Bridge at the northern end, over the deep channel. In times of peace the roadway could be raised to allow masted ships to proceed up the tideway to Queenhithe, the River of Wells and the westerly *portes* of London and West Minster. In an attack, the drawbridge could be raised as a defence. Martin wondered how Peter intended to deal with that requirement if he got his way, and built a stone bridge. Presumably, he would have to include a drawbridge over the deep channel, so the proposed bridge could never be entirely of stone! He smiled at that thought – a stone bridge incorporating a good elm drawbridge!

Martin then came aware that a boatman was pulling towards the shingley length of the Surrey shore where he was standing. It was a well-known stratagem: if the waterman had no passenger, he would pull in to the bank and pretend – indeed, some men were whipped every year for asserting – that the bystander targeted had commissioned their services. Martin would have waved the man away with a smile and a blessing, and he fully intended to do so until he saw a tongue of flame running along the side of a long, low ship moored alongside the Bridge House. Normally that berth was used by vessels that carried timber for the bridge works. There was no sign of dockers working on or near this particular ship, and Martin found himself wondering if she was indeed the *Star Lady*. Her lines were similar to what Martin had heard of Oskar's ship and it would not be too great a coincidence if the vessel had been impounded at this semi-official berth. Taking it through the drawbridge and occupying a landing point in the vicinity of Queenhithe would incur needless costs, so, in the absence of a timber-carrying barge, the Bridge House wharf was as good as any point on the Thames to hold the impounded vessel!

Martin raised a finger, indicating his acceptance of the waterman's services, and in a few strokes the man had set the nose of his boat diagonally into the shingle. Having by now lived adjacent to the Thames for over two years, Martin was able to leap nimbly from the bank into the skiff, and as soon as he had adjusted his balance the man pulled powerfully away from the bank. Martin's attention turned again to the fire on the vessel:

"Is that the *Star Lady?*" he enquired.

"I've no idea what sort of lady," the waterman replied, "but she'll soon be a dead duck!"

"How so?"

"Well, Brother, you've got eyes in your head like what I have and a nose what can smell wood that shouldn't be afire ... them Welshmen have done it, like what they said they'd do!" The waterman's mention of Welshmen made it clear that this was indeed the vessel that Martin's instinct had told him it must be.

Martin asked urgently:

"Are there children ... babies ... or women left on board?"

"You know a lot, Brother, for a Bermondsey monk what can't have heard yet what's been going on at the north end of that bleeding bridge!" said the waterman.

"Don't you want to know where I want to be taken to?" asked Martin, and the man's face revealed plainly that he also was so preoccupied with the blazing ship that he had forgotten to find out.

"Botolph Wharf, just over the river. That was my destination. But first, let us go as close as is safe to the burning ship, to see if there is anyone that should be conveyed to safety," said Martin.

"That's a very proper Christian thought, Brother, if you'll permit me to say so," said the man, obviously opening a longer sentence that Martin curtailed by saying:

"Of course I permit you, my brother!" Martin's pre-emption of the mode that the waterman had chosen for the conversation caused the fellow to consider how to go forward. Into the vacuum, Martin injected a query:

"How can you be sure that the women and the children – and all those Welsh sailors – are off the ship?"

"The women and children were taken off in two boats – of which this, my dear Brother, was one – on last night's high tide to the Oldbourne!" For long enough to make sure that this response produced a suitable reaction, the waterman's eyes met the preceptor's. Then he looked around, to verify that no other boat was in the vicinity, after which he rowed powerfully towards the ship that now seemed to be ablaze in every plank and from stem to stern.

The tide was just beginning significantly to rise. The men working in the coffer-dam would be conscious of the fact, and be as anxious for the order to cease working as their foreman would be keen to get the most work done before evacuation was essential. Martin looked towards the dam, and thought of Tom and his companions, working well below the level of the river water, then the boatman eased his oars, and the skiff glided with only slight deceleration towards the burning ship:

"It was the Welshman without the beard, the little one, that said they'd take the ship if they didn't get their wages. He shouted it to the reeves' man, Edgar, when we'd fetched the two women and the children off, and the bags that they wouldn't leave behind, that must have had the wage money in ... though I've never heard of a ship with wages on board! That's a good way for the master to get his gizzard slit, out at sea – man overboard!" The boatman grinned at his own display of worldly wisdom; then he added in a confidential manner:

"I'm not sure that Edgar understood the Welshman. He shouted loud enough, so the clerk must have heard him; but I'm not sure that he knew English, and the Welsh have a funny accent anyhow."

"I'd never presume that Edgar is ignorant of English, if I were you!" warned Martin. He was not confident of his friend's full mastery of English, but a man whose children roamed Cheap Ward must have picked up the language that they brought home. The colloquialisms of the polyglot community within which Edgar's offspring played were English, and many of the merchants with whom Edgar dealt – both professionally and domestically – must be Anglophone.

Martin's own English impressed the waterman, so he nodded sagely at the suggestion. He had got his skiff on to the panel of those that did fetching and carrying for the reeves, largely on the basis that he was competent in French. Edgar had tested his French, and had always issued instructions in French. The waterman reinforced his mental note to be sure not to make the mistake of speaking carelessly in English when a reeve hall official was in the boat, as he dipped an oar in the water to keep his boat at a safe distance from the burning vessel:

"I saw the Welshmen come ashore – well, they went to the north bank, and entered the city by Dowgate – less than half an hour ago, all four of 'em The boat they was in was full laden too; so they've taken their dues in kind, I'd say ... Burning a ship is a spiteful thing to do, but she looks out of date to me ... She certainly burns well," he added.

Martin could feel the heat of the fire on his face and hands, and unbidden the waterman paddled a few light strokes away from the flames. Other boats, some with passengers and others whose watermen had simply become curious about the blaze, were gathering around the burning ship at about the same safe distance as Martin and his boatman had settled for. Having come from the Surrey shore, Martin's waterman was positioned near the prow of the ship, so much of the smoke now billowing above it was being blown past Martin towards his preceptory by the light southerly wind, so he could still see the Surrey side of the ship. Sparks from the conflagration were beginning to fly in among the woodpiles on which Peter of Colechurch's schedule of works depended. Surely someone should be doing something about that?

Martin asked the boatman to pull nearer to the shore. The man accordingly turned the boat to face east, into the rising tide, and took a few strokes before steering with the last pull on the right-hand oar towards the bank.

Craning round in his seat, Martin could discern between the billows of smoke a group of men – he fancied he saw Fulk among them – hacking at the ropes that secured this danger to their livelihood to the bank. Others were ready with poles to push the ship into the tideway, no doubt hoping that the currents of the river would carry it away.

They might thereby reduce the danger to the Bridge House wood yard, but up above the smoke, on the bridge itself, its bridgemaster would be all too well aware that the rising tide could carry the burning ship against the wooden structure of the bridge itself. Over twenty years of rebuilding could be undone in twenty minutes. The same south wind that carried the ever-increasing volume of smoke from the vessel to the north bank was also fanning the flames that licked all the way up the mast, throughout the rigging and along the entire deck level of the hull. If the ship became lodged against any of the bridge piers, it would be a disaster; worst would be the second pier from the southward end of the bridge, where there was a vast superimposed cat's cradle of timber scaffolding to enable the men to fetch their materials from the top of the bridge down to the coffer-dam. In less time than it could possibly take to hack away the scaffolding, fire could jump from the ship, fanned by the breeze, and would surely spread into the main frame of the bridge.

"Look!" called Martin to the waterman. "They're trying to cut the ship free, to save their timber. If they succeed she'll be on the tide, and she'll fire the bridge before she sinks! Is there any way we – all these boats that have gathered – can stop that?"

"What's it worth?" asked the man. He had already easied his oars before Martin spoke, and he had seen what Martin had seen. The look that he bestowed on Martin was not unfriendly, but it was defiant. Martin was in no position to threaten a whipping if the man failed to endanger himself and the frail craft on which his livelihood depended. Nor could he imagine what – if anything – Peter and the priests of St Mary Overy would be willing to pay to save their bridge.

Loud shouting from the Bridge House staithe confirmed the evidence of Martin's eyes: the moorings had been severed and the ship was being poled out into the river. The stock had been saved, but at the probable cost of the ultimate source of their livelihood:

"Can it be done?" asked Martin. There was no point considering price, if there was no prospect of performance.

"Miracles don't come cheap, Brother!" commented the man. But he spun the boat round as he said this, so that its nose faced the stricken ship. The flames and smoke were billowing ever higher as the trail extended north eastwards towards the Hackney Marshes.

Again Martin felt the proximity of exceptional heat burn his face, as the waterman put the prow of his small skiff between the bow of the ship and the staithe from which it was already separated by twenty feet of water.

"How much?" asked the man again.

"Twice what this boat is worth," said Martin.

"That's your promise?"

"That is the promise of the preceptor of Bellins Gate."

"Fair enough! ... You can be the hero, and I'll pull away if there's any danger to this boat. Understood?" asked the waterman.

"Understood!" answered Martin.

"Right, grab that, then!" The waterman pointed to the forward mooring rope, trailing from the ship for about eight feet with the final three drifting on the surface of the water:

"You hold that, and tie it to the seat when you've got enough of it ... I'll call some other watermen, and we'll keep the ship from the bridge until the rope burns through at the ship end. You'll just have to hope that the ship's too far gone to go anywhere, before that bit of her gunwale is afire."

For reasons Martin could never subsequently explain, the fire seemed not to favour the starboard bow quarters of the ship, from which the mooring rope depended. He pulled in the sodden line, wound it twice round the seat, and sat on it. He then held on to the rope as the boatman's strokes made it taut; the ship was beginning to drift on the tide, and its momentum would soon be vastly greater than was achievable by a one-man-powered skiff pulling in the contrary direction.

Others came in response to the boatman's calls. One of the watermen came up to Martin's boat, and his boatman backed up so that the mooring line slackened. Lesser ropes were produced by the other boatmen, all of whom had some means of tying up their craft while awaiting customers. Soon eight boats were interconnected and the men strove to keep the ship from moving upriver. Slowly they succeeded. More and more small vessels gathered around, offering varying advice. Martin became conscious of the strain on the structure of the boat that he was in, before the momentum of the ship responded positively to the impetus provided by the boatmen's oars.

The heat from the flames was truly intense, but it got no greater. The ship blazed away, with yellows and reds competing for predominance among the flames; greys contested with black within the torrent of smoke that engulfed the flotilla of the rescue boats between the zephyrs of the breeze and then rose to follow the preceding pollution, spreading over the city and the flatlands beyond.

Then the blazing mast collapsed, making a huge crack that startled everyone around. Flame and sparks shot upward, in the biggest flurry yet, and the main portion of the mast completely smashed a boat floating off the port side of the ship to give two Southwark whoremongers a ringside seat. The passenger who could swim and the waterman were saved; the other passenger was the only fatality, and his women subsequently rejoiced at their liberation.

The collapse of the mast broke the back of the ship. The stern two-thirds rose in the water, then sank beneath the surface with a huge hissing as the flames were extinguished, and much gurgling as trapped air was expelled from the hull. The bows, still relatively unaffected by the fire, gave intimation of its mortality and Martin looked around for the man who had tied the knot.

He felt, and he showed, panic. He found himself desperate not to follow his exposure to the flames with an involuntary and probably permanent descent to the bottom of the river. He knew that the tide had already risen by several feet, and did not know how much depth of water there was in the river at that point even at low tide. However, a quick calculation convinced him that if a third of the ship sank while it was still attached to this skiff, the skiff would be dragged under water. The boatman had seen the danger also, probably more quickly than Martin. He called on his companions to untie their boats from his, and called for a knife to sever the mooring line:

"You won't do it in time!" shouted the man who had made the knot and whose boat had thereafter been tied alongside Martin's skiff. The second boatman leaned over into the skiff, while Martin knelt on the boards and prayed. The first waterman backed his boat closer towards the sinking prow, to slacken the rope and give a chance of survival to himself and to the fellow waterman who was addressing the knot, with the two vessels still attached together. Martin watched this process carefully, and suddenly he saw the convolutions of the knot clearly. Martin pulled hard at the relevant place, which could not be reached from the second boat, and the man commended him. He pulled a second time ... and the rope, suddenly detached from the boat, was drawn from their hands with a skin-stripping, rasping force and huge velocity as it followed the bow section of the ship to the bottom of the Thames.

The smaller segment of the ship made much less of a show, and much less noise came from the quenching flames and trapped air as it slid out of sight. Once it had vanished, there was a moment of total silence; then from the bridge came a mighty cheer, taken up at the Bridge House – where the men had quickly recognised the dramatic dilemma that had been generated by their own pragmatic action – and then by the attendant boats, and thence by thousands of voices, so it seemed. The bridge and the riverbanks – particularly on the city side – were crowded with people. Rumour, supported by the smoke of the fire, had told the people of London that 'the bridge has gone up again!' It had almost been true. No doubt Peter would be able to refer extensively to the incident in his attempts to persuade officials who were too young to remember that last fire – including the king himself – of the relative merits that would attach to a stone bridge. Martin had felt for himself the heat of a small ship afire; a bridge whose structure was hundreds of times greater than the ship could burn just as easily, with terrifying force and terrible effect.

The watermen must have the credit – and the cash – for their heroic work this day. In a sense, the bridge was their competitor, but they knew that any increase in the river traffic that resulted from the destruction of London Bridge would be neutralised by the setback to the entire regional economy that the closure of the bridge would cause. The watermen had prevented the potential disaster that the reaction of the Bridge House management had created through a remarkable feat of skill, courage and strength.

Martin – in the midst of the incident – had been alarmed, intrigued, enthused, terrified and now elated as the sequence of events had unfolded. He wondered how long had past ... Did it take hours, or just minutes for a ship – or indeed for a vast structure like the bridge – to hiss and crash its way beneath the rising waters?

Martin looked towards the Surrey shore. Amazingly, he was within about forty yards of where the waterman had picked him up. From his memory of the water level the tide had risen by three feet or more likely two. So the whole thing – the fire and its suppression – had taken significantly less than one hour.

"Where to, Brother?" asked the waterman.

"These boats, all that took part, must come to the Bridge House staithe. There the bridgemaster must have your names and the location of your homes, so that you may be rewarded justly for your efforts," said Martin, in his loudest voice, first to the right and then to the left. Martin knew what he had promised the now-grinning waterman, who headed his skiff in response to Martin's instruction; but the preceptor had no idea whether or not it was a fair remuneration, or whether the proprietors of the bridge would pay it. If not, Martin would pay the man from the Bellins Gate chest, and take the consequences, provided he was assured that he was not being deceived over the valuation of the boat.

Martin had made no bargain with the other boat owners who had participated in the rescue, and he had no estimate – nor basis for estimation – of the value of the service that they had rendered. The price for an hour's rowing would be less than a penny a man, at the normal rate for normal work. Setting a value on the great bridge was impossible in itself, so it would be for Peter of Colechurch and the Overy priests to determine the quantum of any award, which to all but the first waterman must be simply an ex gratia payment.

Willing hands grabbed the boat as it came to the staithe, and a strong arm reached out to help Martin ashore. Tom had thrust himself forward to greet the monk who had once more saved the joiners' livelihood. Behind him, Tom's father-in-law stood with the other men who had loosed the ship from the staithe. Some looked furtive, and some defiant. No one else came close to them and they stood aloof from the foreman who had made the decision that they had all warmly endorsed at the time.

Another knot of people in the yard was composed of the clerics: the canons of St Mary Overy, Peter of Colechurch and the parish priests of St Olaf and Christ Church. One by one, the watermen secured their boats and came ashore, all following Martin towards the bridgemaster, a familiar figure to all of those who passed beneath his bridge many times on a normal working day.

Peter presented Martin to the *praepositus* of the canons, and Martin stood aside to present the watermen. They gave their names, from which Martin learned that his waterman, who had performed so well, was Walfrun of the Oldbourne. After giving his details to the remembrancer of the Bridge House, Walfrun turned to Martin:

"That's why I got the job to go up the Oldbourne with those people yesterday. From my address, Clerk Edgar could be sure that I knew the way ... I'd no idea then quite how exciting this business would turn out to be!"

Martin waited until all eight boat owners had given their particulars before explaining that in the heat of the crisis he had promised Walfrun twice the value of his craft if he could find a way to secure the bridge, which he had done.

Peter raised an eyebrow at this, and muttered into the ear of the *praepositus* that as far as he was concerned it was more likely that Martin had told the fellow what to do.

"Neither fire nor water is my element, Father bridgemaster," said Martin smiling, "and after this day I will be even less sure which of them

I fear the more ... It was certainly Walfrun who showed his mastery of the situation and it was the common efforts of his colleagues, here present, that saved the situation when a mixture of skill and strength could alone prevail."

"What you have promised shall be given," said the *praepositus*. Then he added, ruminatively, "I have no idea of the value of the bridge, but we get above a hundred pounds a year in tolls. If it will take forty years completely to rebuild it, at a cost greater than the income in each year ... then you can compute the value at forty hundreds and at least the same again. To spare us such a loss is indeed a mighty deliverance ..."

Turning from Martin to the watermen, the *praepositus* said, still speaking French and in a sing-song, sermonising sort of voice:

"What Father Martin promised to Wal ... Walfrun he shall receive ... What Martin says the other men have earned, they too shall have ... A great deed has been done today ... A model of river-craft handling and a deed of great courage have been witnessed by this great crowd of people ... We will repay!"

Sotto voce the *praepositus* added to Peter the comment that this payout must come from the Bridge House fund, as it was the folly of the men there that had released the destructive force.

Peter asked, rhetorically, who had assented to the *Star Lady* being moored at the Bridge House staithe, at which the *praepositus* raised his head to get a fix of where the sun was in the sky, set his jaw as a deterrent to further impertinence, and declared that it would soon be time for the midday Office. Prayer would, very conveniently, prevail over any further involvement in mere business so far as the canons were concerned. The secular priest who was in their employment would be left to settle up the earthly accounts.

Chapter Ten

Peter of Colechurch had no more idea than Martin of the value of a waterman's skiff, or of how that compared to a year's wages for one of his own artisans, but he could make an estimate of the loss that would have been suffered if the Bridge House and its wood yard had succumbed to the conflagration, or the bridge itself had been severely damaged.

His dealings with workmen had taught him to be prompt and pragmatic in decisions on pay, especially for unusually dangerous work. He was quite sure that all these watermen would have cut loose and pulled their boats speedily away from the stricken ship if they had felt themselves to be mortally hazarded in the rescue operation, but they had stuck with the task even after the collapsing mast had destroyed the onlookers' boat. Several of the sightseers had put their craft in much greater hazard than the boats that had been roped together ahead of the blazing vessel, and their only reward would be telling the tale in the alehouse or reminiscing in the dark after curfew in winter.

The man who already had Martin's promise of payment could be dealt with last. To the others, Peter said:

"To each of you, I will give a fat sow in pig and five shillings ... and to you," he turned to Walfrun, "I give what Father Martin promised you, plus a fat pig for yourself and your household."

Seven times five shillings was no great burden to his coffers and the pigs, he later confessed to Martin, were to be drawn from a couple of dozen he had ordered from Epping Forest to give to selected men as a bonus at the end of the season. At this time of year the sows would all be carrying young, and a family that was given such a beast at this stage of the year could fatten and sell the young by Christmas. Peter's own men would be getting an empty sow, or a young pig, at Michaelmas when the main bridgework stopped for the winter. So the bounty that was being given to these watermen was significant, while falling within the bridgemaster's budget.

The watermen's smiles indicated their satisfaction at the reward, and Peter gave the Bridge House foreman the task of arranging for the sows to be conveyed from Epping. It was a familiar chore for him, but on this occasion he received the order with the mental calculation as to whether this implied that he and his own gang would thereby be deprived of their pigs, come September time. But he saw a positive aspect too – the instruction indicated Peter was not going to sack him for forgetting the bridge when he saved the yard. He knew that he should have considered the state of the tide, before the ship had been cut loose. Most materials were floated from the Bridge House staithe to the bridge and depended on the tide, so for the foreman to have forgotten the tide was inexcusable, yet Peter appeared to be willing to recognise that a genuine mistake had been made – and, mercifully, had been rectified. The foreman made a mental note to ensure that all the boatmen got good, healthy sows.

"Do you want a ferry over to Botolph Wharf now, Brother? I won't charge you, not after this!"

Martin accepted Walfrun's offer, and this was the signal to the other watermen to return to their boats, which were blocking in Walfrun's craft at the staithe. There were still many onlookers, up on the bridge – where tolls had been suspended during the emergency – and on the riverbank. There were cheers and applause as the rescuers' boats pulled out into the stream, but this was also understood to be the end of the drama, and the vast majority of the loiterers turned away from the excitement and back to their lawful avocations.

Walfrun's boat probably passed over the wreck of the *Star Lady* as it made the crossing. Martin was pretty sure that it must be somewhere on a line from the Bridge House staithe to Botolph Wharf, near the preceptory. But there was no turbulence in the steady flow of the tidal stream to give a hint of any obstruction. Neither of the sunken sections of the ship was big enough to be a hazard to navigation at high tide. No doubt, in the coming days, boats would explore the spot at the lowest point in the ebb to check that there was no chance of ripping out the bottom of a careless skiff. The watermen must have a way of disposing of such obstacles to their earning power, and Martin determined to look out from the preceptory at low tide for the next couple of days to see how they might perform the task.

Martin landed at Botolph Wharf, and in the course of his short walk back to the preceptory it was clear to him that many people on the north bank of the river had presumed that he had been directing proceedings among the little flotilla of skiffs that had saved London Bridge. He was greeted as a local hero, and though he constantly reiterated that the watermen had done it all, he recognised from many faces that people considered his statements merely a formality. Whether they thought it fair or false modesty, Martin preferred not to know.

He met the same reaction in the preceptory, where the entire establishment had turned out to see the incident and identified Martin as the black-habited central figure in the rescue.

The *praepositus* of the Southwark canons had anticipated noon by almost half an hour, for just as Martin entered the yard at Bellins Gate the bells of the city and riverside convents began to call the various communities to the Office. Martin presided in his usual place, trying not to notice a level of excitement among the monks that certainly did not emanate from the daily recitation to which their full commitment of brain and spirit should have been devoted. Reviewing the events of the morning, Martin remained convinced that his role had been passive; and that he had been in no mortal danger, save when the vessel had threatened to pull his craft under. The other moment of real fear had occurred when the planking of Walfrun's tiny boat had taken the shock, at the moment when the inertia of the drifting ship had been challenged by the power of the combined oarsmen, but the boat had held together. If it had not been so strong, Martin would have been precipitated into the river, where he would have had to swim. His youthful swimming lessons had been in the often-treacherous Severn around Gloucester, swelled by rain in the Welsh hills. Martin hoped that he had enough skill and stamina in the water to cope with a Thames tide, but he was relieved that he had not been put to the test.

Once the Office had ended, there was time for Martin to check that Brother Elias had fully performed the official necessities of the preceptory during his absence. He looked out on the placid river, with the tide slowly sweeping all before it, and could see absolutely nothing that hinted at the morning's excitement.

The reading over dinner was a particularly apposite injunction to avoid earthly vainglory, to live among men as before God, and to take no credit for God-driven earthly achievements. Martin hoped that his brethren realised fully that he was applying every word to himself, but this hope was challenged by his own inner spirit as being itself a vain speculation. Earthly glory he could most certainly avoid, but involvement in purely earthly concerns excited his divinely allocated senses. He would sin against his Creator if he denied this. If such involvement made him known to people whom it was convenient to know, such as Edgar at the Reeves' Hall, the bridgemaster and the canons at St Mary Overy, or some of the king's closest counsellors – then that, too, was a God-given gift that enabled Martin the better to contribute to the easement of the human condition. The sort of concupiscent tendencies that Brother Felix had to suppress were directly contradictory to his profession as a monk and it must be concluded that God had implanted lust in the man as the basis on which he must test and develop his resistance, so as to fit himself for immortal bliss.

Martin often questioned whether his differentiation of Felix's class of temptation from his own was appropriate, or whether it was merely self-indulgent. He always came down on the side that favoured using his modest talents to serve humanity; and he defended that option on the grounds that he did not have the objective of committing sin when he became involved in some crime or puzzle. Quite the contrary – he became involved in these matters to suppress wickedness and to expose and elevate the truth. If Felix felt he could avoid observation, he would respond to one of his urges by deliberate and explicit fornication – an undoubted sin and a direct contravention of his personal oath. Martin had no such motivation; at all times he sought to avoid committing any sin in the course of indulging his abilities to serve frail humans. Reflecting in this way, once more he achieved a rationalisation of his own activities that enabled him to hear out with equanimity Brother Elias's rather deadpan reading of a papal sermon. Martin need not change the curiosity in his nature to match the requirements set out in this text; and for any tendency to self-indulgence in his activities, he had the absolution of Father Zebedee. His subsequent actions about the Bridge House and London Bridge would not be considered sinful, even by Prior Osbert, who would have heard much about them before Martin could present his own account of the blazing ship to his direct superior.

Martin had not sent Fulk any message countermanding his invitation to come and view the Galway documents that afternoon. Conscious that if Fulk did come, the documents might depart quite speedily for Ireland, Martin called Elias to join him in the great chamber of the tower after dinner. There Elias carefully copied the Latin that Martin believed to be a synopsis of the Great Charter of the City, while Martin himself made rough copies of the jottings and notes that were the substance of the lesser documents.

Elias had seen pages of bark used by monks from Spain, and had heard of its use as a writing sheet in the east also, but he was intrigued by the Irish bark, saying:

"It isn't like cork, Father, so it has not really the elasticity to serve as a document ... and it certainly can't bear folding, as that piece with the names on it shows too well."

Regretting the need to damage a scarce resource, Martin cut a piece of new parchment to the size that he presumed the thrice-folded and largely decayed bark sheet had been and asked Elias to copy what could be discerned from the bark fragments on to it:

"This original, I think, we will keep, so the Galway people will need a copy. The other documents they should have in the original, so we need a copy of each," said Martin. He wondered for how many hours the copies would be in his care before King Henry's officials seized them. Long enough, he hoped, for Fulk to have got the master copies well away from the Thames, and en route to their proper place in the Galway Town Chest.

Elias enquired whether the copies should be in fine handwriting, or whether they could be taken as sketches. Given the time constraint, Martin could only specify the latter, "But then, if you have time, Brother, please do your best to make a note of the hand – or hands – in which the originals are written; it could just help us to attest the authenticity of any other documents that might miraculously appear – after all these years – to refute some of this little lot!"

Elias smiled in appreciation of Martin's foresight. He might have thought of it himself, even within the time that was available for the copying, but he was by no means confident of this, and he was pleased that his was a worthy chief. The interests of the Abbey of St Peter, and of its preceptory of Bellins Gate, were in capable hands, so Elias could anticipate advancing age with greater confidence than he could inwardly allocate to his prospect once his mortal coil had been abandoned. Elias had done no deed of significant evil ever in his life, but he was tentative in his acceptance of the tenets of the Christian religion. He was a monk because being a clerk – in the dual senses, of possessing literacy and being professed in the church – was the most comfortable earthly existence that he could aspire to. He wanted terrestrial comfort to continue for as long as possible, so the temporal health of his community was of greater concern to him than were contemplation of the infinite or anticipations of immortality. So he quickly made accurate and complete notes of the jottings and numerals from the

Galway documents, and then made a fair copy of the actual writing that had been used. He made the letters about three times as big as the originals, thereby emphasising their individual features.

"Would the style be that of the Abbey of Citeaux?" asked Martin.

"I don't think I know that one, Father," said Elias, ruminatively; "I'd say it's an out of practice writer, who had been well trained ... And from a French school, certainly. You can see that in the numerals, more than in the letters; the spacing of a 'v' and an 'i' – look here, at this xiv – is quite different from English usage ... See, where I've copied the numbers I did it the English way, without really thinking. That's the way the portreeves' office expect them to be rendered; but the spacing is quite different in the French way!"

An underused epistolary talent, with French training; it might, then, be possible to substantiate the stories surrounding Simon of Galway – later Simon the Hermit of Tower Hamlets. Perhaps the son of Simon, whose head reposed uneasily at Chad's Well, had known the truth. Perhaps he had passed it on to someone now living. If so, that person was likely to be in Galway, and might be willing to disclose the facts to Fulk once he was restored to the trust of the community as the rescuer of its licence to exist.

Elias performed his tasks of penmanship with enthusiasm, finding them far more interesting than sermon-copying in the little scriptorium off the preceptory yard. He understood the Latin of the charter summary, and on the reverse of the copy he copied a few of the cursive Irish words, again to provide a basis for comparison with any subsequent forgery. A forgery might well contain very much reduced rights for the citizens, or a time limit on their tenure of the site, or a ban on barriers and gates. All these provisions were in the Latin summary of the charter, but there was no way that Elias could assess whether the Latin was a fair synopsis of the Celtic text. If there had been time, he would have welcomed the challenge of copying the oddly rounded Irish letters, but he had barely begun the execution of a fourth mysterious word on to the parchment when a servant entered the chamber to ask if the preceptor would see: "One Fulk ... and a woman."

The unique nature of the preceptory, as a *porte* on the Thames, made it necessary to allow women to enter the tower. The Queen of England herself had ascended to this chamber, and been bedded by her lord in the room above. Martin gave his assent, and Fulk and Joanne were shown in.

"Tom's with the baby," explained the mother, "I wanted to be with Dad."

Martin realised at once that Joanne's kinship gave her the insight that, if her father was convinced that these documents were of importance for Galway, he would take them there. He could be shipwrecked, the town could have been invaded by the King of Connaght or be suffering epidemic, or Fulk could die before Joanne could see him again, if he set off to Galway.

At this moment, unbeknown even to Edgar, Brother Felix was obeying Martin's command to find any ship that might be going to an Ulster or Munster port from London, and see if the master would accept payment to extend his voyage to Galway. Martin had no idea of the frequency of such journeys, but there was a fair trickle of overnight arrivals at Bellins Gate *porte* from Ireland throughout the course of the year, so at least a few dozens of vessels must be engaged on that commerce. If anyone was about to depart for Galway, Felix would find it out.

Martin showed the documents to his visitors, explaining what each of them portended. Neither of them could write, but both had enough business acumen to recognise numbers up to xx and the letters of their own names. Fulk pointed to his own name, on the fragment of bark, with no prompting from the Benedictines.

"Am I anywhere else?" he asked. He did not ask for the other names that Martin had given to him to be delineated; he accepted that list as fact.

"There's an FK by some of these numerals, that could be you," said Elias.

Martin had not noticed this, but it had been blatant to the expert copyist. Fulk looked towards the end of Elias's pointed finger and agreed that he saw the letters. He made no comment indicative of comprehension of the juxtaposition of the letters with a number, nor did he do so when two other samples were shown to him. Joanne looked over his shoulder, nodded sagely but stayed silent. Martin asked no leading question, as he did not wish to embarrass Fulk by extracting an admission of the joiner's illiteracy and strictly limited numeracy. Very few laymen could write, but Fulk would be hesitant to admit that he conformed to the norm, after he had showed he could identify the letters that formed his name.

"And this one, perhaps, you may recognise?" Martin removed the large blank parchment on which he had spread the fragments of the bark document, to reveal the main charter.

"Maybe ..." said Fulk, hesitantly.

"I believe that it is the Great Charter of the Liberties of the City; the original charter," said Martin.

"Indeed so!" chimed in Elias, giving unsolicited attestation to his preceptor's pronouncement.

"That's important!" declared Fulk.

Elias indulged him:

"Why so?" he asked. It was clear that Martin thought so, too, and Elias was interested to plumb the depth of an artisan's comprehension of such matters. Fulk obliged, displaying as he did so his fitness to serve among the guildsmen of an emergent town:

"Well, Brother, the Irish have decided that they don't like towns that get ideas of their own ... At least, that's the message that we received in Galway from other places such as Limerick and Wexford – though the east coast cities are much longer settled, by Norsemen who handle the Irish kings better than we French seem to have done."

"Why did the king grant you a town charter, if he doesn't like towns?" asked Elias.

"One, it wasn't the same king. Two, the towns weren't as rich as they got once they had the charters. Three, the towns started allying with the other kings – not the local king – and with Canterbury, of course ... So bishops and kings both took against us, especially in the west." Fulk's explanation was a model of clarity and of verbal economy. Elias had expected a partially evasive, rambling answer; and he looked to Fulk with genuine respect. This man did know what he was at, both in his craft and among his civic community:

"May I?" asked Fulk, and he took up the large document with its heavy wax seal at the lower left corner. The wax was pressed on to the document, not attached as an appendage as had become the fashion with papal, imperial, French and English seals:

"Yes, I've seen this before ... I'm on it!" Fulk returned the charter to the table so that he could run a finger along the lines of the text, beginning about two thirds of the way down; Martin and Elias both recognised the name of Simon in the Irish script, then a Thomas and a Guillaume and a Fulk. Fulk's finger stopped moving; the man certainly had found his own name:

"It's it, all right!" he declared. "My name is in just the right place."

Joanne came closer, with a more intense look on her face, to behold this evidence of the once important status of the father who would soon part from her. She would be able to tell her sons and her sons' sons of this – that their forebear had been a charter citizen of Galway, and not merely an artisan journeyman at the Bridge House in Southwark. Tom himself had been made a Freeman of Galway before they had fled the town; his sons too would have status there. Joanne prayed that her family could soon be reunited, as she read in her father's face an increased determination to return to Ireland.

"There is only one proper place for these documents," said Martin gently.

"I know it, Father, for I made that place – with Jed Smith to bind it in iron and furnish the grand lock. Not even here in London will you find a stronger lock, with a smoother turn of its barrel, than there in the Galway Guildhall!" Fulk's pride in the chest that he had himself constructed was reinforced by the reminiscence of the hinges, lock and metal corner plates with which the strong woodwork had been embellished and reinforced.

"How will you travel to Galway, Father? How will you find a vessel?" asked Joanne, but her eyes looked beyond Fulk towards Martin, for whom the question was framed. Fulk, too, looked to Martin and offered no response.

"One of my brethren is enquiring at the *portes* and wharves at this moment," Martin replied, "unless he has already located a ship. If he should fail utterly in that quest, he will go to the Reeves' Hall and there enquire whether any departure for Ireland – other than to Leinster, whose wars with Connaght are well known – is forecast for the coming days."

Joanne looked relieved that no imminent sailing for Ireland was known, while Fulk looked concerned and asked how long it might be before Martin could tell him of an opportunity to do his duty.

"Your guess is as good as mine, Fulk, but I will give you the longest notice that I can, of any sailing that I learn of. Then I will ask if you still want to undertake the mission," promised Martin.

"I will most surely want to go, Father Martin. I have done my duty by Joanne and the babe, and now I can do my other duty, to my community – and to the memory of her mother." Fulk's invocation of his wife's memory was received in silence by his daughter, who recognised that for the old man it was a clinching argument.

Fulk asked if he should take the documents now, and await a call from Martin to be ready to depart at a moment's notice. Elias's eyes cast an unspoken plea to the preceptor to retain the charter, at least for a few days during which the scribe could copy the Celtic script for posterity in the abbey archive, but Martin was most concerned that the original documents should not be lost to the Galway community and therefore he kept to his decision that Fulk should take them now.

Within minutes, father and daughter were descending the spiral stair from the chamber, and Martin decided that good order and discipline in his little community would best be served – in this rare instance – by him revealing his reasoning to his colleague Elias.

"Sit down, Brother. I will explain to you ... The Irish cities are not really Irish at all, but settled by Vikings, or by English and French. As you well know, they adhere by the Pope's admonition to Canterbury because of the Irish church's Celtic eccentricities. To develop, the towns need the licence of the local king, which may be granted in such a charter as you have this day held. But then the burghers might ally with another Irish king – or even with a dissident chieftain – to weaken the power of the local king to revoke the charter or to enforce his rights over them ... For us in England, there is also an Irish Problem. The king has reputedly received from Pope Hadrian an authority to make himself Lord of All Ireland. I have not seen it, so I do not know the form of the authority, but I have heard more than enough to believe that it exists. The Irish kings have already been putting pressure on the townsmen. I have myself recently viewed grim evidence of this. If the towns ally openly with the King of England, in rebellion against the Irish kings, those kings will see no reason to give quarter to the rebels if our king's venture is slow to succeed. So the people of each town must be free to assess their own fate, and declare their loyalties at the time that is best for them ..."

"So if Henry of Anjou had possession of the Galway charter, he could impound it – or replace it with his own – and in either case the local king might believe that the Galway citizens are Henry's subjects, before it is safe for them to be so!" said Elias, keen to display his comprehension. "Let us hope, then, that Felix is felicitous in his quest for a passage for Fulk," he added, smiling at his own conceit.

"Indeed, yes ... Keep the documents that you have in copy over there in the press, so that they will not strike anyone who catches sight of them as being of special significance."

Elias was surprised at Martin's instruction. He had been expecting to store them in the locked chest, probably sealed in a calfskin cover, as were the deeds for the preceptory itself in the Muniment Room of West Minster Abbey. It was obvious, though, that Martin's idea was better. If the king should sacrilegiously send an officer to search for the documents at the preceptory, they would look for something such as Elias would have prepared in the place where Elias would have put it … Of course, that depended on the king's officer having been told of the existence of the documents, but in a world of tyrants and torturers, kings did have a way of discovering the things that they felt were germane to their best interest.

"And this," here Martin tapped the fragment of the bark document that seemed to be the least fragile, "this will go in my chamber above."

Elias knew that half of the top floor of the tower, above the room in which the two monks now were and in which his daily clerical routine was performed, had been used by Martin's predecessor for the decoction of medicines and for the preparation of a powerful spirit according to highly novel techniques. Martin had given away the still, and Elias presumed that Martin used the place for study. So he might well have documents – even books – up there, in which case it would be a reasonable place to conceal this item among several.

The extraordinary business of the afternoon was completed, and it was almost time for Vespers. Martin suggested that Elias might care to spend the intervening time tidying the press, and the scribe gratefully accepted this menial prolongation of his remission from copying the sermon. Martin looked down at the bark fragments, still set out on a sheet of parchment but now slightly out of alignment, and wondered how best to store them. They should certainly be laid flat, not rolled or folded. He searched through the pile of parchment offcuts retained for note-taking and to repair damaged documents, and selected one that was slightly larger than the four intact segments of the bark. This he put in the corner of a linen handkerchief left by the Archbishop of Rouen, laundered and kept aside for a special occasion – or against the return of the Archbishop to claim his lost possession. Martin put the bark fragments on to the parchment, watched by Elias, who had abandoned all pretence of work on the press.

"There," said Martin, "I've gathered it all together. Wrapping such things is more in your field of competence than mine, so I'll leave it to you!"

The preceptor descended the spiral staircase, and by the time he reached the yard he had quite convinced himself that he had acted wisely. Elias would surely make a better job of wrapping the fragments than he himself would have done. He might even work out a way of tying or sealing the package that would damage neither the rare handkerchief nor its contents.

There was probably half an hour until Vespers; certainly not more. Martin felt the urge to be active. His flow of spirits had progressively stabilised since the morning peak, but he was still not ready to relapse into the quietude of monastic routine, much as he told himself it was his duty to do so. In the mood that he was in, indeed, the knowledge of what was his duty – combined with the fact that he was not doing it strictly according to the Rule – was an added irritant, which perversely served as an additional stimulant to the excited state that made him keen to find some proactive thing to do.

He looked towards the door of the scriptorium, beyond which two of his colleagues would be at work, probably envying Elias's secondment to other duties. Any intrusion there by the preceptor might exacerbate the monks' sense of ill usage, rather than be taken as an indication of managerial solidarity with the toilers. The kitchen would be busy with supper and the appearance of the preceptor there at this hour could be understood as a sign that the standard of meals had slipped recently – though indeed the reverse was the case, for the coming of summer had provided ample raw material after the dearth of the long frost. The current drought could cause famine in the future but, for the present, supplies were plentiful and the cooks knew what to do with them. The ale, too, was brewing well, though the hot weather shortened its life, and Martin suspected that some of the servants were taking advantage of the principle that it was better to drink up than throw away. He had asked Brother Phineas to keep an eye on this situation, and knew that he should not intervene personally until his elderly colleague reported back.

All of two minutes were absorbed in deciding not to enter the scriptorium or the kitchen. It was not Martin's habit to stand vacantly in the yard; some brother monk or servant would soon observe him and enquire if he was in need of something, indicating that his behaviour was perceived as out of the ordinary. He had to move, in some direction; and wherever he went, he felt that he must appear to have a purpose.

The dilemma was resolved by the arrival at the gate of Brother Felix, anxious to avoid censure by being back in the preceptory well in time for Vespers. He had evidently hastened – probably run – because he was flushed, and beads of sweat were visible on his tonsured head and on his face:

"There's no one going to Ireland from any *porte*, staithe or harbour on the river, Father; and I've just run from the Reeves' Hall, where Edgar says he knows of none!" He gave all the negative information in a single deep breath, then panted heavily. His eyes had a glint that Martin had learned to be on the lookout for. Felix had told the truth, but there was more to be told, with a little coaxing.

"Recover your breath, Brother, then I must hear the means that you have discovered for resolving this apparently intractable situation," said Martin.

Getting his one sentence out seemed to have seriously impaired Felix's respiratory system for the next couple of minutes. He nodded an acknowledgement of hearing what Martin had said, and breathed deeply to bring his inhalations under control. Martin wondered if Felix could have heart trouble, which had become manifest in his unwanted exercise, but he discounted the possibility, as the monk before him gave no indication of feeling pain or pressure in the chest or abdomen. He was simply blown, and this self-rectifying condition merely had to be indulged.

"Well, Father ... there is a Manxman, whose ship will be emptied by tomorrow's first tide and who reckons he won't hang around for a part load to take on somewhere. He ... well, he sort of hinted that if the pay was right he'd sail almost anywhere ... that's all I could find out." Felix would have extracted a price from the man if he had known enough of Martin's intentions to do so, though he realised that in specifying the voyage he would have given the captain information that the sailor might have been able to make use of.

"Where is his ship?" asked Martin.

"At Queenhithe. He's fetched wine from Bordeaux and that's the best place to land the barrels, so he said."

"He's totally dependent on the tide, then, to get down river," said Martin. The ship could not get into the main stream except when the small harbour at Queenhithe had been filled by the tide, then vessels could leave by the deep channel, through the raised section of London Bridge, and so past the preceptory and the hermitage to the sea.

After Vespers, Felix accompanied Martin to Queenhithe. The Viking captain spoke good French though his English appeared minimal, as could be heard from the remarks he was making to struggling stevedores as the monks approached the side of his ship. He switched to French and said to Felix:

"Ah, Brother! ... So you were interested in doing a little business! Come on board, if you wish ... or would you rather be away from these nosy bastards?" He waved a hand in the direction of the dock workers. Neither monk made any move towards the ship, so the captain said cheerfully:

"Right then, it's agreed: I come to you!"

With this, he stepped over the side of the vessel on to the quayside; which was about the same height as his deck, with the ship lying beached.

"The matter is confidential," said Martin.

"It always is, when monks come in twos to negotiate," responded the captain, adding, "I know the rules, that's how I got a ship of this quality!"

He looked lovingly, over Martin's shoulder, to his ship. Martin and Felix both turned to follow his gaze, though all they could see was the deck with the open hatches, through which could be seen the few score barrels that still had to be lifted from the hold. There was a raised cabin at the stern of the ship, with a command position on its roof, and in front of that the mast with its elaborate rigging. Only when Martin compared the deck area with the size of his room, and the aperture of one hatch with the dimensions of the large oak table in the chamber at the preceptory, did he appreciate how large a vessel this was. It would surely cost a great deal of money to hire it, and although he had considerable discretionary resources at the preceptory it would be difficult to argue that the welfare of the Mother House at West Minster urgently required a large disbursement to be made for such a purpose as Fulk's proposed return to Galway.

Martin allowed that consideration to present itself in his mind, as the proper thing for an accountable official of the abbey to do. Then he firmly shut it out. Prior Osbert would certainly not wish the abbey to be embroiled in the politics surrounding the king's decision as to whether or not to invade Ireland. As a cousin and a counsellor of the king, Osbert would have his say, but that was a personal commitment, and the community must not be engaged in influencing the courtiers' deliberations. From what he knew of Osbert, Martin believed that the prior would prefer Fulk and his papers to be safely conveyed to Galway to greet the king there, should Henry of Anjou choose to visit. Securing the settlers' control of Galway might be seen by the war party as a strong additional incident that helped to tip the balance in favour of the proposed operation. If the abbey was instrumental in that achievement, while Osbert remained personally equivocal about the invasion – or staunch with his friend, Henry of Winchester, in opposing war – the prior could be vitriolic towards those of his community who had compromised his position. But then he would let the dust settle, and if the king won his extra territory Osbert would surely claim the credit for the help that the preceptory had provided.

So Martin guessed that when it came to the point where he had to account for the unusual expenditure, the prior's complaint would be formulaic rather than recriminatory, provided that the aim was achieved without embarrassment to the Mother House.

Martin's focus returned from the ship that was the apple of the captain's eye to the eye itself – both eyes – as he asked:

"How much would it cost to carry human cargo – returning refugees – to a certain city in the west of Ireland?"

"Is that all?" asked the captain.

"That is all."

"Just a few days extra on our journey home?"

"Exactly."

"And you'll obviously want guarantees that the people get there, not like the bastards who take pilgrims' or would-be crusaders' pennies, and feed them to the fishes?"

"Precisely."

The way in which the captain took the lead in expanding and making explicit the proposition confirmed to Martin that this man was indeed used to doing confidential business with merchants and monks who expected evidence of performance. The captain was so well versed in these affairs that he recognised the stage to which Martin's cognitive processing of the conversation had arrived, and said:

"I've worked with your lot, in France, and with the Templars; so you can be quite content that I'll only expect full pay on proof of delivery; but that means, obviously, that my prices ..."

"Are special!" Felix's completion of the captain's sentence was his first intervention in the conversation, and it drew smiles from both other participants. Now it was the captain's turn to say:

"Exactly, precisely!" He said both, in amiable mimicry of Martin, who smiled more broadly at the implied compliment:

"I'll take two pounds with the cargo, for feed and water; then I'll take twenty pounds when I bring you the proofs that we agree upon ... so, where will I come for my money?"

Felix gasped at the price. Twenty pounds would probably buy a ship! He gasped again as Martin coolly gave directions to the preceptory, and said that the proof would be a note of receipt of the cargo, with the town seal of Galway and the attested mark of Edmund Skinner.

"Son of Guillaume ... I know him!" declared the captain. "He's the provost of the town; not that it's been much of a town these last few years. If refugees are going back there, that'll be a good thing ... But I'd not want my family going to settle where there's likely to be a battle ... and that sets my nose smelling to seek out the real reason why some so-say refugees' return may be worth twenty pounds to whoever you gentry may represent! Don't worry though, once I make a deal, I stick with it; and I'm not open to counter-offers ... So, do we have a deal?"

The captain looked from Martin to Felix, and back to Martin. The younger monk was evidently the superior of the pair, both intellectually and in status within whatever sort of place Bellins Gate preceptory might be. As a seaman, the captain knew the purpose of the *porte*, and had many times seen it from the river. He had not conveyed passengers who had used it, but now that he had encountered these representatives of the establishment, he was interested to find out more – but that was for the future. Experience told the sailor that landsmen were not usually adept at making contracts for maritime ventures, so he specified terms for the deal:

"The arrangement is that the cargo must be on this vessel at low tide tomorrow morning. I will provide a direct passage to Galway, and the merchandise is left against Edmund Guillaumson's receipt. I will be on your doorstep with that proof in a couple of months' time, after we've worked on the ship at our home port, and then been again to Bordeaux."

The rendering of Edmund's name in the Viking manner had briefly confused Martin, but he nodded assent to the agreement. The captain spat on his palm and pressed it against Martin's, who returned the handclasp. The contract was made in a pagan fashion that Martin recognised, and he accepted that this form of contract-making could survive to the last trump.

Felix, the sole witness to the deal, had no idea who the passengers for Galway were to be, so was in no position to correct the captain's impression that they were plural. Martin saw no need at this stage to say that one man would be travelling alone – provided the captain got his money, he benefited by having fewer mouths to feed.

The ship was called *Mona*, which the captain explained was one of the names that men gave to the Isle of Man:

"There's at least thirty *Monas* that I know of; great and small; so you remember this one is Andrew Erikson's *Mona!*"

There was no point hanging around to watch the perspiring dockers, or to hear the abusive broken English with which the captain constantly chivvied them. Martin and Felix set off on their way back to the preceptory.

As they crossed Dowgate in their progress along Thames Street, Martin felt his personal intuitive tingling run through his body. There was something that he should have noticed among the sticks and stones of the buildings or among the human activity that swirled around them. He stopped abruptly, and Felix had gone a few paces onward before he realised that the preceptor was no longer at his side.

By the time Felix looked round Martin was hastening into Dowgate Hill. Felix followed him, sensing that there was now a new twist to the adventures of an uncommonly interesting day.

Martin hurried past two women, who supported a toddling child between them. The younger woman carried a smaller child and a bundle, the other was the bearer of several bundles strapped about her person. As Felix caught up with them, Martin turned to confront them. In what seemed to Felix a bizarre opening, Martin simply said:

"Oskar!"

The women stopped. One turned round, as if assessing the chances of simply running away; she saw Felix and her face fell as she turned back to face the black monk who had confronted her. Martin had certainly made an impression with his opening utterance. The women looked scared, and the toddler sensed their anxiety and began to whimper as it clung to the legs of one of the women.

Martin could not guess what language within his capabilities these women would speak or understand. He knew no Irish, no Welsh, no Norse and he knew that many cultures discouraged women from learning alien tongues or expensive foreign ways. These women might speak no French nor English; even though they had lived on shipboard and travelled widely, the Welsh crew would have given them no exposure to any major trading language. Martin was sure that the women would also have been guarded carefully from potentially dangerous contacts when the ship was in port:

"*Comprenez-vous Français?*"

The woman who appeared to be the younger, from her bearing within the festoon of clothes and luggage that surrounded her, gave a shrug that indicated the negative. Whether she did not even understand the question, or whether she understood it and gave it a negative response, was immaterial.

"Do you know any English?" he asked. A word that could have been "little" came from the other, the older woman.

"Why have you left the sanctuary of St Bartholomew's?" asked Martin. Both women looked to the ground, and the baby woke up and squawked.

"It is not wise – very, very dangerous – to go to Sewel of Dowgate. The reeves of the port will have him under observation!"

The older woman whispered to the younger, presumably a translation of Martin's warning.

"Sewel in danger?" asked the woman.

"You in danger, if you go to Sewel. You in danger ... guards watching!"

The elder woman passed the message on to the younger. They both looked expectantly to Martin. Nothing was said, but the mix of defiance and pleading in both faces was unmistakable. The little child, too, looked up towards Martin with big, shy eyes, then ventured a smile that told him she was female, precocious and clever.

"Come with me, to a ship for Ireland .... The captain is Manx, he will confirm my promise to you ... You leave tomorrow. Oskar will follow ..." Martin had to repeat each sentence before he could be sure that the translation from the old woman to her daughter made the sense that he intended.

By virtue of her position as Oskar's wife and the mother of his children, Hela was the decision-taker among the quartet. She indicated assent, and her mother translated:

"We go ... you ... ship."

"Your ship is burned. The Welsh did it," said Martin.

"We hear ... even Bart's we hear ... we come claim!" The old woman's English was robust enough to get her core point across, there was no doubt about that. News of a ship afire had spread rapidly to West Smithfield; the column of smoke would have been visible from there, snaking about the city to the east of St Bartholomew's Priory. Probably the name of the vessel and the cause of its destruction had soon become known. The women had concluded that they had lost so much, they had little more to lose by confronting the Welshmen through their patron. Hela expected the Welshmen to be at Sewel's house on the simple assumption that they had nowhere else to go, once they had burned their accommodation. The crewmen had not been paid off, because Oskar's gold was deposited in Sewel's chest, while the Viking's modest float of silver coinage was divided evenly between the pouches that the women both wore within their skirts. The reeves' removal of the women from the ship had taken away the crew's last chance of being paid off before Oskar's release, and they had vented their spite against the world in a manner that was destructive primarily of their own interests.

Hela had not quite known how to confront Sewel, or what to say to the crew if Sewel had let her meet them. At the worst, the crew might set upon them, to rob and even murder them. At best – and most improbably – Sewel would provide full compensation for the recklessness of the crew that he had assembled for Oskar. Hela had a woman's feeling that she must seek the confrontation nevertheless, even though she would put at risk all the valuables that she and her mother were carrying, most especially her own children.

The black monk had appeared from nowhere, to forestall a mission that no one had known about; and to offer her another route. Hela did not want to believe that it was the product of divine instructions to the monk, because that would mean she and her doings were under a special degree of heavenly scrutiny such as no one would invite upon themselves. Stainhood and martyrdom seemed to be too closely related to have any appeal for a half-Viking, who had found more empathy with the sagas of a heathen past than with stories of Irish and alien saints. But she had no earthly explanation for this monk's knowledge of her identity and her intentions.

Perhaps Oskar, learning of the torching of the boat, had guessed how she would react and asked this monk to act for him? But how could the monk know where she would go; and with what intent?

The monk was a smallish, youngish, down-to-earth-looking sort of a fellow. Hela recognised and differentiated the sounds of the French and English he had spoken, even though she did not understand more than a few words of English. If he could speak two languages, using that of the conquerors first, he was probably quite an upper-crust sort of a monk. That might bode no good, or it might mean that the monk had privileged access to wherever Oskar was being held.

Before she could entrust her children and her own person to his protection, even though the offer of it seemed quite providential, she decided to test out her assessment on him. Passers-by were already dawdling to see what this somewhat strange group of two burdened women with children was, with a pair of Benedictine monks, one before and one behind them. A crowd could rapidly appear and she would have to move, but Hela needed some measure of reassurance. She asked her mother to translate a question; to the best of her limited ability, the old woman complied:

"Where's Oskar? Oskar you leave?"

Martin presumed that the woman meant 'send' when she said 'leave' and replied on that basis, with an economy of truth that he hoped would maximise the chances of the women trusting him:

"Oskar is safe, but a prisoner. I responded to the call of the corncrake – the birdcall."

The old woman looked puzzled as Martin said this, and her face showed her lack of comprehension, as she translated to her daughter. To the mother's surprise, and to Martin's relief, the mention of the bird caused an involuntary relaxation of Hela's taut features and she smiled:

"We will go with him!" she told her mother, who passed the message on:

"We come you!"

Martin offered to carry some of the woman's load, was offered the baby, declined that responsibility, and took on two satchels whose heavy weight surprised him. Felix's face showed similar surprise at the bundles that he took from the older woman. They must indeed have been driven by desperation to carry such tremendous loads from one far corner of London almost to the other. Several of the passers-by watched the unusual sight of monks taking women's loads from them, but they left the little party to move on in peace.

"Just keep an eye out for any of the Welshmen who might recognise you," said Martin to the women. His plan might be undermined if one of the crewmen should follow them, and discover their ship.

When they came to Queenhithe the old woman said:

"That good Norse ship. We sure now!" She translated her own observation to her daughter, who nodded assent and muttered something soothing to the tired and confused toddler.

Captain Erikson was used to passengers chopping and changing their embarkation arrangements. Thus he was not surprised that the monks returned so soon with passengers other than the one for whom conveyance was already reserved.

"There is one more to come tomorrow, but these women need secure accommodation for this night," said Martin.

"Aye, and a good rest, by the look of them!" said the captain, picking up the little girl and setting her on the ship's deck, which the incoming tide had already raised well above the quayside.

Martin did not tell the captain the destination to which he wanted the women taken, so he assumed they were the Galway passengers. By the time Martin and Felix left the dock both women had spoken to the captain in Norse, of a variety distinct from his own Manx but fully comprehensible to him, and this affinity ensured their welcome and their safety. Most Irish towns were Viking settlements, and while Andrew Erikson did not personally know any Galway Vikings, he had no reason to presume that there were none. The women certainly looked like refugees and if they wanted to go back, even if they were being used for some political purpose by the English, that was their affair.

The monks retraced their steps along Thames Street to Dowgate, then walked down Dowgate and left into the alley where the lodgings of Fulk and his family were to be found.

"Watch at the gate; see if there are any loiterers who might be following us," said Martin. He did not believe that they had been followed, either to or from Queenhithe; he liked to think that he had a powerful instinct for such things. But he wanted to keep Felix from knowing too much of what was afoot – the less any one of his brother monks knew, the less trouble could be stirred up with either the civil or the abbey authorities. If some disaster resulted from Martin's interventions, he must bear the blame alone; none of the brethren must be so deeply or broadly involved as to be branded an accomplice. Elias knew some things, and had made the copies. Felix knew some things – and he had found the ship and delivered passengers to it. That was ample, for each of them: both could assert that they had simply obeyed their superior, in ignorance of his true intentions.

Martin went into the yard, to be recognised at once by a child from the family who owned it. He ran into the main house calling out: "That monk's back, to see the joiners!" while Martin approached the open door of the cottage where Fulk lived.

On the table was a large canvas toolbag, and in it a few tools, some clothes, a knife, a mug, a wooden plate, a wooden candlestick and a small leather purse. Rolled and folded clothes were on the table ready to be put in the bag to cover and protect these few treasures. The parchments were doubtless right at the bottom of the bag.

Fulk and Joanne had clearly been arguing about what the old man should take; he wishing to leave as much as possible to support the future of the family, and she determined that he should not find himself walking into an empty shell of a workshop with all his personal possessions and tools stolen by thieves and scavengers.

"Edmund promised all would be safe!" the old man said, with his back to the door, as Martin's shadow fell across it.

"It's you, Father; welcome." Tom, the embarrassed co-beneficiary of his father-in-law's generosity and of his wife's acerbity in response to his rare interventions in the debate, greeted Martin's arrival with relief.

All three participants in the family quarrel looked sheepish, wondering how much of their noisy debate the preceptor had heard before he disclosed his presence.

"There's a ship sailing tomorrow, on the next tide ... a Manx vessel called *Mona*. Andrew Erikson's *Mona*. She looks a good strong ship and voyages regularly to Bordeaux."

The announcement had the desired effect of overriding the debate, and focusing the minds of the household on the impending departure of Fulk, and on the possibility that they might never again meet in this life.

"Be at Queenhithe two hours before the tide is full tomorrow morning; I will await you!"

With this Martin allowed them to make tearful apologies for the unnecessary passion with which they had shown their stress, then left. He had half an hour before Compline in which to take a late supper with Brother Felix, who was in great good humour after a day of considerably greater activity than was normal. Missing the suppertime at the preceptory meant that they escaped also the prayers and admonitions that accompanied the meal, and this rare treat delighted Felix almost as much as did his reflections on the day's doings.

Chapter Eleven

At the dockside of Queenhithe the next morning all happened so easily and in so orderly a fashion as to be prosaic. A reeves' officer checked that the ship was only carrying a human cargo, and that none was a runaway from Anglo-Norman feudalism. The vessel was then cleared for departure, and lifted slowly off the harbour bottom by the rising tide, eventually taking its place in the little queue of ships that lined up to sail through the raised section of London Bridge.

Joanne, with the baby at her breast, and Martin were the only witnesses to the departure. Fulk had been told not to give away to the captain that he had no previous acquaintance with the other passengers, and the women made no move either to accept or reject the old craftsman on his embarkation. Three to five days would be the journey time, according to the captain, dependent on wind and weather. Then, with wind and sea supporting much of the homeward trip, the vessel should make it to Man in only a couple of days from Galway.

Tom had been persuaded by Joanne to go to work, so that he could announce Fulk's departure to the foreman and collect the large axe that Fulk opted not to bring home nightly with his other tools. She also wanted the moment of parting to be hers – and the baby's. Like Zebedee, she recognised the importance of the baby in the formulation of Fulk's resolve to return to Galway.

Joanne did not want Tom to sense the depth of the emotion that she would feel on seeing her father carried away on the tide. Fulk would not notice the profundity of her feelings, for to him familial affection was his due; but Tom would sense his wife's commitment for another man, and might even be jealous. Her husband was not a demonstrative man, but Joanne recognised in him greater sensitivity than was in her father, and as she was set to spend the rest of her life serving Tom and his children, she was convinced of the wisdom of encouraging Tom to make his farewell to Fulk before he left for an ordinary day's work.

Joanne would compose herself by the time Tom came home, bearing the axe that would then be his own property, and she would have a nice fresh fowl to feed him with, in gratitude – so she would say – for his facing up to the embarrassing task of clearing Fulk's precipitate departure with his employers. Formally, Fulk had been employed on a daily basis, but in practice the bridgemaster's scheduling required the men to commit themselves at least by the season. Fulk had followed Joanne's lead on this point, praising Tom for his goodness in taking news of his father-in-law's defection to the foreman. So Tom would come home feeling that he had borne his full share in the burdens of the day, and Joanne would provide his reward in his trencher and afterwards in bed. The absence of Fulk from the single room of the cottage would make cohabitation less inhibited, and Joanne was herself looking forward to that part of the proceedings even as her emotions focused on the old man waving from the departing ship.

"Well, Joanne, my daughter, the great adventure for your father begins – and you must get home with this grandchild of his!" said Martin.

Joanne was surprised that a celibate man should so clearly have recognised the role of the baby in making Fulk's decision – she had no doubt that this was the inner meaning of his statement.

"Thank you, Father ... Do you mind if I walk alone ... well, with the baby ... and my thoughts?"

"Not at all. I have errands to perform anyhow, errands that had to wait until your father was down river from the preceptory, which he will be within five minutes, or about the time it takes me to walk to my next port of call!" To these words Martin added a farewell, after putting forward his finger to be squeezed by the baby's grasping hand.

Martin had decided to go first to the Reeves' Hall to tell Edgar that the women who had been quarantined at St Bartholomew's were believed to have sailed overnight – or perhaps even yesterday – to foreign parts. From time to time, riverside gossip came to the ears of the preceptory monks and when it touched on smuggling or illicit migration the word was passed to the clerk Edgar, who accepted all intelligence with gratitude. He had learned not to be overly particular in enquiring after the original sources of information or speculation that was passed on by his regular informants and would not ask Martin where his information came from.

At the hall, the sergeant of the guards greeted Martin with the comment:

"He's popular with the clergy, today, for one as ran away from them!" Martin guessed Edgar had received other ecclesiastical callers that morning, and found he had guessed rightly: Father Frederick, the flabby, friendly and shrewd sub-prior of the Priory and Hospital of St Bartholomew, was seated in the best chair in Edgar's room. He begged Martin's indulgence for not rising to greet the Benedictine, "for I'm quite out of breath with rushing all this way".

"What brings you here, Father Martin?" asked Edgar, waving the preceptor to a chair and pouring another mug of ale from the jug that had been fetched to assist Father Frederick to recover from his trot from West Smithfield to Aldermanbury.

Edgar was acutely aware that when Martin became involved in affairs too many apparent coincidences occurred for all the component incidents to be quite coincidental.

Frederick had just reported that the women and children from the *Star Lady* had gone missing from St Bartholomew's. Edgar had discovered that the canons' idea of keeping people in quarantine was to allocate them to a small ward, and give them a day's food and drink every morning. They were shown where they could witness the priory services through a squint, so that they did not need to break their isolation, and unless they asked for medical attention or spiritual direction, they were left to their own devices. No check was made between feeding times and medical observations as to whether they remained in their allocated places:

"We are a hospital, not a prison!" Frederick had declared.

Edgar's riposte was that this attitude was all well and good from the hospital point of view, but it did not constitute what the city authorities necessarily meant by quarantine. Edgar recognised that he had failed to test whether the authorities at St Bartholomew's took the same interpretation of the word as he did: that quarantine was a form of preventative detention. The reeves' office could not now blame the prior or his canons for having let the women go, though he expressed surprise – indicative of incredulity – that two women and two children, together with most of the impedimenta that Edgar had fetched with the women from the *Star Lady*, had decamped from the hospital completely unobserved.

"It must have happened soon after Matins, Edgar," explained Frederick, "as no one gets in or out of our walls during the night."

Edgar had accepted this assessment and shared Frederick's consequential assumption that the women would be in or very near to the city.

Thus far had the conversation progressed when Martin joined them. Both looked expectantly at him, confident that this visit was germane to their discussion, but what he said surprised them:

"The women who were left in St Bartholomew's Hospital are rumoured to be at sea. For that to be so they must have left the priory before curfew last evening and in that case, they are fair and far off by now! ... I think that Father Frederick's presence confirms my rumour."

Frederick, who was ignorant of the rules that surrounded the passing of gossip to the Reeves' Hall, asked Martin:

"How did this news come to you, Father? ... How did your informant know you to be in any way interested in the women?"

Martin was ready for the question, and responded with true statements that enabled him to avoid telling the truth almost completely:

"I was engaged in trying to save London Bridge from the burning *Star Lady* yesterday. Hundreds – perhaps thousands – turned out to look, and dozens of them knew who I was ... So, if the women from the ship were seen later, by someone who knew who they were ... I might hear about it."

Frederick heard this as an explanation of what had actually happened. Edgar interpreted it as probably constituting a clever evasion of the direct question. He had heard several reports of Martin's involvement in the rescue of the bridge, and had intended to make time this day to go to congratulate the preceptor on behalf of the civic authorities. It would be remarkable if Martin's presence near the *Star Lady* at just the crucial moment had been another pure coincidence, though Edgar dismissed any idea that the preceptor could have colluded with the Welshmen in firing the vessel. If he had seen Martin alone just to talk over the rescue, the preceptor might have told his friend what had led him so opportunely to the scene of potential disaster. But now the more urgent issue of the disappearance of the women had come to the fore, so it was less likely that Edgar would ever get a full elucidation of Martin's role in all the steps of the saga.

"At sea before curfew, you say?" said Frederick, having by now fully assessed Martin's opening statement.

Martin nodded, and sipped the ale.

"So, we've lost them ... and whatever use they might have been," said Edgar.

"True," said Martin. "And now that you have been able to confirm the rumour of the women's flight, it would be much in the interests of your masters, the reeves – and also of the bridge proprietors at St Mary Overy –

if you could pursue the Welsh crew of the *Star Lady*. They were witnesses to all that went on in the ship, and are much more likely than the women still to be in London. Get them in hand, and you apprehend the criminals who destroyed a ship. Already one of the Welsh crew is in the Wardrobe, and yet another is also held captive ... So if you are able to persuade Sewel of Dowgate to give you the rest, you will serve your masters well if you can discover what drove these men to such action." Martin found that a tendency to prolixity could be persuasive with literate men; and even more so with the tiny minority of holy nuns who were as literary as they were literate, and who could on occasion be useful and inventive allies.

Edgar knew that he was being cajoled, but Martin's courteous manner and the obvious good sense of apprehending the former crew of the *Star Lady* were even more persuasive. By their thoughtless action, born of frustration tinged with malice, the crewmen had threatened London Bridge with devastation by fire for the second time in a lifetime. Martin and the watermen were the heroes of the day, but Edgar could gain a share of the kudos if he did his part, and apprehended the miscreants. He had no fear that Martin would claim any of the credit if he seized the men with a minimum of fuss, so he decided to act quickly.

So it was that, barely a day after Martin had told Hela that the guards might be watching Sewel's house, a small detachment was actually doing so. Then Edgar ordered the sergeant to beat on Sewel's street door to demand admission. Besides giving *post facto* veracity to Martin's statement of the preceeding afternoon, the visit proved successful. Two of the Welshmen, the pair who had proposed and started the fire, had got away on a ship on the night tide assisted by Sewel's neighbour; two others were wasting time on the attempted seduction of Sewel's scullery maid when Edgar's detachment arrested them.

The hangdog look and the apprehension in the Welshmen's faces and demeanour convinced Edgar that these were mere stooges in whatever games were played around them; but they were without doubt material witnesses to the firing of the *Star Lady* and whatever other activities the ship had taken part in. They were marched off to incarceration in the city jail, while one of the guards was despatched to the Royal Wardrobe to inform the Father preceptor of Bellins Gate that two fat birds had flown, but two runts had still been in the nest.

Martin meanwhile had walked on to the Wardrobe – to find out if any message had come back from Rulf at the king's court, or what further evidence Oskar or the Welsh prisoner had given to their captives, and hopefully to get to Oskar the news that his women were safe in a Viking ship en route to Ireland.

When he arrived Angelina le Court was still waiting for news as to the success or failure of her messenger to reach her husband before he spoke to the king's officials. She had made no further attempt to interview Oskar, and had decided that the Welsh seaman who had been arrested with Oskar was best interrogated by someone who really knew how to do it.

Martin asked if he could see Oskar to check on his condition, and Angelina listlessly acceded to the request. She had slept little for several nights, and in her exhaustion saw no reason to accompany Martin to the small room where Oskar was being held.

"The women and your children are in a ship bound for Ireland. You need have no fear for them!" said Martin as soon as the servant who admitted him to the cell stood aside to allow the preceptor to enter.

Oskar looked up from his position flat on the floor. As the room was devoid of all furniture, its occupant had decided to rotate standing, squatting, sitting with his back against the wall and lying down. His face showed challenge, then enquiry, then acceptance. Oskar weighed up whether the information was a ploy by his captors, but concluded that the a balance of probabilities was in favour of this monk telling the truth – he would live on in his progeny, even if his own life was soon concluded. He could face his end free of the shadow that his loved ones might be damaged as a consequence of his actions.

"The captain is a Manxman, and the vessel is a large, strong one ... You heard about your own ship, I suppose?"

Oskar's face showed that he did not. He bounded to his feet, asking simply:

"What?"

"Be calm! You can do nothing! The day before yesterday your family were taken to St Bartholomew's Hospital, on my advice. They were put in quarantine ... isolation from other people ... I said there might be a possibility of infection – which is true of anybody at any time. If you had been adjudged a spy they could have claimed the sanctuary of the priory ..."

"The ship!" interjected Oskar. Martin continued the narrative as he had planned it, but answered what he guessed was a major part of Oskar's question:

"All your possessions of value and of interest were taken to the priory; and all that Hela and her mother could carry are with them on the ship to Ireland ... The Welshmen told the portreeves' men that they were unpaid, and demanded pay. They even threatened action against the ship – another good reason why your children were well out of it!"

Martin knew of no threat made by the Welsh crewmen before the children had been removed from the ship, but it would enhance Oskar's acceptance of the situation if he inferred that there had been a dangerous situation while the family was still on board. The Viking was looking intently at Martin, taking in every word, with the muscles around his jaw twitching with frustration. Speaking as clearly and as economically as he could, to ensure that Oskar fully understood him, Martin concluded the story:

"Anyhow, yesterday morning the Welshmen fired your ship; it sank about half an hour later, after breaking in two. Your wife left her sanctuary, to seek out Sewel and confront the crewmen. I was able to meet her in time to dissuade her, having already located the Manx vessel. She agreed that the best plan was to go to Ireland and prepare for your return ... I think that you would agree that for your family to walk into Sewel's house in Dowgate would not be wisdom?"

Although Martin ended with a question, he had no expectation that Oskar would focus upon it. The Viking had a vast picture to take in to his mind; of his family at sea and his ship at the bottom of the Thames. He turned away from Martin, his face in his hands, and took a couple of paces towards the far wall, stopping short of the corner that contained his stinking faeces:

"The ship was not really mine; it was funded by King Diamuid ... but I have much of value in her, and nothing elsewhere ... you say they are safe: the women and the bairns?" he asked.

"Safe and well, and very strong, judging by the weight of the bundles and bags that Brother Felix and I assisted them with yesterday." Martin had the impression that the content of the bundles mattered as much to Oskar as did his own children, perhaps even more. Some men take the view that as long as you live you can get more offspring, while the chances of acquiring gold occur rarely in some lives and never in most.

"So you think it's down to me now?"

"Yes, Oskar, to you."

"What are my chances?"

"It depends who the king sends to examine you. If it is Becket, or another of the no-war party, they have a simple choice: to execute you for your desecration or to send you back to Ireland with a message that there are some around the King of England who discourage the proposed expedition to Ireland."

"Or?" said Oskar.

"Or if it is the pro-expedition party whose agent the king sends to see you, you will be wise to offer your services to Henry of Anjou; and watch your back all the time, for the daggers of those who want the king to ignore the siren calls to become Lord of All Ireland!"

"Well said, indeed, Brother!" A voice totally unfamiliar to Martin reminded him that the cell door stood open behind him. He had not noticed approaching footsteps, so intent had he been on his conversation.

Martin turned to the voice, and saw an elderly cleric in a rich habit with a large double-cross in gold with many jewels on his breast. Martin knew he must be an archbishop, and therefore Theobald of Canterbury – a leader of the party that had procured the papal licence for an invasion of Ireland. If he had just heard the last bit of Martin's advice to Oskar – which the preceptor more fervently hoped was the case – then the opening remark could be taken in its simple meaning, with no ironic overtone.

Martin knelt on one knee and the archbishop smiled as he presented the large ring on his gloved hand for Martin to kiss. The strong smell of horse from the archbishop's clothing indicated that he had ridden direct to the Wardrobe from wherever he had passed the proceeding night.

As Martin rose, he saw behind the archbishop one of the king's closest associates, whose name he could not recall:

"I've seen you before, Sir Monk!" the man declared. "I have it – you run that place down on the river, where we came with the king when he had to pay a quick visit to London from France ... Father Martin ... You don't remember me, I suppose?"

"By face, sir, yes; but I thought you of the inner household," said Martin.

"A valet or some such, you mean?" answered the courtier. "Well you could easily think that, sometimes; especially when the king travels light ... I'm his steward, Bisset: Menasser Bisset!" He held out a hand in greeting, which was uncovered as he carried the gauntlet in his other hand. Martin shook the hand, recognising as he did so that Bisset was confirming to Theobald that this man was to be treated as noble, reliable and on side with the king himself. Theobald nodded, almost imperceptibly. Bisset went on:

"Well, Brother, you seem to be well on the way to doing our work for us: but first we need to be brought up to date on the situation here."

By now Martin had recognised Rulf le Court among the knot of people just outside the doorway to the cell.

"All will be well, Oskar; if you make it so!" said Martin, as the others preceeded him out of the cell. Oskar had seen Martin's obeisance to the older man and he had heard all that had been said: if Father Martin was known to the king, and these men were here by the king's command to determine his fate, then he had the agonising decision to make as to whether he could trust the advice that Martin gave to him.

Again the Viking wondered whether this was all a rehearsed show for his benefit. The arrival of the visitors immediately after Martin's tale of the *Star Lady* made the whole recital seem very far-fetched ... Yet all the details were consistent – it would take several days for the king to send those who would give effect to his response to Rulf le Court's report, and Oskar, like Martin, had seen Rulf in the cell doorway and knew that he had returned. Oskar had to assess the credibility of the story for himself.

Edgar, the reeves' clerk, would have been happy to tell Oskar at any time that coincidences collected around Father Martin of Bellins Gate, but that counsel was not accessible. Oskar was abandoned to his own turmoil of thought and calculation. He knew that only a short time would elapse before he was brought before these new arrivals. He needed to have his options clear in his own mind, but there was so much to assimilate, and so many dimensions that must be compared.

Did he owe prime allegiance to King Diarmuid or to himself? Would the safety of his family be at stake, if Diarmuid heard that he had turned his coat and pledged himself to a new master? Would the English ask him to be a double agent?

The earnest stare with which Rulf fixed Martin, as the monk emerged from the cell, indicated profound gratitude. From the silent signal, Martin could infer that Rulf had indeed been able to present in Oxford an account that would not be discredited by the new information in London. The Welsh seaman who had ridden pinioned as a pillion passenger to Oxford was being brought back, still bound, by the more amenable mode of river transport – he was no longer important in Rulf's eyes, so he could be dealt with later in accordance with whatever treatment was meted out to the man whom Martin and Angelina had correctly identified as his principal. Rulf had now recognised, peering into the cell over Archbishop Theobald's shoulder, that the Viking was obviously a more significant and sinister figure than the Welsh sailing master.

On his arrival in Oxford, Rulf had deposited his prisoner for safe keeping in the castle and had obtained a night's lodging for himself and his attendants in one of the decaying former canons' houses in the castle precinct. There Angelina's messenger had found him, before noon the next day, before his solicited meeting had taken place with Richard of Ilchester, one of the king's clerks who could direct Rulf along the right official channel. Hence the story that Rulf told Richard was rather different from the one that had been rehearsed in his mind overnight, but it was much more interesting than the original would have been to Richard, a supporter of the war party largely because of his loathing for Becket on the other side. Richard of Ilchester had called in Menasser Bisset to hear Rulf's story, and he had taken the matter to Theobald.

Regardless of whether or not King Henry would finally take up the gauntlet that the Pope had proffered to him, Theobald took seriously the papal authority that he had inherited over the maritime towns and cities of Ireland. The headless body could be one of his flock, the severed heads certainly were, therefore the affair was the business of the See of Canterbury regardless of whether or not the king seized his Irish opportunity.

Theobald had in any case need to return to Canterbury within a few days, so he took Rulf with him into the royal presence. There he sought the king's consent to advance the date of his departure so as to have time in London, en route to Kent, to sort out this trivial but intriguing incursion of Irish politics into the Tower Hamlets.

King Henry agreed, subject to Bisset going with Theobald and returning directly to report back to the king on what had been discovered. Henry was intrigued and highly amused by the tension developing between Becket, his own chancellor and archdeacon of Canterbury, and the Archbishop of Canterbury. Henry guessed that Theobald's increasing assiduity in looking to the affairs of his diocese was deliberately directed to check-mating any incursions by the archdeacon into the archbishop's prerogatives or resources. So when Theobald asked that this whole business should be kept a secret from the Chancellor of England – for a while, at least – the king guffawed and assented. The more these clerics scored points off each other, the less of a menace they could be collectively to the Crown. Individually the bishops and upper clergy were useful to the monarchy: they had independent income, were mostly literate and often intelligent; some even had diplomatic and political skills; some were good at fortification, and a few were competent field commanders. Provided these talents were individually and severally accessible by the king, on his terms, they were beneficial to him. Should the clergy ever take it into their heads to form a party of their own, that would spell danger to the king: but it was not going to happen, because Becket was already at odds with many of the most senior clerics, and thus was driven to develop his successful role as the king's most loyal advocate and judge.

Occasionally the king found that throwing a reward in the direction of Becket's opponents and challengers was essential for keeping them in the wider king's party, so handing the investigation of this trivial matter to Theobald was an easy decision for him to take. It would be justifiable even to Becket – if he ever came to hear of it – in terms of Theobald's legitimate interest in the affairs of any Irish port.

Thus, with Bisset to act as eyes and ears for the king, Theobald rode with Rulf to London, arriving at the Wardrobe in the City of London just as Martin went into Oskar's cell.

Angelina briefed the arrivals on what she and Martin had heard from the Welshman who remained in the Wardrobe and from Oskar. Martin then gave them a carefully tailored account of the quarantining of Oskar's family, the firing of the ship and the flight of the family; and tentatively expressed the view that Oskar could be turned to serve King Henry.

"But there would be no hostages, then!" said Bisset. It was spoken almost as a condemnation of Martin's suggestion – how could Oskar be let loose on any sort of engagement, if there was no sanction to ensure his compliance?

"Does that matter, Father?" said Martin, addressing the Archbishop. "If the king is persuaded not to follow the admonition of the Holy Father, there is no loss to us in a potential agent in Ireland reverting to his former loyalties if he is able to avoid exposure. On the other hand, if our king is set upon being Lord of Ireland, then Oskar will have no resort if it is ultimately found that he has failed in a pledge to assist the venture."

"I think you may be right, Brother ... er ... Martin; I think you may be right!" Theobald went deep into thought, and the others stood respectfully around him. He had declined to take a seat, after so long in the saddle, so the others perforce stood also. At length, he announced his decision:

"Master Bisset, you will be better able than I am to define a task for a turncoat, so please do so ... Father Martin, I charge you to come to Lambeth – I shall go there presently – to tell me what has been decided. Then, on your way back to the city, you may report on the matter also to your prior ... I presume your abbot is still whoring and skulking in Essex?"

Martin bowed, which could be taken as an affirmative gesture, but avoided any verbal confirmation of the archbishop's crudely expressed though wholly accurate assumption. Theobald was evidently a schemer, who practised the fine art of protecting his rear at all times. In indicating his clear wish that Martin should report on this business to Prior Osbert that afternoon, he was doing what was necessary to retain the goodwill of another key player in the counsel of the king. And Osbert could not in future complain that there had been anything underhand in the transaction. Martin, for his part, hoped that Osbert would be in one of his more communicative moods when he heard his preceptor's report, and would reveal something of his opinion of the Primate of All England.

All those present bowed low as Theobald bade them farewell, and an almost audible sigh of relief followed his back. Bisset nodded to Rulf, and said:

"So there you have it, my friend. We are to test whether this fellow Oskar may be useful to the king when the Irish venture is launched."

He looked around, and saw that Angelina had raised her eyebrows at this statement and the slim-built monk's mouth had gone in a straight line, as if he would question the point also. So he added:

"Believe me, madam, it will happen. Not because of the Pope's decree, nor the Archbishop's pretensions, nor even the murderous conflicts that sully the land; it will happen because the king must have an empire. He wants defence in depth – if he is attacked in France, he wants Welsh archers and Irish spearmen to call upon; and if the Vikings should try to take Ireland from him, he wants knights from England and foot soldiers from Anjou to be at his beck and call. *E pluribus unum.* It is an old phrase that is not usually applied to our situation, but out of many, there shall be one monarchy."

Martin was slightly surprised to hear a layman speaking Latin, even to quote a tag that evidently had political currency at King Henry's court. More significant was the determination – clearly distinguishable from dogmatism – and pragmatism with which Bisset spoke.

Rulf punctured the rather charged atmosphere that the courtier's statement had produced, by coming forward to shake Martin's hand and thank him "for helping Angelina". Again his eyes conveyed volumes of words that he would not utter in the presence of Bisset; he could not jeopardise his future in the king's party by displaying how his precipitate judgement of his captives from the hermitage might have compromised what was now a promising opportunity to contribute to the winning side in the policy debate.

If Oskar were to prove willing to work for the English, ahead of the expedition being mounted, he might materially assist the entire enterprise ... If Oskar failed the English, and Henry nevertheless became Lord of Ireland, then Oskar would have to flee over the waters to the legendary lands of the west, never to return. Rulf was not worried about this; the choice would be for Oskar to make. Should Oskar offer his services, the king was unlikely to miss such an opportunity if Bisset knew his mind and had reported his cerebrations accurately.

Rulf looked admiringly at Angelina. If she had been a less loyal, less able, less determined wife, their situation would have been very different. He must find a special way to thank her, especially as her mistress, the king's mother, was reputedly in the antiwar party and might reject her lady of the chamber on grounds of disloyalty on a matter of high politics.

Angelina read his look accurately, and then took an initiative that surprised and thereafter greatly pleased him. She said:

"My lord, gentlemen, you have men's work to do now. May I withdraw?"

She curtsied and left the room. Bisset gave no reaction; if he thought of it at all, he would be of the mind that it was proper conduct in a female. Martin and Rulf each separately thought that she could have taken a part in the ensuing proceedings as useful as any of theirs, and she could have brought insight that the remaining participants would not generate. But in terms of consolidating Rulf's reputation with Bisset and his royal master, Angelina had certainly done the right thing. Angelina, too, knew that she could not influence Oskar's response to the proposition, so she might as well do the wifely thing, in public, and await the outcome in seclusion.

Rulf told the servants to bring Oskar from the inner chamber that had served as his cell. The room where they waited, like the other chambers in the building, was used for storage. Documents were arrayed in racks around the walls and up the middle of the room, and the three men stood by the large trestle table used for spreading out rolled-up documents for classification or reference. There was one high stool, for use by clerks working with the documents. Bisset gestured to Martin to take the stool; he declined, so the trio remained standing when Oskar was brought into their presence.

"Leave us!" Rulf ordered the servants. They did so, while Bisset made his first visual assessment of the prisoner.

The clothes that he had taken from the crewman were filthy and ragged, but it was obvious that they were too small for him. Even the poorest of seamen would have clothing of roughly the right size. Rulf was incredulous at his own failure to have seen this, even in his haste to do something significant speedily after the midnight arrest of the men. He was satisfied that Martin would not betray his stupidity to Bisset, but he did not like the monk knowing something so embarrassing. Such secondary considerations had to be set aside, however, as the core business of the day was addressed.

Oskar's hair and beard were unkempt, and he was dirty, but he impressed all with his lucidity and self-possession. Bisset had no English, so relied on Martin's translation and his own keen eye for body language. Rulf's English was good enough for him to make small direct contributions to the dialogue.

Within forty minutes, Oskar had told his captors that, in his view, King Diarmuid of Leinster was in a precarious position. He might well be willing to accept King Henry as overlord of Ireland if the English king would lend him support against rebellious forces. Surely it would serve the English purpose to have friends ruling the parts of Ireland that faced Wales and England?

And what if Diarmuid would not agree, or he was deposed, as Oskar seemed to think probable?

Then Oskar would report the state of things to whoever became his controller, on each of the trips he would regularly make to London in the vessel that the English would give to him as a replacement for the one that had been lost while it was under the control of the London portreeve.

Menasser Bisset bristled again at the prisoner's demand, but Rulf said: "There's still a couple of William of Ypres' ships on the Thames. They've had a few tenders put up to buy them, but they've got a funny Flemish rig and London mercers don't like 'em. If you have the king's authority, you can release one of them to Oskar. It'll be a positive use of a wasting asset!"

"Not with a Welsh crew, though!" said Martin, in English, so that Oskar understood the assertion before he said the same in French. Oskar replied:

"Perhaps Welsh for a one-way trip; if I can round some of those filth up! ... The ones who destroyed my ship! ... I've nothing against the Welsh in general, nor against those who were ashore with me when you took us. But as to the firebugs, that's a very different story!"

He had either understood some of the French conversation between his interviewers, or he had inferred from Martin's one remark in English that he was to have a ship.

Bisset looked thoughtful, then said:

"Give him the smaller ship! ... On lease from the crown, of course."

Rulf's wink to Martin, which Oskar saw though it was concealed from Bisset, indicated that this was thought to be the better of Ypres' rotting leftovers. To Bisset, Rulf said:

"He'll need cash to repair the rigging and sails, and to get stores for his first trip – as well as furnish a crew."

"Do you hold any Crown money here?" asked Bisset. He probably knew that there was a small reserve held in this secure royal refuge in the middle of the capital; he might even have seen the amount in Rulf's latest return on the Wardrobe, submitted to the Chamberlain at the King's court. Rulf had to admit it, and he would have to release funds if Bisset so ordered though he had not previously let the thought enter his head.

"Do it! Use the least possible, of course. Send the account to Bishop Nigel, and I will confirm the authority for spending it directly to him." Bisset made it clear that both parts of the order were equally important.

"I have business at West Minster, then I ride for Oxford," said Bisset, signalling that now his decision was announced he would leave the entire implementation of the project to Rulf. He gave a curt but friendly farewell to the monk and to the custodian of the Wardrobe, sent his compliments to Angelina, and departed. Within three minutes the clatter of hooves from the courtyard confirmed his departure. Martin, too, said goodbye to Rulf and descended the stairs to set out for Lambeth Palace.

The small cluster of buildings inside a wooden palisade that formed the archbishop's base were on the south bank of the Thames, almost facing the royal palace and abbey of West Minster. To get there by land, one had to cross London Bridge and pass from Southwark through the Surrey lowlands to Lambeth. There were a few hamlets on the way, but no major settlement to match the buildings that provided an almost continuous pattern of houses and gardens along the northern strand of the Thames from the city to West Minster.

The Surrey lanes near the river would be passably dry in the present drought, but normally they were awkward to traverse and sometimes waterlogged. London residents tended not to consider the overland route to Lambeth, especially if they had no horse to ride. The river was the obvious choice, particularly if the tide was running strongly upstream.

Martin decided to see if the waterman Gutrin was available to take him; it was useful to employ one man regularly. A client who provides a steady source of income and pays modest tips can ask a man to go a long way or work at night – and keep his mouth shut about the errand. Gutrin had a few such customers who were very far from holy men, and it had balanced the ethical account a little when the preceptor of Bellins Gate became one of his regulars.

A ragged child at Gutrin's hut told the monk that Dad would be waiting for work at Botolph Wharf, if he was not busy. There Martin spotted him and in calling to him drew attention to himself. Martin realised from the way folk pointed and looked at him that the reminiscence of the previous day's fiery incident would follow him around the riverside for a while to come.

With slack water at high tide, Gutrin would be working against the effluent river for much of the journey to Lambeth, but in compensation the stream would be behind the oarsman on the return journey to the city. Martin would require Gutrin to wait while he was in the archbishop's compound – a boat was the only means to get from Lambeth to West Minster.

Martin had never before passed West Minster in a boat; normally his journeys ended at the Palace Stair. The complex of royal palace and abbey looked powerful, if haphazard, set on Thorney Island well out in the main stream of the river. To the east and west of the buildings, indentations in the riverbank showed clearly where the margins of the island formed residual waterway defences around the whole site at high tide. There were ditches to the east and the Tyburn – a tributary at least the size of Wallbrook – entered the Thames to the west of the palace after collecting the waste of the abbey and the court.

The river frontage gave the king's palace direct access to the tidal seas.

Martin reflected that it was the sea that linked the cities of the earthly trading world – the Manxman Erikson's ship linked Bordeaux with London, and both with Galway. A king who lived here, if only for a few weeks in the year, would see and smell the rising tide and be reminded of the power of the sea and its trades. He had only to step on to a ship and his next footing on dry land could be in Spain, Norway, Normandy or Ireland.

Gutrin was pulling the boat now towards the small Saxon tower of the parochial church next to the palace of the archbishops, with its halls, kitchen, stables and servant quarters. The archbishop, no less than a king, would be conscious of the pull and the power of the sea far more keenly here, than when he slept a dozen miles inland at Canterbury.

The tide drove high water up the Thames, twice in every twenty four hours, to bring the commerce of the world to London and to challenge London to set forth to seek more. It was so easy: wait for the tide to flow outward and it would carry you and your wares to sea. With this perception of elemental forces that must be working upon the human psyche, to underpin and to challenge any rational evaluation that a king might make of the benefits of an Irish expedition on a purely rational basis of computation, Martin formed a conviction – which he found strangely gloomy, even doom-laden – that the Irish venture would indeed be pursued.

Gutrin brought his boat close to the uppermost exposed step of a ramshackle wooden stair, and Martin jumped on to the still wet and slippery surface. Gutrin pulled back, looking for spot where he could rest on his oars in the time that the monk was at his business in the palace. The waterman envied some of the goings-on to which he took the burghers of London in Southwark, but he could not even begin to contemplate the sort of thing that the likes of Martin might engage in at West Minster or here in this gloomy complex of buildings. So he would dream of home, of a warm fire and a full belly, of his children growing up to prosperity, and of remaining fit to ply his trade for many years to come.

Martin crossed the shingle bank and a riverside lane to the open gate in the palisade surrounding the primate's palace. Small wooden turrets had been built at each side of the entrance, more to emphasise the importance of the premises than for defence. The Archbishop and his predecessors clearly took the view that this was not a defensible site; if an archbishop were in danger he had castles to which he could flee.

In times of peace, such as King Henry's reign was well set to be, the palace provided a comfortable base from which the archbishop could make his contribution to the counsels that the King received. In sight of West Minster Palace, but discreetly on the opposite bank of the river, the archbishop's base signified his position at court: close to the crown, but with a clear measure of independence. As the river flowed between Lambeth and West Minster, so the clear difference between ecclesiastical and civil authority perpetually distinguished the archbishop from others of the king's close council.

A man at arms at the gate greeted the Benedictine by name, though incorrectly:

"You Martin of Bells Gate? ... He's waiting for you. Over the court, in the new palace!"

The man pointed to a stone hall. As Martin approached, a priest came to meet him:

"Father Martin? ... I'm so glad! He's been getting crotchety ... He is awfully nice to everybody in words, but his looks are lethal and the servants are terrified. Someone's likely to get a whipping when he is really being polite! ... Be careful how you handle him, if it's not good news!"

Martin forbore to ask what would constitute good news. He guessed that the staff here at Lambeth knew nothing of their master's recent activities, and little of his current principal concerns.

The chaplain led Martin up a flight of steps to the raised floor level of the new hall, and through the doorway with its elaborate dogtooth-carved stone arch. Although the day was quite warm, a fire burned in the hearth. All the shutters were open, giving brightness to the room, and the archbishop was seated at the large table with the fire behind his high-backed chair:

"Ah, Father Martin! Approach!"

The archbishop handled diffident visitors and new acquaintances by giving them explicit instructions, while smiling that ambiguous smile. It was not a treacherous smile, as Father Athanasius of Paris had had; it was undoubtedly meant to convey reassurance and priestly empathy, but behind the smile the eyes were restless, searching, demanding – almost countermanding the soft surface look and the kindly words that accompanied it.

Martin approached, and knelt to kiss the archbishop's ring, then obeyed the instruction to sit. A servant poured wine from the ewer on the table into a waiting goblet before him, then brought a plate piled with cuts of meat, setting them next to the wine. Then he backed away and Martin realised that this interview was to be conducted in strict confidence; the chaplain and all the servants had left the room.

"Eat, Brother! It is past dinner time, and you have had no opportunity for a repast," said Theobald.

Martin realised that it would be unwise to take a mouthful, as he would surely be asked a question immediately, so he took a sip of wine – and heard his host enquire:

"Are you acquainted with the Chancellor of England?"

Martin held his eyes in the line that they faced, avoiding raising his glance to meet the Archbishop's gaze.

"I saw him, once, at West Minster," answered Martin,

"Good!"

Theobald seemed to relax. When Rulf le Court had told his tale about the head at the hermitage to a small circle of the faction who favoured positive action in Ireland, Theobald had discovered that the king knew of the preceptor of Bellins Gate. Theobald knew that the king could be as devious as any subject – while Henry reposed full confidence in Becket to bring the country uniformly into submission to the king's justice, he retained close links with old courtiers who showed antipathy to Becket and had even made a few new friends from among those who indicated a similar tendency.

Martin's extremely low-key response to the Archbishop's question was enough to convince Theobald that Martin was no agent or affiliate of Becket, who Theobald felt had betrayed his trust in becoming a close confidant of the king. The bishops suspected that Becket's intentions included some attenuation of the rights and immunities of the church, under English law; and they were already preparing arguments and alliances against the time when he took a positive move in this direction. Theobald's purpose in assessing whether or not Martin was under Becket's influence was to ensure that the plan involving Oskar did not become known to the Chancellor.

Until Oskar was safely out of the country, Becket could have him arrested and dispatched, then face out with the King any problem that the execution might cause to the proponents of the invasion of Ireland. Once Oskar was out of the country, his value lay partly in returning regularly with confidential information for the war party in

England: again, he could be endangered if Becket knew of his role and discovered anything of his movements. Theobald had no doubt that among the thronging population of the capital city there were those who had been associates of Becket *père* and would willingly gather information for his son. Hence it was highly desirable that only Bisset, the le Courts and a friendly preceptor of Bellins Gate shared Theobald's secret about Oskar. The king must be told, but at a time and in circumstances that minimised Becket's chances of becoming privy to it and undermining the plan. Theobald was quietly confident that the Lordship of All Ireland was a prize that the restless, ambitious young king would not reject, but it could take several years to bring him to the point, and anything that could be done in the meanwhile to precipitate the Irish situation into greater chaos would make the fruit seem more ripe for the plucking, and less costly to access.

Theobald listened attentively as Martin briefly recounted the events that had taken place at the Wardrobe after the archbishop's departure. Theobald then urged him to eat, and withdrew through a door at the end of the hall. The servants returned, and went about various tasks while keeping an eye open for any requirement of their master's guest. Martin found his appetite to be small, and he declined a further goblet of wine. He sat and wondered how long he would be expected to wait for the return of his host. Then the chaplain entered in a stately manner, approached Martin's chair and announced that he was ready to escort him to the gate.

Obviously Theobald, once he had extracted what he required from the conversation, had moved on to deal with the business from his Surrey estates that had accumulated during his sojourn with the king. Martin's service to him was complete, and the Benedictine was pushed to the back of the primate's mind to be used again, as and when it suited the archbishop's purposes to do so.

The chaplain was amiable enough on the brief walk to the exit, but he was merely carrying out his master's bidding and made no attempt to excuse the discourtesy of the host.

At West Minster stairs, Gutrin exchanged strong language with watermen who were blocking the landing, but at length Martin set foot on land and Gutrin again pulled away to find a spot where he could secure the boat for the hour or more that the preceptor estimated that he would be closeted with his superiors.

The porter's greeting to the preceptor of Bellins Gate indicated that an embellished account of his activities on the river on the previous morning had reached the abbey. The servants grinned at him as he passed them on the way to the prior's lodgings. Two of his fellow monks similarly smiled as they greeted him, though a third gave him a disapproving stare.

At the prior's lodging the servant who answered Martin's knock on the door also smiled, but was sufficiently professional – or scared of his master – to avoid any comment. The prior's amanuensis, Brother Gandolphus, came to greet Martin in the antechamber:

"Ah! Brother preceptor ... and the guardian of London Bridge, as well as of our own modest *porte!*" His words could have been ironical or even carried a sneer, but such was the rapport that events had brought about between these two essentially differing characters that the intention to express good humour was unmistakable.

"He'll see you now!" said Gandolphus. "I've been sent out, with an errand; but I'll be back before you leave!"

The slightly skittish way in which Gandolphus spoke of his service to the prior again raised in Martin the question as to the basis of his relationship with the prior. It was almost such a remark as the women of a house would address to a visitor. But Prior Osbert's absolute commitment to chastity was well known. Martin again consigned the question to the 'too difficult' portion of his memory, and knocked once on the oak door to the Prior's inner sanctum:

"Come!"

As Martin entered the room, a servant came up behind him with wine, bread and fruit, a more frugal meal than the archbishop had offered him, but a sign that Osbert – like Theobald – had worked out that Martin had had no opportunity over the midday period to take any dinner.

Martin accepted the invitation to sit, accepted wine – Osbert would otherwise have been offended – and took a piece of dried apple.

"You have not come to tell me boating stories I am sure!" began the prior.

Martin smiled.

"I dare say that what has come to us is much exaggerated. If you had either been endangered, or massively heroic, the stories would have greater realism!" Osbert returned Martin's smile, then sat, with his hands characteristically folded and his big bald head glistening in the light from the window, waiting for Martin to tell him the reason for his visit.

"I suppose, Father, I have come to seek your permission – retrospectively – to spend quite a lot of money on shipping a refugee and another family back to Ireland."

"To Ireland." Osbert repeated the words in a slightly surprised tone, as he might have used had Martin sent the people to the moon.

Martin explained how Fulk and his family had come, as refugees, by way of the Bellins Gate *porte* last year, how Fulk had remained homesick and that a fortuitous opportunity had arisen to help him, "and, perhaps, help the king to keep his options open, on Ireland".

"Here your story interest me greatly," said the prior. "I assumed that it must connect to a certain issue of state. In order that you may tell me the facts in a manner that I find coherent, let me tell you my position. Edward the Confessor was a man of peace. Defensive battles must be fought, of course: that is the way of the world, but the Saint Edward teaches us that aggression – in territorial, as in sexual matters – is sinful. Rape is rape!"

Martin wondered how far Osbert said these things for effect, and how far his obvious obsession with sexual purity invaded his thinking about other areas of life. He seemed sincere, and his determination to secure the canonisation of Edward the Confessor was so transparent that to refer to Edward in any contest was tantamount to saying that he meant his point absolutely.

Martin decided that Osbert was declaring an antiwar stance – at least until the king decided in favour of an invasion or until Osbert convinced himself that the establishment of the feudal system in Ireland would end an era of rape and murder. So Martin told Osbert the full tale of the past few days, emphasising how Fulk's return of the charter to Galway would help to keep the field clear for the king to decide whether or not to obey the papal and primatal admonitions to seize Ireland.

Osbert needed the favour of papacy to get Edward the Confessor canonised, so he would not speak out against any papal ruling openly, but Pope Hadrian had recently gone to his final judgement, and his Italian successor would surely have many priorities that he ranked higher than the pretensions of the See of Canterbury to control the Irish ports' religious affairs. The new pope would not repudiate Hadrian's grant of the Lordship of Ireland to the most powerful ruler in western Europe, but he might be rather relieved if it became a dead letter, along with so many other nugatory grants and requests of past pontiffs. The cause of King Edward was transcendental to the prior, and he would do anything within his power to keep that case in the forefront of the relationship between England and the Holy See.

"I do not presume to enquire into affairs of state, Father: but when it is placed in my hands to decide some little thing that may be a pawn in the great game, I try to act in the manner that best conduces to safety." Martin hoped that this did not sound smug, or prim.

The prior propped the hinges of his jaws on the base of his two thumbs, his elbows on the table surface and his forefingers caressing his cheeks. He beamed towards Martin and said:

"You are evidently an apt pupil. You have understood one of life's important lessons: if there is doubt about the wisdom of a proposed course of action: delay decision. And if one's role is modestly to assist the mighty, then the prolongation of the status quo is always preferable to precipitating activity – unless a complete pre-emption of the situation is possible. I think it would be ... unfortunate ... if the king was ever to know that the Galway Charter had been at Bellins Gate ... most unfortunate ... ever ... Do you think that your fellow, Fulk, will appreciate this?"

"I do, Father. He would prefer the impression to be maintained that the Galway Charter was ever at Galway," said Martin.

"As it should, most certainly, have been," agreed Osbert. "And Fulk's family, who have stayed in London?"

"Have every reason not to draw attention to themselves," said Martin.

"Indeed yes! ... And Rulf le Court – and his wife – know nothing of the charter?"

"Nothing, Father."

"The hermit?"

"Cannot read, and did not see the unfurled document anyhow," said Martin.

"So there is Brother Elias – on whom we can both rely, and you, who have managed this business quite satisfactorily ... Yes: I do authorise the expenditure that you have committed to ... er ... to ensure that the charter remains in its proper place, at Galway. And now tell me what really happened at London Bridge yesterday. I am bound to be asked about it, as it has become quite a sensation."

Martin gave a brief summary, while Osbert read his expression carefully:

"Becket's London sources will certainly report the incident to him. You must expect a visit from the Chancellor of England, when next he deigns to visit the capital ... May I suggest that you suppress your natural modesty, and give him a somewhat vainglorious account of the events. Make exaggerated statements about the proximity of the fireship to the bridge and the fragility of the vessels that made the rescue. If he thinks you vain, and limited in percipience, he will find that consistent with his mental picture of a man who takes physical risks. If he should gauge your real character, and find you materially resourceful as well as perceptive, he will target you as a potential antagonist. You will be watched, and that could limit severely your usefulness to me and to Abbot Gervais – we who know that we are likely at any time to be under observation by the king's enemies, and the king's friends, for that matter!"

Osbert sighed, ever so slightly: the smug sigh of one who frequently reminds himself and others of the exceptionally elevated birth that ensured that his activities would always be of interest to somebody.

Martin suppressed a smile at Osbert's unusual failure to speak of the interest of the abbey rather than of its principal officers. Osbert saw the muscular tension in the younger man's face, and declared his recognition of the cause of it:

"You are quite right, Brother! I do normally speak – and mean properly to speak – of the interests of our House, to which we are all dedicated within the wider community of the Benedictine Order and of Holy Church herself: but you also understand that I do have a role in the affairs of state that is partly derived from my personal position. Some would say that my occupation of my post here is due to the origins that I cannot repudiate. I cannot agree with that patronising calumny, and you are too wise to make any comment on it – even by gesture."

Having picked Martin up for his body language, Osbert was now telling him that it would not be held against him if he relaxed a little and involuntarily let some spontaneous reaction be manifest.

Instead of accepting that opportunity, Martin decided to risk Osbert's wrath by asking:

"The archbishop asked me about Becket; and now you warn me of him, Father. Is his threat increasing?"

Osbert's face stiffened. He calculated visibly and decided to be indulgent, but only to a limited extent:

"He threatens nothing. He is intermittently discourteous: but so are many great and good men. One must admire his apparently total dedication to the king, even if one deprecates his failure to proceed to priest's orders and to serve his church as well as his king ... You know, as well as I do, Brother, that the threat – as you call it – is the unknown! One has the feeling, in his presence, that he has no real empathy with any man. His wolf – a dog that has the look and the manner of a wolf – is said to be his only close companion. He rides and drinks and goes whoring with the king, but there he is a shadow only; he follows the king and does what he thinks the king wishes him to do. Is that a threat?"

If Martin had ventured a reply, Osbert would have weighed it carefully before disagreeing with some part of the argument advanced. That was his familiar technique when he was bored with a conversation, or felt a subordinate was tending to impertinence.

A faint tap on the door indicated the return of Gandolphus; he would not enter unless told so to do when the prior was conversing with a visitor.

"Come!" said Osbert, very quietly and with a twinkle in his eye. Gandolphus' ears would have had to be very particularly attuned to his master's voice to hear the word through the solid oak door. It opened instantly nevertheless and the monk entered, looking expectantly towards the prior. Would he learn what had been the business that brought Martin to the abbey? Gandolphus knew his man well enough to be sure that Martin had not come to retail tales of derring-do on the Thames; had Martin done so, Osbert would have evicted him from his chamber long before this.

"Gandolphus, pray make a memorandum for Brother Celarer, to note that the preceptory of Bellins Gate has by my order expended twenty pounds on a matter of charity for the relief of refugees."

Gandolphus was as sure that this was true, as he was convinced that the truth was told with extreme economy. He knew from Osbert's phraseology and expression that no more would be said of it, so he guessed that it was a matter of state and a matter of delicacy.

Martin must, he surmised, again have stumbled into some complex matter, and handled it in a manner that Father Prior considered satisfactory – for the time being. But should it turn out unfortunately, when failure became manifest the prior would distance himself absolutely from what Martin had done. Martin would then have to take the full responsibility for his action and keep all the blame well away from this abbey and its principal officers.

Gandolphus would like to know what it was all about, but he knew that the prior would expect him not to know so that, if needed, he could swear to ignorance with a bland smile and total conviction.

"Shall I write the memorandum now, Father?" he asked.

"After you have escorted our preceptor to the door, yes, my son." Osbert's tone struck his acolyte as patronising; he was gloating at having another secret that was not for sharing with his closest associate, and Gandolphus had no comeback. The power of the prior was absolute, both in the formal structure of the abbey and in his ability to exclude Gandolphus from his favoured position at the prior's side. Martin saw the situation clearly, and gave silent thanks that he occupied neither of these men's positions hierarchically or personally. The relationship was surely celibate, sexually, which made the intellectual and emotional interplay between the participants all the more intense.

Martin took the reference to being shown to the door as his dismissal, and stood up.

Osbert smiled towards him:

"Send word to Stebenhithe, to the priest, to expect a funeral, and to your friends at Chad's Well, to deliver the remains ... I suppose the crabbing season is over, at the hermitage?"

"Yes, Father." Martin's answer covered the question together with the instructions.

Introduction

I feel that this book is long overdue.

As a parent *Scout Leader Badge Book* is based on a personal perception of what, in my experience, leaders could be up to when the kids are doing their own badge work if they weren't the professional and hard-working volunteers that they are.

Why should the young people be having all the fun? Whilst they're earning their badges the grown-ups could be busy earning theirs. The great advantage of this to leaders is that there is no one to tell them that they haven't done enough to earn a particular badge; at the end of the day it's entirely down to them! If they feel they've earned it then they should be able to have it. Everyone knows that leaders' kids get all the badges so why shouldn't the leaders have a chance also?

One last thing - *Scout Leader Badge Book* is not meant to be taken too seriously. It's just a bit of fun. We all love our leaders dearly and greatly appreciate what you do. If you do take offence then I would respectfully suggest that you probably shouldn't be working with young people for I'm sure, given the chance, they would be trying to earn some of these badges for themselves. Now there's an idea!

Karen

"Success in training the boy depends largely on the Scoutmaster's own personal example."
Robert Baden-Powell

ANGLER

Angling is great hobby for a scout leader. It gets you out of all those interminable meetings with the hierarchy. Just tell them that you've had to go and do a risk assessment on something or other and off you go. You don't need to buy any expensive equipment, just a small tent (which you can borrow from the scout hut but make sure that you have all the poles and pegs) and a camp chair.

To gain your badge

1. Find a pond or small stretch of water. This could be in your garden but it should be somewhere where you can't easily be found so best to be a little further away.

2. Erect your tent on the bank. Place it so that the entrance is right on the water's edge. This prevents any unwelcome visitors from coming round the front and looking inside and seeing what fishing tackle you have, or more likely don't have.

3. If this makes it difficult for you to enter and exit easily then turn the tent around so that the entrance is facing away from the pond. Enter the tent and with a sharp knife cut a door shape in the far end.

4. If you have them, spread a few tin boxes around the outside of the tent, a flask and a packed lunch wrapped in greaseproof paper or foil.

5. Open the camp chair and put it in the tent facing the pond or stretch of water. Sit on chair.

6. Remain in tent for at least four hours before collapsing chair and tent.

7. Return home via Tesco's having bought some fish.
8. Don't forget to duck tape up the tent before returning it or just hide it under the other tents. No one will notice.

Notes
You may use a pop up tent but you will never be able to sit in it, nor will you ever get it back down again.
Make sure that you buy fresh whole fish. Scampi and other breaded fish, seafood or cod in a bag of parsley sauce will arouse suspicions.

ARSONIST

Setting fire to stuff is one of the highlights of being a scout leader.

To gain your badge
There are two alternatives. Select one of them and complete all the tasks.

Alternative One
Accidental
Either
1. Throw a container of something on the camp fire with the intention of extinguishing it. Suitable containers would be a fire bucket, bottle or mug and the contents have to look like they are water but are in fact petrol because someone couldn't find the correct container.
2. Do not try to find anything to extinguish the furnace that you have created. Run away and let someone else deal with it.
3. The furnace has to set light to something accidentally so make sure that there is a flammable object nearby that can be incinerated. This could include a camp chair, table, woodpile or even a tent - especially if it's one that the scouts are going to be sleeping in.
Or
1. If it's a particularly hot summer, build a camp fire in a wood especially where there is a thick pile of dead leaves.
2. Ideally the fire should burn the wood down completely so once the fire is lit leave it unattended and go off on a hike or similar activity that will take you temporarily away from the area.

Alternative Two
Intentional

Set fire to something that you can justify with, "I just wanted to see if it burned," or "I just wanted to see what it looked like." Whilst it may be more satisfying to set light to a building it is sufficient to set light to something that is considered of value to some but is, in fact, worthless. This could include risk assessments, safeguarding reports or anything dreamt up by a committee.

Notes
Never intentionally set fire to people or animals (unless they are dead.)

Never set fire to dead people (unless you work in a crematorium), just dead animals and then only after they have been prepared for a grill, pan (frying or sauce), spit, barbecue or oven.

ARTIST

This is a particularly common badge for a scout leader to gain because it is not a difficult one to achieve. Many scout leaders gain this badge after a very short while. Most are artists of the highest order before becoming leaders. Those that aren't soon become them. No painting or drawing or other creative ability is needed.

To gain your badge
There are three alternatives. Select one of them.

Alternative One
This badge will be awarded automatically in conjunction with any other badge that has been correctly carried out.

Alternative Two
Attend a Leaders Only camp for at least one night.

Alternative Three
Drink an excessive amount* of alcohol before leading a scout meeting. This must be carried out on three occasions, ideally in consecutive weeks.

Notes
* "Excessive amount" would normally be defined as that which results in the scout leader not being able to stand unaided.

ASTRONAUTICS

Space travel and exploration continue to make scout leaders yawn but for those few who are interested in the physical universe beyond the earth's atmosphere this is the badge for you. Gaining this badge is a fantastic achievement and you will always wear it with pride.

To gain your badge
1. Explain what the verb "To moon" means. Give a practical example to a scout.
2. Pronounce "Uranus" correctly at a scout meeting without smiling. This must be in the context of astronautics and not as part of the scouts' Hygiene or Know your Body badges.
3. Explain why a famous vocalist (now deceased) in a rock band named Queen may have had a planet named after him.
4. Be able instantly to tell a scout whether the moon is waxing or waning. (You don't have to be correct, you just have to sound as if you know. If the scout contradicts you and is likely to be correct tell them that you are long-sighted cross-eyed and beyond only a few feet images are laterally-inversed.)
5. Suggest a name for a new planet that is offensive but credible.
6. Ask a scout, "What planet are you on?" without smiling. Ideally ask the scout that looks most like someone from another universe.

7. Point to a bright star in the night sky and tell the scouts that it is the International Space Station. Best to make sure that it is at least moving.

8. Get most of the scouts to wave at the International Space Station. If you are asked if they can be seen tell them that they have very good telescopes on board.

9. Let off a firework, preferably a rocket, without you or any of the scouts saying, "Wheeeeeee!"

Notes
If you do 9. indoors then you do not have to do the other requirements.

ASTROLOGER

As this badge is often confused with **Astronomer** badge they are now interchangeable. That is to say, if you fulfil the requirements of **Astrologer** you can gain **Astronomer** and vice-versa.

To gain your badge
There are two alternatives. Select one of them.

Alternative One
Use a telescope to gaze at the sun. Ideally only do this once and with only one eye.

Alternative Two
1. Use a telescope to gaze at the stars. You may have to set your telescope up outside Harrods or Harvey Nichols (daytime) or any London nightclub (night-time).
2. Identify at least three stars (minimum B-list) and their surface finishes e.g. lipstick colour, tanning level (real or fake), any exposed areas, any sparkly bits.
3. Get a sample of each star using scissors without causing any long-term damage to the subject and without getting arrested.

Notes
Any "London nightclub" does not include establishments in an SE, SW or NW postcode.

ASTRONOMER

As this badge is often confused with **Astronomer** badge they are now interchangeable. That is to say, if you fulfil the requirements of **Astronomer** you can gain **Astrologer** and vice-versa.

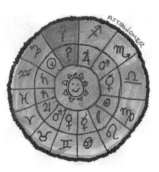

To gain your badge

1. Explain why there are thirteen signs in the Zodiac but only twelve for the purposes of astronomy.
2. Ask the scouts what their star sign is and if they don't know assign them one of the following without asking for their date of birth: Scaries, Sorarse, Goldeneye, Canker, Lielow, Vertigo, Leaveher, Scorethepoo, Saggytarius, Crapricorn, Hilarious and Piesneeze.
3. Think of at least twenty-four words that can be used as characteristics and assign them to the scouts. Two per sign. Include words such as fat, lazy, incompetent, smelly, unloved.
4. Make at least one scout cry by using the words from 3. If you are in the unlikely situation of having no success then you will need to think of some more.
5. Write out twelve horoscopes for the day that you are doing this badge. You will need to see into the future or just make them up and assign them to one of the star signs. An example would be, "You are going to come into some money. Make sure that you spend it wisely because you are likely to want to fritter it away."
6. Check up one week later to see if any of the horoscopes have come true. If they have then you will need to try again until they don't.

ATHLETICS

Keeping yourself fit and feeling healthy is achieved for the greater part by immersing yourself in track, field and team events.

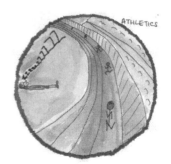

To gain your badge

1. Choose up to three of the following disciplines:

FIELD	TRACK	TEAM
Discus	10,000 metres	4×100 metres relay
Hammer	100 metres	4×400 metres relay
Heptathlon	100 metres hurdles	
High jump	110 metres hurdles	
Javelin throw	200 metres	
Long jump	400 metres hurdles	
Marathon	400 metres	
Pole vault	800 metres	
Shot put	1500 metres	
Triple jump	3000 metres steeplechase	
	5000 metres	

2. Find your local athletics club or ask one of the scouts.
3. Choose a nice sunny afternoon, preferably in summer and go to the club.
4. Locate a pleasing grassy knoll in a quiet corner.
5. Do some warm-up exercises with a newspaper, book or smartphone.
6. Sit or lie down and watch your chosen discipline(s) for at least an hour.

Notes

It may well be that if you attempt 6. after a good lunch you may well fall asleep. This does not matter and in fact is encouraged.

ATHLETICS PLUS

As the name implies you can only attempt this badge if you hold the **Athletics** badge.

To gain your badge
Building on the **Athletics** badge you need to choose up to three disciplines but not the one(s) previously chosen and carry out the requirements as before but you must watch for at least two hours and you MUST be asleep for most of that time.

BALDING

This is easier for some male scout leaders but this should not put the females off from attempting this badge.

To gain your badge
Keep a check on your pate and when you notice balding on the hairline or on top of the head you must show one of the scouts and get them to touch it to verify that you are going bald.

Notes
If you are female or balding has yet to commence and you wish to earn this badge you can hurry it along through the application of Immac or some other proprietary hair removal cream. However, if hair grows back the badge will have to be surrendered. To avoid this process happening several times and for a more permanent solution you will need to use electrolysis.

BARBECUE

This is a very popular badge but plenty of work has to be done before it can be awarded. There is however no need to go to any great lengths to prepare for this badge.

To gain your badge

1. Get yourself invited to a barbecue. This may be by one of your friends or if they are in short supply try a local church or club or society during the summer.

2. Get to the event early and offer to do a turn on the grill. If the host declines your invitation go into the garden or wherever the barbecue is situated and start to fiddle with the tools. In view of the opposition that you may encounter it is always a good idea to bring a set of cooking implements with you. These should include as a minimum a spatula, a fork and a pair of tongs.

3. If the heat source has yet to be lit, do it. It will most likely be either gas or charcoal. Familiarise yourself with both methods beforehand or ask someone, but not a male as they may try to take over.

4. With the barbecue lit continue to look busy. When more guests arrive send one of them into the kitchen area to get the meat. Spoken to with authority the guest will not think to question your request, nor will they ask the host. A compliant guest will take it upon themselves to find the meat, even looking in a fridge on their quest to be helpful. By this time the host will be getting too occupied with guests arriving as well as salads and accompaniments to be taking too much notice.

5. If using gas, turn it up full, if charcoal, make sure that it is still flaming.

6. With tongs in one hand and spatula in the other, start with the chicken and flash cook it - no more than one minute. Gas will give the skin a black colour, charcoal will coat the chicken with carbon. These are both signs of a successful barbecue.

7. By now someone should have brought you a drink. If not ask another guest to get you one. If you already have a drink ask for another one. This should continue at regular intervals. If anyone question how many drinks you've had ask someone else. If this is not possible tell the querying person that working the barbecue is hot work.

8. You can now add all the other meat to the barbecue. Throw it on then space it out so that it looks very neat, separating sausages, chops, ribs etc.

9. Keep patting the meat with the tongs and the spatula. You don't have to do anything more. Do not turn anything over as this may encourage someone to think that something is cooked.

10. Add some herbs for flavour. You should be able to find some in the garden or again use a compliant guest. If you can't find any use any shrub or flower that is nearby.

11. You may find a small group of men gather around you. This is fine but do not put the tongs or spatula down otherwise you may soon find yourself out of a job.

12. If anyone asks when the meat will be ready tell them that the chicken's done and give them a piece. They won't trouble you further.

13. Now is a good time to let someone else take over. Do not ask for anyone just quietly announce that you're popping to the toilet and will be back in a minute. When you return you will find several people tending to the

barbecue. One will have the spatula, one will have the tongs and at least one will be poking the fire with a stick, even if it's gas. They will also have turned all the meat over. Tell them it doesn't look very well done.

14. Leave the barbecue area and go and tell the host that several people have been sick. With luck you may get your job back.

15. Under no circumstances is it necessary to offer to clean the barbecue. This is a disgusting job and should be left to a scout.

BEER

This is often a very difficult badge for some scout leaders to attain. The main reason appears to be that they try too hard. Approach this badge, as with the others, with determination and tenaciousness but without going "over the top."

To gain your badge

1. Identify the different types of glass for beer. These may include pint (UK only), tankard (may be pewter), mug, stein (Europe and pretentious London beer kellers), goblet, tulip, pilsner and plastic (violent pubs and international scout camps).
2. Select a beer that would be ideally suited to each of the glasses that you have identified.
3. If possible, visit a public house in order to experience putting the selected beers in the identified glasses.
4. Sample the beer.
5. Try putting the incorrect beer in the selected glasses.
6. Sample the beer.
7. You may find that having a spirit before the beer enhances the taste of the beer. Choose a popular chaser such as tequila, rum or whiskey.
8. Sample the spirit. All of it. Then the chaser.
9. Try the selected bears after the spirits in a identified gloss.
10. Try putting the incoherent bear in the incoherent glass and chase it.
11. Tell the barmaid that she looks pretty.

12. Go home or back to the campsite. Try to remain on two legs.

Notes

The above does not apply to male leaders who are mostly exempt from having to earn this badge as most will have already earned it whilst a scout.

BIRTHDAY

You don't achieve this badge simply by having a birthday. That would be silly! Instead, read through the requirements and see if you can meet the rigorous tasks. If so then you're definitely deserving of the badge that everyone should have but many don't achieve.

To gain your badge
1. Know when your birthday is and tell someone. (Real birthday, not the one that you've put on Facebook.)
2. Act your age.
3. If a scout meeting falls on your birthday, cancel it unless someone promises to bring a cake. You may want e.g. Mandy's mum (or dad) to give you one but if you get one from e.g. Mandy herself then you must say "Thank you" and eat it without grimacing.
4. Get the scouts to sing "Happy Birthday" to you and smile throughout.
5. For your scout meeting nearest your birthday take everyone to the local pub (in the summer this can include the beer garden) and buy everyone a pint of lager shandy with alcohol-free lager. This won't just look funny (which is something that is acceptable on your birthday) but may, if you're lucky, result in a flying visit from the police. This will mean that the scouts will be able to complete some of their Emergency Aid badge at the same time as you do yours.

Notes
Always carry a breathalyser kit for this badge as there will always be several scouts who will tell their parents on pick-up that they are drunk. Mind you, they might be if you give them your drink by mistake.

BOOT BURNING

To gain your badge
There are two alternatives. Select one of them and complete all the tasks.

Alternative One
Accidental
Sit in front of the camp fire once the scouts have gone to bed and stretch your legs out. Your boots do not have to be wet but you may have to explain what you've been doing all day if they're not. It may be that your boots are genuinely wet after a day hike through the undergrowth and they need to be dried out. More likely you are relaxing after a good dinner (i.e. not one that originated in the mess tent, camp fire or anywhere else on the campsite). You may be fiddling with some of the logs although a stave or other long stout stick would be preferable. Wait until another leader points out that your boots are smoking. Say, "That's just the steam coming off," but you know that they're alight because the other leader either throws a bucket of water over your feet or they come over and pull your seat out from under you then pull you away.

Alternative Two
Intentional
1. Select a pair of boots to burn. You may burn one boot if it comes from a new pair.
2. Put them on and sit near to the camp fire. If you have borrowed a pair from a scout and they don't fit simply put them next to you by the fire and keep bringing them closer.

3. Slowly get as close to the fire as you can without it being too uncomfortable and stretch out your legs. It's a good idea for you to undo the laces just in case matters get out of hand and you have to take them off quickly.

4. When they start to smoke wait for another leader to tell you that it looks as though your feet are alight. At this point kick them off and into the fire with a lot of screaming and shouting. This way, not only will you gain the badge but you will also be able to claim a new pair of boots on the camp insurance with plenty of witnesses to the "accident."

5. If you have borrowed a pair and you are not wearing them, continue to push them nearer the fire. Eventually they will catch fire, especially if you have filled them with some vegetable oil, a few firelighters or some paraffin that has been siphoned from the Tilley lamps.

BREAKFAST

It is not important who makes your breakfast, just that you eat it. If you can't eat it you can't function probably. Many scout leaders do eat it but still can't function properly. This is probably because they're waiting for lunch. This badge will normally be earned on camp. You cannot earn it, under normal circumstances, at home.

To gain your badge

1. Wait until all the scouts are gathered in the mess tent for breakfast then ask them what their favourite cereal is.
2. When they have told you, and the answer will mostly be "Coco Pops," ask them if they are allowed to eat them at home.
3. When they have told you, and the answer will mostly be "No," produce a packet, preferably the one kilo size, open it, pour yourself a large bowl, add a load of milk and start to eat before announcing, "Then you're not going to start here either."
4. When you have finished your bowl, unless you want another bowl, go and put the rest of the packet in your tent.
5. It is usual to have a cooked breakfast on camp. It is not expected that scout leaders prepare it, that is why parents are invited on camp; all you have to do is make sure that it tastes okay. For this reason it is important that you do not serve the scouts first, let *them* have the scrambled egg scrapings, the burnt sausage, the bacon bits and the

hardened beans. You go first and make sure that it is all edible. Eat it if it is.

6. If it isn't give it to one of the scouts. They won't notice that you've eaten half the sausage.

7. Don't forget a couple of slices of bread. It has to be white sliced otherwise it doesn't count. Use one slice to wrap something in such as the sausage, the egg or the bacon, maybe all three. Do not wrap the Coco Pops. That doesn't count either. Use the other slice for wiping around your plate when you've finished.

8. Make sure that you drink a cup of tea although a cup is the last thing that it will actually be served in and tea is the last thing it will actually taste like. It will be a mug at the very least or any kind of drinks bottle except glass.

9. The mug / drinks bottle should be personalised with "Chief Scout" or "Tiny's mug - hands off." If not write something on with a Sharpie. Even if it has already you can always cross it off.

10. Leave the washing up for the parent helpers. Pop back to your tent for a quick nap after you've cleared up all the Coco Pops that one of the scouts will have poured down your sleeping bag.

BRIGHT IDEA

Bright ideas are always welcomed in scouting. Make your voice heard and gain this badge.

BRIGHT IDEA

To gain your badge

1. Have a bright idea.
2. Communicate it to someone who doesn't laugh.
3. Put your bright idea into action. This should be over several weeks.

Notes

Your idea doesn't have to be particularly bright but if it is, once you have gained your badge, you can forget it again.

THIS BADGE HAS BEEN DISCONTINUED

BUNGEE JUMPING

Gain this badge and you'll be the envy of your fellow scout leaders! With a few basic materials you will be able to have hours of fun with the most incredible adrenaline rushes!

To gain your badge

1. Obtain a length of elasticated rope or other thick cord. Ideally you will need at least two hundred feet. If you use standard polypropylene rope you will ideally have 20mm thickness as a minimum. If not it is essential that you do your jump over water, otherwise wear a helmet.
2. Furthermore, if using polypropylene rope you will need to have some elasticity built in to avoid a dead stop. Cut the rope in at least two places and tie in lengths of bicycle inner tube using a reef knot as this is the simplest.
3. Tie one end of the rope around your waist using a clove hitch.
4. Find a bridge or climb a crane. You will find many cranes dotted around various parts of the country, especially London. If you are some way from London consider staying overnight in one the parks as part of your unofficial Survival badge.
5. Tie the other end to part of the crane or the bridge railing using a knot of your choosing. Jump.
6. If nothing happens, you have tied the wrong end. Untie it and tie the other end. Jump.
7. If the bridge or crane is high enough you should bounce. If you have used a bicycle inner tube you may find that you bounce back to higher than where you started from. If you

don't bounce but just keep on going you have probably untied your clove hitch instead of the knot of your choosing. It would be suggested that in this case you may like to have another attempt but it may be a bit late.
8. If your jump is successful and you are conscious lower yourself to the ground using a penknife to cut the rope above your head. Aim to land / enter the water on your feet.

BURPING

Master the art of burping, especially
in a confined space! Use a foodstuff
for assistance, such as a carbonated
drink or airy food including apples
or a soufflé.

To gain your badge
1. Open your mouth and suck from your throat. Pull until
you feel an air bubble enter your throat.
2. With your mouth still open let the air bubble rise. You
may need to encourage it by relaxing your lungs.
3. When you feel the air bubble about to emerge reshape
you mouth to make an interesting or unusual sound.
4. Once you have practiced a few sounds move onto
something a little more challenging such as the alphabet or
numbers one to ten or try to make a sentence. Maybe try
saying some strong words and see if the scouts can guess
what you're saying.
5. Once you are proficient teach the scouts. They will thank
you by burping non-stop for the rest of the evening or, if
on camp, for the rest of the weekend including throughout
the night.

Notes
Each time you prepare for a burp you swallow a small
amount of wind. After a very short time you will be
presented with a huge burp that is an accumulation of all
these mini bubbles that you won't be able to control. These
huge burps can often bring with them the contents of your
stomach so for maximum impact practice some burps
straight after eating.

BUSHCRAFT

"Best left to the experts," is what
the bushcraft community will tell
you. Don't listen to them! Anyone
can be a bushcraft expert. There's
more than one way to skin a cat,
that's what we say.

To gain your badge

1. Take a tent and go and spend a night or two in a wild or
uncultivated part of the country. This could be your back
garden or a scout hut grounds. Open a can of beer.
2. Whilst you can sleep in your tent you may wish to
consider cutting it up and making a "bivi" which is a type of
temporary shelter. Drink the can of beer.
3. Set a trap for a wild animal whilst you sleep or bring
something with you. This can be a fillet steak or a chicken
drumstick but it would be better if you had something that
needs preparation such as a whole fish, a pigeon, a
squirrel. If none of these are to hand then consider
bringing a cat, especially if you've killed it first. Or set the
trap and hope that the cat gets caught in it. Sharpen your
knives. Open another can of beer.
4. Build a camp fire and light it. Drink the can of beer.
5. Meanwhile prepare your meal. You will mostly be
plucking in the case of a bird or skinning in the case of a
squirrel. To skin a squirrel hold its nose down and make a
sideways cut below the grommet, aiming for the anus. Cut
through the hide and with your knife feel for a joint in the
spine by the tail and cut through. Step on the tail, hold the
squirrel by its hind legs, and pull in a slow, steady motion.
When you get all the bare meat exposed remove the hide

then the paws and head, then extract the innards. The process is similar for cat. Open another can of beer and drink it. Repeat.

6. As your fire will have now gone out and it will be getting late go and get a take-away. Throw your skinned animal / plucked bird into the undergrowth. It will be gone by morning. And so will you.

CAFFEINE

Get your daily fix and achieve your badge at the same time.

To gain your badge

1. Name two foodstuffs that contain caffeine apart from energy drinks, dark chocolate, Anadin, diet Coke, cough syrup and slimming tablets.
2. Make a drink with what you have found. Alternatively get someone else to make them. To help you identify them, one is found in tea bags and the other rhymes with toffee.
3. When you have made your drink, look around and if anyone is looking at you say, "I'm sorry. I should have asked if you wanted one." Then turn back round.
4. Put it in a reusable mug and carry it around with you for no more than one hour. You do not have to drink the contents.
5. If you are obliged to ask someone if they would like a drink and they reply, "Yes. Do you have any decaf?" always reply, "Yes, of course." Fiddle around with any jars and / or packets that you have at your disposal before making them a caffeinated decaf.
6. Ensure that the caffeinated decaf. is made extra strong then sit back knowing that irritability, sleeplessness and possible anxiety may be triggered as well as causing diarrhoea.

CAMP TOILET

To gain your badge
There are two alternatives. Select one of them and complete the requirements.

Alternative One
1. Use the camp toilet at night after you have been asleep in your tent for a while.
2. Think, "There can't be anyone about at this time of night," then get up and wander down to the toilet in just your underwear.
3. Explain to the night warden who is patrolling the site why you are wandering around in your underwear or shut your eyes, hold your arms out horizontally in front of you and walk straight past the warden moaning softly but ever-so-slightly menacingly.

Alternative Two
1. Stay in your tent and use one of the following: Fizzy drinks bottle, reusable drinks bottle, water carrier, plastic carrier bag, toothbrush holder (make sure that the holes have been taped up).
2. If you can achieve 1. without exiting your sleeping bag then you will not have to complete any further requirements.
3. Transport your container to the nearest bin without being caught. Most can be discreetly wrapped up in a towel but a large plastic fizzy drinks bottle will probably stick out.
4. If questioned by a scout tell them that it's Tizer. If they want to know why you're taking Tizer with you to the toilet

tell them that it's good for settling the stomach after a night sleeping in a tent.

5. Ask them if they would like to have it as you have plenty. Offer them the bottle and if they mention that it's a lighter colour tell them that it's been watered down for greater effect.

CAMPER

One of the mains reasons for scouting, the camper badge is central to its aims and values and is therefore a very important badge to achieve.

To gain your badge

1. Obtain a tent. Ideally you will be sleeping alone if you're male or with another female if you're female. Males usually never share tents with other males, females nearly always share tents with other females. Even if you're male make sure that you have a minimum two-man tent. This is so you can store all your scout leader boys toys stuff. Females don't have so much of this sort of stuff. Apart from hairdryers.
2. Put up the tent. This can be in your garden or someone else's garden although it's best if you know them and / or have told them but it's not essential if they're on holiday. If you do it on the front garden you may receive some unwelcome attention so best to go round the back. You can also use a field or a camp site. If you have trouble erecting your tent you may enlist the help of a scout or two. Scouts should be told that a tent erection should take around twenty minutes and not three hours.
3. Put down a floor for insulation even if you have a groundsheet. This could be rubber matting, rug or fitted carpet; maybe all three.
4. Open up a camp bed and add a mattress.
5. Unroll a foam roll or two and place on top of the mattress.

6. Unroll your sleeping bag and place on top of the foam roll(s).

7. Unroll a duvet and place on top of the sleeping bag.

8. Add a pillow or two.

9. Add a small bar area, a mini-snacks corner, emergency plastic bottle (or Sheewee and Peebol if female), smoking area.

10. Remember that there is space under the camp bed for you to store boys toys stuff such as pen knives, torches (head and hand - two types of each), badges for swapsies, mug, hot water bottle, radio, 'phone and charger and items that you have to bring but won't use - e.g. risk assessments, safeguarding information etc., extra prosecco if you're female.

11. Get into sleeping bag and go to sleep.

12. If you are in charge of scouts they will wake up before you so instruct them before you go to bed on how to use the gas hobs so that they can cook their own breakfast in the morning and give you a bit of a lie-in.

CAR SHARE

This is a badge that the parents can achieve but most don't. Usually they will have no idea until you present it to them.

To gain your badge

1. Read the emails and other correspondence that is for you and which gives you all the information that you need for your scout to have a happy and exciting time on camp or other activity.

2. Do not ring up the scout leader the night before the event and ask where it is or what time you have to be there.

3. When the information suggests that you car share do so. Speak to the other parents and organise how you are going to get the scouts to the meeting place efficiently and with the minimum number of car journeys.

4. Arrive on time and wait until the event is completely finished before collecting your scout and taking them home.

5. Wear or bring suitable footwear for the meeting place so that you can jump out and be ready to offer to help or do anything that you're asked to do.

6. On pick up it is not necessary to ask your scout how they managed to get so muddy and you do not need to ask them why they think it's acceptable to get into your car in such a mess.

CAVER

Explore the delights of an underground world whilst staying firmly on top of it!

To gain your badge

1. Buy a bus. If a double decker - which is preferable - the following applies to both upper and lower decks.
2. Paint all the windows with a black gloss paint.
3. Paint them again.
4. Put scaffolding boards from seat to seat across the aisles then down the aisles on top of the existing boards with a small gap at either end
5. Put scaffolding boards from tops of seats to tops of seats either side of the aisles and then across the aisles all the way down leaving a small gap at either end.
6. Put four courses of bricks on the top level of boards all the way down, one third in from either side to create three channels.
7. Board all the way down the bricks leaving a small gap at the end.
8. Board down the stairs.
9. Paint CAVE BUS on the front and sides in large capital letters.
10. Mark ENTRANCE by one set of doors and EXIT by the other. It doesn't matter if there is only one set of doors because the scouts will normally enter and exit both ways.
11. Tell the scouts to enjoy the caving experience and say that there's plenty of room for all of them whilst you jump in the driver's cab and have forty winks.

12. After one hour go to the back of the bus (you will need a ladder if it's a double decker) and open up the back using the emergency external window.
13. Extract all the scouts.

CHEF

Knowing how to keep yourself and your fellow leaders and the scouts fed and watered is essential for a happy and content scouting experience. With this badge you will feel confident with what you are doing to make it so.

To gain your badge
1. Write up a menu for a weekend's camping.
2. Include the following (which you can add to but is sufficient on its own so why try to reinvent the wheel?):
Scouts:
Breakfast - Coco Pops
Lunch - Spaghetti and sauce
Dinner - Pasta and sauce
Supper - Hot chocolate
Repeat.
Leaders:
Breakfast - Full English from down the road
Lunch - Two pints and / or glass of prosecco from up the road
Dinner - Curry take-away (delivered)
Supper - Leaders' coffee.
3. Know how to ask one of the scouts to put a pan of water on the stove, light it and heat the water so that the lunch and dinner (not breakfast) can been heated up. Supper can be cold.
4. Find a manhole cover, lift it up and pour away all the excess spaghetti / pasta.
5. Using the water from 3. clean the pans.

CIRCUS SKILLS

Being able to entertain your fellow leaders can be difficult. With this badge you will be able to keep them chuckling through to the early hours when the scouts wake up.

To gain your badge

Select two skills from the following list. They should come from different sections and be things that you haven't attempted before. (This includes something that you may have attempted but haven't succeeded in.)

CLOWNING

Showing a scout how to put up a tent that you've never put up yourself before.

Getting into the wrong tent.

Getting into the wrong sleeping bag.

Putting your boots on that are outside the tent whilst you are still sitting inside determined not to stand on the groundsheet.

Trying to pump up a blow-up mattress in the middle of the night without it making any noise and sounding like you're having a cardiac arrest or an asthmatic attack.

Trying to find your torch in the middle of the night.

Trying to repair a blow up mattress in the middle of the night in the dark because you've given up looking for your torch.

Trying your best not to spill a drop in the middle of the night whilst using a plastic drinks bottle in your tent.

Trying too hard and getting your glans stuck just as you realise that your plastic drinks bottle is too small for three pints and firing the bottle like a pressurised water rocket through the tent wall and straight into the mess tent where a couple of scouts are having an earnest late-night discussion.

JUGGLING

Working out how, as a scout leader, you're also going to have time for a day job.

How to deliver scouting with only two hours every week.

How to get a decent meal when the scouts are cooking.

How to write a risk assessment that doesn't preclude you from doing anything that's the least bit fun.

How much petrol to charge the group when you've been driving around for an hour trying to find the campsite because you didn't check beforehand and the sat. nav. is trying to send you into a lake.

Verbal

Trying to speak to another leader without saying any swear words.

Speaking to a scout leader and using a swear word but then trying to disguise it when you realise a scout is listening. E.g. Fudge if you haven't gone too far, or Fork if you have, although you may then have to explain to a scout why you want to fork the object of your sentence.

Trying to remember to use alternative words to swear words which sound like they are but aren't. Fuksheet is part of a sail, Knobstick is a truncheon, Shittah is a type of tree, and Wanapin is a plant.

Ground

Crawling around the campsite, because your legs have given way, trying to find your tent.

Spending the night in a sleeping bag in a survival bag (sleeping bag and survival bag optional).

Falling backwards off your camp chair and cracking your head open.

Alcohol

Pouring a frisky can of lager or bottle of prosecco into your camp mug and trying to explain to the scouts why your coffee is foaming.

Pouring a whole bottle of rum into the wrong hot chocolate and serving it up to the scouts before realising your mistake when they start singing, "Dinah, Dinah show us your legs," which you had taught them the previous evening when you had poured the previous bottle of rum straight into yourself not bothering with the hot chocolate.

CLIMBER

Getting to the top isn't about teamwork, you can do this on your own. You just need to butter up a few people further up the ladder and before you know it you will be at the top of the pile with a long, fancy job title and no kids to worry about apart from maybe your own!

To gain your badge

1. Go to every scout meeting that is arranged (other than the ones for your scouts - they don't count) in your local area even though you may not have been invited. Don't worry though, no one will turn you away.

2. Find someone with not many badges on their very new scout shirt. They're usually quite senior as they've not spent much time taking scout meetings but have spent plenty of time taking scout leader meetings talking about scout meetings.

3. Alternatively find someone who's not wearing a scout shirt. This will normally mean that they're quite senior also but they haven't even bothered climbing, they're probably best friends with another senior person who's got them in. Be warned though, they may be someone extremely lowly who has either merely forgotten their shirt or they're running the bar.

4. Explain that you have plenty of time on your hands and would be interested in attending a meeting at the next level up. Say something like, "I'm very interested in how all the levels fit together and what everyone does." If you're

talking to the right person your invitation won't be long in coming. Like straightaway.

5. When you do receive the invitation make sure that you attend and tell everyone that you were invited, because you were. Repeat 4. At this level everyone is worth speaking to because there will probably be some very senior people at this meeting. Don't wear your scout shirt but consider wearing a scout scarf (a very old and faded one if you can because this will imply that you are part of some sort of dynasty, a new clean crisp one simply means that you can use an iron). Wear the scarf over your jacket and / or an obscure enamel badge in your lapel. This may be a cracker freebie or a broken piece of jewellery that you picked up in a charity shop, but no one will know. They will glance at your accessories and think, "This is someone who's going places."

6. Do not wear a name badge. These are most definitely for those who not only have yet to get out of the badge collecting habit but also are under the mistaken belief that name badges confer authority and prestige. They don't.

7. Continue until you find yourself at a meeting at which the monarch is present. If they produce a sword, don't panic. You're being knighted for, "Services to Scouting" although "Services to Climbing" would be more appropriate! Well done! You've certainly earned this badge having climbed all the way to the top!

COMMUNICATOR

Communication is at the heart of scouting as it enables people to speak and to socialise. Continue to advance in both of these areas by gaining this badge.

To gain your badge

1. Make sure that your smartphone is fully charged at all times.

2. If not, make sure that you have the means to charge it, especially when on camp. This will normally mean having a battery pack which has been charged.

3. If not, borrow one from the scouts. When in the mess tent tell them that you're thinking of buying a battery pack and ask which one has the highest milliampere hour. They will be very keen to tell you whose is the most powerful. Say, "Make sure you keep it somewhere safe," and they will respond with something like, "It's fine; I've hidden it in my rucksack," which will mean that you will be able to charge your 'phone in the morning whilst they're out.

4. If at a large camp where there are buildings, make it your business to find out where the electricity sockets are. Often they can be found in cupboards or under metal flaps in the wall or on the floor. If in a wall plug your 'phone in and sit on the floor with the socket tucked under your arm. If on the floor lie down and pretend you are unconscious. In this latter case make sure that you lie down in the recovery position or some well meaning scout may try to move you. For this reason it is better to have someone else with you, maybe someone who also needs their 'phone charging.

5. Although sockets can be found in all sorts of unusual places, if you venture into a kitchen just be careful if you're pulling out a plug to accommodate yours as it could easily be a freezer and this normally causes added problems.
6. Once your smartphone is fully charged resume communications with it by either staring at it for hours on end or playing some mind-numbing games whilst the scouts are playing some proper ones.

CRAFT

With a desire to make something unusual, using just your hands, you will find that you will soon be the envy of all your friends!

To gain your badge

To gain your badge It should be something that, although unusual, will be practical in your scouting life.

Notes

Here are some things that you make like to consider or you can do something similar that isn't listed:

A container that is shaped like a pint or wine glass using wood, paper, plastic, canvas or fibreglass.

CYCLING

There's nothing better than to get out in the fresh air and enjoy some quality time with your bicycle. This badge will be the reward for all that bicycle knowledge.

To gain your badge

1. Get hold of a bicycle. You can buy one from any cycle shop on the high street or you could go to Cambridge with a good pair of bolt cutters and take your pick. Make sure that you've sharpened them though and be quick about it or you may find yourself at the wrong end of a quant.
2. Prepare your route. It should be for four hours or two two hour sessions. You should aim to cycle past at least seven public houses. You can include cafes and other eating establishments but four as a minimum must be licensed.
3. Know what to say if you stop at all seven public houses and have a couple of pints of bitter or glasses of prosecco. Practice saying, "It's okay I'll push it home; I only live a mile away," to the landlord / lady without slurring.
4. Learn how to cycle in a straight line afterwards and know where to find a toilet at short notice.
5. If you cannot find a toilet, learn how to position a bicycle by the side of the road so that you can have a quick pee next to it without anyone realising what you are doing until you have finished.
6. Once you near home, know how to hide the bicycle quickly if you hear sirens.
7. Learn how to dispose of the bicycle in the local pond / river / canal.

DIGITAL CITIZEN

An understanding of, and being able to communicate via, digital platforms is vital in this day and age. Having this badge will show to the world that you are a well and truly a person of the 21st century!

To gain your badge

1. Know where to find someone who can turn on your PC, laptop or tablet.
2. Remember to have a password that is easy to remember when logging on and for accessing various websites, especially online banking. The easiest to remember is 1111 or 1234 if it's a number or aaaa or abcd if it's letters. If it's a combination try 1234abcd. Once you've set a password or found someone to do it for you, write it down on a Post-It note and stick it on the edge of your computer screen so you will always be able to find it.
3. Know where to find someone when you need to load a piece of software.
4. Know where to find someone when you need to connect a printer to your device.
5. When sending a private email to one person know how to "cc" everyone in your address book, then do it - maybe several times, one after the other in quick succession just to make sure that you know what you're doing.
6. Find five websites where you can access material that interests you and that are new to you. Share them with someone if you can.
7. Know how to get a virus and get one.

8. Know where to find someone when you need to get rid of the virus.

9. Know what to say when the person that you have found to sort out your virus says that it's not worth trying to deal with it because your device is too old and the best thing that you can do is get a new one.

10. Know where to buy a new PC, laptop or tablet.

11. When buying your new device know what to say when you are asked what processor you want, how much RAM you require, what size hard drive you would like, what graphics you need, what software you would like pre-installed, which anti-virus you fancy and which broadband package or know where to find someone who can answer all these questions for you.

12. Pay twice as much for the device as the ticket price once you have added on all the extras and take it home with you.

13. Open the box and find that along with your new device you have at least twelve cables and various plugs that you haven't a clue what to do with them.

14. Know where to find someone who can turn on your PC, laptop or tablet.

15. Put the kettle on.

DIY

Be the envy of all your friends with this badge. This badge shows that you are a dab hand in the art making repairs in the home rather than having to employ a professional.

To gain your badge

1. Find out what at electric shock feels like. This can most easily be achieved by sticking a screwdriver into a wall socket, sticking a metal knife in a toaster when it's on or putting your fingers instead of a light bulb into a live lamp holder.

2. Find out how well water conducts electricity by taking a hair dryer into the bathroom whilst it is plugged in and dropping it into a bath full of water. Your investigation will be more conclusive if someone is in the bath at the time.

3. Know what happens if you pour a bucketful of concrete down a toilet and leave it for a day. Experiment with different quantities and see if the result is the same.

DRAGON BOATING

There's time on the water for you too. Just make sure that you remain on it and don't end up in it. This is an activity that you can do with the scouts as there is plenty of space and loads of roles (well two) for everyone. A dragon boat is a cross between a very long canoe and a very long rowing boat with raised ends and a large drum.

To gain your badge

1. Identify the two raised ends and ask the dragon boat captain which end he sits at. Sit at the other end. Do this before the scouts embark to avoid one of them taking your space.
2. Just before you launch, jump off and approach the captain and ask to borrow his drum. If he doesn't let you just take it, cutting the rope with your penknife if he has it secured around his neck, and return to your seat giving the boat a quick push as you get back on. The boat will leave the jetty and the captain won't be able to do anything. If the captain tries to give the command for the scouts to row back to the jetty just shout out the opposite of what he is saying until you are in the middle of the lake.
3. If the captain continues to want the scouts to row back to the jetty threaten to drop his drum overboard. That will keep him (it's always a him) quiet. Dragon boat drums are very expensive. Make sure that you make a hole in it first with your penknife otherwise it will float.
4. The rowers will follow the drum beats so a good sense of rhythm is essential for the boat to follow a straight

course. This is unimportant though so just enjoy the experience. If your drumming is too erratic you may find the scouts capsizing or sinking the boat. You are to avoid this at all costs as you will also probably get wet.

5. When / if you return to the jetty (this return may be assigned to the captain otherwise you may be on / in the lake for the rest of the day) make sure that you are first off with the drum.

6. Run with the drum and hide it either in your car or, if at camp, on your campsite. In this latter instance, when the captain comes looking for it send him away with the word "Safeguarding" ringing in his ears.

DRIVING

An essential badge as having completed the requirements you can award yourself the Diving badge also because it sounds sufficiently similar (even though it doesn't even exist). Two badges for the work of one. Fantastic!

To gain your badge

1. Go to the local driving range. If you drive there that is sufficient to gain this badge.
2. Buy a bucket of balls in the pro shop. You should also be given a driver but don't worry if you're not as it is not going to be used.
3. Find a cubicle that faces out over the driving range. Upstairs is better as it's quieter (because many golfers cannot climb stairs and have to resort to buggies). Put down your bucket of balls and driver and go and find the bar. There's always a bar at the driving range. It's probably a legal requirement.
4. After about half-an-hour return to your cubicle. You should find that your balls have been taken. If not simply kick the bucket over (unless you are on the first floor as a ball on the head often offends, let alone fifty or one hundred. In which case offer them to someone else explaining that you over-ordered.)
5. Return the empty bucket and driver to the pro-shop. If they ask how it went say, "I shot a few good'uns."
6. Return to the bar.

DUCT TAPE

Duct tape is an essential part of every scout first aid kit. Keep it zipped up inside your bag. It should fit even if you have to take everything else out. Don't worry! Most of the consumables are hardly ever used and go past their expiry date before they are ever pressed into service. In any event duct tape can be used for most emergencies.

To gain your badge

Use duct tape in at least three different emergency first aid situations. Some examples are given below or you can devise your own.

1. If a scout comes to you and is bleeding cut a length of duct tape twice as long as the wound and stick it over the top and press down.

2. If the cut is longer or deeper than one inch use two lengths.

3. If a scout faints cut a length of duct tape, at least six inches, and stick it on their hair. Take hold of one end and pull firmly and vigorously. You may not remove all the hair but they should wake up.

4. If a scout breaks a bone wrap the affected area in duct tape. For an arm or foot go round twice, for a leg go round four times, for a back six times. Anywhere else 'phone for an ambulance.

5. It a scout is feeling sick tape their mouth up with duct tape. Go around the head twice as a minimum to prevent any discharge escaping.

6. If a scout is screaming or making some other distressed noise, for example if they have sustained a burn or a scald, use the duct tape to tape from under the chin around the side of the head, over the top of the forehead, down the other side and back under the chin. Repeat until the mouth is firmly clamped shut.

7. If a scout gets a splinter that has no part exposed don't leave it - cover it up with duct tape. One layer should be sufficient.

8. If you go to use the first aid kit and there is no duct tape available, don't panic. Help is only a 'phone call away! Telephone a local office supply company and put in an order. If you're lucky you may get next day delivery and almost certainly before next week's meeting.

DYING

This is a badge that everyone eventually earns whether they like it or not. When exactly you earn it can be down to you but there should be no rush as once you have earned it you will not be in a position to sew it onto your uniform - although someone else may do it for you.

To gain your badge

1. Stop breathing.

EARPLUGS

As essential part of the kit for the bathroom when you drop the toothbrush cap down the toilet. They are also very useful when on camp. Anyone who goes on camp should be able to gain this badge without trying.

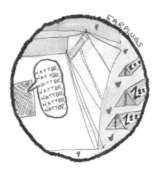

To gain your badge
1. Purchase one pair of earplugs plus a few spare for every scout that you take on camp.
2. When on camp hand out the earplugs on the first evening over hot chocolate. Show them how to roll the curved end between thumb and index finger to make them more pliable and flatter. This makes them easier to insert.
3. Once the scouts have finished their drinks tell them to go to the toilet, clean their teeth then go to bed.
4. Remember to tell them to put in their earplugs.
5. Talk all night as loudly as you like.
6. It is not necessary to wake the scouts up in the morning. If the earplugs have been inserted properly they may not appear until teatime the following day.

ENTERTAINER

Do you think that you have a magnetic personality? Do people always stop to listen to what you have to say? Do you make people smile and laugh? Probably not otherwise you wouldn't waste your time being a scout leader. No one can make you a more humorous person but entertaining isn't just about laughter - if you shock people that can work just as well for the purposes of this badge.

To gain your badge

Do something entertaining. It may be that you have a particular situation in mind that you feel could be classed as entertaining. Alternatively use just one of the following. Do not use more than one otherwise you may find yourself a scout leader no more.

When parents are picking up their scouts at the end of a meeting and you are handing out the notices say,

- And hopefully I won't be quite so drunk next week, at least not at the beginning of the meeting, or
- Who would have known that [name of scout] could knock back a pint of lager in under ten seconds? or
- I hope you enjoyed making cocktails this week. If you have a bit of a headache later just drink some water, or
- Remember that rolling your own cigarettes does take quite a bit of time to master so don't be too disappointed with your efforts. We'll have another go next week. Maybe we'll practice on some sushi first, or

- Blowing smoke rings is so cool once you have had a few more tries. I'll bring some cigars next week because they create more smoke. If you take a huge puff you will be able to exhale several, one after the other, if you get really good, or
- I'll bring my circus knives in next week and then you can have a proper go a knife throwing. We'll rig the round table up a bit better so that it rotates more evenly when we have someone strapped to it. It's probably just as well we were only using penknives this week! or
- I hope that you enjoyed learning the A to Z of swear words. We'll have a recap next week just to make sure that you haven't forgotten them and if you haven't I can give you some more, or
- We'll finish off the swear word crossword next week once I've taught you some that you obviously don't know.

Notes
See **Swearing**

ENVIRONMENTAL IMPACT

This is such an important badge in the current climate. It is everyone's responsibility to make an impact on our beautiful world. If we all did our bit locally this would add up to making a huge difference globally. Do your bit and by gaining this badge show everyone that you really don't care.

To gain your badge
1. Think of all the single-use plastic that you put out for recycling every week. Much of it doesn't get recycled at all due to its being contaminated (that is to say it hasn't been cleaned / rinsed properly).
2. For plastic and glass bottles with a cap fill them with water and replace the cap. For trays, take-away foil, tin cans put them into a black sack, add a house brick or some stones and securely tie.
3. Find a large stretch of water (lakes work well, canals less so because they are occasionally dredged) and throw the plastic, glass and black sacks as far as you can aiming for the middle. This will ensure that no further energy is wasted trying to recycle it.
4. With over 70% of the world's surface covered in water (and not just because it has rained) there are always plenty of places available for disposal of recycling other than the recycling bin. Remember this figure for when someone tells you that we should be recycling more.
5. When on camp there are always a number of black bagfuls of rubbish generated that no one wants to take

home. Don't be the one who has to take them home for drip-feeding to the bin men every fortnight for a year. The campsite's had your money, let them sort it out. Offer to take them home and ask the scouts to put them next to your car but not too close. When it's time to go home make sure that you are last off or that it's dark. No one can see so simply drive off. They will soon be disposed of by someone, just not you. Foxes do a good job but by then it's not your problem.

EQUESTRIAN

Hone your skills with this popular badge. Horsemanship is not necessary.

To gain your badge

1. Find a racecourse, preferably one that accommodates horses as opposed to cars or athletes.
2. Learn how to place a bet, what odds mean, betting terminology.
3. Tell the parents that you're going on a visit to the New Forest and that scouts are to bring a packed lunch and ten pounds for the shop.
4. Visit the chosen racecourse, preferably when there is a race meeting taking place. Tell the scouts that they have five hours' free time and don't spend all their money at once.
5. Purchase a race day programme, look at it and let your eyes glaze over.
6. Before each race go to the parade ring and look at what the people on the opposite side are wearing. If someone comes up to you and tries to engage you in conversation tell them that you cannot discuss any of the horses as you are a race marshall.
7. Having learnt the terminology approach a bookie waving a twenty pound note and say, "I would like ten pounds each way on the brown horse." Make sure that you are given a ticket.
8. Watch the race then go back to the bookie waving your ticket to ask if you have won. You won't have done. It may be that a brown horse did win but it won't be yours.

9. Find the bar and waving a twenty pound note say, "I would like ten pounds each way on a pint of Guinness." This way you will be assured of a win.

10. If the barmaid looks at you with a quizzical expression say, "I would like one pint to come in first place and another pint to come in second place."

11. When it's time to go home confiscate all the scout's winnings. You can be sure of a profit as there will be only a few that have lost their money and so will have nothing to give you but there will be plenty who will have won. Tell them that they're not to tell their parents as they should not have been gambling and if anyone finds out they will be in big trouble.

12. If any parents ask you how the trip went tell them that you saw loads of ponies but unfortunately their child lost their money.

13. Take the scouts' winnings back to the racecourse the following week on your own and lose it all.

EXHAUSTED

For those for whom scouting is their life and not just a hobby, this badge should probably be awarded automatically after a couple of years, but for the rest of us it is more of a case of simply having to appear exhausted. This means, in practice, sitting down most of the time and complaining that you're exhausted. If you want to make the effort to gain this badge legitimately then try one of the following.

To gain your badge
There are three alternatives. Select one of them.

Alternative One
At a scout meeting when the scouts are going to be doing something outside ask another leader / helper if they can oversee the activity. Tell them that you have something urgent that needs doing. Once everyone is outside sit down and have a rest. This can also be applied if everyone is outside and they are going to be going inside for an activity (unless it's raining). You can wait until someone finds you whereupon you tell them that you've just finished and were just about to come and find everyone, "but I was exhausted." If anyone asks what you were doing say that it's confidential or a "safeguarding matter." That always avoids further awkward questions.

Alternative Two

On camp get the scouts to put your tent up then tell another leader / helper that you have to go and sort some paperwork out. This can mean an absence of at least an hour. Hopefully you've chosen a campsite near a pub.

Alternative Three

If you are on a camp with some other scout groups you can often disappear for the whole weekend and just reappear when everyone is packing up. In this instance you could even go home.

Notes

Hiking is self-evidently a more difficult situation as if you're not careful you may end up genuinely exhausted. But if you can plan a route that involves not being too far off the beaten track then put the scouts into teams with a leader each and send them off at staggered times. If you've organised this well no one will realise that you're last to leave and you have no scouts. Then it's a case of jumping on a bus or even taking a taxi to your destination. Keep out of the way until some of the groups have arrived then slip back into the crowd.

EXPLOSIONS

Blowing stuff up is one of the highlights of being a scout leader.

To gain your badge
There are two alternatives. Select one of them and complete all the tasks.

Alternative One
Intentional
1. Put something flammable in your trouser pocket or rucksack (depending on size) such as a gas canister, petrol or paraffin can (filled), or firework (at least one).
2. Stand next to a roaring camp fire with the inflammable item closest.
3. Wait until you hear a hissing sound before taking off your trousers or rucksack, dropping them to the ground and running.
4. You will know if your explosion has been particularly effective if the fire brigade turn up within the next ten minutes. If you explosion is not successful put your trousers / rucksack back on if there's anything left of them and try again.

Alternative Two
Accidental
Either
As Alternative One but someone else has put the flammable item in your pocket or rucksack without your realising it. If successful both you and the other person will gain this badge.

Or

Build a large reflector camp fire next to the gas cage with the cage acting as the reflector.

Notes

Do not keep wearing trousers / rucksack when you hear hissing otherwise the badge will probably have to be awarded posthumously.

FACILEBOOK

A hugely popular badge for old people. Be part of the social media revolution!

To gain your badge

1. Like / follow / join every scout-related page and group you can find.

2. All your posts should be trolling - starting quarrels or upsetting readers with controversial opinions.

3. Comment on absolutely every post with irrational, barmy, senseless, inflammatory, poorly thought out arguments that are littered with speling errors and not good grammar.

4. Keep it up even when everyone else is asleep.

5. Continue all day, every day, through Christmas Day, New Year's Eve, summer holidays with the same old idiotic, mindless, vacuous drivel.

FARMING

Becoming more self-reliant as a nation is probably a good thing and so knowing how to make the most of the land is to be encouraged.

To gain your badge
There are two alternatives, one for arable and the other for pastoral. Select one of them and complete all the tasks.

Alternative One
Arable
1. Identify your crop. Barley is best followed by wheat as these are both used in beer production.
2. Find a large gap in the hedge. You could consider using a more orthodox method of entry such as a gate but you need to make sure that this entrance is well away from the farmhouse.
3. For a small crop you can cut using a scythe but for anything substantial you will need to obtain a combine.
4. Although these can be fairly hefty machines they have the advantage of combining three separate harvesting operations, namely reaping, threshing, and winnowing, into a single operation. Do it.
5. Tie bundles of barley together and leave them to dry for several weeks.
6. If working by hand you will now need to thresh and winnow your crop.
7. Store whilst you find a buyer or use it to make some homebrew.

Alternative Two

Pastoral

1. Identify your animal. This will normally be a cow, pig or lamb.
2. Find a large gap in the hedge. You could consider using a more orthodox method of entry such as a gate but you need to make sure that this entrance is well away from the farmhouse.
3. Borrow a large trailer and park in the entrance with the back positioned inside the field.
4. Find your animal and guide it into the trailer. Once in, lock it.
5. Unless you are going to slaughter the animal yourself, take it to a local abattoir and ask for a carcass.
6. If you are going to slaughter the animal yourself you will need to stun it first. To do this obtain a captive-bolt pistol for a cow, electric tongs for a lamb, or gas with a high concentrate of carbon dioxide. The process for stunning and slaughtering is outside the requirements of this badge.
7. Store the meat. If using the meat for camp it is useful to know that a cow will give you around 1,750 burgers, a lamb will be in excess of fifty pounds and a pig around double that - which is a load of bacon! You could consider setting up a stall. "Organic" always helps sales.

FAST FOOD

Fast food is a necessity in today's world and knowing how to get one's hands on it is so important for a scout leader's sanity. Go for this badge and gain some expertise in the meantime.

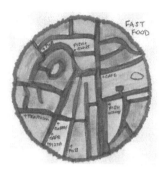

To gain your badge

There are three alternatives, one for scout meetings, another for hikes and a third for camps. Select one of them and complete all the tasks.

Alternative One

Scout Meetings

1. Identify the location of fish and chip shops within a mile or so of the scout hut.
2. Obtain funding for six large bags of chips from each shop.
3. Take the scouts on a chip shop challenge whereby they have to purchase some chips from each shop, taste one each and mark them out of ten for look, smell and taste.
4. Tell the fish and chip shop owner that you are doing a chip shop challenge and the one with the best chips will get a certificate and a mention in the local paper. (This could just be a newsletter to the parents - or maybe just tell them, or some of them, or think of doing so).
5. Only purchase one bag of chips. With luck the owner may try to give you some more in an attempt to bribe you. This is perfectly acceptable. Tell them that you would rather he slipped a large cod in with the order.

6. If you do not get a large cod you will have to buy one but make a note that this fish and chip shop now cannot win.

You can also complete this alternative by substituting rice for chips and a chicken korma for cod in a curry house or garlic bread and a pepperoni pizza in a pizzeria.

Alternative Two

Hikes

1. Identify the location of fast food outlets where you are going to stop for elevenses (cafe), lunch (anything) and tea (tearoom).

2. Once you've started the hike walk round the corner and ask if anyone is hungry yet. Someone will say that they are.

3. Stop for at least half an hour. This should give the scouts long enough to drink everything that they have.

4. When you arrive at the elevenses stop the scouts will all be thirsty. Go into the cafe and say that you will bring twenty scouts in and they will all buy a drink if they can oblige you with a free cappuccino. Be unfailingly polite and you may well get a bacon sandwich also. Tell the scouts it's almost lunchtime so that they will eat their sandwiches.

5. When you arrive at the lunch stop the scouts will all be hungry. Go into the fish and chip shop or similar and say that you will bring twenty scouts in and they will all buy something to eat if they can oblige you with a large cod and chips. If the owner doesn't bat an eyelid keep on going. Say as much of the following until their facial expression changes, "and a wally and a pickled egg and a pickled onion and a buttered roll and a small saveloy and a can of diet Coke," and if you get this far and they still haven't said anything, add, "and a portion of scampi. Thank you."

6. When you arrive at the tea stop the scouts will all be hungry and thirsty again. Go into the tearoom and say that you will bring twenty scouts in and they will all buy a drink and a cake if they can oblige you with a free Earl Grey and a large slice of Victoria sponge.

7. When you finally get home, in addition to the **Fast Food** badge award yourself **Exhausted** also.

Alternative Three

Camps

1. Identify the location of a fast food outlet within a mile or so of the camp site.

2. Although it is expected that the scouts prepare their own dinner it will not be particularly "fast" and it probably won't be "food" either so there is no obligation to eat it. Washing-up is a good time to slip out and have your fish and chips. Don't overlook the fact that pubs often do excellent bar snacks also.

3. When you return to the camp if any of the scouts ask you where you've been say, "Have you finished the washing-up yet?" If they say, "No," tell them to stop asking questions and go and finish what you told them to do. If they say, "Yes," go and have a look (it will all still be out on a rack or the table) and tell them that's it's still covered in smears of food and they will need to do it all again.

4. You could at this point go back to the pub for another pint and to finish off the requirements of the **Beer** badge.

FIRE SAFELY

Knowing how to set fire to your scout hut safely can be fraught with danger, especially if you are looking for a new one and are hoping to claim on your insurance. You may have your own ideas and that is fine but if you try one of the options below you shouldn't go far wrong. In both instances check your buildings insurance policy and make sure that you are covered for explosion or fire.

To gain your badge
There are two alternatives. Select one of them and complete the task.

Alternative One
Explosion
Advantages: Quick. Effective.
Disadvantage. Loud. Will blow up everything else nearby.
To blow up the scout hut you will need a large gas canister, preferably 15kg, a hammer, chewing gum, condom, matches, large candle. Put the gas canister on the ground floor in the middle of the hall. Whack it smartly in the middle with a hammer so that a crack forms. Work quickly now. Press chewing gum around the crack and then stick the end of the condom to the chewing gum so that the condom starts to inflate. Make sure that no gas is escaping outside the condom. Go to the end of the hall by the main door, put the large candle on the floor and light it. Leave the building, lock the door, put more gum in the lock to deter anyone from trying to enter, and leave. Preferably

run. You should be far enough distance away from the hut when the expanding condom reaches the candle and the gas ignites causing the pressurised gas to explode. Keep running; there will be nothing left of your scout hut.

Alternative Two
Fire
Advantages: Quiet. Can be used in a fairly confined area
Disadvantage: May take too long to completely destroy the building. Evidence of arson may be detected.
To set fire to the scout hut you will need one gallon of petrol, plenty of newspaper and matches. Pour the petrol onto any flammable surface up to ten. Roll up individual lengths of newspaper and scrunch up. Starting at the main door run a line of scrunched up newspaper to each petrol point inside. When you are ready light the first sheet of newspaper. Leave the building and lock the door. Remember to take the petrol canister with you. There is no need to run.

Notes
This badge is not suitable if you meet in a church hall as ecclesiastical insurers are very adept at investigating deliberate fires. Only take this course of action in consultation with the local priest and, if possible, get them to do all the work. You will still be able to gain the badge though.

FIRST AID

So very vital that you know who to turn to when there's a first aid incident and what to do with the kit when there's not.

To gain your badge

1. Make sure that you have the largest first aid bag you can find. It should be green with a large white cross on it. It doesn't have to have anything in it as others are loath to open someone else's bag even when there's a proper emergency. And you're not going to be opening it.

2. Just in case anyone does think about opening it, lock it and lose the key.

3. If someone suggests slitting the bag open say, "There's no time for that; the scout obviously needs to go to hospital. You obviously know what to do so off you go. Now!"

4. That said, make sure that you do always have someone with you who knows what to do.

5. Carrying a large first aid bag around will get you into places that others may find impossible. These include back stage, after-show, last night and celebrity parties and VIP areas of every description. Wearing an oversize yellow / green jacket with hi-vis silver stripes and PARAMEDIC printed across the back will make a big difference. Don't smile, look serious, determined, be confident and walk straight past security as if they're not there.

6. Once you are where you want to be head for the toilets and get into a cubicle as quickly as you can. Stuff your

jacket in the first aid bag having pulled out your party clothes.

7. Tuck the bag under your arm and go and find reception. Ask someone to look after it for you. They always will and they will never ask any questions. They will just assume you're off-duty which you are, albeit permanently.

8. Under no circumstances get caught up in a real first aid situation. If something serious has happened just leave. Quickly.

FOOTBALL

This is not a badge about playing sport; this is a badge about talking sport. It is said that a Premier League football match is a game played by 22 men in need of a rest and watched by 50,000 in need of some exercise. You don't have to be one of those 50,000. Even if you know nothing about football you just have to go through the requirements methodically and with the appropriate facial expressions when speaking to an aficionado to earn this badge.

To gain your badge

1. Arsenal, Liverpool, Manchester United, Everton, Tottenham Hotspur and Chelsea are the only teams never to have been relegated from the Premier League. Don't make a statement like "Everton are doing okay this season," as they may be bottom. Ask a question, ask for an opinion, something like, "What do you think of Everton's performance this season?" That way it won't matter where they are in the table. Use "Everton" or any of the other clubs mentioned above.

2. Remember always to refer to Manchester United as "Man U" and "Tottenham Hotspur" as "Spurs."

3. Say, "The top four clubs have all got a quite good defence this season," or, "The top four clubs have all been scoring quite well this season."

4. Say, "The bottom four clubs have all got quite a bad defence this season," or, "The bottom four clubs have not been scoring well this season."

5. Say, "I'm looking forward to that new guy who's supposed to be joining [name of one of the six clubs mentioned above] shortly. Apparently he's really good." If someone asks his name say, "It's something like 'Arbonamende.'" The person you are talking too will probably just nod as you won't be talking to the brightest star in the sky.

6. Remember not to use any of the above out of season (i.e. June and July).

FUNDRAISING

This is a badge that you should be earning with your eyes shut. It's so simple to fundraise especially when you have a few scouts around looking sweet. Remember also that much of the money that is given will be cash so no need for it to go anywhere near a bank account.

To gain your badge

1. Decide what you're going to fundraise for. You obviously but you can't really say that as it doesn't encourage much response. How about a collecting tin with " For the scouts' " written on the front? On the back put " Leader ". It's not you problem that people don't look around the back and just complain about a misplaced apostrophe that is nothing of the sort. You don't have to mention it though.

2. If someone persists and asks what the scouts are going to do with the money say, "They'll be giving it away to a good cause." You do not have to say that you are the good cause.

3. Buy loads of packets of cookies from the pound shop. Take them home, open all the packets and put them in small brown paper bags. Maybe tie them up with a piece of ribbon.

4. Borrow a few scouts to go up and down some roads near where you live and knock on doors. Research has found that around 80% of responders buy on the doorstep if it's a scout selling something that can be eaten. (Not necessarily edible.)

5. Use the sweetest-looking scouts and remember to tell them that they will be paid.
6. After all the cookies have been sold pay the scouts and pay them well. You can run this activity as often as you like so long as you don't go back to the same round more often than once a month. The rest of the money is yours to spend as you like.

GEOSTASHING

Knowing where these little nuggets have been secreted around the country is vital for a positive hiking experience. Use the Geostashing app to find out exactly where.

To gain your badge

1. Download the Geostashing app and find the section for Scout Leaders.
2. Plan your hike so that you go within around 100 metres of a Geostash location every hour or so.
3. Make sure that the Geostash locations that you aim to use are a good mix depending on whom you have leading the hike with you. You should opt for lager, wine, vodka and tonic, and cigarettes.
4. When you are on your hike, stop near the Geostash and use the app to find the exact location. They are not difficult to find. The location will be something like, "In the hollow of the first tree on the left as you enter the park."
5. Say to your fellow leaders, "I'm just going for a stash." They will know what you mean and the scouts hopefully won't. Remember that other leaders may also be working towards this badge so take it in turns to go for a stash unless you are desperate.
6. When you have consumed the stash put the empty can, bottle or packet back where you found it.

Notes

Remember that Geostashes are maintained by local scout leaders for your benefit. Consider adopting a stash or two yourself so that you can give something back to those who are hiking through your local area.

GHOST STORIES

Use your creative juices to make up then tell the scouts a very scary ghost story. This is best achieved on camp so that they don't go home and wet the bed.

To gain your badge

1. Write a ghost story. It doesn't need to be very long or very good for that matter, just scary.
2. To achieve maximum scariness use some or all of the following:
   - Anticipation
   - Facial expressions
   - Tone of voice
   - Isolation. Put the protagonists into a situation where they are cut off from help
   - Slow build up
   - Sudden climax
3. Tell the story to the scouts.
4. Create a scary atmosphere. On camp this can include cold, damp, dark, late. Consider waking them up just as they've gone off to sleep to tell them the story.
5. If you are in a mess tent make sure everyone has a hot chocolate in their hands. They will grip it tightly like a comfort blanket.
6. When you come to the climax watch out! BOO! The hot chocolate will go everywhere!
7. Then send the scouts straight off to bed saying, "I don't know about you but I certainly won't now sleep a wink tonight!"

GHOST STORIES PLUS

Once you have gained your **Ghost Stories** badge advance to **Ghost Stories Plus** with a ready-made story that you can adapt to fit your environment but it is meant to be read on camp.

To gain your badge

1. Tell the following story on camp.
2. Have at least half of the scouts either stay awake all night, cry, wet their sleeping bags or ask to go home.
3. If someone asks if ghosts really exist, say "Yes."

There was, many years ago, a tragic accident that occurred at this very campsite. In fact, now I think about it, the scene of the accident was more or less where we're sitting now. [Look around you.] Yes, I think this was it. A group of scouts, much like you, were on a weekend's camp. They were excited, lively, keen and great fun to be with. On the Saturday afternoon they had been receiving some instruction. They were learning safety in saws, knives and, most crucially, axes. When it came to axes they were taught how only one person should be near the axe when it is being used and that they must put the wood to be chopped on a raised block. The free hand should hold the wood at the end further from the block and chip away carefully. The axes had all been put away in a metal box and were being stored in a cupboard in a building. In fact it was that building over there [point]. The scouts had been told that under no circumstances were they to use the axes without adult supervision.

87

There were three scouts. One was called Simon. They decided that while the leaders were in the mess tent they would take the axes and go and practice chopping some more wood. They found the metal box and Simon took out the largest axe. It was one that none of them had used before. The three of them walked over to the chopping block and put a thick bough on it from one of the nearby trees. "I wonder if it's possible to cut through the branch in one go," said one of the boys. "I should think so," said Simon. Simon offered to hold the bough so while he bent down to get a good grip, one of the boys picked the axe and passed it to his other friend. This boy was standing behind Simon and he raised the axe as high as he was able [do actions]. From the highest point he brought the axe down as hard as he could. CHOP! Simon screamed. For his friend had missed the branch completely and there on the ground lay Simon's hand with blood pumping from his wrist. The boy that had chopped Simon's hand off threw the axe at his friend and went running into the dark whilst the other boy stood rooted to the spot. Soon Simon stopped screaming. He turned to see his friend holding the axe before collapsing to the floor just as some leaders came running. "There's been a terrible accident," the boy said, "and Simon has chopped his hand off." Nothing could be done to save Simon. The axe was thrown to the middle of the lake. The two boys never spoke about it again but suspicion always rested on the friend who was holding onto the axe.

Some years later there were some scouts camping on the very spot when... [look up at the door / into the distance] "Hello Simon." Simon looked quizzically at the scout leader. "W...w...what do you want?" No one apart from the scout leader and one other could see Simon. "I think you owe me an apology," said Simon.

"But it wasn't me." Simon walked slowly towards the scout leader. "Oh yes it was." The scout leader looked all around [look all around] but it was obvious that no one else apart from one other could hear Simon either. "There's been some mistake." "Oh no there hasn't." It was then that the scout leader noticed that Simon was holding the axe and that it was wet and blood was dripping from it and that one of his hands was missing and blood was pouring from his wrist. "It know who is to blame because I saw them holding the axe just before I died."

"It wasn't me," said the scout leader trembling. "It is time for me to tell you the truth for the world to know and so that you can finally rest in peace. It was....[turn slowly round and point to one of the other leaders] YOU!"

GLOBAL ISSUES

Be aware of what is going on in the
world. See what you can do to
make it a better place.

To gain your badge

1. Many people in the world today
are not paid very much. Millions live
on less than two dollars a day. Help alleviate this situation
by going for a curry in your local Indian restaurant more
often. If this is not possible consider ordering a take-away.
2. Around one third of the world's population does not have
access to the medicines essential to their health and
survival because of the high prices. If you can't beat them,
join them. Next time you go to pick up a prescription refuse
to pay for it. If you are challenged tell the pharmacist that
you are pregnant. If it is pointed out that you are a man
tell them that they are so behind with the times and that
anyone can be pregnant now.

GO-KARTING

This is a very popular badge to earn. Go-karting can be dangerous but by going along with the scouts you will be assured of something soft to crash into as well as having someone else to blame. However, the main aim is to ensure that you and your fellow leaders can have the track all to yourself.

To gain your badge

1. Book a go-karting session at your local track.
2. Under no circumstances are you to put your hand in your pocket. Some tracks will allow one free place for every ten or so paid places. Alternatively make sure that you load what the scouts have to pay in order to cover your place. If you can get away with two places this will mean that you get twice as many rides as everyone else.* If you can add a bit more to cover the cost of a beer / prosecco or two after the event so much the better as there are always plenty of stories to be swapped with the other leaders. This can be justified, although you have no one to justify it to, as a debriefing session. If an awkward parent (and you know who they are) checks the prices and notes that they are having to pay more tell them that you are obliged to purchase additional insurance.
3. Forget to give a waver form to the parents to sign. Any child who turns up to race that doesn't have a completed form will not be allowed to race. Some parents are on top of this sort of thing and may look up the form themselves, others will ask you for a copy. The rest will just have to sit

and watch. For this reason bring plenty of leaders and mates to take their places. Go-karting is expensive!

4. Before having the safety talk tell the scouts that the reason that they have to have such a talk is because go-karting is extremely dangerous. After the talk remind the scouts that they don't have to take part if they don't want to; it's entirely up to them. Given that half will already be on the benches, don't be surprised if at this stage several more voluntarily drop out.

5. Ensure that there is a leader near the front at the start of each race. This will mean that on the first corner they will be very well positioned to "nudge" one of the scouts into the barriers. This will scare a few more off and they will retire shaken but otherwise uninjured. Don't forget to tell the race organisers that in your opinion these individuals should not race again. As scout leader you won't be contradicted.

6. If you have any scouts left - scare them! Drive like maniacs. Treat the circuit as if it were a bumper car circuit. Turn round if you must and go the wrong way!

7. Now you can have a race with your fellow leaders and mates. If there are any scouts left on the track that is not a problem as they will have passed the unofficial test in being fearless and they will probably go faster than you anyway.

Notes

If one of your fellow leaders wants to gain this badge wait until all the fuss has died down from the parents before you rebook.

*To make effective use of time courses will often have the next team in the pit stop ready to go onto the track the moment the last person comes off from the previous race.

Make sure that you have a word with the organisers so that you have a go-kart waiting for you at the back in the pit stop so that you can jump straight out of yours and into the next.

***

GO-KARTING PLUS

Hold the **Go-Karting** badge.

To gain your badge
Come first.

HAIR ALIGHT

Hair alight is a fairly regular occurrence when there are young people around, especially when long hair, curiosity, matches and petrol are involved. You may not actually be present when petrol is around as you may have told the scouts that petrol is banned at scout meetings as it is extremely flammable and explosive but this will often result in their going straight home and getting out their parent's petrol can for the lawn mower and wandering down the garden with a box of matches in order to find out just how flammable and explosive. However this is not a badge that can be gained by mistake; you need to be actively involved in hair catching alight in order for it to be awarded. But don't panic! Hair does not actually burn, it singes and as it grows from roots inside the scalp new hair normally grows back without any problem.

To gain your badge

Ensure that someone in your care catches their hair alight. Remember that the longer an individual's hair the easier it is to catch alight so focus your efforts on these scouts. There are two alternatives. Select one of them.

Alternative One

Get a camp fire going not very well then tell the scout to bend down and get as near as they can to the fire and tell them to blow gently with their eyes shut. Encourage them to get nearer. Nearer still. As they are blowing gently you can blow as hard as you like from the other side. This should send the flames over your scout and before you know it you've earned your badge. (Having their eyes shut not only saves them from being blinded, it also hopefully ensures that they have no idea what you were up to.) If they do accuse you, say something like, "I'm sorry but I thought you had finished / given up." However, given that they will probably be otherwise occupied for some time they probably won't say anything.

Alternative Two
Any other planned incident that causes hair to catch alight. Candles are a good place to start.

HILL WALKER

Hill Walker is one of the more challenging badges for scout leaders to gain as it involves a much greater degree of preparation than most to ensure that nothing goes wrong. Only attempt this badge if you are committed to achieving it by completing all the requirements.

To gain your badge

1. Using local knowledge identify a hill. This is normally described as, "a natural elevation of land, higher than a mound but not as high or craggy as a mountain."
2. Make sure that the top of the hill is accessible by car or other form of motor vehicle.
3. Using an Ordnance Survey map plot your route. Ensure that you don't miss any opportunities for a sit down and / or refreshment.
4. Start your walk by driving to the top of the hill. Preferably get a lift otherwise you will have to walk up the hill later to collect your vehicle. This should not be attempted under any circumstances.
5. Once at the top of the hill make sure that you have your first aid kit in your rucksack. This should include cigarettes, hip flask (full) and four cans of beer or a bottle of wine*.
6. Start your walk down the hill walking at a steady pace. Don't forget to make regular stops for a sit down and / or refreshment. The Highway Code recommends a driver stopping at least every two hours and having a break each time for at least fifteen minutes. However, as you are walking it is recommended that you stop at least every

fifteen minutes and having a break each time for at least two hours.

7. Aim to cover (with breaks) about four miles every nine hours.

* "A light load is a happy hiker." Offload the liquid as soon as you can, preferably into your mouth. It will quickly sink into your bladder. This will lower your centre of gravity and make you much more stable.

HITCH-HIKING

One of the greatest delights of hitch-hiking is getting around the country without having to pay. This is achieved by using private transport that stops by the roadside. You can't simply ask your spouse to give you a lift.

To gain your badge

1. Find a suitable place to catch a lift. By the side of the road is a good start, preferably at a junction where vehicles have to slow down.

2. Put the scouts into pairs along the road. It is very unlikely that an empty coach is suddenly going to pass by and stop so you need to be fairly certain that anyone who stops can accommodate two people. If, however, they can't then don't worry. Send just one scout having ascertained whether the other one can travel in the boot. This is often overlooked but it a perfectly acceptable way to travel - unless you are a scout leader.

3. If you find that very few vehicles are stopping, if any at all, then you will need to take emergency action. Hide all the scouts behind some large trees or in the undergrowth and put one of your more *attrayante* young people on the side of the road by themselves.

4. Get her to smile and wave at drivers. Someone will soon stop. At this point the bait will open the back door and as she does so two of the scouts must be ready to emerge from their hiding place and dive straight in. The driver, if he realises, will normally too polite to eject them. Continue

with the other scouts until all have lifts. You will be last. You can get a taxi.

5. Make sure the scouts all know where they are going as if you lose some it may take a considerable amount of time to locate them and even more time explaining to their parents why they were lost in the first place.

HOBBIES

A hobby is a leisure activity that someone does regularly for pleasure. Winston Churchill once said, "To be really happy and really safe, one ought to have at least two or three hobbies, and they must all be real." So think about what you

do or would like to do regularly for pleasure and you'll already be well on your way to gaining this badge.

To gain your badge

1. Identify three hobbies that you currently do or would like to do to.
2. Plan how you're going to do your hobbies, when and where and stick at them for at least three months.
3. You will need to be motivated and enthused by your hobbies.
4. Choose the following areas:
   - Drinking. This could include indulging at various different venues. For example the local pub, another pub, a restaurant ("I'll just have a drink if you don't mind"), your home. If you find you are having difficulty with some of these venues try your car or your shed. Make an in-depth study of what you are drinking. Have at least half a dozen and ascertain whether you notice any changes. Do you feel like getting more involved with your hobby or is the floor moving? If you are up the road how do you intend to get back home without falling over? Would you do things differently next time?

- Gambling. Take at least one hundred pounds to a local betting shop. Decide which horse you are going to put your money on. Put the money on and get a betting slip in return. Realise that this is the only thing that you are going to get for your one hundred pound bet. Return the following week and be told, "You didn't collect your winnings last week sir. 'Who r u kidding?' came first at fifty to one so you've won five thousand pounds." Wake up in a cold sweat and realise that you were having a dream, or more likely a nightmare.
- Relaxing. Find a nice comfy sofa and sit in it. Better still, sit in an armchair so that no one can sit next to you and disturb you. Turn on the TV if you haven't already. Fall asleep for at least three hours.
- Lap dancing. Visit a lap dancing bar. Don't forget to take a credit card and rack up a huge debt drinking Champagne, smoking ginormous cigars and being treated like you're someone special when you're not. Return home and cancel the credit card (unless it wasn't yours in the first place). In case your husband sees the bill go to a place that's called "Sewing Kit" or "Baking Ingredients" so that he doesn't suspect. He will have no idea how much these things actually cost. If he presses you tell him that you had a "same-day, personal delivery."
- Anything else that you can think of.

HYGIENE

With infectious diseases all around us as much as ever before it is important that you are practising what you preach, especially on camp. At large scale events where norovirus is one disease that can quickly take hold it is important to ensure that hands are kept clean.

To gain your badge

1. When preparing food, especially on camp, and you haven't had time to wash your hands after you've been playing "toss the cow pat" with the other leaders make sure that you get rid of as much of the dirt as possible by wiping them in some long grass. If you can't find any long grass nearby go and look for a tree as there is often long grass around the bottom of the trunk although no one really knows why.
2. Alternatively you can wash them in the washing-up water for the crockery and cutlery if it is ready.
3. If you forget to wash your hands and one of the scouts complains that they're dirty (which they won't) flick your fingers up and down your top a couple of times reminding the scouts that it's not soap and water that kills bugs - it's friction but it only works for leaders because only they know how to do it properly.
4. Hands may be dried by waving them in the air although this is not so effective on winter camp so you can always dry them on a tea towel to speed up the operation.
5. If you have a cough or a cold, when coughing or sneezing aim for a large billy, preferably one that is cooking

pasta or a stew. Aim from a standing position and do not get too close when sneezing otherwise you may end up with a face full of Bolognese sauce.

6. If you need to go for a pee whilst cooking remember that it's only the thought of it that's off-putting: the sound will be drowned out by the bubbling of the pasta or the gurgling of the Bolognese. During the winter months this can be a bit tricky as you may end up with frost-bite down one leg. However if you're on summer camp preparing a salad you may have to contrive to make some French dressing and shake it vigorously in a bottle for as long as it takes. Make sure you're wearing shorts / skirt though.

INSTRUCTOR

Being an instructor is far beyond
the call of most scout leaders but
obtaining the badge isn't. This is
because you aspire to be at a level
higher than instructor which means
that you don't need to instruct, just
manage. This badge is best
attempted at a large camp gathering.

To gain your badge

1. Dress appropriately for the activity that you've chosen.
Normally this will be a large distinctive red jacket with loads
of pockets and florescent strips.
2. Have plenty of accessories. These could be any of the
following, or all of them: at least one lanyard, whistle,
bunch of keys around your neck, walkie-talkie, clipboard
with pen attached (either clipped or dangling), torch (even
during the day), stern expression.
3. Find your chosen activity and walk straight in (unless it's
water-based).
4. Ask who the lead instructor is then approach them and
say, "Alright?" followed by, "How's it going?" They should
respond by giving you a run down on how the activity is
progressing.
5. Once they have finished speaking say, "I'll just have a
quick look around," and then do so, especially the places
that are marked for authorised personnel only.
6. If, when you are leaving, say, "It all looks good to me,"
and the lead instructor responds with anything other than,
"Who are you?" or similar then you can also be awarded
the **Instructor Plus** badge.

INSTRUCTOR PLUS

See **Instructor** badge.

INTERNATIONAL

Don't think that travelling to the nearest coast to where you live is as much as you can manage. Look further afield to a place that involves travel over water! This can include anywhere that is classed as an island, even though it may not now be.

To gain your badge
1. Find somewhere that involves navigating over a stretch of water either on foot or by car / train.
2. The place that you choose should be somehow connected to the mainland, usually by a bridge although even then this may not be necessary. Suggestions include:
South East: Isle of Grain, Isle of Sheppey, Isle of Thanet, Canvey Island, Foulness Island
South: Hayling Island, Portsea Island
South West: Isle of Portland, Wales via M4
Wales: Anglesey
North West: Walney Island
Scotland: Isle of Skye
Northern Ireland: Inch Island
If you already live on one of these islands - go the other way.
3. Travel to this place.
4. Immerse yourself in the local culture. This could include a visit to a pub and sampling a local beer or pie. Perhaps visit a local art gallery and ask, "Who buys this ****?"
5. Try out the language. Learn a few words* beforehand and try them out on the locals. Even better, you could try

to copy their accent to see if you can be thought of as one of their own.

6. Get to grips with the currency. Maybe bring a couple of notes back with you as a souvenir (except in Scotland).

7. You do not have to stay there. A cup of tea will suffice before returning.

*Useful phrases include:
"Don't you know who I am?"
"I have not been drinking."
"He is not my husband."
"I didn't realise that I had to pay for it."
"I didn't know that it was an offence here."
"Don't worry, I won't be coming back."

INTERNATIONAL PLUS

To gain this badge you have to hold the **International** badge.

Broaden your horizons still further! There are now no limits to what you can achieve internationally!

To gain your badge

1. Find somewhere that involves navigating over a stretch of water by boat or ferry. (You do not have to do the navigating yourself.)
2. The place that you choose should not be connected to the mainland. Suggestions include:

Isle of Wight

Channel Islands

Isles of Scilly

Lundy

Isle of Man

Loads of islands off Scottish coast

3 - 7. As per the **International** badge

INTERNATIONAL PLUS PLUS

To gain this badge, one of only two Plus Plus badges, you have to hold the **International** and the **International Plus** badge.

Now you're flying! Metaphorically speaking.

To gain your badge

1. Find somewhere that involves flight.
2. Get hold of some travel brochures. You could try a local travel agents although these are sometimes hard to find. Explain that you would like to research somewhere really exotic and spend loads of money. You should then be able to return home with an armful.
3. Sit down in your favourite armchair or curl up on the sofa with a European lager or glass of prosecco, a plate of tapas and with your passport in your back pocket.
4. Flick through the brochures admiring the hotels.
5. Make disparaging remarks about the prices, calculate how much it would have cost to have taken your spouse / partner / friend on a trip and sit back in your seat feeling very smug that you have saved so much.
6. The following day wonder why you cannot find / make contact with your spouse / partner / friend.

IT'S "ON THE TENT!"

This badge can easily been gained on a weekend camp.

What do you say to the scout that asks a stupid "Where do I put" question? They all do it. Do you give them a straight answer? No, because this doesn't teach them to think for themselves. Do you sigh? No, as this implies that the scout is stupid. Do you refuse to answer? No, because you should be engaging with the scout and not making them think that their question isn't important. Mostly your response or lack of will inadvertently led to your also gaining the **Safeguarding** badge which is great but you won't be getting this one.

To gain your badge

1. When a scout asks you a stupid "Where do I put"*question you must not refuse to answer or sigh or respond with a straight answer. Instead say, "On the tent."** You have thus given them an answer but one that will make them think for themselves.

2. The scout must then take the correct action and not take you literally.

3. You must answer, "On the tent," at least five times in a twenty-four hour period.

* Possible question include:
"Where do I put this rubbish?"
"Where do I put this washing up?"
"Where do I put this drying up?"
"Where do I put my sleeping bag?"

110

"Where do I put my towel?"
"Where do I put my cutlery / crockery?"
"Where do I put my wet / dirty clothes?"
"Where do I put this opened milk / juice?"
"Where do I put my boots?"
"Where do I put my sick?"

If "On the tent" is the correct answer, such as in response to a question like, "Where do I put this dolly?"* then you could just point.
***"Dolly" as in a wooden tent dolly that goes on top of a tent pole as an attachment for a guy rope and to act as a rain cap. If, however, the scout is waving a rag / stuffed dolly as in a child's doll around see 1.

KNOTS

This is another of those badges that should be extremely simple to earn as you have so much choice. Recent research has suggested that there are over four thousand knots. You only have to learn and use ten!

To gain your badge

1. Think of ten knots* that have been of most use to you.
2. Use them in situations that are suited specifically to these knots. You cannot use a knot that is not suitable.
3. Do not select the easiest knots. Have a mix of ones that are easy, medium and others that are more difficult.
4. The knots must be completed. Do not get half way and then give up.

*Notes

The following is a good selection:

Easy

Do knot do that.

Do knot say that.

Do knot touch that.

Do knot go in there.

Medium

I told you knot to do that so why have you done it again?

I told you knot to say that so why have you said it again?

I told you knot to touch that so why have you touched it again?

I told you knot to go in there so why have you gone in there again?

Hard

I told you knot to do that so why have you done it again? I will tell you this for free - if you do it again on this camp you will probably go blind.

I told you knot to say that so why have you said it again? It wasn't funny then and it's even less funny now. (To be said without smiling.)

I told you knot to touch that so why have you touched it again? Now you have two burnt fingers,

I told you knot to go in there so why have you gone in there again? She didn't want you in her tent the first time so what makes you think she's changed her mind?

LIBRARIAN

The British Library holds over 13 million books. Think of all the cataloguing that has to be done in order to make it as easy as possible to find any one particular book. To gain this badge you don't have to go quite so far yourself.

To gain your badge

1. Obtain a book. You may not have one at home so try a bookshop although they're not so easy to find these days. In London you could try Charing Cross Road, otherwise you may have to try a bit harder. In a church you may find that if the vicar is around he will let you have a Bible if you look interested and tell him that you're searching for a good book. You could try a mini-library that many railway stations have or how about a disused red telephone kiosk that has been converted?
2. Take it home and have a look through it. If you've chosen well you will have one with plenty of pictures. If you've chosen badly you will have one with only pictures.
3. Learn how to catalogue. With a felt tip pen write "1" on the spine and then file on a shelf. If it's a book with only pictures it will probably have to go on a top shelf.
4. Next time you're out see if you can get yourself another book.
5. Continue until you have ten books.

LIFESAVER

In a dire emergency, having a lifesaver to hand is all but essential in order to avoid troubling the emergency services.

To gain your badge

1. Learn the different types of lifesaver.
2. There are different lifesavers for different situations. Know when to use which one. It may be that an occasion demands more than one.
3. Lifesavers and when to use them can include:
   - Microwave. When it's Christmas Day and you've forgotten to defrost the turkey.
   - 24-hour supermarket. When you've forgotten to buy a turkey.
   - Keys to the scout hut. When you've run out of cash and there's no loo roll, bbq briquettes, gas cylinders, tea and coffee, soap, washing-up liquid indoors.
   - The back way into the garden centre. When it's gone five o'clock and you've suddenly realised it's your wedding anniversary.
   - Vodka. When you arrive on camp in the pouring rain and find out that you and your fellow leader thought that the other was bringing the tents.

LISTENING

Being able to listen is the mark of a good scout leader but you need to find the right things to listen to - don't listen to any old nonsense. You don't have to - it's not necessary.

To gain your badge

1. Find a situation where you feel you will be comfortable listening.
2. Start to listen.
3. Listen for as long as you feel is necessary.
4. Stop listening and respond.

Examples for listening include:

- The television although this may involve watching as well.
- The radio, especially Jo Whiley or similar on Radio Two or Radio Five Live when there's a Premier League match on.

Examples for responding include:

- Television: Laughing or giggling.
- Radio Two: "Oh I love this track!"
- Radio Five Live: "GOOOOOOOOOOOAAAAAALLLLL!!!"

5. On no way should you ever listen to any scouts, their parents or anyone in management. If someone in one of these groups insists on talking to you as a last resort stick your fingers in your ears and start to hum loudly.

LOCAL KNOWLEDGE

With a compass and Explorer series Ordnance Survey map in your hand you will be able easily to navigate your way across whatever the geography of an area throws at you even if you're somewhere totally new to you, especially if you have a GPS app on your 'phone. But everyone has to start somewhere and where better to start than where you live?

To gain your badge

1. Show that you know the area around your scout hut up to around a mile in every direction. This can be achieved by drawing a map showing fields, woods and roads. Then add as much of the following as you are able:

Pubs: Mark all the main entrances and exits. Show that it is possible to lead a group of scouts, send them around the outside whilst you walk through the pub and with a bit of swift arm action knock back a pint or a vodka and tonic then rejoin the group at the back.

Restaurants: Especially those that will serve you in scout uniform so that you can pop in for a quick bite to eat after a scout meeting, or maybe even during it.

Cafes: A good cafe will have an English breakfast waiting for you at all times.

Toilets: With public conveniences at a premium this can now include behind bushes and (up) trees, churchyards, telephone kiosks (even if they are now mini libraries or information hubs), post boxes or anywhere in a park.

Bicycle sheds: To include other similar constructions where you can have a cigarette where you are hidden or that are, in fact, legitimate. Fortunately the smoking ban on indoor venues now means that there are plenty of new areas where you can indulge, maybe having a pee at the same time (see Toilets above).

Benches and other places suitable for a forty winks.

2. Use your map to plan a route that takes in at least one pub, restaurant, cafe, toilet and bench.

MARRIAGE

In the Bible it is written, (Proverbs 18:22), "He who finds a wife finds a good thing." In Genesis 2:24 it states, "...a man leaves his father and mother and is united to his wife, and they become one flesh." If you wish for a long and happy life this will be most achievable, if you are to marry, in a Christian marriage between man and woman where your marriage is a gift from God and one that should never be taken for granted.

To gain your badge

1. Take time to find someone who truly loves you and whom you truly love. This could be in a church, at work, in a pub, maybe at a party. There is more likely to be someone out there for you than not. It is one of the miracles of life that there are roughly an equal number of males and females in the world.

2. When you feel that the time is right ask your girlfriend / boyfriend if they will marry you. Although ninety-five percent of proposals come from the man if you want to have something to talk about for the rest of your life - propose to your boyfriend!

3. Don't be scared to ask. If you don't and she doesn't you will never know. One survey found that one in four women have turned down a proposal although one in four of those later regretted saying, "No."

4. Get married in a church surrounded by your friends and relatives.

5. Stay married together for better, for worse, for richer, for poorer, in sickness and in health until one of you dies. If that's you then you won't ever get your badge but you will have had a life filled with love and laughter.

MARTIAL ARTS

Martial arts help you to become subservient, dominated and put upon but these are all necessary for a quiet life.

To gain your badge

1. Get married to someone whom you love but also get on with very well.

2. Find areas in which your spouse responds in a way that surprises you. These could include saying that you're just popping up to the pub but not inviting them or forgetting a birthday or anniversary. If you are really brave try forgetting Christmas or pick Christmas Day for just popping up the pub. Maybe invite a load of mates round to watch the cup final (male) or for females have a girls' evening and drink all the bottles of Champagne that he's saving up for Christmas for when he comes back from the pub. Better still, for the females you invite a load of male mates round to watch the cup final or for the males have a boys' evening and drink all her prosecco that she has stashed. (All females have a stash of prosecco. Favourite places are those where they think that you will never look such as their underwear drawer. If only they knew. Look behind the books etc. on a book shelf. If a book is particularly large look inside it. Have a quick peep in the washing machine, dishwasher, tumble dryer and microwave. Then try her shoeboxes, under the sink, and finally in the sofa between the seat and the back cushions. If you are looking for his stash they only ever use the shed or the barbecue.)

3. Work out a strategy and employ it. This may include:

Subservient - Say "sorry" and buy her a large bunch of flowers or him something that is cordless.

Dominated - Say "sorry" and buy her a large bunch of flowers or him something that is cordless.

Put upon - Say "sorry" and buy her a large bunch of flowers or him something that is cordless.

4. If you are successful your spouse will smile and forgive you and say no more about it but if she continues to nag or he continues to go on then go back to 2. and try again. When you get to 3. consider a more generous response. For her pay for her to go on holiday. If this fails suggest that firstly you don't go and secondly that she can take half a dozen mates with her. For him buy him a shed. If this fails build it for him.

MASTER AT ARMS

Do you like shooting things? If so, this is the badge for you.

To gain your badge

Join a club. Preferably this would be rifle shooting or archery but if you're in London and a bit posh you may want to consider The Athenaeum or Brooks (although Brooks is for aristocrats so that excludes most scout leaders). No further action is necessary on your part. If anyone asks how you earned your badge just tell them that you were awarded it automatically because you are / were a member of a club.*

Otherwise,

1. Attend regular (at least two) sessions in archery or rifle shooting. One of the more popular Master at Arms disciplines among the scout leader fraternity is darts. This involves attendance at a club also (for the purposes of having a good excuse, although in this context this could include a Working Men's Club) but is mostly going to be the pub.

2. Show an improvement between the sessions. To make this a little less onerous you may wish to consider being deliberately useless during your first session. There is no limit as to how useless you can be. For archery aim to miss the target and, if you think you can get away with it, the large security backdrop. If you can get the arrow over the backdrop then anyone up to half a mile away won't be safe. For rifle shooting a .22 bullet can travel up to a mile. A .303 can go twice this distance. Just make sure that you

miss the target and fire the bullet into the sand beneath. A good ruse is to scream loudly and fire the bow / rifle straight up into the air. Apologise profusely to your instructor, say that you saw a mouse or some other frightening character. Firing straight up into the air has the added excitement that what comes up must come down so be prepared to dive under shelter whilst you wait to see how straight you had fired. For darts try to embed the dart in the wall. Added excitement can be gained if the dartboard that you are throwing at is seated inside a rubber car tyre. Great amusement can be had if you can hit the tyre. If you dart does not have a honed point it won't embed itself but rebound often in a random direction causing other patrons to scatter if not you yourself.
At the second or subsequent session, whatever your discipline, at least hit the target.

*NB. Golf club membership does not count even though golfers are mostly quite violent and like throwing things. Anyone can become a member of a golf club.

MECHANIC

Never get caught out with a dodgy car. Always know what to do in an emergency. Don't rely on others except when it's vital. Know what everything does "under the bonnet." Get these things right and you will be well on your way to being a first-class mechanic.

To gain your badge

1. When buying a new car offer half what is being asked for. You probably won't get it but you might.
2. When buying a used car always kick the tyres as you walk around the outside. Shake your head and inhale through your teeth at each wheel. You don't have to say anything - your actions and noises will tell the seller all that they need to know and that is that you know what they know and that is that the car is not worth what they're asking for it. Then offer one quarter of what is being asked for. You probably won't get it but you might and you will be able to drive the car home safe it the knowledge that you have saved enough to pay for a new gear box when it goes the next month and a new engine the month after that.
3. At the petrol station put the wrong fuel in the tank. When it won't start you will need to call out a specialist misfuelling service to drain the fuel and flush the lines through with a cleaning fluid. When you're asked by your spouse how you could be so stupid tell them that the petrol / diesel was on offer so you thought that you would fill up saying, "I didn't think it really mattered which one you put in."

4. If you get a puncture don't bother stopping and having to go through all the rigmarole of having to change a tyre on the road. You probably won't know where to put the jack under the car anyway and before you know it you'll be driving home with a large hole in the footwell. Drive home and get one of the children to do it.

5. There are two main caps under the bonnet. One is for oil, the other is for screen wash. Getting them mixed up will be sure to make a journey much more interesting. There are three more caps that you need to be aware of. They are for brake fluid, engine coolant and power steering fluid. Getting these mixed up with the other two can make a long journey even more exciting. This will be for various reasons but could include:

a. The car has broken down

b. The car has burnt down.

b. You've crashed.

6. Shouting at other motorists is a great stress reliever. If they haven't done anything wrong don't look at them whilst you're shouting. Keep the window wound up and the radio turned up. You'll feel much better and you won't have been thumped.

MEDIA RELATIONS AND MARKETING

This is probably the badge least worth having. It's completely meaningless. As with children who read these subjects at university (more likely the old polytechnics as no self-respecting university would offer these as degree courses) yours is not worth the paper it's written on or the badge material that it's woven into. Other leaders will wonder how you had the audacity to sew it onto your uniform.

To gain your badge
There are two alternatives. Select one of them and complete all the tasks.

Alternative One
Media relations
1. Write to a newspaper.
2. Online you could post a comment to a news item.
3. Tell them what a good job they're doing.
4. Send them a press release about yourself or your scout group. If you struggle to think of anything newsworthy then simply make it up. You don't have to get it published.

Alternative Two
Marketing
1. Go shopping. This could be a street market, an indoor market, an antique market, a flea market, a fish market or if you're struggling how about a supermarket? If you're still really stuck attend a car boot sale.
2. Buy something.

MESS TENT

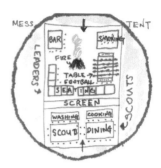

A mess tent is an essential piece of kit on any camping trip (although if you are hiking or on an expedition it is best left behind). It is at the centre of everything that's going on. It can be the cooking area, the eating area and the socialising area.

Originally it was known as a messy tent due to the state of the scouts who would appear in it after they had been on some activity or other. They would come in, often soaking wet if they had been kayaking or other water-based activity, looking for food, often with nothing on their feet. They would dump all the wet kit on the tables and start hunting out the biscuits that they would then proceed to fight over leaving crumbs scattered all over the tables. Alternatively they would bring their own food and drink into it. Drinks would be spilt and food wrappers would litter the ground. Individual bags of crockery and cutlery that were meant to stay in the sleeping tents would be left, unbagged, on any surface they could find. Random bowls with half eaten food would be left lying around. Messy tents became a magnet for foxes and badgers that would invade in the night adding their own individual calling cards.

Something had to change.

Now the more enlightened scout groups ban scouts from the messy tent and it has been renamed to the above.

To gain your badge

1. Know how to erect a mess tent. Impart this information to the scouts when they first arrive on camp whilst you sneak off for a beer or glass of wine.

2. Know the various possible configurations of a mess tent to include a cooking area, eating area and socialising area. Impart this information to the scouts once they have erected the mess tent whilst you sneak off for another beer or glass of wine.

Note that the central poles can be removed to make more space. The mess tent will not collapse. However it is best to ensure that you place tables under the central connectors (or put slits in tennis balls and shove on the ends). Otherwise any scout who passes underneath and then suddenly raises their head will find that they have a tubular hole in their skull.

3. Make sure that you have enough pegs so that the mess tent stays attached to the metal frame in high winds. Give the pegs to the scouts and get them to secure the mess tent all the way round whilst you sneak off for yet another beer or glass of wine.

4. Come back from the pub and tell the scouts that they need to erect their tents while you prepare supper. Sit down in your comfy chair for a couple of minutes and fall fast asleep. You won't be woken up because if you've done your job properly they won't dare come back in unless you've invited them.

5. When it's time to strike camp do the above in reverse.

Notes

If you have a brand new mess tent and don't like the colour of it and want to mess it up a bit, invite the scouts in one evening, give them a mug of hot chocolate each and tell them a **Ghost Story**. At the climax SHOUT! Any hot chocolate that has yet to be imbibed will end up coating the inside of the mess tent.

METEOROLOGIST

Research has shown that the average British person spends around nearly ten minutes every day talking about the weather and that over half of us have the weather as our go-to topic when making small talk. No wonder we're so boring if all we can say is, "It's warm / cold / wet / dry for the time of year." With the **Meteorologist** badge you can big talk small talk with clouds, wind and temperature.

To gain your badge
1. Cumulus is a type of cloud. It's the only word that you really need. When someone says, "It's cloudy today," or anything that mentions clouds look up and say, "Cumulus." There are several types of cumulus. Estimate whether the clouds are high, low or in the middle somewhere and call them "High cumulus," "Low cumulus," or "Mid-range cumulus." If there is no cloud you can refer to it as a "Minimal cumulus day." It will make them look stupid and make you look knowledgeable.
2. The same with wind. Beaufort is the word that you need. When someone says, "It's windy today," don't worry about the thirteen levels of the Beaufort wind scale. After all, who's going to know whether it's moderate gale, near gale, fresh gale, strong gale, severe gale or whole gale? Estimate the basic levels and call them "Low Beaufort," "Medium Beaufort," and "High Beaufort." If there is no wind call it "Minimal Beaufort."
3. Temperature is another area where you can succeed. Nearly everyone will say, "It's hot / warm / cold / freezing

for the time of year." Show them your knowledge, not with the Centigrade or Fahrenheit scales as some may know a little about these. There is a third - Kelvin. Use this one. Unlike cloud and wind there is always temperature. You can have, "High Kelvin," "Low Kelvin," or "Medium Kelvin." Don't in your haste get muddled up with a similar rather ugly boys' name and refer to temperature as "Kevin."

4. If someone mentions rain, pressure or humidity don't get involved as this is having to learn to much. Refer back to 1, 2 and 3 above.

NAPPING

The **Napping** badge is one of the few badges that you may find yourself gaining whilst you're asleep and so is a popular badge that is worn by most. In fact if you don't wear it people will only ask why you don't have it. So make sure that you gain it at the earliest opportunity. There's plenty of choice.

To gain your badge
1. Find a comfortable chair on camp and sit in it. This can out in the open, under a dining shelter or in a mess tent. If you are in your tent this doesn't always count. If you are in the hours of darkness this doesn't ever count.
2. Choose a nap. Choose wisely. If you just slouch into a chair and close your eyes you will feel no benefit and you may miss a meal. A good nap has to be planned. Set an alarm. Choose from the following:

The Early Riser Nap
Benefits: Boosts your energy levels, helps you to focus and increases mental ability. Gets you out of washing up.
How Long: Twenty to thirty minutes.
When: After lunch between 2 and 3pm.
Detection Rate: Low. If you need a nap this is the time to have it as plenty of others will be at it also.
Hassle Factor: Low. Make sure that you tell everyone before you find a comfy corner that you were first up "doing stuff."

The Espresso Nap

Make and drink an Espresso quickly before finding a place to snooze. This is not recommended as a regular type of nap.

Benefits: Gives a quick boost to your energy levels if you're feeling really tired. You will wake up just as the caffeine kicks in. You will have relieved some of the sleep and tiredness pressure but make sure that you go to bed earlier the next night.

How Long: Twenty minutes maximum.

When: Mid-morning or mid-afternoon.

Detection Rate: Lowish.

Hassle Factor: If you have been up late entertaining the troops you will be forgiven.

The New Mother Nap

Sleep when your baby sleeps. If it's good enough for them it's good enough for you. You may find yourself wide awake in the middle of the night though if your baby is very young.

Benefits: You'll get plenty of sleep.

How Long: As long as your baby is asleep.

When: Whenever your baby is asleep.

Detection Rate: Nil.

Hassle Factor: Low. Other leaders should understand if you are found out. Otherwise move your tent so that is next to theirs and don't feed baby in the night for half an hour when it wakes up demanding sustenance.

The Night-Owl Nap

If you're heading out for a very late one that's going to zap the energy levels, maybe you're roller-discoing or nightclubbing, then you need this nap. This is also not recommended as a regular type of nap. It's a serious nap and not at all good for your sleep pattern if you keep doing it. You body craves sleep rhythms and this means going to bed and getting up at the same time every day. Don't be tempted to have a lie-in. Get up at your usual time and you will be bright and breezy when the rest appear, even if you do need to have an Espresso nap later in the day. Go to bed at your usual time. Don't do two Night-Owl Naps in a row.

Benefits: It will give you the stamina to keep going until the small hours without dropping off and crashing into the D J or, worse, one of the bouncers.

How Long: One to two hours in your tent.

When: Early evening. Give yourself half an hour at least once you wake up before you go out.

Detection Rate: High.

Hassle Factor: If you're going with others it won't matter. If you get up bright and breezy the following morning you have nothing to lose.

The Scout Nap

Scouts are of an age where their internal clocks want them to go to bed late and get up late. If you're getting them up early offer them a mid-afternoon nap so that they can catch up.

Benefits: The campsite is quiet for a while.

How Long: Twenty minutes otherwise the scouts won't want to go to bed at all.

When: Around 3.30pm.

Detection Rate: Low because everyone will be doing it, including the scouts.

Hassle Factor: None

The Siesta Nap

This is a serious nap! In hot weather it's a complete change to the usual routines in the UK although in other parts of the world it's expected. In countries like Spain the shops and offices all close up in the early afternoon for an extended lunch and chill out.

Benefits: Start early and finish late with a great big sleep in the middle! It's more like each long day being two smaller ones. It means that you can stay out even later than if you have a Night-Owl nap.

How Long: Three hours.

When: After an early lunch. One to four pm is a good time.

Detection Rate: High.

Hassle Factor: Very high and that's why it's a good idea to get the other leaders doing the same.

The Sports Nap

This is a great nap if you're going to be involved in any sort of energetic sporting activity or game, maybe a football match or playing tag.

Benefits: A nap before a strenuous event may pay dividends. You will receive a physical and mental boost for a short time with no sleep lethargy (that is waking up feeling groggy) unless you really were tired.

How Long: Fifteen minutes. If you sleep for too long you may experience sleep lethargy upon waking and unless you give yourself time for this to wear off you may suffer a negative effect and instead of being bright and sparkly you will be sluggish and lethargic. If you want to gain an edge, suggest to your opponents that they have half an hour's sleep then wake them up just as you're about to start the activity.

When: Afternoon or early evening. It doesn't work well in the morning when you should be fairly alert anyway.
Detection Rate: High but inconsequential as you have a good reason.
Hassle Factor: Low, but don't try and do it before a game of cards or tiddlywinks.

Notes
Warning: You may awake to find that someone has already awarded you the badge.

***

NAPPING PLUS
Gain the **Napping** badge then repeat - not at camp but at a regular meeting or on a hike, or gain the **Napping** badge twice with two different types of nap.

NARROWBOATING

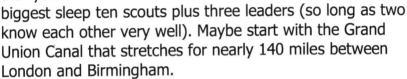

Try your hand at narrowboating - a leisurely 4mph chug along the canals of the United Kingdom.

To gain your badge

1. Book up the longest narrowboat that you can find. Some of the biggest sleep ten scouts plus three leaders (so long as two know each other very well). Maybe start with the Grand Union Canal that stretches for nearly 140 miles between London and Birmingham.
2. Have a couple of hours' familiarisation with the vessel so at least you know how to start and stop.
3. Pile the kids onboard and head off.
4. On a straight stretch see how fast you can go, especially when passing moored boats. Fishermen on the bank will greet you with whoops and plenty of hand gestures.
5. At full speed see if you can take a tight corner. If you time it well any scouts that are sitting on the roof may find, when you nudge the bank with the stern, that they are suddenly on the bank themselves if not in the field beyond.
6. When approaching a lock and the narrowboat is travelling downstream go full speed. (Make sure that the scouts are all sitting on the roof.) This means that it may be possible to force open the lock gates at the far end and experience a Niagara Falls effect as the narrowboat drops twenty feet or so without waiting for the lock to empty in a more controlled manner. Once through the lock rescue the scouts from the canal.
7. When approaching a lock and the narrowboat is travelling upstream go full speed. (Make sure that the

scouts are all sitting on the roof.) This means that it may be possible to force open the lock gates at the far end and experience a Niagara Falls effect from above as the water cascades violently down. Once through the lock rescue the scouts from the canal if the narrowboat hasn't sunk.

8. For a proper theme park ride, when going downstream don't shut the upstream lock gates. When the downstream gates are opened the narrowboat will emerge from the lock like a cork out of a Champagne bottle. If those that are operating the lock gates aren't quick they will find themselves walking quite a long way and they'll be the first to be arrested so make sure that you put on lock duty someone you don't like.

NATURALIST

In the good old days in would have been perfectly acceptable for a male scout leader to jump naked into a pond with the male scouts, but not anymore. If you were to try that now you would probably be chucked out straight away and have to face all manner of additional sanctions including being arrested. Times have changed and as a result this badge is extremely difficult to earn. Any scout leader who sports it should be accorded immediate respect from those around them not least of all because they're probably no longer a scout leader.

To gain your badge
Complete one of the following:
1. Jump naked into a pond with the scouts whilst on camp. You may be arrested and if convicted of an offence you will have to sign and will appear on the Violent and Sex Offender Register. To be prosecuted it would have to be proved that you intended that someone would see you and be caused alarm or distress. All male scout leaders naked would cause distress and so this is a very high risk strategy. You could jump into the pond then take your shorts and underwear off. This would count but you run the risk of letting go as you hold them under the murky water and then not being able to retrieve them. How you would get out of this situation is anyone's guess. You could stay there until nightfall or ask an understanding leader to fetch you a towel but more questions may be asked over

how you managed to get into the pool clothed but somehow mysteriously lost your clothes once you were in.
2. On camp, not a naturalist camp, go to the toilet from your tent and return naked. This is achievable if there's a new moon and you keep to the trees. You must not go to the toilet in the trees - the toilet needs to be a temporary or permanent building and not a tree. The main danger is whilst you are in the toilet so you are permitted to take a towel and wear it whilst in the toilet. If anyone asks say that you're just about to take a shower or if it's been raining say that you have just had a shower. If the other person says that there are no shower facilities say, "Oh dear. And I went to all this trouble of getting prepared."
3. Go to another campsite, strip off in your car and go for a wander around in broad daylight. There must be other campers present. You will be screamed and shouted at and someone may call the police. You could leave before they arrive but either way explain that you thought that you were at The Natural Naturalist and you must have taken a wrong turn.

NATURIST

The study of animals and plants is probably one of the most boring things that you can do as a scout leader. This makes for a badge that is not often awarded. Unlike with some of the harder-to-achieve badges if you sew this one on your uniform you will most likely be laughed at.

To gain your badge
1. Watch the scouts eat their dinner whilst on camp. Work out which animal they most closely resemble.
2. Identify six famous British plants. Choose from:
Robert Plant
Lynda La Plante.

NOSE PICKING

You may wear this badge with pride or you may be acutely embarrassed to gain it. If you fall into this latter category when you are asked what the badge is for you don't have to say "Nose Picking" but "Rhinotillexomania" instead - a medical word that makes the act sound almost romantic, as they normally do.

To gain your badge

1. Find a generally dirty and dusty place, one of the boys' tents (when they're not in it) is a good place to start. Other places include camp fires, incinerators, lofts, behind beds, curtains, behind fridges, freezers, garages and sheds.
2. Inhale. Deeply. Loads of times. Through the nose and never the mouth. Unless your nose is completely blocked up of course. Then it would be fine to breathe through the mouth. Robert Baden-Powell in "Scouting for Boys" wrote, "...Mr Catlin in America wrote a book called, 'Shut your mouth and save your life'... Breathing through the nose prevents germs of disease getting from the air into the throat and stomach, it also prevents a growth in the back of the throat called 'adenoids' which are apt to stop the breathing power of the nostrils, and also to cause deafness."
3. If you haven't done so as part of 2. expose yourself to a bit of moisture. This is not too important though as mucous membranes in the nose cavity constantly produce a wet mucus. This will line the cavity and remove dust and pathogens from the air that flows through.

4. Wait an hour.

5. Find a quiet spot where no one is looking and have a good poke.

6. For the optimal experience try 5. in a public space without being seen. How about in a car, in a restaurant, in the mess tent, at a meeting, on a video conference call? These are all places where some scout leaders think that they're not being seen - but are.

***

NOSE PICKING PLUS

To gain this badge you need to hold the **Nose Picking** badge. One of the advantages of this badge is that you can usually gain it at the same time as **Nose Picking.**

To gain your badge

1. Get to 5. in **Nose Picking.**
2. Eat it.

NOSE PICKING PLUS PLUS

This is a very special badge. It is one of only two Plus Plus badges. To gain this badge you need to hold the **Nose Picking Plus** badge. One of the advantages of this badge is that you can usually gain it at the same time as **Nose Picking Plus.**

To gain your badge
1. Convert someone who expresses disgust to rhinotillexomania to the point of picking (they don't have to eat at this stage).
2. In "Gastronaut" Stefan Gates discusses the eating of dried nasal mucus. He says that 44% of those he questioned said they had eaten their own dried nasal mucus in adulthood and said they liked it. As mucus filters out airborne contaminants it could be thought that eating it is unhealthy but Gates says, "...our body has been built to consume snot," because the nasal mucus is normally swallowed after being moved inside by the motion of the cilia that are tiny hairs at the back of the nose. Professor Friedrich Bischinger, an Austrian lung specialist said that nose-picking and eating could actually be beneficial for the immune system. Impart this information to your "someone" in 1. then get them to eat. Keep a small supply spare in case they have none left to pick.

OBESITY

This is a badge that you don't really have to think much about: it comes quite naturally and can be reached without much effort. Look around you and you will see that most scout leaders have reached their goal already. Scout meetings and camps are places where you can get a good start.

To gain your badge
1. Go to the NHS website and search for your BMI (body mass index) healthy weight calculator.
2. Input your height, age, weight and sex.
3. Press calculate to find out whether you are classed as underweight, a healthy weight, overweight or obese. If you are already obese congratulations, you have gained this badge. If you are not you need to complete the following also:
4. At every scout meeting, when it's refreshment time, sample everyone of each type of biscuit at least three times. If you don't have a refreshment time, start one.
5. On camp tell the scouts that you always eat what they're eating, so do, only a double portion. It's usually pasta or spaghetti with some stodgy pudding. When they've all finished you will find that there's normally a large billy full of untouched pasta and another of Bolognese. Eat it. Repeat for breakfast and lunch.
6. After the scouts have gone to bed, order a curry for four for one. You. Eat it.
7. At the end of camp give the scouts all the leftover fruit and vegetables, nuts and pulses (if they were even brought

in the first place) and take home the biscuits that you hid, the cake that you hid, the sweets that you hid and any uncooked spaghetti and pasta.

8. Once home, cook it and eat it.

9. Repeat at every weekend whether you are on camp or not.

10. If you are not on camp aim to drink as much alcohol as you can.

11. Under no circumstances are you to take any exercise whatsoever.

12. After three months repeat 1,2 and 3. If you are not obese you are not trying hard enough. Scout leaders will laugh at you for not having this badge. Redouble your efforts.

ORIENTEERING

Orienteering is an exciting outdoor adventure sport that is suitable for all ages and fitness levels. The aim is to navigate between various checkpoints or controls that are marked on a special large-scale orienteering map. There is no set route. In competitive orienteering the challenge is to complete the course, that could be up to over ten kilometres long, in the quickest time.

To gain your badge

1. Invest in a lightweight top, Lycra leggings and footwear with a good grip.
2. Join your local orienteering club.
3. Attend your first event.
4. Orientate your map. Rotate your map so that you can relate the features on the map to those that you can see around you. You can use a compass if you need to.
5. Think about the scale of the map. Things may appear much sooner than you realise. Think about your pace - if you are going to walk at a brisk pace you will cover two yards every second and a mile every fifteen minutes walking at four miles per hour.
6. Look at the map colours on the legend. Open land is yellow and easy forest is white. After that the thicker the forest the darker the green.
7. Fold your map so that you can easily see where you are. Put your thumb on your position at the start.
8. There is no mass start. When it is your turn to go 'punch' the control. This starts your timer.

9. Go in the wrong direction.

10. Find a pub. Sit down and have a beer or glass of wine.

11. Return to the start and tell the organisers that you got lost.

***

ORIENTEERING PLUS

To gain this badge you need to hold the **Orienteering** badge.

To gain your badge

As per **Orienteering** badge except at 11. instead of returning to the start simply go home. The organisers will spend hours looking for you and will continue into nightfall if the course involves going around water. Why not put on a disguise and return to join in the search? We quite like the idea of someone joining in a search for themself. This means that you can tell the organisers that the missing person is a friend of yours and that you will take responsibility for reporting the disappearance. You can then mysteriously reappear the following day. This way the authorities will not need to be troubled and you can report to the organisers that you have been found.

PAINTBALL

This is a competitive team shooting game in which players attempt to eliminate those on the other side(s). This is achieved through hitting them with round capsules of "paint" fired from high-velocity airguns. The paintballs usually break upon impact.

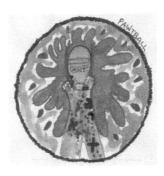

To gain your badge

1. Book some paintballing sessions at a local course.
2. Add several pounds to the cost for each scout. This will enable you to purchase extra paintballs.
3. Try and get an extra gun if you can or smuggle one in. You're going to need it in order to use up all your paintballs.
4. When at the course, when you are dealing out the paintballs the usual way to count is, "One for me, one for you." This way you will have the same number of paintballs as the total that all the scouts have put together. These are in addition to the extras that you have bought.
5. If a scout buys extra paintballs off his own bat make sure that you count them out using the method in 4. above.
6. The organisers will probably say that when one is hit they have to retire immediately from the playing area. This does not include scout leaders so you can ignore this instruction. If one of the scouts complains shoot them even if they are on the same side as you.
7. When you've had enough sell your spare paintballs to the highest bidder. If no one has brought any money wait

until a game is in progress then empty the paintballs into the rucksacks of your "favourite" scouts. Then sit on them.

PAINBALL

A hard man or woman's badge that can be achieved in one of two ways.

To gain your badge

There are two alternatives. Select one of them and complete all the tasks.

Alternative One

As **Paintball** only use large marbles.

Alternative Two

This is similar to air hockey. You will need a pool table for this one. Fellow leaders will greet you with, "Marbles or pool balls?" when they see you sporting this badge.
1. Stand one end of a pool table with your opponent at the other.
2. One will hold in their hand the white cue; the other will hold the black ball.
3. Scatter the remaining balls on the cloth.
4. Using the ball in your hand hit the other balls without letting go so that they go down the two holes at your opponent's end whilst defending your two holes. (The middle pockets don't count so maybe tape them up.) You can use your fingers so long as they are wrapped around your ball. Try not to get them crushed between two balls. If you let go of your ball you are disqualified.
5. The person who knocks more balls down their opponent's two holes is the winner and gains the badge.
6. Play from the sides and have three holes each.

7. Play on a full size snooker table (that can be up to twice the size of a pool table) and involve all the scouts.

Notes
Be sure to choose a pool table that is situated near a hospital and have an ambulance on standby.

PARASCENDING

Parascending is a very adventurous activity much loved by scout leaders. You will learn to fly a canopy that is towed into the air by vehicle or winch before gliding back down to land. Heights of over two thousand feet can be obtained.

To gain your badge

1. Attend a parascending course and learn how to:
   - Use the equipment properly
   - Self-release the tow line
   - Launch
   - Land safely
   - Collapse and field pack the canopy
2. Attend your first parascending flight.
3. Put on your harness and adjust it to a comfortable fit.
4. Tell your instructor, "You're not getting me up with nothing more than a dodgy old parachute even though I love the colour. It looks far too dangerous."
5. Go and find the on-site café. Most of them do a cracking Victoria sponge.

PASSING WIND

Passing wind is when a build up of gas ("flatulence") escapes from the digestive system and out of the back passage. It is commonly known in scout leader circles as "farting." This badge can normally be gained whilst a scout leader is asleep and you should not be surprised to find it shoved down your sleeping bag when you awake in the morning - even if you are sleeping alone - along with the **Snoring** badge. Passing wind is not a rare occurrence. The NHS estimates that the average is between five and fifteen times a day.

To gain your badge
1. Go on camp.
2. Sleep.

Notes
Men can gain this badge also.

PASSING WIND PLUS

To gain this badge you need to hold the **Passing Wind** badge. With not much effort, but certainly more than the **Passing Wind** badge, you can gain this Plus badge too.

To gain your badge

1. Produce an extremely smelly fart. This can be achieved by swallowing air (by design or through smoking, chewing gum, sucking hard sweets or on pen tops) or eating foods that are more difficult to digest such as the stuff that you will be given on scout camp. If you are having difficulty producing a corker try stopping doing any exercise and keep up with the camp diet once you have returned home. Eat large meals and quickly and don't drink peppermint tea as this won't help.

Food and drink that can help you fart include:

- broccoli
- Brussels sprouts
- cabbage
- cauliflower
- dried fruit - raisins or apricots
- fizzy drinks and beer
- food or drinks containing the sweetener sorbitol
- onions
- pulses - beans or lentils.

2. Although 1. can be executed anywhere, you may like to try letting rip on a bus or other enclosed space. A lift is a good place to start. Don't worry if you make a noise, simply look at one of the other passengers and sigh deeply.

Notes

A gentleman would apologise for a fart in an enclosed space even if it wasn't theirs. You are many things but you are not a gentleman. Do not get caught up in this sort of behaviour.

PENKNIFE

A good-quality penknife is the mainstay of a scout's kit. Make sure that yours is bigger and better than any of theirs.

To gain your badge

1. Buy a penknife. Since 1897, the Swiss Army Knife has been a trusted tool of adventurers around the world.
2. It's all about features and you need to have a penknife with the most, certainly more than the scouts. One Swiss Army Knife has seventy tools including an altimeter, a fish scaler, a pharmaceutical spatula and a digital watch. It weighs 350 grams.
3. Alternatively try the Wenger Giant with eighty-seven tools including a cigar cutter and a compass. It weights 3.25 kilograms. Get it!
4. Attach it to a belt loop and swagger around with your 3½ inch (minimum) monster dangling.
5. Watch as your trousers fall down.
6. Sew your badge on whilst at the police station.

PHYSICAL EXERCISE

The wording for this badge has been taken from "Scouting for Boys" by Robert Baden-Powell. It is a rarely gained badge; the reason for this will probably become self-evident.

There is a great deal of nonsense in fashion in the way of bodily exercises; so many people seem to think that their only object is to make huge muscle. But to make yourself strong and healthy it is necessary to begin with your inside and to get the blood into good order and the heart to work well; that is the secret of the whole thing, and physical exercises should be taken with that intention.

To gain your badge

1. Make the heart strong, in order to pump the blood properly to every part of the body and so to build up flesh, bone, and muscle.

Exercise: The Struggle. Two players face each other about a yard apart, stretch arms out sideways, lock fingers of both hands, and lean towards each other till their chests touch, push chest to chest, and see who can drive the other back to the wall of the room or on to a goal line. At first a very short struggle is sufficient to set their hearts pumping, but after practice for a few days the heart grows stronger and they can go on for a long time.

Exercise: Wrist Pushing. By one man alone. Stand with both your arms to the front about level with the waist, cross your wrists so that one hand has knuckles up, the other knuckles down. Clench the fists. Now make the lower hand press upwards and make the upper hand press downwards. Press as hard as you can with both wrists gradually, and only after great resistance let the lower push the upper one upwards till opposite your forehead, then let the upper press the lower down, the lower one resisting all the time.

These two exercises, although they sound small and simple, if carried out with all your might, develop most muscles in your body and especially those about the heart. They should not be carried on too long at a time, but should be done at frequent intervals during the day for a minute or so.

2. Make the lungs strong, in order to revive the blood with fresh air.

Exercise: Deep breathing. Deep breathing is of the greatest importance for bringing fresh air into the lungs to be put into the blood, and for developing the size of the chest, but it should be done carefully, according to instructions, and not overdone, otherwise it is liable to strain the heart. The Japs always carry on deep breathing exercise for a few minutes when they first get up in the morning, and always in the open air. It is done by sucking air in through the nose until it swells out your ribs as far as possible, especially at the back; then, after a pause, you breathe out the air slowly and gradually through the mouth until you have not a scrap of air left in you, then after a pause draw in your breath again through the nose as before.

3. Make the skin perspire, to get rid of the dirt from the blood.

Exercise: Bath, or dry rub with a damp towel every day.

4. Make the stomach work, to feed the blood.

Exercise: Cone or Body Bending and Twisting.

159

Standing at the "Alert" raise both hands as high as possible over the head, and link fingers, lean backwards, then sway the arms very slowly round in the direction of a cone so that the hands make a wide circle above and round the body, the body turning from the hips, and leaning over to one side, then to the front, then to the other side and then back; this is to exercise the muscles of the waist and stomach, and should be repeated say six times to either hand. With the eyes you should be trying to see all that goes on behind you during the movement.

5. Make the bowels active, to remove the remains of food and drink from the body.

Exercise: Bond Bending and Kneading the Abdomen. Drink plenty of good water. Regular daily "rear."

6. Work muscles in each part of the body, to make the blood circulate to that part, and so increase your strength.

Exercise: Running and walking, and special exercises of special muscles, such as "Wrist Pushing," etc.

The secret of keeping well and healthy is to keep your blood clean and active. These different exercises will do that if you use them every day. Someone has said, "If you practise body exercises every morning you will never be ill: and if you also drink a pint of hot water every night you will never die."

Notes

If you have managed to get this far and you are still alive well done. You are indeed a very rare scout leader. Are you sure scouting is really for you? If you are dead you will be awarded this badge posthumously.

PIONEER

Scouts love constructing with wood and so will you! Think big! How about getting hold of some pallets and letting your creative juices flow?

To gain your badge

1. Learn a few lashings and knots. It doesn't matter which ones as they all normally come apart anyway.
2. Build your structure. Choose from:
   - Bar
3. Stock the bar.
4. Cheers.

Notes

It's not necessary to complete the bar so long as you have an idea of what it's going to look like in your head.

POKER

It's very important that you always have a great game idea to hand, especially on those long, cold, dark nights at camp. Card games are ideal because they are easy to learn and the scouts love playing them.

To gain your badge

1. Learn how to play a few card games.
2. Choose from Poker (there are many versions but you need those that involve a banker), Blackjack or Baccarat.
3. Make sure that the scouts that are playing have something to play with. This would normally be cash but you should be flexible and take any asset from a teddy bear to a tent.
4. Remember to hold your nerve. In the medium term you, the banker, will always win.
5. Make sure that you have brought a few survival bags for those scouts who have lost their tents to sleep in.

PULLING

There are two types of pulling badge for the scouts and they are sliding seat rowing and static seat rowing. You, on the other hand, have only one. This can be gained at almost any scouting event but how about taking it out of your immediate surroundings and try to gain it with someone new, such as on an international camp?

To gain your badge

1. Complete one of the following:

Slide up to that desirable scout leader...

...in the bar,

"You have a fine collection of badges on your shirt. Would you like to tell me about them over a beer?"

Or,

"I like your woggle. I would love to have one like that. Did you make it yourself? Would you like to show me how it's made over a glass of wine?"

Or,

"You look like you've been in scouting for quite a few years. Either that or you've put your shirt through too many boil washes. Can I have a guess how many whilst I buy you a drink?"

...walking through the campsite,

"Is that your tent? It looks like a two-man 1980 Zango double strength macchiato canvas with zumo all-weather zip and built-in double M groundsheet. Fantastic! Mind if I have look inside? Perhaps you would like to show me? I'll take my boots off first." Or,

"Excuse me. Do you do badge swaps? I have available a limited edition triangular diamond jubilee hare challenge survival camp and I would like to swap it for your group badge and a cup of coffee with you."

...on the minibus,

"I'm really looking forward to going white-water rafting although I'm a little bit scared. If you let me sit next to you in the raft I'll buy you a cup of tea afterwards to warm you up because looking at you I reckon you're just the sort of person who's going to fall straight in."

Or,

"I wonder where we're going to end up on this mystery trip? Perhaps we could go around together. I'm useless at directions and am hopeless with a compass. Honestly I've no idea why I'm a scout leader. I'll buy you a stick of rock to say, 'Thank you.'"

2. If you receive a positive response you've pulled and you can award yourself the badge.

QUARTERMASTER

Sounds boring? It is boring! Making yourself responsible for your group's kit and equipment is a boring and thankless task but it's another badge so go for it - you'll have no competition!

To gain your badge

1. Ensure that the tents are stored in a dry area and in order of size; keep ropes hanked and stored in order of length; make sure flammable materials are kept together, ideally outside in a cage; all cooking equipment / utensils should be clean and dry; everything else should have an appointed place for storage.

2. Lock the door to the stores and put a sign on the door stating, "No admittance. Quartermaster only."

3. Draw up an inventory of kit and equipment that your group holds.

4. When a section leader would like some supplies for a camp hand them an inventory form and ask them to tick what they require.

5. At the next scout meeting unlock the door to the stores and get the scouts to locate the items and pile them up in a corner of the scout hut.

6. After the camp check through all the items. Pay particular attention to rips and tears in tents, frayed ropes, empty fuel containers, dirty / wet cooking equipment / utensils.

7. Unlock the door to the stores and get the scouts to, "Chuck it all in."

8. Lock the door to the stores and give the key to someone else telling them that you've done your bit for long enough and it's now someone else's turn.

RAFT BUILDING

However many times you teach the scouts how to do this properly they never seem to be able to succeed. Lead by example and show them how.

To gain your badge

1. Find a deep lake.
2. Lay four long pioneering poles (staves) on the ground in the shape of a rectangle, with corners overlapping.
3. Lash them together using square lashings or another random knot you can think of. Or make one up.
4. Put a fifth pole across the two long poles in the middle to form a two-rectangle figure of 8.
5. Lash.
6. Put plastic drums in or on the rectangles.
7. Lash the drums to the poles using lots of rope and then some more.
8. Leave any spare rope dangling down.
9. Turn the completed raft over and head for the lake.
10. Carefully place the raft on the lake and jump on.
11. Paddle to the middle of the lake.
12. When you are in the middle of the lake you will probably find that you are sitting on an oil drum / a pole / nothing. Turn round and see the other poles, drums and rope bobbing about in the water.
13. Sink.
14. Once you have swum back to the water's edge or been rescued by the scouts explain to them that what they've just seen is how not to do it and that you expect them to

do it properly and if they don't they'll find that their toes will be nibbled by the resident terrapins.

15. Go back to the mess tent and have a coffee whilst sewing on your new badge.

SAFEGUARDING

Safeguarding can be boiled down to one sentence and that is, "Avoid one on one situations." However, to gain this badge you need to have actually been in a one on one situation so it's best to sew this badge on the inside of your shirt otherwise you may be told off to say the least. You know the badge is there but no one else will know unless you use a brightly coloured cotton and they're looking for it. Then you may find another scout leader sidling up to you and with a knowing look mutter, "Safeguarding?" By way of response all you need do is almost imperceptibly nod.

To gain your badge
1. Have a cigarette with a scout behind the toilets. See **Smoking**.
2. Any other one on one situation.

***

SAFEGUARDING PLUS

It is far too easy to gain this badge. You need to hold the **Safeguarding** badge.

To gain your badge
Get suspended.

SAFETY WITH AXES

Axes are great fun to play with;
make sure that when you are
playing with one you know what
you're doing. Chopping wood for
the camp fire is one of the main
uses of an axe.

To gain your badge

1. Get hold of the sharpest axe you can find. A long
handled and heavy axe is ideal.
2. Sharpen it.
3. Check to make sure that no one is within an arm's length
of you by holding the axe in your hand and walking round
in a circle on the spot swinging the axe wildly about
yourself. If you don't hear any screams you are fine to
continue.
4. Place a branch across an upturned stump.
5. Holding the branch with one hand attack it with the axe
in the other hand by coming down hard on the part of the
branch that is resting on the stump.
6. If the branch is moving about too much hold it nearer to
the stump or rest your hand on the branch on the stump.
7. If you are not making much of an impact on the branch
take the axe over one shoulder and bring it down heavily
on the branch with a blood-curdling yell. This sudden
release will help focus your energy onto the branch.
8. With the axe hand wrap your severed hand in a plastic
bag, place in a cool box with some ice if you have any and
drive to A&E. If you have a manual car you may need
someone to drive you.

SAFETY WITH KNIVES

Knives are great fun to play with; make sure that when you are playing with one you know what you're doing. Stripping bark from wood to use as tinder for the camp fire is one of the main uses of a knife.

To gain your badge
1. Get hold of the sharpest knife you can find. A long and chunky bushcraft knife is ideal.
2. Sharpen it.
3. Check to make sure that no one is within an arm's length of you by holding the knife in your hand and walking round in a circle on the spot swinging the knife wildly about yourself. If you don't hear any screams you are fine to continue.
4. Place a branch across an upturned stump. Birch is a great wood as it has an oily bark that burns very well.
5. Holding the branch with one hand attack it with the knife in the other hand by pressing the cutting edge on the bark at a forty-five degree angle and sweeping away as if you are peeling a carrot.
6. If the branch is moving about too much on the far side hold it nearer to the stump or rest your hand on the branch on the stump.
7. If you are not making much of an impact on the branch bark place the knife, angled towards you, on the far side of the branch and pull sharply towards you with a blood-curdling yell. This sudden release will help focus your energy onto the branch bark.

8. With both hands grab any cloth or other material that you have with you, stuff as much of it into the wound as you can and drive to A&E.

SAFETY WITH SAWS

SAFETY WITH SAWS

Saws are great fun to play with; make sure that when you are playing with one you know what you're doing. Sawing wood for the camp fire is one of the main uses of a saw.

To gain your badge

1. Get hold of the sharpest saw you can find. A chain saw is best if you can get hold of one.

2. Sharpen it or buy a new chain.

3. Check to make sure that no one is within an arm's length of you by holding the saw in your hand and walking round in a circle on the spot swinging the saw wildly about yourself. If you don't hear any screams you are fine to continue.

4. Place a stump across an upturned stump.

5. Holding the top stump in place with a foot attack it with the chain saw in both hands by pressing down on the stump.

6. If the top stump is moving about too much hold it in place nearer to the centre with your foot..

7. If you are not making much of an impact on the stump take the chain saw over one shoulder and bring it down heavily on the top stump with a blood-curdling yell and with the chain at full speed. This sudden release will help focus your energy onto the stump.

8. Chain saws cut very quickly and you won't initially feel a thing. With both hands wrap your severed foot in a plastic bag, place in a cool box with some ice if you have any and drive to A&E. If you have a manual car you may need someone to drive you.

SCIENTIST

Blowing up campfires and even scout huts is very satisfying but you can only usually get away with it once so work on this badge when you have no more to collect or you are ready to retire.

To gain your badge
There are two alternatives. Select one of them and complete all the tasks.

Alternative One
Campfire
1. Build a campfire and do what you need to do on it - s'mores, sausages, popcorn - that sort of thing.
2. Wait until the scouts have just gone back indoors for flag down. You will find that the fire is glowing just nicely thank you. Make a small hollow in the embers, an approximate 100cm circle and place a gas canister in the void. Pierceable 190g butane / propane gas canisters work well. They're quick to explode and very effective.
3. Go back into the scout hut yourself and shut the door.
4. The explosion (which is caused due to a build up of gases) is loud and destructive. It's one way of putting the campfire out without using any water although you may find that you have started several little fires all around.

Alternative Two
Scout Hut. See **Fire Safely**

1. Put a large steel gas canister in the middle of the scout hut. A fifteen kilo butane / propane / butane propane mix all work well.
2. Whack it hard until it cracks.
3. Put the open end of a condom around the crack.
4. Roll well-chewed gum into a long mini sausage and stick the condom to the canister.
5. Light a candle two metres away from the canister on the side of the condom.
6. Shut the door and run.
7. The explosion will be heard from five miles away.

SMARTPHONE

Generally speaking scout leaders hate the scouts having their 'phones at meetings or on camp. They're antisocial and a distraction. Ban them! But you need yours; it's essential. Make full use of it and gain this badge.

To gain your badge

1. If you don't have a smartphone confiscate one. If no one has one on display say to the scouts something like, "Who can be the first to find out when Queen Victoria died?" When the 'phones come out take them all and tell the scouts that in accordance with your rules they will get them back at the end of term. If their families can afford to give them a smartphone then they'll probably just buy them another one. Don't try this too near the end of term though. The best time is at the beginning of term, especially just after Christmas.

2. Choose the best one. Change the cover. Sell the rest.

3. When at scout meetings spend the whole time looking at it.

4. When on activities with the scouts spend the whole time looking at it.

5. When on camp spend the whole time looking at it.

6. When in your tent on camp set the alarm for 6am. Make sure that you select the noisiest one. The cockerel is a good start. A piercing electronic whistle is especially annoying. Turn the volume up to full before you go to bed.

7. Sleep through it. You can be sure that someone else will get up and put the kettle on.

SMOKING

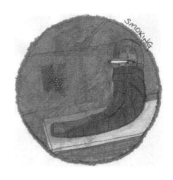

Smoking in front of the scouts is frowned upon. Your campfires can smoke, your cooking can smoke, everything can smoke apart from you. The problem is that all scout leaders smoke. Those that don't currently smoke are either ex-smokers or future smokers. Smoke is so much part of scout leaders' lives that they are all strangely drawn to it at some point. Gain this badge and wear it with pride - even if you do have to cover it up.

To gain your badge
There are two alternatives. Select one of them and complete all the tasks.

Alternative One
1. At the scout hut going off for a cigarette is easy. Just tell another leader that you need to pop out for a bit of fresh air. Go and hide behind the gas cage for your smoke. No one will look behind there. Just don't start to play with the on / off dials on the canisters whilst you're smoking though otherwise the scout hut will not be there for you to re-enter and the scouts will find out what it feels like to be a fireball.
2. On camp there's often a wood that you can go and hide in or go behind the toilets. Be careful though. You may find some scouts there. However there's nothing to be worried about as you would both be in trouble so make the most of it. Perhaps you could make the most of the situation to teach them some new tricks such as how to blow smoke rings, the ghost inhale, the French inhale and the bull ring?

If you encounter just one scout you may be able to gain the **Safeguarding** badge also.

3. On camp have a cigarette in your tent. This is best done at night otherwise someone may call the fire brigade or douse you with several bucketfuls of water. Do make sure that you open the main zip first or the air will be like someone who lights a wood burning stove with damp wood or a blocked chimney.

Alternative Two
In any of the three situations above substitute regular tobacco with cannabis leaf. However, although this is a possibly a more fun way of gaining the badge it may also lead to your being arrested for possession so this is not recommended unless you are in a bit of a rush.

***

SMOKING PLUS
To gain this badge you have to hold the **Smoking** badge.

To gain your badge
Smoke a cigarette whilst cooking breakfast on camp in a mess tent with no one realising.

Notes
It's best to burn something beyond all recognition first to disguise the smell.

S'MORES

No doubt you know that s'mores originated in America, a country known for its inability to spell words in their entirety. S'mores or more accurate Some Mores are marshmallows that are gently roasted over embers until browned then squeezed with a square or two of chocolate between two sweet crackers.

To gain your badge

1. Roast a large marshmallow at the end of a metal skewer over an open fire. Don't wait until there are just embers, smoke is fine.

2. When the marshmallow is black and alight, sandwich it between a chocolate digestive biscuit, thrust it into your mouth and bite on it.

3. Unless you have remembered to remove the pointed and red hot skewer you will need to go to A&E for a stab wound at the back of your throat and through your neck with a third degree burn on your tongue.

SNORING

Snoring is when your tongue, mouth, throat or nasal airways in your nose vibrate as you breathe. You are most likely to snore if you are overweight, you smoke and you drink too much alcohol. This is an extremely easy badge for scout

leaders to gain and can normally be gained whilst a scout leader is asleep. You should not be surprised to find it shoved down your sleeping bag when you awake in the morning - even if you are sleeping alone - along with the **Passing Wind** badge.

To gain your badge
1. Go on camp.
2. Sleep.

Notes
Men can gain this badge also.
This badge can also be gained during most scout committee meetings.

SNOWSPORTS

Are you a winter sports enthusiast? Do you love skiing, ski jumping, snowboarding, sledging, snowmobiling, that sort of thing? If so then this is the badge for you! It's not for the faint-hearted though and you have to work hard at it to get your badge. That's not to say that it's out of reach of most scout leaders because it isn't. Simply practise then apply yourself and soon you will be there.

To gain your badge
1. Find some snow.
2. Put on some warm clothing and a good pair of gloves.
3. Go outside.
4. Find a car that is covered in snow and draw a silly face on it.
5. Scoop up some snow in both hands, cup them together, compress and mould the snow into a ball. Throw it at someone.
6. That's enough! Go back inside for a hot drink and a brandy.

STATUE

Fed up of seeing that statue of that person that you know nothing about even if you do know their name that you go past whenever you're in your home town? Maybe you just don't like their stupid grin; maybe they are a little bit too  smug-looking; perhaps they may have said something once that you disagree with. Then it's time for them to go!

To gain your badge

1. Find a suitable statue for toppling, the bigger the better. Someone (they're normally male) astride a horse makes a good target.

2. Make up some spurious reason for them to be removed. No matter what they're known for, maybe a local benefactor or doer of good deeds, bad stuff (even if it's not even true) outweighs the good.

3. Publicise your reason as much as you can making full use of local papers, social media and left-wing councillors / MPs if the person was a Conservative or right-wing councillors / MPs if the person was a socialist. You will soon find many people doing your bidding for you.

4. Tell your local elected representatives that the arguments have been going on for far too long, at least ten years (make sure that the statue has been up for at least ten years) and that if something isn't done soon you will be forced to take direct action.

5.You may strike lucky and the elected representatives may take it upon themselves to organise the statue's dismantling. If not, take some of your scouts to the statue one evening after dark and get them to practice their lassoing over the statue's head.

6. Once lassoed get the scouts to all pull on the other end of the rope. If you have chosen well (i.e. made of metal as they're usually hollow) the statue should come off its plinth very easily. If not try tying the end of rope to the tow bar of a stationery bus, lorry or digger that may be parked nearby. Then run! But do be sure to return later to check that the statue is down and to retrieve your rope if it doesn't look like you're going to be in any imminent danger of arrest. Well done! That's another statue down that's spoiling the view!

***

STATUE PLUS
Hold **Statue** badge.

To gain your badge
Topple another. Don't worry – there are loads to go round. There are over three hundred in London alone.

SUNBURN

Sunburn is red, hot and sore skin that is caused by too much sun. It may mean a bit of discomfort on the way to gaining this badge but it will be worth it in the end as it takes courage to get sunburn.

To gain your badge

1. Whether on camp or at home arrange to be in the sun between 12 noon and 3pm.
2. Take off as many clothes as is prudent.
3. Do not put on any sun cream.
4. Do smother yourself in tanning oil. If you do not have any use any oil that you can lay your hands on. This could include olive oil, any other type of vegetable oil, nut oil, plant oil, engine oil or WD40.
5. Sit or lie in the sun.

SUNBURN PLUS

Take sunburn to a new level with added complications. You will need to have the **Sunburn** badge.

To gain your badge
1. Repeat 1 - 5 of **Sunburn** twice.
2. Once your skin is properly burnt add petroleum jelly.
3. Then put ice or ice packs on your burnt skin.
4. If you get any blisters pop them.
5. When skin starts to peel pull it off.
6. When skin starts to become itchy scratch it.

SUPERMARKET VOLLEYBALL

This is one badge that you can gain with the scouts playing the game for you.

To gain your badge

1. Take your scouts to a largish supermarket and put them in teams of five.

2. Give every pair of teams a loaf of bread.

3. Send each pair of teams down two aisles that are separated by a line of groceries.

4. Teams then have to volley the bread over the centre shelving. (It doesn't usually reach to the ceiling.) Points are given to the team that manages to volley the bread to the ground that the other team is guarding.

5. The winning team is the first one to ten successful volleys or when you are chucked out - as you will be eventually. However you be surprised at how long you can play for before someone intervenes.

SWEARING

Everyone's at it these days but no one's supposed to be. If you hear a scout swearing you reprimand them. If they hear you swearing you get a badge. So speak up!

To gain your badge

1. Learn at least one swear word for each letter of the alphabet.

2. Use them all during the course of one scout meeting.

Notes

Swearing is supposed to relieve physical pain. Knowing this may help you to get out of a tight situation.

TENT

Big tents, little tents, old tents, new tents, one-man tents, two-man tents, three-man tents, bell tents, mess tents, patrol tents, toilet tents. Avoid looking foolish when putting up any of these.

To gain your badge

1. Get out a tent.
2. Tell the scouts to put it up.
3. If they say that they don't know how don't pander to them, tell them to, "Work it out." They'll get there eventually even if it does mean missing supper.
4. When it's time to take it down undo all the guy ropes. Say, "That's how you start it - now fold it up." If they do so and it doesn't fit in the bag tell them to do it again.

TENT BLOWN AWAY

Imagine coming back to your tent and wondering where it was. "It was here when I left it." People will nod knowingly if you're sporting this badge. We've all been there - don't get left out.

To gain your badge

1. Get hold of one of the cheapest and nastiest pop-up tents that you can find.
2. Wait for a particularly windy day.
3. Find a position that's at the top of a hill, in the open.
4. Pop the tent up.
5. Put nothing inside it.
6. Do not "do" the guy ropes.
7. Zip the tent up.
8. Wait for a good gust of wind. The tent will act like an oversized balloon and take off, find a thermal and disappear into the distance.

Notes

Group together with a few leaders and see whose tent goes the furthest. Maybe put your name and contact details on a slip of paper and zip it up inside the tent, a bit like a message in a bottle.

TENT ON FIRE

So many scout leaders have this badge but are ashamed to admit it. This is hard to understand why as modern tents are very flammable. Gain yours and wear it with pride!

To gain your badge
There are four alternatives. Select one of them and complete the task.

Alternative One
Have a cigarette whilst tucked up in your sleeping bag but fall asleep half-way through.

Alternative Two
Put a small gas stove in your tent and light it before accidently knocking it over.

Alternative Three
Try out your new flint and steel using the fluff from your tummy button. (Remove the fluff first.)

Alternative Four
Take a few embers from the camp fire to warm your tent up.

Notes
This badge may be awarded posthumously.

THAT'LL DO

Every scout leader must have this badge. If you don't have it you'll be constantly asked why not. Scouts are implored to do their best but leaders aren't, so don't waste time doing so.

We've all been there - gone on camp, arrived late, laid the mess tent out, sorted out the poles, done the roof, raised part of the walls, added the canvas, finished the walls, gone inside, noticed a very bad smell, realised that the tent's positioned over a cesspit, taken the tent down, moved it, sniffed, started to put the tent back up, the scouts are arriving and not one of the pegs or guys are in place. The tent's flapping all over the place. You sigh. "That'll do," you mutter.

To gain your badge
Whatever you are doing, whether it be erecting a tent, washing up or any other task that you've been assigned to do, mutter, "That'll do," so that another scout leader can hear. (You don't have to be looking at them.) If they agree or say nothing then you can award yourself the badge. If they disagree then you will have to finish the task in hand and try again later.

THAT'LL DO PLUS

To gain this badge you have to hold the **That'll Do** badge.

To gain your badge

As for the **That'll Do** badge only you have to mutter these words before you've even started the task that you need to do / have been given to do, such as leave the mess tent in its bag or not begin the washing-up. Again, to gain this badge, you have to say "That'll do," so that another scout leader can hear. If they agree or say nothing then you can award yourself the badge. If they disagree then you will have to start and finish the task in hand and try again later with not starting something else.

TIME IN THE WATER

This badge is also very popular amongst scout leaders. Not everyone who goes for water sports, anything from boating to yachting, will gain this badge. Leaders have to put some effort in themselves.

To gain your badge
1. Take a water vehicle onto a pond, river, lake or sea. This could be a boat, canoe, dinghy, kayak, paddleboard, raft, that sort of thing.
2. Fall in.

Notes
You do not have to accidently fall in, you can go in on purpose. You have to remain in the water for at least ten minutes without being rescued.

***

TIME IN THE WATER PLUS

To gain this badge you need to hold the **Time on the Water** badge.

To gain your badge
1. Once you are in the water, swim away from your vessel and any rescuers.
2. Remain the water for at least one hour.

TOMOHAWK THROWING

A tomahawk is a type of long-handled axe that is used for throwing at targets, mostly not human.

To gain your badge
1. Get hold of an axe, it doesn't have to be a tomahawk.
2. Find a target, preferably wood. You could consider using a purpose-made target or a tree but a fence, shed or summerhouse will do just as well.
3. Holding the axe by the shaft, take it over one shoulder, bring it forward and when in line with the target let go.
4. Imbed the axe into the tree or building.

Notes
Try throwing at a target that borders a neighbour's garden so that you have a bit of a run-off in case you miss.

***

TOMOHAWK THROWING PLUS
Hold the **Tomahawk Throwing** badge

To gain your badge
Throw the axe at the tree so many times that it falls down, or at the shed / summerhouse so that it collapses.

VEGETARIAN

Don't stand for it - The one scout who comes on camp with a letter from their parent telling you that they've just become a vegetarian! Don't they realise that you have enough to sort out? This is how you can deal with it.

To gain your badge
1. Prepare a cooked English breakfast comprising bacon, sausage, black pudding and nothing else apart from maybe some kidneys just to set the whole thing off. Tell the vegetarian that no one can have beans, egg and mushrooms unless and until they eat the first bit.
2. After breakfast ask the vegetarian that if they like animals so much then why do they keep eating their food?
3. Beef sandwiches for lunch. Tell the vegetarian that they can have crisps, fruit and a biscuit once they've eaten their sandwich.
4. After lunch tell the vegetarian that cows are vegetarians so they don't have to be.
5. Cake for tea for those who ate their breakfast and lunch.
6. Before dinner ask the vegetarian if they are still one. It doesn't matter if they say, "Yes," or "No," give them spaghetti Bolognese for dinner. If you're concerned about how little the vegetarian has had to eat you could give them spaghetti Bolognese made with Quorn instead of mince but if they accept it wait until three o'clock in the morning then ring their parents to tell them that their child has been violently sick in their sleep and that they need to pick them up NOW! Tell them that they will find their child

in their tent and not to disturb you. The child won't know anything about being sick so pour a few mashed up carrots and potatoes with milk over their sleeping bag while they sleep.

7. If the parents haven't turned up by the time that you get up call social services.

8. Enjoy the rest of the camp.

Notes

If a scout comes on camp with a note telling you that they're vegan send them straight home after you've told them that veganism isn't a life choice but an illness and you're not a doctor.

YOU DON'T WANT TO BE DOING IT LIKE THAT

Everyone loves a know-all. And if you're a know-all this is your badge.

To gain your badge
1. Go up to a scout leader that is doing something either that you consider is the wrong way or that can be done better another way.
2. Say to them, "You don't want to be doing it like that!"
3. When you come out of A&E you can sew the badge onto your shirt.

scout leader badges

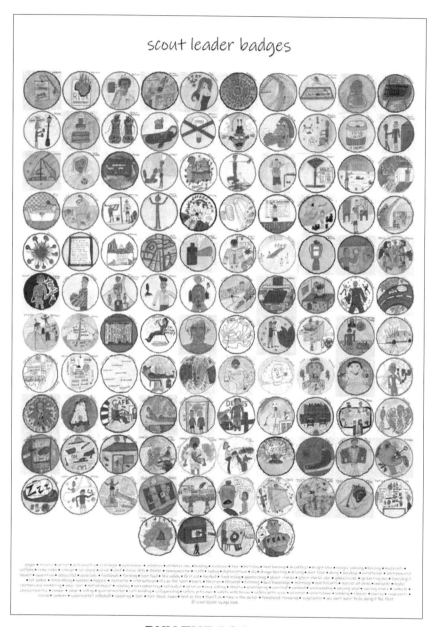

BUY THE POSTER!
https://www.searchlinepublishing.co.uk/product-
page/scout-leader-badges-poster